Corrupted

Southern Watch, Book 3

Robert J. Crane

Corrupted
Southern Watch, Book 3

Copyright © 2014 Midian Press
All Rights Reserved.

1st Edition

This book is a work of fiction. Names, characters, places and incidents are products of the author's imagination or are used fictitiously. Any resemblance to actual events or locales or persons, living or dead, is entirely coincidental.

The scanning, uploading and distribution of this book via the internet or any other means without the permission of the publisher is illegal and punishable by law. Please purchase only authorized electronic editions, and do not participate in or encourage electronic piracy of copyrighted materials. Your support of the author's rights is appreciated.

No part of this publication may be reproduced in whole or in part without the written permission of the publisher. For information regarding permission, please email cyrusdavidon@gmail.com laughter carried on the hot wind. Last week, the carnival had been in Mobile, and the wind had come off Mobile Bay with a little cool air. Here it was dead and stifling, like someone had opened the oven and fanned the heat out at him.

He started to say something to Mandy but stopped. Turned and half-opened his mouth before he caught himself. Didn't have nothing but dumb things rolling through his head, and it was driving him nuts. Here was this pretty young thing next to him, and Mick's brain couldn't come up with nothing but stupid to spit out.

"How much do you travel?" Mandy asked, breaking the silence between them.

He glanced over and saw those sweet cheeks—man, what was it about cheeks? Her eyes were nice too, kind of a green that still had a little dancing to it, like she hadn't been out in the world and seen how shitty and mean it got. They kind of bounced, like she was excited about things still. And her Southern accent was pretty good, too. Slipped off her tongue and made everything double sweet, like it was rolled in sugar and fried.

"We get around a lot," Mick answered, and his voice sounded deeper and huskier than usual, like he was trying to sound all grown up instead of half-scared out of his goddamned mind. "Every week, it's somewhere new."

She looked past him. "That sounds amazing."

Mick could feel his chest puff up inside, as if he'd taken in a real deep breath and was holding it, pride threatening to burst him open. It was amazing, wasn't it? Living on the road. If it looked cool to her, it must be pretty good. "It's not bad. Seen some nice places along the way."

"Where are you going next?" Her singsongy words captivated him. That and the dancing green eyes now.

"I don't remember," he lied. "But we're packing up tonight. Gotta get on down the road, you know."

She looked away from him now. "I know."

They walked across the fresh field, cutting between the cars. There were ruts here and there from where people had been parking the last few days, the smell of fresh upturned earth in the air all around them. Mick took her hand to help her over one rut that looked real muddy, still wet from a rain a couple days ago. She smiled at him, and he felt

Prologue

Hobbs Green, Alabama
August 1984

Mick had picked the girl up on his way through town. She was tall and pretty, long hair and long legs, shown off by a pair of jean shorts that cut off mid-thigh to reveal smooth, tanned skin all the way to her ankles. She'd told him her name was Mandy. Mick liked that. Liked Mandy.

He'd met her a few days earlier when he first got to town, walking around through the square. He'd seen her while he was killing time away from the carnival after setup was done. She still had that baby-faced look, that little bit of childish chub in her cheeks coupled with innocence in her eyes, even though she said she'd just turned eighteen. That was what had done it for Mick, drawn him in like a fly to one of those new zappers. That innocent look.

It was awful hot, like it got in Alabama in summertime. Mick felt the sweat creeping down everywhere but mostly along his back and forehead. He gave Mandy a half-assed smile, but he could see she was sweating a little, too. They walked along toward the field outside of town where the carnival had set up. It was getting toward late as they approached, field full of cars all the way to gates, where the lights were already all on.

The Ferris wheel was a big one; took a truck to move it even when it was disassembled. Mick had helped put it up, unpacking and getting the pieces and shit together. It was a good day's work, but now it was done, and it lit up the night as it made its slow spin. The sound of the tingle in his hand as he held hers. Once she was over the rut, he didn't feel inclined to let it go, so he held on.

They passed out of the field and cut between two bright, red-striped tents where the freak show and the bearded lady were set up, and Mandy let out a little giggle as she saw the sign. Mick grinned, showing her some teeth. He liked the sound of her laugh, too, liked that she still thought the bearded lady was some kind of novelty. He'd been dealing with her for years, and she was a real bitch. He supposed he might have been, too, if he'd grown tits or something unnatural he couldn't shake.

The lights were bright as they walked past the roller coaster. Mandy's eyes got all big as she looked at it. "You never been to the fair before?" he asked.

"Not like this," she said as the car came round a turn and a half-dozen screams filled the air—excitement and fear, all mixed up in that nice way that they got when they didn't have something shittin'-your-pants-bad to deal with. There really were two different kinds of screams; he'd heard both kinds and damned sure preferred these.

Mick took her up, nodding at Wyatt who was taking the tickets. Mandy's eyes flashed once when they passed Wyatt without so much as handing him a stub, and she smiled at him like they'd done something they shouldn't have and gotten away with it. Mick just smiled back, trying to be cool.

They rode the roller coaster twice, and he listened to her scream. She clutched his hand hard when it started to move and didn't let go the whole time. Mick just smiled; he'd been on the coaster more times than he could count, and it was old news by now. He could see the fear the first time, knew she'd never done anything like this before. The second time it wasn't quite old hat but close, and she laughed between the occasional shout. Giggles between the screams.

When they got out, she took his hand again and smiled at him. He could feel the natural sway of their hands as they walked, and he caught the sly looks she gave him, the smiles, the abrupt "look away and push her hair out of her eyes" thing she did. He liked her hair, too, that honey color. They walked past the booth with the funnel cakes, heard Reg hawking them to everyone that passed. The smell was rich, and somehow it fed the moment, him smiling at her, her smiling at him. He stopped short and went for a kiss, and she returned it, pressure on his lips and the hint of her tongue somewhere in there.

When they broke, he smiled at her again. "That was pretty good," she said.

"A-yup," he agreed. "Wanna ride the tilt-a-whirl?"

They rode the tilt-a-whirl and went through the haunted house and held hands all the while. There wasn't much conversation, but there was breathless excitement after each experience, and more kisses, here and there, breathless as the first but more satisfying. He started to slip her the tongue, that so-called French kissing, and found it was real good. He'd never tried that before. She got a little too enthusiastic about that, but it was okay. She couldn't stop smiling, and that was okay, too.

"Ferris wheel?" he asked her as they almost passed it, still walking hand in hand. He was getting dirty looks here and there from the people who knew her, but he didn't care. He liked the faint smell of her sweet shampoo that was now a little eclipsed by the fresh smell of sweat. He took a sip of the Coke they were sharing and felt the sweet, syrupy taste linger on his tongue. It was so goddamned hot, but who gave a shit? He had a pretty girl hanging on his hand, it was a glorious damned summer night, and life was good.

"Let's go," she said, her eyes alight. They were always alight now, had been all night, and he loved it. Maybe he loved her, who knew? It was like the night was running away with them, and his head was swimming from it.

They passed Richie, who was manning the Ferris wheel, but by now doing that didn't even get her to turn and look at him, it was just how it was. No ticket, no worries. The carnival was their damned oyster, whatever that meant. He helped her up into the box, and she smiled at him. The lights were bright outside and shining kind of dim in here. Mick caught Richie's eye and gave him a nod, full of meaning. He got the look back from Richie and knew he was good to go. If their positions were reversed, he'd have done the same for Richie.

Mick held Mandy's hand on the first few clicks up the wheel. He could feel the sweat now, slick on her palm, and he wondered if it was his or hers. They came up about forty-five degrees on the rotation—what Mick called first position—and stopped as Richie went to unload the people in the next car down below.

He had some time. Lots of time, thanks to Richie.

"Wow," Mandy said, looking out the window. "It's real pretty up here."

"Wait 'til we get to the top," Mick said, throwing it out there with the aura of assurance. "You ain't never seen nothing like it, I promise."

She turned her head from the window, and he caught her as she turned around, kissing her full on the lips. She returned the pressure and opened her mouth. She'd gotten used to this by now, he thought, and she seemed to like it. If he'd tried it on their first kiss she might not have gone for it, but now she pushed her tongue into his mouth like she was poking a finger in his eye. He ignored the abruptness and the force of it and tried to smoothly, slowly show her how to do it right.

They sat that way for a couple minutes until the car started moving again, and Mick broke it off, taking a deep breath as he did so. He had about ten minutes left as the car stopped in second position—three o'clock on the wheel. Richie was taking his time. "You know, I'm leaving tomorrow." He said it quietly and a little sadly.

"Yeah." Mandy nodded her head, and she was clearly a little sad too, no faking. He kissed her—gentle and brief this time, not giving her enough time to cram her tongue in his mouth like she was shoving a cat in a sack. "I know," she said as their lips parted.

"You make me feel something, Mandy," he said, trying to keep his eyes on hers. The trick was to not say it cheesy, like one of those big-city Lotharios that would lie to get what they wanted. The trick was to mean it, behind his eyes. He really did feel something for her. Something.

"You make me feel too, Mick," she said. He knew she meant it. She had a hand on his chest, running over his light shirt. Felt good.

He kissed her again, tonguing her first this time, before she could beat him to the punch. He moved off her mouth and to her cheek, and she froze as he gently put a hand on her breast. It wasn't bad, that's for sure, and he could feel the bra just under the cotton shirt. He could feel her tense up, but she didn't scream, didn't swat his hand away, and that was a damned good sign.

He put a kiss on the side of her neck, sucking gently on the salty skin there. Ran his tongue over her flesh and felt her get goose bumps. He left the hand on her breast and squeezed gently against her bra. She was maybe a B cup on a good day, and the padding on the thing interfered with the sensation, but she moaned a little as he did what he did. Very good signs.

"Wait," she said and brushed his hand off her. He withheld the cringe he felt inside as she did it and managed to smile through it. She took a second, caught her breath, and it rattled a little between gasps. "I ... I can't."

"It's okay," he said, and ran a hand through her hair. "I just ... want to show you how I feel." He leaned in to kiss the side of her neck and she pulled away.

"I can't ... I just ... I've never—" she said finally, and her eyes looked frightened now, like a scared animal about to bolt for the woods at the sight of a hunter.

But she couldn't bolt, because he still had almost ten minutes left. And like he hadn't already known she'd never done it before? It was as obvious as the innocent look in her eyes. "It's okay," he said again, and ran a caress over her cheek. "I understand." Which he did. He leaned in and put an arm around her. "I just thought maybe we could ..."

"It's not that I don't want to," Mandy said, leaning into him. He could smell that sweet hair shampoo again, mingled with that little hint of sweat on her scalp as he kissed the top of her head. "I just ... what if somebody found out?"

Music to his ears, like AC/DC out of a speaker nearby. "Nobody would have to know," Mick said. "Just you and me."

He could hear her swallow, could sense the gears turning in her mind. "I'd be so embarrassed. And if I got—"

"You won't," he said, putting all his soothe into it. He tried to make his voice low and confident. "I can make sure that doesn't happen, a friend of mine taught me how."

She glanced at him sideways. "Really?" That innocence was working in his favor.

"Really," he said. Not really, though. Not a chance. But once she said yes and they did it, it wasn't his problem anymore.

"O-okay," she said, and that was all he needed, just that quick half nod. He could see the reluctance in how she held herself, still stiff and uncertain, eyes downward.

Mick leaned in and kissed her again, sucked on the side of her neck, and now she got tense from that and not the reservations pinging around in her head like the ball in that game he'd seen once on somebody's TV, bouncing off the little lines. He ran that hand up her shirt behind, tips of his fingers running over that lightly sweaty skin, slipping their way up to the fastener for her bra.

She gasped when he popped it loose in one. Reached his hand up to the promised land as he helped her slide out of the seat and onto the bottom of the metal car. It was a little rough, true, but he felt her warmth, felt his weight against her. She was going along, but she had that look on her face, still scared. He smiled, trying to reassure her as he knelt down. She just lay flat on her back like she knew how it was all going to play out. Worked for him.

He leaned in and kissed her again, and again. She wasn't the one forcing the tongue anymore, maybe because she was all nerves and no energy. That was just fine, though, and he slid her shirt up and pulled the loosened bra down to expose perfect, slightly browned nipples against her pale flesh. Her legs were all tanned, but she had dark lines that ended where her shirt collars came, and everything south of there was near-white, nothing like the brown skin of her arms outside the sleeves.

She drew a ragged breath as he looked her in her eyes—still innocent, still scared—and kissed her nipple gently. She sighed, and some of the fear melted into pleasure. Some. He kissed her more deeply, and she stirred, moaned. They'd clicked another forty-five degrees up, and Mick knew the Ferris wheel was like a ticking clock—but he still had plenty of time. He let his hand drift lower while his mouth stayed occupied, and he unfastened her jean shorts.

She helped a little, shifting so he could pull them down. He didn't go too far with them at first, just to below her knees. He left her white panties just where they were. Damned things covered all, but it didn't matter because now he could get some fingers down in there. It was sweaty and damp, maybe just from the heat, but Mick didn't care. The moistness turned him on and he suckled harder on her nipple as he started to explore the crotch of her panties. Her moans got a little louder now as he took his time, warming her up gently, soothing on the outside before he even thought about dipping a finger in.

She was moaning within a few minutes as they clicked into the twelve o'clock position on the Ferris wheel. Mick could feel how damned hard and ready he was, but he wasn't gonna take a chance and botch this. Rush and she might get cold feet. Warm up her pussy and everything else would stay ready for him when the moment came, too. She was getting into it now, he had one finger barely into her while he was rubbing her clitoris and had his lips on her nipple. She had a hand over her mouth, though, like she was trying to keep her heavy breathing from being heard by anyone. His tongue was occupied by her left nipple now, though, or he would have told her that nobody could hear them.

He could feel her desire rising and wondered if she ever did this to herself. If not, he was just giving her all the gifts tonight, wasn't he? Doubtful she'd appreciate it, though, after he was gone. He glanced up and saw her bite down on her own wrist as she nearly cried out, and he knew it was time.

Mick let her breast fall out of his mouth and pulled away from her. He stared at her eyes, saw the reluctance, the *Why'd you stop?* He tugged her panties all the way down to her shorts and then wrapped his fingers around them as he pulled them down to her feet and worked them free of one of her white cloth shoes. He noticed the green grass stains on the shoe and smiled. She was helping him get them off and when he unfastened his pants and pushed them down to his ankles, she watched him the whole time with a hungry look.

He walked on his knees up to between her legs, awkward as the metal stung his kneecaps with each movement. He ignored it, because who gave a fuck right now? Other than Mandy. She was about to give a fuck.

Hopefully a hell of a fuck.

He could see her wince a little when he pushed in the first time, even though he tried to be gentle. There was only so gentle you could be and still break through, though; at least, that was his experience. He was leaned down over her, his pelvis on hers, weight on his knees which were letting him know they weren't all that happy about the metal bottom of the car they were resting on. He still didn't care.

He went slow at first. Felt her biting her lip because it probably still hurt. She was damned tight, tight and a little dry to start, but she got wetter as he went. By the time the wheel clicked down again to between ten and eleven o'clock, he could feel things starting to build. His dick was leaden, and when he thought it couldn't swell anymore, it damned sure did, the pressure building. He was still a good ways off, though.

Mick felt his eyes roll as he kept going. It was all through him now, the pleasure. How could this feel so damned good? He didn't know, didn't care, just wanted it. His head was rushing, too, both of them, but the one atop his neck was getting into the act. Any minute now, it was going to open up, going to—

Here it went—

Mick felt his mind expand as he ground his cock into Mandy. Before it was like he could just feel her, here in the box and car of the Ferris wheel, locked in between ten and eleven o'clock on the arc. His dick was calling out its pleasure, every nerve shouting its enjoyment of the sweet slide in and out that he was grinding out on her. He could feel his pubic hair matted and pushing against hers with every thrust, could feel his balls slap just below her pussy.

But when his mind opened up, suddenly he wasn't just living the pleasure in the car on the Ferris wheel.

He was elsewhere, too.

He could sense the girl in the car at twelve o'clock, twenty-two years old, sitting next to her boyfriend whose name was Mark. Hers was Caroline, and she had dark hair and small tits, and Mick could feel himself in her, too, like he was there. He could hear her moaning in his mind, her body slumped against the back of the seat with her boyfriend beside her. She smelled like peaches, tasted like cinnamon and sugar when his tongue met hers, and she wasn't nearly so sweaty as Mandy. She'd fucked before, knew what it felt like, and she leaned into him as he put it into her. Her moans were stronger, her whole feel was stronger, and she was ignoring the boyfriend next to her in favor of the strange sensation of amazing pleasure sliding into her, blotting out everything else around her—

It was the same in the car below, with a woman married twenty years to the same man. Her name was Gail, and Mick could feel her too, feel her at the same time he could feel Mandy and Caroline. She had an older-lady perfume, but he didn't care. She was ready as he entered her, throwing her head back and moaning as he did it, her eyes glazing over as he kissed her neck the way he did with Mandy.

Her husband was next to her, said something to her, but she didn't even hear it because she was completely wrapped up in Mick and what he was doing to her.

Mick could feel his mind expand away from the Ferris wheel, covering the ground around him. He was with all those women at once, every one of them, and it felt SO. AMAZING. Like it had with Mandy by herself but times a hundred, then two hundred as more and more of them found their way into his path. He could feel his brain expanding like a balloon getting blown up and more and more women feeling him inside. Too many to name, even though he tried. Jillian, Cathy, Michelle, Patty—old, young, who gave a shit? It felt so damned good.

So.

Damned.

Good.

The Ferris wheel started to move again as Caroline above them moaned so loud Mick could hear it with his waking ears down below. He wondered if Mandy noticed, but he didn't care as his mind expanded again to the town around them. He could feel them all, all the women who'd had any awakening, who'd felt this kind of passion, he could feel every last one of them, and he was inside them, could smell the perfumes and the sweat and the night air and taste their skin and tongues and salty sweetness as he moved toward that explosive climax—

When he came, he didn't pull out, not at all, just felt himself jerk in Mandy and keep going until it was done. He could feel the cum shoot out, squirting like he'd had his balls in a tight grip and then someone had loosened it. His body went slack, and he lay his head down on the girl's shoulder, sweaty hair against the sheen of perspiration.

The world shrunk around him, and he said goodbye to all the women he'd just loosed himself in. His breathing was heavy, and he was still in her, still in—what was her name? Mandy—and he didn't want to move even though his knees hurt like fucking hell.

His crotch was sticky and damp, pubic hair matted down where it touched hers. He felt the soft cloth of her t-shirt against his chin and wished he'd been able to take it off so he could rest his cheek on her soft, pale shoulder where the sun hadn't tanned her skin. But they were clicking into the nine o'clock position now and he only had a couple minutes before they were down and Richie was opening the door to let them out.

It kind of tickled and kind of hurt when he pulled out, that sticky, dried out feeling like his dick had gotten glued into her. She cringed when he did it and he saw the hint of blood tingeing the swollen, red-purple skin around the head of his cock. "Damn that was good," he whispered. She didn't answer. He had a feeling she didn't feel the same.

He got up on his knees and pulled his underpants up first, felt his dick stick to the cloth, still hard. He'd still be hard when he got off the Ferris wheel, there was no avoiding that. Walking around with a big old hard-on was embarrassing, but he had no concern about it. There was this dim sense of relief over him now, like all his cares had just gotten washed away—or more likely, gotten shot out at the end of their little tryst.

Mick fastened his pants and put his ass up on the seat. He didn't spare a glance to Mandy, who was still lying flat on her back, watching him, with her jean shorts and white cover-all underwear hanging off of one foot, bra pushed down and her shirt up to expose small, pale breasts. "Ride's gonna end soon," Mick said matter-of-factly. "Might want to get dressed." He let out a long, heavy breath and felt all the tension bleed out of him.

"Okay." Her voice was small, and she extended a hand toward him so he could help her up. He glanced at it and ignored it, putting his eyes to the slatted window that afforded him a view of the fair beyond. They'd missed the view from the apex.

Mick could feel the last of his cum drying in his underwear like concrete. It always hurt to clean that off later, but it was worth it. After a moment of waiting, Mandy sat up on her own and fumbled to fasten her own bra. It took her a minute, and Mick wondered idly why they didn't make them fasten in fucking front.

"Ohhh," Mick said, like a man who'd just let a huge burden off. He had, really. He put his arms up and folded his hands behind his head, and watched Mandy fumble back into her underpants and shorts out of the corner of his eye while he sat like a fucking king who'd just gotten crowned. "Damn, that was good."

Mandy was looking at him; he could see that from the little he was watching her. Looking at him like she was a dog he'd kicked, not sure if she should come around him again. "Was it?"

"It was," Mick said, nodding. He could feel his sweaty, tangled hair against his hands, and the faint aroma of her pussy was still on his fingers, he could smell it all the way around the back of his head. The whole Ferris wheel car smelled a little like sex, and Mick fucking loved it. There was nothing like these moments after the urge was relieved. If he could have taken a nap right now, he would have and loved it.

"Was I ..." Mandy's voice was small, "was I ... good?"

"Hell, no," Mick said, almost laughing, "you were terrible. You just lay there, like a dead body or something. That ain't sexy."

Now he looked at her full on, and that innocence, it was all damned gone and replaced by a stricken look that turned to horror in the eyes that had been so sweet before. "I ... I ..."

"Don't worry about it," he said breezily as the car clicked down to the last position between seven and eight o'clock on the wheel. "It's not like I needed you to be amazing or anything." He thought about petting her on her tousled hair but didn't want to move his hands from cushioning the back of his head against the metal car wall. "Still, learn to move, baby. Get into it so you're not so boring for the next guy."

"Next guy?" Her lip quivered with her voice.

He shrugged. He could say something fiercely mean and utterly truthful to that, but what was the point now? He'd got his rocks off, she'd let him use her to expand his mind, and it was all good for him. She was sitting there with her pants halfway pulled up, little trail of blood and other ooze working its way down her inner thigh. He stared, thinking about how he'd like to do that again but knowing he couldn't because even if she'd wanted to—and he was under no illusions she would—he was leaving town in just hours.

"I thought you ... felt something for me," Mandy said quietly. It was all hurt from her, like she'd got shattered by what he'd said and did. Mick could pick up on it; hell, a deaf and blind man could have picked up on it from this distance.

"I did," Mick said with a laugh, "and it was called a raging hardon." He waggled his crotch at her from where he sat. "Thanks for helping me take care of it."

The Ferris wheel started to move that last time, ratcheting down to the six o'clock starting point. Full circle. She started to speak again, but the sound of Richie unlatching the door from outside stopped her, and she turned her head like a rabbit toward its hunter as the door opened.

"Hope you had a good ride," Richie said with a knowing smile. Mick knew if Mandy had been a little older and a little wiser, she'd have figured out it was all a big setup. "Everybody out."

She wasn't that old, though, and she wasn't that wise, though she was getting there now, Mick knew. She looked crushed as he stood up and hopped out of the car. His feet hit the solid ground, the subtle rocking motion he barely noticed anymore stopping as he landed. He didn't put out a hand to help Mandy down, not this time, just walked away from her without a care or a goodbye. He didn't need to look in her eyes to know that innocence he'd thought was so wonderful earlier in the evening was gone, blissfully and blessedly. He'd taken it. Taken it and loved every minute of it.

He passed Gail, the housewife that had been in the car below them, leaning against a railing on the edge of the platform. She was still flushed in the face, and her big, fat husband was next to her. "I just don't know what came over me," she was saying as Mick passed. She started to say something else but stopped and stared at him as he went past her. He didn't say anything to her, didn't even look at her, but he could tell she knew. He didn't care, though. He got those looks all through the carnival as he made his way out—women being attended by the guys they were with, all of them wondering what the fuck had happened that had left them all weak in the knees and uncertain.

Mandy would probably feel it the worst tonight, though, Mick knew as he threaded his way between the Fortune Teller's tent and a ball-throwing game. But he didn't need the Fortune Teller's crystal ball—she was a fraud anyway, that old bitch—to tell him that they'd all be feeling it tomorrow, and the day after, and in the weeks and months to come.

***

Mandy woke up the next day still feeling it. And for the next weeks, too. Her mother called it "being blue," but she didn't know the why. Not that it mattered; she thought it was just a little lovesickness. And then a regular sickness, when she started to throw up in the mornings a few weeks later. It took about a week for her mom to work it out after that.

It took another week for them to put together that every woman her age and older in the town who hadn't already been pregnant was now. Married, single, even the divorced ones. Young and damned near impossibly old.

Mandy had cried for weeks, and when she found out she cried some more. When she found out she wasn't alone, she cried again, like that wasn't any consolation at all. It was still terrible, still a fresh wound, still the end of her world like someone had burned down everything and killed everyone that mattered to her.

But then, nine months later, all of Hobbs Green really did burn down, and everyone that mattered to her got killed.

And all that was left was Mandy—and she damned sure didn't feel innocent anymore.

1.

"This is such a fucking goddamned mess and a half," Sheriff Nicholas Reeve opined, standing in the middle of Berg Street. Arch might have shared that assessment, minus the colorfully added swear words, but he didn't feel a need to voice it now. It was a mess and a half, no mincing words on that score.

"I know we've seen some weird shit this last week," Erin Harris said, standing off the curb, straddling the cracking pavement as the sun beat down on the trio, "but this is monumentally fucked. Not quite the Mount Rushmore of fucked, but maybe like the Lincoln Memorial of it."

"Ahuh," Arch said, more than a little preoccupied, and not just by the grisly mess in the middle of Berg Street. There was blood every-dang-where, splattered all over the pavement like it had been dripped on a canvas by a painter trying to make a statement— the statement being, *"Let's drench this beast!"* Though some avant-garde painter who covered an entire canvas in red probably wouldn't use the word beast.

Still.

"I've seen a lot of traffic accidents in my day," Reeve said, shaking his head, "but I ain't never seen nothing like this shit." He waved a hand at the remainder of the body. "If he didn't have his damned wallet on him, you'd never even know that was Tim Connor."

Arch nodded and caught Erin doing much the same out of the corner of his eye. Tim Connor had been a pretty active guy, always running. He wasn't gonna be running no more, that was sure and certain.

"Whoever fucking did this had to be going a hundred and twenty on a residential street," Reeve said. "Kids play here, people jog—like

Tim." He indicated the remainder of the corpse. "This is so goddamned reckless I can't even define it." Arch could tell Reeve was shaken because he was dropping the Lord's name in vain at ten times the usual rate. Arch had gotten over flinching every time the sheriff violated the Third Commandment by now; if he hadn't, dealing with Lafayette Hendricks would have been well-nigh impossible for him.

Arch shook off the thought of the cowboy-hat-wearing demon hunter and looked back at the sack of butchered meat that had been Tim Connor. He'd been a middle-aged guy, in good shape, always drinking protein shakes whenever Arch ran into him somewhere. He'd seen him at the diner a few days ago, and the guy ordered a bare fish, no fried topping.

"He was such a healthy motherfucker," Reeve said. "Always running, eating right, trying to push the damned envelope." Reeve unconsciously reached for his own belly, which hung over his belt. "Son of a bitch should have outlived me by a long shot, but he didn't because some cocksucker ran him down going a hundred miles an hour in a thirty. This is whole fucking town is turning into a fucking slaughter fest out of goddamned control—"

"Sheriff," Erin said, catching Arch's eye as she spoke. Probably to avoid looking Reeve in the eye. "It ain't your fault."

"I'm the law in this goddamned town! When *County Administrator* Pike," Reeve put a special sauce of sarcasm on that title, "gets wind of this, the blame's gonna come one way, and it's mine."

Arch drew a breath and felt a certain tightness that had nothing to do with how well his shirt fit. Unlike Reeve, he did tend to do that whole exercising, eating right thing. Or had, until a couple weeks ago when things had got suddenly busy in his life. "Still ain't your fault," Arch said.

"I appreciate your support," Reeve said without an ounce of sincerity, "but I doubt the voters are going to share your enthusiasm for the results of our law enforcement efforts this last month. Disappearances, kidnappings, entire families getting wiped out, some sort of crazy highway massacre, and a hooker that got burned alive from the inside. Not to mention those security guards up on the Tallakeet Dam." Reeve pulled his hat off his head and ran his fingers through thinning hair. "Yeah, I can't see how I could possibly be blamed for anything."

"At least the town didn't flood," Erin said sympathetically. She shot Arch a sidelong look that was full of meaning—and the meaning was "What do you say at a moment like this?" Arch didn't say anything because he didn't know either. It wasn't Reeve's fault.

It wasn't like he'd set out a sign inviting every demon in North America to Midian, Tennessee. Heck, he probably didn't even know that was the source of his problems. It wasn't like mass murders and slaughters and burnings of people alive automatically brought to mind the idea that demons were real and walking among humans like regular people. That was crazy talk.

But then, these were crazy times.

Arch glanced at Erin and found her looking at him. Thought maybe she was thinking the same as him—that they were both crazy and bound for the same asylum. "How long 'til the corpse wagon gets here?" Erin asked, drawing her gaze back to Reeve.

"Who fucking knows?" Reeve said, and for a moment, it looked like he was gonna spike his hat.

"We should probably get back out on patrol," Arch said, shrugging his shoulders. "Unless you want us to stick around to help you guard the scene?"

"Get the hell outta here," Reeve waved his hat at them. "Maybe you can do some good elsewhere, because there ain't nothing going on here other than me trying to keep the lookiloos from peeking at the hamburger someone made of Tim."

Arch's gaze danced over to Connor's body again. Hamburger wasn't far off. Limbs were missing, knocked clean from the body. There was a straight line of blood from the site of the impact some fifty feet or more from where the body rested now to where it had started, and the terminus of that line near the corpse was filled with the evidence of a long, skidding roll that it had undertaken before it came to rest in its current position. An arm was missing at the elbow, and one of the legs was hanging by a string of flesh so narrow it looked like an onion straw. But drenched in blood.

Nope, that wasn't a good way to go.

"Get on out of here," Reeve said again, waving his hat at them. "Go patrol, just … get the fuck outta here."

Arch didn't need to be told again. He'd never really seen Reeve in one of these moods before.

He thought about trying to say something else reassuring, but he still couldn't think of anything. So instead he just fell into line with Erin as they headed toward the barricades set up just past the site of Tim Connor's launch. They stayed quiet all the way 'til they were on the other side of the first blood splatter, and Arch knew that was as far as he was gonna get before Erin said something.

***

"What the fuck do you think did this?" Erin asked. She had the sick feeling in her stomach that came from knowing something the sheriff most assuredly did not but being totally unable to voice it to him. It made her feel bad, made her feel—if she admitted it to herself—a little bit excited, too, like she was on the inside for a secret that no one else knew.

"No idea," Arch said, the big, stoic man that he was. He was stalking away from the scene in a hell of a hurry, his eyes hidden darkly under the brim of his hat. She couldn't tell if he was trying to be shadowy and shit or if he was annoyed with her.

"But it was a demon, right?" Erin asked a little louder than she intended and realized a moment later there were people out on their porches all down the sides of the street.

Arch played it cool and didn't even bother to turn his head to look, like she hadn't just said anything. He was a cool customer, Arch. "Probably," he said in a low voice that was probably more appropriate to the situation than hers had been. Erin kicked herself mentally. She should have been a little more circumspect, she knew. "But it's not like I know enough about them to tell what kind."

Erin thought back to that book of Hendricks's that she'd pilfered a couple days ago, before the dam. It had all types of demons in it. Crazy shit. She was sure it meant he was crazy, too, but then she'd seen a guy breathe fire out of his mouth like some kind of dragon, and suddenly the ex-Marine didn't seem quite so insane. "You think Hendricks would know?"

Arch just looked tense now. "Maybe. If not him, maybe his new buddies."

"You mean Lerner and Duncan?" Erin shot him a coy smile. Lerner and Duncan seemed all right, even though they were demons.

Or Officers of Occultic Concordance, as they'd pronounced themselves when she'd gotten the full intro. Lerner had said it with a swagger. Duncan hadn't said anything at all.

"Yeah," Arch said tightly as they crossed through a gap in the barricades to where their patrol cars were parked on the other side. "Them." Arch's Explorer's lights were flashing, and so were the dashboard lights in Erin's car—which had until really recently been the sheriff's own. She didn't exactly consider this a moment appropriate to smile, considering how straight-to-shit things had gotten in Midian lately, but the thought of having her own car was almost worthy of one, even under the circumstances. Even if it was still missing the driver's side mirror.

"How did you explain that mirror to the sheriff?" Arch asked, like he could read her fucking mind or something.

"I haven't," she said. "Figured if he had time to notice it, it'd be the least of his problems. He hasn't said shit about it yet."

Arch paused next to his car, lowered his voice. "What about those spent shells from the rifle in the back?" He kept his cool gaze on her. "He find out about those yet?"

"The gun's clean," Erin said. To this she smiled, though politely and coolly rather than with any kind of satisfaction. "Cleaned it myself after I took it to the range. Bought some replacement ammo while I was there, so no need for anyone to be the wiser about that little ordeal." Because losing a mirror was one thing but discharging an AR-15 in a gun battle with a demon on top of Tallakeet Dam was the sort of thing Reeve might pay attention to, even in his current state. "What about those big .50 cal rounds hiding up in the tree line near the dam?"

Arch didn't even flinch. "Picked 'em up myself the day after." He opened his driver's side door and got in. He shot her a little half-assed look of pure chagrin. "No need to leave that thread hanging out for anybody to yank on."

***

Hendricks was running down the goddamned hill at a high enough speed that it ought to have scared the shit out of him. Maybe it did a little, but after clearing doors in Ramadi a few times, the fear factor for running down a steep hill turned down a few notches. It was like being afraid of getting in a bicycle accident after learning to drive a car at a hundred and ninety miles an hour; it could still happen, but it wasn't something you gave a lot of thought to.

Tree branches whipped at him as he descended the slope, hauling ass and all else while whipping around tree trunks and shit. He wasn't winded, not yet, but he wasn't in near as good a shape as he'd been in the Marines, either, so it was bound to catch up with him soon. He thought that, anyway, as he ducked his head slightly to avoid a low-hanging branch and nearly fucking toppled. That would be an embarrassing thing to have to cop to—*yeah, I rolled down a fucking hill while chasing after a demon. I'm a serious demon hunter, all right.*

He'd busted down the front door of the demon's home as impolitely as he could. About like he imagined Arch would do, crashing in some meth dealer's house if he had to. Knocked it off its hinges before his companions could volunteer to do it for him; he was always more of a DIY guy, hating to delegate shit. Do it yourself it gets it done right. He wasn't an officer, after all.

Now he was damned near pinwheeling his arms to keep from getting that weightless sensation as each foot left the ground. It was a steep fucking hill—foothill, he guessed—somewhere near the bottom of the King Daddy mountain in these parts, Mount Horeb or something stupid. His mind defaulted to calling it Mouth Whore-ebb, though that wasn't exactly how the locals said it.

All this kept flashing through his mind as he ran. Busting down that door, sword in hand, ready to deal damage to a demon only to have the scrawny bastard flash those eyes at him and cannonball out the nearby picture window into the gulch below the house—all of it played along with a commentary in his head that said, *Holy shit, what the fuck am I doing?*

And the answer was: *Trying to make this town a safer place, one demon sonofabitch at a time.*

The wind kicked up a little as he came over a slope. He grunted and adjusted his feet to compensate. He still felt like he was out of control, but his legs were keeping up so far. It was a crazy fucking feeling, not quite as bad as tear-assing down a steep road on a bike but close, and his quarry was at least a hundred feet ahead of him, busting branches of the trees with his arms as he ran. Hey, it cleared a path for

Hendricks, and he wasn't choosy about the kind of help he was getting, especially lately.

Especially lately.

He didn't have enough breath to shout insults at the thing or he would have. All he had was the focus to keep his eye on the damned ball, on the damned demon, and his mind out of the possibilities for all the shit that could befall him should he fall. He wasn't sure if there was a tonic that could undo all the fucked-up damage his body would take if that would happen, and he didn't want to find out.

The wind kept a coming, blowing in his eyes and making him squint. It was a hot damned day, and he was sweating like he was on Parris Island again, just wishing it was some morning PT. It wasn't quite as bad as Iraq, though, that was certain. The ground was all dried up, too, which was weird as hell, he thought idly as he went, because only a couple days ago it had rained hard enough to flood the fuck outta the whole county.

"On your left!" came a voice from—big surprise—his left. Hendricks would have tossed a look of disdain but instead he tucked his left elbow again, even as he kept dodging down the slope, his big black drover coat billowing behind him and his cowboy hat still clinging to his head.

***

Lerner surged past the cowboy without much effort. Hendricks had a good lead time because the dumbass had jumped out the window behind the fleeing demon—a quantel'a, as near as Lerner could see—and Lerner wasn't willing to do something that stupid. It wasn't exactly a point of pride, like he was too good to go leaping out a window. It was more like he just shook his head at the two of them for being fucking morons and made his way down with his partner, Duncan, in tow. Like civilized people and not fucking animals.

They were running like animals now, though, he and Duncan. And cursing like men. Well, he was, anyway. Duncan was still stoic and approaching on Hendricks's right, though he hadn't bothered to announce himself. He'd often pondered why Duncan was such a mild-mannered sort of fellow when he really could have cut loose— like Lerner did every now and again. He hadn't come up with any answers on that front, not even after a hundred-plus years. That was probably some sort of answer in and of itself, but as long as Lerner had pondered it he hadn't gotten to the bottom of it in any way that satisfied.

Now Lerner was watching the world whip past him as he ran down what felt to him like a mountain, hoping he didn't take a misstep. Smashing into a tree at this speed could be potentially career ending for him. And by career ending, he meant breaking open the shell that held his happy demon essence in that rough covering he called a body. It would not make for a joyful day, not for him. He could kind of imagine showing back up in the underworld, earthly form busted and burned up, and imagined the reception he'd get. It made him watch his steps just a touch more carefully.

The fucking quantel'a that had started the whole foot chase wasn't getting away, but the strung-out dipshit was damned sure making a good show of it. Whatever he was on was letting him run a lot farther and faster than he should have been able to. Fear would probably do that to a quantel'a. Fear and meth.

"You getting a reading?" Lerner called out to Duncan and saw a shake of the head in return as Duncan passed Hendricks. The cowboy started to do a double take and halted as he cut left around a tree, its big-ass, low-hanging branches causing him to swing wide just behind Duncan. "Sons of bitches. I catch that fucking screen Spellman selling those fucking clouding runes to anyone, I'm gonna expose his empty-ass innards to the light of day."

"Would it do any good?" Hendricks had started to gasp now. Lerner wondered how much longer the cowboy could run.

"It'd do my heart some good," Lerner said blackly. That screen—just an empty vessel that could talk like a man, used as a veil by someone from the other side to transact business with earthly creatures—that sonofabitch was the cause of all his problems for the last few days. All of them. And they couldn't even find his ass now, nor the asses of most of the other troublemaking demons in town, because the fucking screen had been selling runes that hid them from Duncan and his sensing powers. "Yours too, based on how much huffing you're doing, meatbag."

"I'm not used to running mountains every day," Hendricks answered, and Lerner could hear him trying to rein in his heavy breathing. He hadn't known the cowboy for more than a few days, and already he could see the pride just oozing off the bastard.

"Wouldn't matter if you did," Duncan answered matter-of-factly, missing Hendricks's look of ire, "he's faster than you." Duncan turned on the jets and blew down the slope.

Lerner wanted to laugh at Duncan's sudden burst of speed, but he had enough charity in him that he decided not to rub it into the cowboy. Poor bastard. Instead, he just sped up himself.

***

They were outpacing him like mad now, Lerner and Duncan, and Hendricks could feel his face burning not just from the heat of the run but from shame. Sure, they were demons, and they damned well ought to be stronger and faster than him.

That didn't make it burn any less, though.

Duncan broke loose a tree limb ahead of him, sending it spiraling down the slope with a hard hit of the wrist. The crack echoed down the mountain. Hendricks could see a field somewhere through the trees up ahead.

He knew they had to catch this bastard soon. Duncan was closest, was closest and almost there—

The demon juked right as Duncan was almost close enough to lay a hand on him. Hendricks would have held his breath if he hadn't needed every one of them at the moment. Duncan missed a step and tumbled, his shoulder hitting the ground hard enough to break bones.

If he'd had bones.

The demon burned hard right like a receiver in a football game. He snaked out of view for a second behind a low fir tree. Hendricks picked up on him again as he turned back down the slope.

Hendricks was beyond winded now, beyond tired. He wanted to go back to his hotel room and pass out and wake up without any of the pains he knew he was going to. Beyond any rationality, he wanted Erin to massage his hurts away, wanted to get down and nasty with her. That second bit would probably happen anyway, based on how often they'd been fucking the last couple days.

He filed that thought away for later as he rounded the pine and swooped down the slope after Lerner. He didn't look back to make sure Duncan was all right. He was sure the demon was, though he'd probably messed up his lime-colored suit.

Lerner was a good twenty yards ahead of Hendricks by now, and about ten behind the demon. The fucker was doing everything in his power to not run a straight line, and he could have been going anywhere based on his movements. Hendricks half expected him to double back and head up the slope.

"Nowhere to run," Hendricks breathed.

"He's proving you wrong on that one," Lerner tossed over his shoulder. Hendricks frowned. He hadn't expected the demon to even hear him. What were they called again? Oh, right. Office of Occultic Concordance.

OOCs.

Lerner was closing the gap with the speedy, dodgy bastard. The slope got sandy and the ground went a little soft, forcing Hendricks to look for better footing. Lerner didn't, though, and missed a step.

Whoosh.

The OOC went sideways down the hill, smacking into a tree with a noise that told Hendricks he did feel pain.

"And then there was one," Hendricks muttered.

The trees thinned ahead and the demon was slowing. Whether it was because he thought he'd gotten away clean after dodging two OOCs or because he had smelled Hendricks coming and didn't think he was much of a threat—well, it didn't matter.

Hendricks passed the last few trees as the last boughs vanished and uninterrupted sky appeared above them. The demon wasn't exactly pulling a Run Forrest Run anymore. He'd slowed and was jogging backward lightly, like he was just leading Hendricks on at this point, standing at the edge of a meadow that stretched all the way up to a fence beyond. There was activity there, but it was far enough off that Hendricks didn't pay it a bit of attention.

"Moves like that, you oughta be playing for the Titans," Hendricks said, slowing to a walk as he entered the meadow. The grass was ankle deep, green and uneven, whispering as he stepped on it.

The guy was all thin and rangy, had meth teeth and black-as-night demon eyes. "OOCs don't let us play sports, can you believe it?" He grinned. "Damn near killed me when I found out as a teen. I was pretty good at football."

"Yeah, well, you don't really have the build to be taken seriously as anything but a kicker," Hendricks said, keeping his distance. The sun was damned hot above now that the trees were behind them. The demon was just treading in place, looking more like a boxer practicing footwork than a runner about to sprint off. "So ... we gonna throw down now?"

"Looks like a fair fight to me," the demon said, still grinning with those spotted teeth. "Now that you've lost your friends."

"Oh, they weren't my friends," Hendricks said. Draw the sword or draw him in? Guy could run, no doubt, and pulling the sword tended to make demons antsy. Wait too long, though, and this bastard was fast enough to put him in a world of hurt.

"You're a human demon hunter hanging out with OOCs," the demon said, shaking his head. "That's not even strange bedfellows man, that's like ... a cat sleeping with a giraffe."

"God, I hope I'm the giraffe in that scenario," Hendricks muttered.

"You're about to be the cat," the guy said, and he lunged for Hendricks.

Hendricks knew in the second the guy came at him that he should have pulled the sword. The demon already knew he was a hunter, already had a feel for what he was capable of, and knew he was hanging out with OOCs. The rumors—they'd damned sure gotten around, and fast, considering he'd just met Lerner and Duncan a couple days ago.

Hendricks knew even as he got his hand on the hilt that the demon would be on him before it was out, would have his teeth buried in Hendricks throat before he could even—

BOOM.

The sound was louder than thunder, like artillery called in from the hill, like an airstrike dropping in from above. The demon that was coming at Hendricks dropped—more like flipped backward, upper body rocked like he'd been hit with God's own hammer right in the chest. Not that Hendricks believed in God, but the way that fucker flipped, it might as well have been an act of His.

The sound of the shot faded as Hendricks closed on the demon. The guy was hurting, plain as anything. Hendricks thought about making light of it, but why? He drew his sword as he stood over the bastard, and smelled the strong scent of smoked meth hanging in the air.

"Not your friends, huh?" the demon asked, with black eyes.

"You know a lot of OOCs that carry a .50 cal Barrett rifle?" Hendricks asked. He smiled, shrugged, and slammed the sword through the demon's chest.

Black fire crept out from the hole, from his eyes, from his mouth, and swallowed him whole like he'd been pulled back into the black depths of hell. The grass beneath him waved lightly with the passing of the storm of ebony flame, then settled undisturbed, the blades just a little shorter in the shape of the demon's figure than the ones around them.

Hendricks watched him go, watched the hellfire recede, his outline still visible like an afterimage. He sighed, long and heavy, before he turned back to the hillside, where one, two ... now three figures threaded their way down, not in much of a hurry since the job was done.

"Alison," Hendricks muttered under his breath, low enough so that only the two OOCs could hear him.

***

Alison Longholt Stan wasn't much for this wilderness stuff. Her daddy had taught her to hunt when she was young, but she'd never really taken to it. She'd mostly sit in the tree stand with him during the season because he liked it, but she passed up most of her shots to let him do it. It was the gutting and the blood and all that mess—just not for her.

The shooting, though? That she didn't mind.

The Barrett rifle she'd borrowed from her daddy's gun cabinet kicked like—well, like something kicked her. An elephant, probably. Something big. She braced it against her shoulder and carried a pad to place between her and the butt of the big rifle, but it still wasn't no peach. Left a bruise on her shoulder that Arch had noticed when they'd had their confrontation after the dam.

She didn't care. She wasn't no little peach herself. No shrinking violet; she'd taken a shovel to a wild dog's head one time when it had rabies and it got after her dog. It was all she had handy, so she did it.

Everything she'd seen since the night those animals had busted down her door reminded her of that moment when she grabbed the shovel. See a wild beast foaming at the mouth, you lay your hands on something heavy and hard.

The Barrett was a fair sight better than a shovel, but the things she was swinging at were a click or two meaner than a rabid dog, too.

She'd watched the cowboy, Hendricks—she was still getting used to him—poke the demon in the belly with his sword. For some reason she didn't understand, that sword or the knife Arch was carrying or the batons those two demon fellows had were the only things that could pop a demon open. She hadn't run across much that a .50 bullet couldn't solve, seeing as it was bigger than her damned finger, but it only put these down—it didn't put 'em out.

She'd come down the slope in the car the OOCs had driven up to the house. She'd waited for them in the back seat until the demon came busting out the back window, then she'd jumped to the front and started the car because it was GO time. She'd stopped about three quarters of the way down the slope and set up, prone, waiting to see if she'd get a clear shot.

Sure enough, they'd let the runner get onto the clear field, and he'd turned to get a load of Hendricks. It hadn't even been tricky at this distance, less than a hundred yards. She'd just plugged him right in the ten ring, square in the middle of the chest. On a human, it'd have been a kill shot.

The fellow certainly felt it, but it didn't kill him.

Alison slid off her belly and adjusted the pad to keep it from falling off her shoulder once the demon was dead. She didn't have much interest in getting up close with one of them again, but greeting them from a distance to put a hurting on them? That was just up her alley, played right to her strengths.

She cased the big Barrett and carried it. Damned thing was heavy, and she struggled a little under the burden. Still, it was her burden.

"Nice shooting, Tex," the slick one—Lerner—said as he caught up with her while she was making her way down toward the field.

"I'm from Tennessee," she said, trying not to take it as an insult. How much could a demon know about geography, anyway?

"Nice shooting, Ten," Lerner said.

She frowned at him. "I don't think they usually call people from Tennessee that."

The corner of the demon's mouth turned up in a smirk. "I bet you've been called a ten once or twice in your time, though."

Alison blushed at that, but she told herself it was because the weight of the rifle was getting to her. She stopped just shy of the edge of the woods, lingering near a tree. She could see across the field where the carnival was setting up, Ferris wheel already sticking off its spoked center, metal bones hanging half-exposed. She didn't mean to, but she felt a little smile coming on. Summertime was usually real nice in Midian, and the Summer Lights Festival was the capstone. Felt like the town could use a little happiness, seeing how grim things had been lately.

Especially considering how grim things had been lately.

"That was a little too out in the open," Lerner said, holding up near Alison. His eyes were on the carnival in the distance, too. She wondered if he could see anything going on over there.

"Thankfully, it's Tennessee, where rifle shots ring out in the middle of day all the time," Hendricks said dryly. The cowboy was wearing a deep frown, and he seemed like he was doing all he could not to look at her.

"You're welcome, by the way," she said, feeling a little irritation springing up from inside.

"I had—" Hendricks started.

"No, you didn't," Lerner and Duncan—that other demon—chorused. Hendricks looked even more irritable.

"I thought you were a professional demon hunter," Alison said. Part of her felt a perverse joy in ribbing the cowboy. Things had been going great before he showed up, after all.

"Yeah, professional demon hunter, not sprinter." The cowboy chewed on that for a moment, looking like he was seething before he finally said, "Thank you." She just nodded at him; she'd already said "You're welcome" after all.

"This is spinning a little off-axis," Lerner said, and Alison didn't quite take his meaning. He glanced at her, probably saw it on her face. "Things are getting out of control."

"It's a hotspot, right?" she asked. "That's ... normal for a hotspot, right?" This time she looked to Hendricks. "Things being out of control?"

The cowboy kind of shrugged. "This one's not been like any of the ones I've been to before. The demons here are a little wilder and more aggressive than past hotspots I've parked in."

"For us, too," Duncan said, his quiet voice and lime green suit making Alison want to giggle a little at him. He seemed so totally strange and harmless that she couldn't really believe he was a demon. "Can't recall a time when anyone's gone and sold runes to keep demons off our radar—and so methodically, too."

"Does seem weird," Hendricks said, suddenly a little tense. Alison wondered if she was imagining it.

"Weirdness is deniable when it's on the fringe," Lerner said, expression dark. "A few deaths here and there can be explained away. But this town is going full-on powder keg, and people dying in droves is not making it any easier to keep the damned match away from the fuse." He looked straight at Alison. "I'm assuming your hubby's current problem is something of the sort that's going to fall into that category."

Alison felt a little heat on her face. "I don't really know; he had to leave pretty abruptly this morning. Something bad happened, but I don't think the sheriff told him over the phone before he took off."

"Erin said something about another body," Hendricks said, and that made Alison blush even more. So Erin had told the cowboy something Arch hadn't told her. She couldn't help the rush of resentment; their argument after the dam was still fresh in her mind, still an open wound. This would probably come up later tonight. Even when she wanted to hold something like this in, it tended to float its way up. Keeping the secret about following Arch with a rifle was the only thing she'd been able to keep from him in their entire marriage. Other than that one credit card she was slowly paying off.

"Nope, this ain't getting any prettier," Lerner said, and the demon was awfully dour. "Come on, let's get out of here before someone reports a gunshot." He glanced at Alison, and he didn't even have to say anything.

"Already picked up my brass," she said, and patted the pocket of her jeans where the massive .50 shell casing hung out just slightly. It still felt a little warm in there. There was a buzz in her other pocket and she fished her phone out to find a message waiting. "Arch and Erin are away from the crime scene—they want to meet in ten minutes."

"Let's get outta here," Lerner said, waving toward where she'd parked the car up the slope. Duncan hesitated, looking toward the carnival setting up in the distance. "What?" Lerner asked. "You got a sudden urge for a funnel cake?"

"No," Duncan said, shaking his head. "Just thought I felt something for a second." He caught Alison looking at him and sent her a reassuring smile as they started to pick their way back up the slope toward where she'd left the car. "Probably nothing."

***

Mick watched 'em go from where he stood close to the half-finished Ferris wheel. He could see 'em a long ways off, those two OOCs and the demon hunters. He'd heard the crack of the rifle and watched the rest. That was a new one for him, he had to admit, seeing someone blast a quantel'a with a big gun so they could get popped by a sword. Not a terrible idea, as far as ideas went.

"Hey, Mick?" A voice came from behind him. It was Jim, that ornery old fucker. A real slavedriver. Not the literal kind, though. Mick could actually still remember those from back in the 1800s. "Need a little help here, man."

"Sure thing," Mick said, tearing his gaze away from the quartet disappearing into the woods. His hand went to his pocket instinctively, and he felt the cold smoothness of the rune he'd bought from that vendor just outside town. Looked like it had been a smart investment after all. And he'd worried as he'd handed over the money that he was getting taken for a ride.

Mick chewed his lip as he stretched like he was hurting. He wasn't; demon flesh had no muscle beneath it to ache, just essence to strain. He just wanted another moment to mark what he was seeing.

Two OOCs, two demon hunters. His fingers traced the lines of the rune stone. It'd keep him out of their way until he got what he needed. He wasn't looking for trouble, after all; he was just feeling the ache, the need to let loose, to dump a wad and taste some innocence. He could almost smell that in the air.

Nope, he didn't need OOC trouble, nor demon hunter trouble either. He'd keep his nose clean, avoid the hell out of them, get his dick wet, and blow town. Just like he always did when he needed to let it loose.

And he needed to let it loose. Oh, how he needed to.

2.

Arch was parked next to Erin's borrowed sheriff's car in the driveway of the MacGruder farm out on Kilner road. The house was up just a little ways, looking empty—as it damned well should, given that its occupants had been killed by demons a couple weeks back. Arch hadn't gotten out of the car like she had; he was just sitting inside filling out his patrol log, waiting for the others to show up. This was about as private and quiet a place as they were going to find without venturing farther out into the county.

He could see Erin out there, just kicking around in the dried, rutted driveway. She was probably waiting for him to get out, or maybe she just enjoyed the pleasant heat of the summer day. Either way, the only thing waiting for Arch out there was more awkward small talk, and he didn't have it in him right now. Not today.

He saw the car coming up the drive as he crossed a "t" on his paperwork. He still didn't get out, though, taking a last breath of the leather scent of the Explorer's interior as the town car pulled up in front of him. All four doors opened, and the trunk popped, and he let out that breath he'd been holding when he saw Alison with them.

Arch could feel the tension running through him as he watched her walk around the black town car to the trunk and haul the big rifle case out. Having her go with them hadn't been his idea. Hadn't been their idea either, he knew. Hendricks had looked a little flummoxed when it all came out, not sure what to say.

Arch wasn't sure he knew what to say, either.

After he'd smelled the gunpowder on her hands after the dam, he'd made a beeline out to the trunk of her car. Popped it open, found the case for a big dadgummed rifle inside. When he'd come back inside and confronted her about it, she hadn't tried to deny it.

"Why would I deny it?" she asked him. "I've been saving your life."

Arch couldn't deny that, but it still felt unseemly somehow that he'd put his young bride in the middle of his dangerous activities of late. Arch considered himself a gentleman of the South, and although he'd never consider anything less than absolutely equal treatment for someone like Erin, who worked with him in a somewhat dangerous profession, he also was the type to still hold the door for her. It was a dichotomy he was still struggling with in his head. And it mainly bothered him because he'd had it driven into his skull from a young age that you were supposed to protect your woman.

So how did that jibe with her picking up a rifle and providing covering fire against the onslaught of demons that had been rolling through Midian?

Arch just shook his head. There was no easy answer on this one. And the arguments thus far with Alison hadn't been pretty. He was man enough to admit that he might have a double standard when it came to how he wanted to treat her versus how he thought others should be treated.

But he didn't have to like it.

***

Hendricks caught Erin lightly in a hug as she came up to greet him. He went for the light kiss on the lips, but she didn't break it off immediately and he didn't stop her. It felt good—long and slow, full of feeling and promise for what was going to happen later. He would have kept going, too, if not for that goddamned wiseass Lerner.

"Humans," Lerner said. "Leave it to you people to come up with creating an intimate greeting using your mouths instead of your genitals."

"Oh, that greeting will come later," Erin said, breaking off from Hendricks long enough to glance at Lerner. "Didn't want to make y'all jealous, after all."

"I'm surprisingly not jealous of your exchanges of unclean bodily fluids filled with viruses and bacteria," Lerner said with more than a hint of amusement. "I mean, don't you think about the smells and the possibly fatal diseases you could be swapping back and forth while you're doing it?"

"With sweet nothings like that to whisper, I'm guessing you'd be really bad at it," Hendricks said and caught a sly grin from Erin. Lerner was a dick most of the time. A useful one, he supposed, but a dick.

Arch was finally stepping out of his car. The guy had been off his game a little lately, ever since the dam. Hendricks hadn't been around him as much, partly because of all the shit landing on Arch from the Sheriff's Department and partly because of their own personal dealings—Arch with his wife and Hendricks with Erin. He just looked glum. Hendricks supposed he was probably besieged on all sides. He cast a sidelong look at Alison as she came up to her husband; Arch gave her a kiss on the cheek that wouldn't have been out of place if she'd been his sister.

"Did you get him?" Arch asked, and even his voice sounded down to Hendricks. Poor bastard.

"Thanks to your wife," Lerner said, doing some sort of exaggerated, dickish bow, like it was some great ceremony. "Sonofabitch rabbited. Nearly got away, too, but not before he decided to take a chunk out of John Wayne over here." He gave Hendricks the nod. Hendricks just rolled his eyes.

"So he was a demon," Arch said, low and pensive.

"He evaporated like one, so I'd say so," Hendricks said, a little tense himself. The new girl in the crowd was a little weird, and adding a couple demons to the mix made things even more uncomfortable. The whole scene just felt strange. They'd never gotten together like this—at least not all of them—ever. He left his arm hanging around Erin's waist and cast his eyes around between the two OOCs, Arch and Alison.

What the hell kind of group was this, anyway?

Lerner was watching Duncan, who was just taking it all in. They'd never had humans working with them before, but then again, they'd never quite dealt with anything like that Sygraath who decided to kill a whole town, either. Something was different about this place. Different vibe, different feel. Lerner had been to hotspots—more than his share, really—and every one of them was a hellhole. Some came out of it better than others, some didn't come out at all. Even in those dark spots, though, when the shit hit the fan there were elements of predictability.

Here, it wasn't even shit hitting the fan. It felt like an entire septic system hitting a jet engine. One hell of a mess was coming, seemed like.

"It was a quantel'a," Duncan said quietly, just like he did everything. "Lower-level hellspawn, if you want to call them that. Strong but not terribly bright. Lot of them have gone criminal because they can't blend easily in polite society."

"Why's that?" This from one of the ladies—Deputy Harris, Lerner thought of her as when he was being formal. Skinny ass, no tits was how he thought of her when he was applying everything he'd learned on earth. It had been an interesting journey.

"They like to eat human meat," Duncan said apologetically. "It's a delicacy, and they go through it like your people go through steak."

There was a dead silence, punctuated by the cowboy's uncomfortable grimace as he looked away. He knew. Lerner knew he knew what was about to come down. He'd probably had this conversation at some point himself.

"I'm sorry ... they eat *people*?" Harris asked. "Does that happen ... often?"

"It's what happened in that lovely scene you found a few days ago," Lerner said. He couldn't help himself, he was grinning. Opening innocent eyes to the truth of the world made him deliriously happy for some reason. It was seeing the awareness settle in, the shock etch the lines of their faces. A grim business, he supposed, but one he enjoyed. "Perhaps you recall?"

"The fucking mess on Crosser Street," Harris breathed. She turned pasty pale under that blond hair, like someone had pulled a plug under her chin and let all the blood drain out of her face.

"Pretty egregious, no?" Lerner asked, feigning sympathy so he could really hit her with the next bombshell he was about to deliver. "Most cities have a good underground market where you can do pickup, or have human meat brought right to your door. It's a lot more civilized than what they've got going out here in the boonies." He sniffed, trying to keep a straight face. "More of a kill-it-and-grill-it yourself atmosphere around here, you know."

Lerner just waited for his asshole comments to land. They did, and he judged it to be worth it. Hendricks blew air out through pursed lips, still keeping his eyes averted from the scene like he was trying to avoid seeing a train derail. Deputy Stan—Lerner still wasn't used to calling him Arch—had a darkening expression on his face, like he had an inkling of all this but didn't like to hear it laid out quite so brutally. Harris was still looking pretty sick and edging toward her boy toy Hendricks. Lerner wondered idly if it would put them off the fuck fest they'd seemed to have planned for tonight.

As for the last one, Mrs. Stan—she was just watching like it wasn't a big deal. He waited, and she stared back at him.

"They ship human body parts like the genitals as a special sort of delicacy," Lerner said, pretending he wasn't watching her. Having demon eyes helped. He didn't have to be looking at her to see her clearly; he didn't have an actual iris, so he could see whatever was in the arc of his eyes. "Cook 'em up, eat 'em raw—they do all sorts of stuff. They even have this version of veal in the high-end stores—"

"That's enough," Hendricks finally said. His girlfriend was three shades of white, all bleached out. He just looked disgusted, like he'd heard it all before and was tired of it. Deputy Stan still had that look of quiet fury in his eyes, and his wife was still just staring straight ahead, listening politely like she was at the fucking country club and someone had told her what was on the dinner menu. No big.

"We got another one," Deputy Stan said, breaking his silence. The big man looked more than a little irritable, and Lerner wondered if he'd had a bad morning already. Probably, the way this town was going.

Lerner was still keeping an eye on the wife, though. Mrs. Stan was an interesting character, and showing zero reaction to the news that humans were a food source to demons? Lerner had his ideas of how a Southern belle should act, and they weren't all based on cable TV viewings of *Gone With the Wind*, either. This chick was different, though. Real different. And not just because she carried a rifle that would make most real men shit their pants and run.

He watched her, and she just listened to her husband. That same polite look, like she was taking it all in, with no reaction on the surface. What Lerner wondered, though, was what was going on beneath the facade?

***

Erin was ready to chuck. She had that sick feeling in her gut like she was gonna, and she kinda just wanted to get it over with, just stick a finger down her throat and start the engine so she could finish and be on with life. The problem was, even if she emptied her stomach, the thing causing her to feel nauseated was still gonna hang around. It was like having your eyes opened so you could watch a snuff film. Not a great thing to wake up to.

"Another what?" Hendricks asked. She was standing inches from him, could tell that he wasn't too happy about the current topic of conversation, either. He didn't look sick, just annoyed.

"Another body," she answered before Arch could. "Another murder." She looked to Lerner and Duncan, those two weird-ass guys. "Another demon."

"Oh, yeah, look at us, like we dragged them to town," Lerner said, eyebrows raised. She didn't have too much sense of the man yet— though she supposed he wasn't a man at all, was he? She had, however, decided that man or not, he was a dick.

"Did I say that?" She was able to keep her tone calmer than she would have thought given how annoyed she was at him. "Or did I just look to you as our resident experts on demonology?" She paused and felt that slight satisfaction dissolve as she thought about what she'd just said. "If that's a thing."

"Heh," Lerner said and glanced at Duncan like he'd heard something hilarious. "Demonology."

"We got a body," Arch said stiffly. More stiffly than usual. He looked a little pissed himself.

"Just one?" Lerner asked, and some of the dickishness dissolved. At this point, Duncan reached up and tugged on Lerner's arm. Erin didn't get even close to the same vibe from him as she did from Lerner. Duncan seemed softer somehow, maybe because his face wasn't quite as lean. Lerner kind of paused as he noticed what Duncan was doing, like he was actively reassessing what an ass he was being. "What is it this time?"

"Looked like a real nasty hit and run," Arch said. "Like someone was going a hundred miles an hour down a residential street, but no one heard an engine rev like that."

Lerner shrugged. "That's not a lot to go on. Could be anything. Could be a car instead of a demon." Duncan tugged his sleeve again and Lerner wavered for a second. "But assuming it was a demon, it could be almost any kind. Strength like the Hulk is not out of line for any number of types of our kind."

"How many types?" Erin asked. "Like, a dozen types? Or—"

"A hundred," Duncan answered, again almost apologetic. "Or at least somewhere between there and a thousand. A lot."

"Well, that don't make it too easy to narrow down," Arch said.

"The worst part is that they're unassuming," Hendricks said, and she could see him adjust the brim of his hat over his eyes. He was projecting the aura like he was old hand at this—which he was, obviously.

"What the kid means with his twenty-dollar words," Lerner said before Erin could ask him to clarify—it still annoyed her the demon did that shit—"is that if a demon did this, there's no guarantee they're going to look any different than a normal human when they're just walking around among you. It's not like they're carrying the muscle mass of Brock Lesnar—it could look like a twelve year-old girl, for all we know." He chucked a twisted smile at Hendricks. "Or like he said, unassuming."

"How did it look?" Duncan asked. For a second, Erin thought she saw irritation flash on Lerner's face, but it was gone in half a beat.

"The scene?" Arch answered. He always seemed to like to take the lead in these things, as best he could. Made sense; he'd been a leader around these parts for as long as she could remember. "Like I said, hit and run wouldn't have been too out of place. Body got hit, went flying about a hundred feet or so—"

"Whoa," Lerner said, lips pursed in an "o" and eyes all squinted. "Like a fucking field goal."

"That's a hundred yards," Duncan murmured.

"Who was it?" Alison asked, finally coming out of her shell a little. She looked reserved to Erin, like she was just taking it all in.

"Tim Connor," Arch said. "Got him on a jog."

"Ohh," Alison looked pained. "He used to come into the store all the time asking for organic chicken breasts. We didn't get too many of them in, just a few, because almost nobody bought them—"

"I'm sure this going somewhere lovely, princess," Lerner said, and there was that dickishness again, "but rather than eulogizing the poor bastard, maybe we should start looking for what killed him." He snapped to face Arch, who didn't look none too pleased at Lerner's behavior toward Alison. "Where did this happen?"

"Berg Street," Erin answered after a few seconds of silence in which Arch did not speak. "The sheriff has the scene cordoned off."

"We'll take a peek after sundown," Lerner said, stretching. She frowned at the demon—Hendricks had said that they were all just bags of contained essence. Why would he need to stretch? Unless he was just trying to look human in his movements? She was tempted to ask him but didn't. Because he was an ass. "Come on, Duncan, let's vamoose on back to the motel."

"Gonna catch some shut eye?" Hendricks asked. She couldn't tell if he was joking.

"Nah, there's a new episode of *World's Deadliest Catch* on that I've been wanting to see, and since we don't have a DVR …" Lerner shot him a toxic smile. "If the world goes to hell, give us a call. Otherwise we'll be at the scene after dark."

"And then?" Arch asked. He was most definitely not sounding happy, at least not to Erin's ears.

"And then we deal with the next thing, and the next thing," Lerner said, already turning away to head back to his town car. "It's always gonna be something here until things calm down."

"When will that be?" Erin felt her irritation with the demon dissolve just enough for her to slip that out.

Lerner actually turned around to face her when he answered. "Hopefully it'll last for a while yet." He wore a kind of twisted grimace that held not one ounce of pleasure. "Because the likelihood is that when it's done, the town is done right along with it."

***

"God, what a cheery fucker," Erin said as the OOCs drove away. She had shuffled closer to Hendricks, and he could smell her light perfume as she slipped an arm into his drover coat and around his waist.

"He's got a point," Hendricks said, watching the town car kick up dust in the driveway. "I've been to enough hotspots the last few years to know. Most of 'em tend to be on a slow burn, things ratchet up a little at a time. Things have already gotten crazy here, what with Hollywood, those demons that came through and ate all those people, plus Gideon, that necromantic cock-spurt. Shit's already getting bad here, and it's not even week two. This isn't a slow burn, it's a fast one." Hendricks shook his head. "Those are the ones that tend to go big."

"You've been in ones like that before?" Arch asked.

"A couple times," Hendricks said, chewing his lip. It gave him a sort of nervous satisfaction to nibble on his lip the way Erin probably would later. "There are always signs when it's about to spin out of control. Enough to let you know to leave, anyway."

"Define 'spin out of control,'" Arch said.

Hendricks felt a flare of discomfort that twisted his face. Worse, he knew he'd let it show. "Well …"

"How bad could it get?" Arch said, pressing him. Hendricks could almost feel the earnestness dripping off the Deputy. It was a funny thing, how Arch could stab a demon with a knife after a knockdown brawl and still have that ring of … naivety? Something. Not quite innocence. "You said Detroit and New Orleans have been hotspots—"

"Low level," Hendricks corrected. "Increased murder rates, some bizarre happenings, I mean all that shit's grist for the mill. They weren't huge spikes because they were slow burners. The towns where you see things get out of control …" He paused. "Well, those are the ones that disappear off the map. You can always tell when it's about to happen because demon activity goes through the roof. You can't walk down a street safely—"

"You mean like how I was laying in my apartment and demons came busting through the door," Arch said dryly. "Or how you got jumped outside your hotel room and she got knocked out." He gestured to Erin.

"I got knocked out?" Erin wheeled on him, and he felt her grip tighten on his belt. "*That's* what happened?"

Hendricks shrugged, feeling the scarlet rush across his cheeks. "Would you have believed me at the time if I'd said it was demons?"

"No," she said, a little mollified. "And I probably wouldn't have laid you, either." Hendricks caught Arch looking away pretty hard on that one.

"It can get a whole lot worse," Hendricks said. "Though I admit I don't usually get run down like that on my first couple days in town. Demons tend to avoid demon hunters until they have to face them or until they've got the numbers on their side. Hollywood was different. He didn't avoid. He confronted because he was a pissy little fucker." It was true; normally it didn't matter if Hendricks got a little plastered in a hotspot as long as he wasn't too far gone.

"Probably wouldn't have been as bad if he hadn't caught you flat-footed while you were chasing tail," Arch said with a little bit of sting. What was up with him? Bad mood, it felt like.

"And just what were you doing that they busted down your door and caught you naked as the day you were born?" Hendricks asked, raising an eyebrow at him. He had a lot of respect for Arch, but he hadn't known him for long enough to take too much of his shit.

"We were trying for a baby," Alison said, completely casual, like she wasn't saying anything out of the ordinary.

That sort of stayed there in the air like a heinous fart in the barracks during basic. Hendricks didn't know what to say to clear it, either.

"This is getting us nowhere," Erin finally said. She looked tired and uncomfortable. "I don't know why we're even bickering now that Lerner's gone. I would have thought that guy took all the asshole with him when he left."

Hendricks had to concede she had a point, even though he secretly kind of liked the particular brand of obnoxious Lerner spit out everywhere he went. "So, this scene you were at … pretty messy, huh?"

"Never seen anything quite like it," Arch said, shaking his head. "I'm getting real used to the sight of blood at this point, though."

Hendricks nodded. "It's not been pretty around here lately, that's for sure."

"Least the carnival's coming," Alison said with a shrug. Hendricks withheld the frown out of politeness only.

***

Lauren Ella Darlington was born in Midian, raised in Midian, lived in Midian, and worked in Chattanooga. She justified this to herself by saying she lived on the far southwestern edge of Midian and worked on the far northeastern edge of Chattanooga, which meant she was only driving about forty minutes per day, and that wasn't too bad, really, was it? Especially not for her to be an attending physician at the Red Cedar Medical Center, floating from the ER to the ICU, depending on the day and the patient load. Red Cedar was not exactly a level-one trauma center, so on any given day the patient load varied from one or two to a handful, mostly old folks on the way out.

On the plus side, she did get the occasional fun job, like suturing up some kid's leg when he wrecked his ATV against a tree. He was lucky sutures were all he needed. Other than a new ATV, she supposed, listening to him bitch about it. Had his priorities firmly in order, too.

The other advantage to being the locally known big-city doctor in Midian was that Lauren occasionally got a call from Sheriff Reeve. She hadn't voted for him—or anyone from his party, ever—but he went to church with her mother and he hadn't ever been an obnoxious asshole to her that she could recall. Plenty had in Midian, especially after a certain time in her high school career. She'd made a list and everything.

But it was ultimately a pointless list, because if she'd gotten a call from any one of them complaining of anything more serious than pink eye, she would ultimately have just sighed and had them meet her at the diner so she could try and judge what was wrong. And then send them to some other doctor if it was serious, because dammit, if they were on the list, she didn't want to deal with them.

She cursed herself for being a little soft, but she knew it was all true. Because there'd been plenty of other people in the town who hadn't landed themselves on that list, who'd helped her, who'd done right by her and cared and sent pies and cookies and God-only-knew what else, and she told herself she'd help everyone because of them, not the ones on her list. Her shit list.

She guided the car onto Berg Street and killed the ignition. She didn't remember to put it in park until after she'd done that, which happened frequently. Lauren said "Fuck!" really loud to herself in the car. No one could hear her, not that it would have mattered. Everyone in Midian had an opinion about her already anyway, and screaming "FUCK!" from the rooftops wouldn't have changed it one way or another.

She grabbed her purse, which was laden with all manner of crap from make-up to tissues, and slung it over her shoulder. Old habit, she realized as she got out of the car. It wasn't like someone in Midian was going to come running up and break her car's window while she was outside talking to the sheriff a couple hundred feet away. It wasn't Chattanooga, after all, and that stuff didn't even happen all that often there. Still, old habits.

Old enemies.

Old lists.

Her heels clicked along on the pavement as Lauren walked, sighing to herself with irritation that she'd gotten roped into this. It was pointless. There was a perfectly good pathologist at the morgue where this corpse was going, and they'd be able to render a much more sensible, well-thought-out suggestion as to what had happened than she would. She tried to come up with a reason why she was doing this for Reeve, any reason at all, and the only one she could summon forth was that she was doing it because he wasn't on the list.

Lauren dodged the blood trail as she made her way toward the sheriff. He looked about as hangdog as she'd ever seen a man who wasn't sleeping in the doghouse, his normally jovial face completely weighed down. It had been a shitty week, she knew, but Reeve was usually a lot more effervescent than this.

"Dr. Darlington," Reeve said as she approached.

"Sheriff," she replied with a veneer of politeness that she didn't really feel. It was a world of ick around her. She didn't get grossed out easily—you couldn't get through medical school and an internship if you did—but this was pretty gross. She'd seen a few high-speed collisions and the results were seldom suitable for an open casket funeral. "What can I do for you?"

"Well, seeing as the EMTs have already pronounced the victim dead," Reeve said, smearing the sarcasm on with a trowel, "I was hoping you might just take a look at this real quick and tell me what you think."

"Other than that he's dead?" Lauren asked. "Since the EMTs told you that." She stared at the body for a second. "I think even if he were still alive, he wouldn't be playing baseball anytime soon."

Reeve turned his head to look at the body. "Ohh, because of the arms getting knocked off. Clever." The way he said it left her in no doubt he didn't find it clever. Or cute.

"I don't know what you're looking for here, Sheriff," Lauren said, shaking her head.

"I'm looking for anything you can tell me," Reeve said, and she caught the hint of desperation. "We've had … so many people die here recently, and I got nothing. Whoever slaughtered those families up on Crosser, they left nothing the lab can point us to. No witnesses, nothing. That catastrophe on the interstate? Nothing. That girl in Melina Cherry's whorehouse?"

"Let me guess," Lauren said, a little hoarse, "nothing."

Reeve held up a hand and made a zero with his thumb and fingers. "It's like whoever who did it just evaporated afterward. People are scared, and now there's this." The sheriff's lip quivered. Actually quivered. "I need to deliver something."

"Because of elections," Lauren said, a little jaded, "yeah, all right—"

"No," Reeve said, and he was firm about it, to her surprise. "Because dammit, we can't live like this! Midian ain't Chicago or Atlanta. This level of carnage, of chaos—we can't handle it. This is beyond a bad run of luck, and I wouldn't blame anyone for wanting to leave town after all this shit just came rushing down like Mount Horeb had the world's largest hog pen up on the south slope. I … need … *something*. I need to bring somebody to justice. Not for my damned job, but because we can't live like this. This ain't us. It ain't our way."

"Yeah, all right," Lauren said, sighing. She'd felt it too, in the air. Midian was on edge lately. Bad. It was actually kind of nice being able to drive to Chattanooga just to get away from it every day. She turned to the body again, picked her way over to it, and looked straight down into the face. "Ohhhh," she said, and it dragged out like a sad little sigh. "It's Tim Connor."

"Yeah," Reeve said, adjusting his hat as he looked at the bloodied mess that remained of the man. "Did you know him?"

"Not really," Lauren said, staring at the earthly remains, "but he wasn't on the list."

***

Erin was driving, feeling the natural pull of the wheel against her hands as she cruised the sheriff's car down Kilner Road. It felt right, even after just a few days, her being on the patrol.

Or at least it felt a hell of a lot more right than filing shit and answering phones for eight hours a day.

Hendricks was in the passenger seat, preoccupied and drifting. He had his hat off, and his sword was sticking out a little under his coat, a pillar jutting up like the world's biggest hard-on. She hadn't thought of it as much of a sword once she saw it, an inch or less across the blade, only a couple feet long. Little stinger of a sword, but she supposed that was all he really needed.

"Whatcha thinking about?" She mentally slapped herself just after asking.

Hendricks roused himself like he was stirring out of sleep. He even looked like he did when he woke. "Mm? Oh, I was thinking about that hooker you were telling me about."

Erin felt a little tingle. She didn't need any prompting to figure out which one he was talking about. "You mean Lucia?"

"I mean Starling," Hendricks said bluntly, and Erin felt more of a cringe, though she hid it. "Something is seriously weird with that woman."

"You mean other than that she's turning tricks in a brothel one minute and fighting demons with you the next?" Erin asked. The whole damned conversation made her uncomfortable. She liked Hendricks, liked him a lot, got all fluttery thinking about him yet. That redheaded harlot wasn't her favorite subject.

"I mean her disappearing act after the dam," Hendricks said, like he was ignoring what she just said. Maybe he was. "I mean, she was there on the dam—"

"And then back at the police station with Reeve, I know." Erin had been the one that had told him, after all. She'd completely forgotten about the redhead in the aftermath of the dam, forgotten she was supposed to be driving her to the sheriff's station. It had caused more than a little heartburn for her once she realized, too, but when she called the sheriff to talk about it, before she even said anything he'd gone off on a rant about "that goddamned lawyer," which she took as the precursor to an ass chewing. When she'd mentioned the redhead, the sheriff had cut her off and thanked her for driving her over so promptly. Without a trace of irony.

Sheriff Reeve was a great many things, but a sufferer of fools and embracer of failures that put his ass in a sling he was not, not either damned one. Erin had worked it out in her head at that point and confirmed it with the sheriff's wife, who had been manning the desk at the time. The redhead, Lucia—Starling—whatever she wanted to call herself this week—had walked into the sheriff's office less than five minutes after she'd disappeared off the top of the Tallakeet Dam.

To Erin's mind that meant she was either a twin, or a demon, or both. Didn't much care which, as long as she didn't have to discuss that flame-haired woman with her new beau anymore.

Unfortunately, that wasn't likely to happen anytime soon. "I was thinking about dropping by to see her at her work," Hendricks said, the look of preoccupation on his face the only thing saving him from getting smacked hard in the side of the head. Erin didn't hit idly, but this seemed like it might be worthy of a little overreaction in that department.

"You want to go visit a hooker in a brothel?" she asked. She knew how to add ice to her tea, but she was a fair sight better at adding ice to her words.

"Yeah, I—" Hendricks caught himself; she could see the dawning realization in his eyes as he turned to look at her. "You just put out a snare, and I walked right into it, didn't I?"

"No, it's fine," Erin said, shaking her head but keeping her eyes on the road as she made a left turn. "Tell me all about it afterward. Just make sure you bring a wad of cash. Maybe somewhere between the big O and pillow talk you can get out of her how she manages her disappearing act."

"I'm not looking for a ... big O ... from her," Hendricks said, lowering his voice when he said the middle bit. "From you, yes—"

"Good luck with that."

"You can't seriously be pissed at me because I want to get to the bottom of this," Hendricks said.

"You mean get into the bottom of her?" Erin raised her eyebrow dangerously.

"No," Hendricks said, "I mean get to the bottom of this weirdness. And by the way, she saved your life that night in the motel parking lot."

Erin felt her jaw clench. "You're not moving any closer to any O, let alone a big one."

"You can't tell me you're not curious," he said. "Come with me. We can talk to her together—"

"I don't have the cash or the inclination for a threesome." She tightened her grip on the wheel.

"Look, I've been doing this demon hunting thing for years, and this is some weird, fascinating shit," Hendricks said, and he was leaning toward her now, eyes all lit up like he was opening a Christmas present early. "She knows things—"

"Like how to give head without smearing her lipstick."

"—things that could help us," Hendricks went on, ignoring her. "And you don't need to be like this—I've got eyes for you, baby. Not her."

"I don't like her," Erin said and realized she'd just stated a painfully obvious truth. "She just gives me a bad feeling about everything." That wasn't wholly true. Lucia didn't give her a bad feeling at all. She was … normal, or as normal as Erin figured a sex worker could be. It was Starling that was the problem. Starling was the wild card she didn't want to turn over. If Hendricks went to go see Lucia, Erin reckoned nothing would happen. Lucia didn't even seem seductive.

No, it was Starling that had something going on—something for Hendricks—that she didn't care for at all.

"Come with me," Hendricks said softly. "It'll guarantee everything stays on the level."

"I've met her pimp or mistress or whatever," Erin said, letting go only reluctantly, and feeling the air almost hiss out of her as she surrendered on the point. "She's not going to let a cop anywhere near Lucia without her listening in. You'd have to go by yourself." She hated every word she was speaking. "And you'll have to pay, unless you want to just kick down the door and bring the law and all hell down on you."

Hendricks thought about that for a minute, and she dreaded what he was going to say up until he spoke. "I don't have to go alone, really. I just have to bring someone with me who isn't a cop ... and isn't suspicious."

Erin frowned at him, staring at him in the passenger seat and wondering exactly what he meant by that, even as she ran through a dwindling list to the only possible person that could fit that description.

***

Alison wasn't waiting for Arch to speak first. She had been around him long enough to know that he was a stoic in addition to being a man who liked to get lost in his own thoughts. If she ever had a need to talk, she'd just talk, that was all there was to it. Passive aggressive only worked on a man who knew you were using it on him. Arch was just as likely to assume during the passive stage that everything was all right and write off the aggressive stage without looking too deeply at the root cause.

Besides, Alison wasn't mad at him, not really. She watched him out of the corner of her eye as he drove the police cruiser. She liked the Explorer, thought it was pretty nice that the sheriff had given it to Arch instead of keeping it for himself or giving it to one of the other deputies. They were all driving the old Crown Vics, and Arch was tooling around Midian in the latest and greatest piece of police equipment the department had bought. Arch had his eyes forward, thoughts bouncing around in his head so loud she could just about hear them without him needing to voice them.

She could tell the thought of the town sinking into Armageddon was weighing on him. All the stuff he'd seen so far was weighing on him, too. All the happenings had shocked the town. She'd seen the people come dragging in through the door of the supermarket now, lethargic, near dead, shuffling around. It was like all their energy had been stolen. Lately everyone knew someone who had been killed; it was unavoidable unless you were a shut-in.

Arch let out a sigh that sounded like he had about ten thousand pounds resting on his chest forcing the air out. She could see the tension etching lines in his face, setting his jaw in place like he was ready to grind his teeth. She unfastened her seatbelt, and he turned in surprise at the click and the sound of it drawing back as she slipped free and leaned over.

She unzipped his pants, and he started to protest but quickly fell silent. She moved her head up and down, up and down in sweet rhythm. He'd been sweating, but it didn't bother her at all. It never had, not for him.

She could feel him keeping the grip on the steering wheel as she worked steadily, methodically, using her hand to support him as she went down on him. He grunted and moaned, and his knee jostled her as he brought the car to a slow, then to a stop, moving her slightly as he threw it in park.

After that he leaned back and let her work unfettered, not saying a thing. She clutched his balls and squeezed, and he moaned again and came as she pushed him to the back of her mouth until he was finished.

His breath came slow and ragged. Her hand rested on his thigh, and she could feel it unclenched now, the tension that she had felt when she started gone. She slowly lifted herself up, pulling off of him and eliciting one last gasp of something that sounded like it was between pleasure and pain before she slid back into her seat and buckled her seatbelt.

She didn't look at him, didn't say a word, and neither did he. He just put the car in gear and drove her home.

***

"Huh," Duncan muttered in the bed next to Lerner.

Lerner shot him a sidelong glance, trying to decide if he really wanted to know or not. If it was important, Duncan would probably say more than, "Huh." Probably. He wasn't the talkative type, but he wasn't a mute, either.

"Huh, what?" Lerner went for the bait. It wasn't like he had anything else to do. He was staring at the TV, hoping something interesting would come on to kill the time until Duncan gave the all clear that the sheriff was gone from the site of the collision.

"Arch just got a hummer from Alison," Duncan said, drawing a sharp look of distaste from Lerner.

"Don't call them by their names like they're our friends," Lerner said. "Like they're coming to a dinner party next week, can we please get a big gravy boat and fresh biscuits and serve after-dinner cocktails." He paused. "He got a hummer, huh? I wouldn't have bet on that. Looked like they had so much tension between them you could fit a full-size refrigerator in the bed between them at night right now. Sideways." Lerner waited. "What about the cowboy? He's getting fucked all over that cheap hotel room right now like he's the bull and she's going for an eight-second ride, right?"

Duncan shook his head. "Not so much."

"Oh?"

"Foot in mouth disease," Duncan said, prompting Lerner to nod. Human guys were always saying dumb things. Lerner wondered if it was a genetic predisposition or something.

"Heh," Lerner said, strangely amused by that. "Sounds like the only play he'll be seeing tonight is the app store."

Duncan frowned as his eyes shot skyward in a reasonable approximation of a man pondering something. "I don't think he has a smart phone."

Lerner sighed—another approximation of human behavior. "It's just a figure of speech."

***

Lauren Darlington's key hit the lock a second before she heard the argument inside. It didn't sound knock-down, drag-out, which was a plus, but it didn't sound like the sort of thing that just resolved itself without a storm out, either. Based on the volume of the voices, Lauren figured slamming doors were in the offing in the next few minutes. She was trying to decide as she turned the lock whether to make her presence known, because depending on where she had to land on it, it could either make things better or worse.

And she wasn't very sure which it would be.

She opened the door as the crescendo of yelling spilled out into the hot summer eve, her heels clicking as they left the old scuffed wood porch and stepped into the darkened hallway. She could smell supper on the stove, the low simmer of gravy going and biscuits baking in the oven. It was just a little sullied by the argument taking place in the same room. Kind of cast a pall on the feeling of home that she usually got when she stepped in the door.

"Young lady, you will mind me—"

"Oh, I mind you! I mind you plenty—as in you annoy the fuck out of me!"

"Watch your mouth, girl! Bad enough you show up late, but then you smart off? You're pushing me to the edge tonight."

"So that's where the edge is?" Lauren could hear her daughter's voice bubbling over with the usual sarcasm. She did it well, credit where it was due. "I haven't seen it in a while because you people pushed me over it a long damned time ago with your rules and your bullshit and your sanctimony—"

"You sure like to throw out the fancy words when you get cornered." Lauren could hear her mother edging closer to the actual edge. Lauren had pushed her over it more than a few times in her day—and even more recently, come to think of it. It wasn't a fun place to linger around. "Seems like if you applied your vocabulary and smarts to your schoolwork, you might not be getting yourself into as much trouble as you're in lately."

"Every word sounds like a fancy word to you," Molly said, and Lauren felt the sting from down the hall. She trudged forward into the fight, even though she didn't want to, heels clopping quietly on the hallway floor as she edged around the corner into the kitchen. Molly stopped when she saw her. "Mom."

"Yeah," Lauren said. She didn't sigh, but she wanted to. Long hours, long days, long weeks and months and years had been leading up to this. She stared at her sixteen-year-old daughter and wondered when the hell she'd found time to grow up. The answer was the same—while Lauren was going to college and medical school and doing a residency—but it was somewhat unsatisfying nonetheless. "You're mouthing off to your grandmother?"

Molly folded her arms in front of her, dark hair shaking as she moved her head to look away. "Again, yes." She could apply the sullen look pretty quickly, too. Probably the age working in her favor. "This shouldn't exactly be a surprise to you."

"That you treat your grandmother with disrespect?" Lauren could hear the quiet echo of her own voice as she dipped her head to look at her shoes. They had a trace of blood on the toe from the crime scene, and she felt a rush of disgust. She'd specifically taken them off at work for a reason, dammit.

"She's not listening to me," Molly said, and the self-importance oozed out of every word. "I—"

"Kid, I don't care," Lauren said, looking back up at her. Stern face. She wasn't very good at it because she didn't do it very often. She didn't need to most of the time. Molly had been so good up until lately. She'd been a champ. They'd been like friends. She put the hammer down when she had to, but it was thankfully rare. "I've never been an authoritarian with you, and you've never acted like this so I'd have to."

"No, because you let grandma do it," Molly said, and again there was that sting.

"That's ... that's true," Vera said, shaking her head. Lauren shot her a *Whose side are you on anyway?* look.

Lauren started to open her mouth, and Molly preempted her: "I don't feel like arguing anymore." She turned on her heel and headed right for her room.

"You're sixteen," Lauren called after her as she ascended the staircase. "You're supposed to be ready for a dramatic throwdown with your mother anytime, day or night." She heard the slam of a door somewhere upstairs. "Well, at least you've got the dramatic part down." Lauren felt the air deflate from her. "I guess I should go talk to her."

"I'd give her a bit to settle down," Vera said, waving her off. "Oh, Lordy, the biscuits are burning." She went for the oven and pulled out a pan that brought with it a smoky aroma to fill the kitchen. The white doughy biscuits looked fine on top but Lauren knew from long experience that the bottoms were singed to the pan. "Well, what are we gonna do now?"

"Eat the tops of them," Lauren said, staring at the biscuits stoically. She just didn't have enough emotion to channel into anything else. "It's not like it's the first time you've burned the biscuits."

"I meant about your daughter," Vera said in a huff. "She's getting—"

"Worse," Lauren said, nodding slowly. She thought she could almost feel the color draining out of her face, but it was probably her imagination. "She's getting worse. I'd ask if I was this bad at her age, but I think we both know the answer is—"

"You were hell on sixteen wheels, girl," her mother said, now positioned by the stovetop and working a wooden spoon through the gravy. "At least she hasn't come home pregnant yet, unlike some people in this kitchen I could name."

And there was the color returning to her face. It was still a slightly raw spot to Lauren after sixteen years that she'd gotten pregnant at sixteen. Now she was thirty-two, and her daughter was where she was when she'd had her. Not an appealing thought when you were watching your daughter veer off the road. "I should go talk to her," Lauren said again.

But she stayed right there in the kitchen and worked her way over to the pan of biscuits sitting on a towel on the table. She nibbled from the top of one and just kept thinking, because at least if that was all she did she wouldn't stir up another storm in the house.

***

Mick was hanging out on the town square. Place was quiet as quiet could get, like a thousand other towns in America, time passing them by and moving all the shops out to the freeway.

He'd seen that a lot lately. Or maybe he was noticing it a lot lately. He'd been around long enough to remember when it was the other way, when everything happening in a town was on the square. There'd maybe be a malt shop, with a buzz of conversation at this time of night, where you could get a tall glass of sweet malted chocolatey goodness slid in front of you with two straws so you could share. Sipping it while you were looking at the person across from you, eyes meeting while you drank it all in.

Mick missed that. It was an easy setup, and a great way to get a girl loose and ready for the finale. He remembered doing that back in the fifties and it had worked really well.

It had been a while since the last time he'd done it. Probably at least ... thirty years? Something like that. Some town in Alabama, if he remembered right. The thing about Mick was, he didn't need it that often. He saw the human men in the carnival, and they could go a couple-three times a night, some of them. That was almost obscene to him. Like rabbits to humans, he figured. No, once every thirty years was good for him, maybe a little more, maybe a little less.

But when he let it all go, boy, was it a doozy.

Mick was swinging his arms as he walked, just a natural rhythm he barely noticed anymore. He'd learned to adapt when he first got here, learned to watch the natives so he could blend in. You walked with your arms straight at your sides, you looked weird. Weird got attention. Normal let you blend, let you fade into the background.

Which was not a bad place for a demon to be.

It was a pretty warm night. Mick had been up north a couple times during the winter for winter carnivals, which was a damned asinine idea in his mind. Staying south during the winter was a winning idea to him, but he just worked here, he didn't run the show.

The light was fading in the western sky, purple and orange kaleidoscoping together for a fantastic view. Mick wasn't exactly a connoisseur of sunsets—he tended not to notice them when he was working—but this one was pretty amazing. The town was so quiet that the only thing he could hear was the sound of one other person walking just across the square.

He caught her eye as he made his way around. She was young, a pretty thing. Porcelain face like a little doll and big eyes. She just screamed with innocence. It was dripping off of her in the way she wore her jeans just a degree too loose for her body, in the way she averted her gaze after she caught him looking.

He sped up and changed directions. If she noticed, she didn't panic, which was good. This was small town America, right? Nothing to fear here.

At least not yet.

"Hey," Mick announced himself once he was within a half dozen feet of her. He'd crossed under some statue in the middle of the green space in the square just to get to her. She had been eyeing him warily as he'd approached but pretended she wasn't. Mick caught it anyway.

"Hey, yourself," she said, still wary. She'd stopped, but her whole body was held at an angle, like she was about to jackrabbit if he took another step toward her.

"My name's Mick," he said, nodding. He'd updated his wardrobe just for this. He always looked young, but some ragged skinny jeans from a thrift store in the last town coupled with a tight t-shirt and some black nail polish gave him a look he figured might appeal to a girl of her age. He called it his tortured-soul look.

"Okay," she said, and he could tell she either wasn't instantly impressed or she was a little too stunned to fall into the rhythm of a proper conversation.

"And you are ...?" he prompted.

"Busy at the moment," she said. She had the arms folded across her chest in a very obvious *fuck off!* manner. Still looked ready to run, though slightly less so than she had. More aggravated. Gave a little flush to her cheeks that Mick found appealing.

"Sorry to hear that," Mick said, nodding his head. He applied the false sincerity like Spackle to try and keep her in place. "I'm only in town for a few days, and I was looking for somebody to show me around."

She stared at him, like she was trying to decide how much more she was willing to tolerate from him. "Okay. Well. Here's the square." She unfolded her arms and waved them around to encompass the series of buildings around them. "This concludes our tour. Bye, now." She started to turn but hesitated, and he caught it.

"Wait," he said, utterly calm. She was right where he wanted her. "What's your name?"

She turned back to him, and here he saw she was torn, like that age-old programming she'd been hit with since she was a child telling her not to talk with strangers was warring with her common sense which was saying, *What does it matter? It's just a name.*

Common sense won the battle. "I'm Molly."

"Nice to meet you, Molly." He smiled at her.

"I gotta go," she said. "See ya later." She walked off but not quite so fast as she had when he'd first seen her.

Mick watched her go, nodding his head. Yep, she'd do. "Yes," he said once she was good and out of earshot. "Yes, you will."

3.

Lerner stood on the street in the warm summer night, trying to pretend he gave a shit about what he was looking at. Which was basically just a lot of blood at this point and not a lot else. "You seeing anything here?"

Duncan didn't speak. He had his eyes closed, sniffing his way through what was left behind here. Lerner blew out air between his lips and made a raspberry noise that Duncan probably pretended not to notice. Ever since they'd come to this town and started mingling with the humans, Duncan had started acting more like them. It was bad enough he didn't like to engage in any edifying discussions of the sort Lerner enjoyed, but now he was starting to pick up some eccentricities of the sort that made Lerner feel ill. "No, that's fine," Lerner said. "Just ignore me. No big deal. I'll just sit here on the street and listen to those cicadas bitching in the distance while I wait for you to finish your guided meditation—or whatever these trendy humans would call it."

"There's a lot of blood here," Duncan said. Quietly, of course.

"That's something I could have told you without the need for guided meditation," Lerner said. He leaned against the town car and tried to look like a government stiff. If he made himself look unapproachable enough, most people—surprise!—didn't try to approach him.

"I can see something hit him …" Duncan said, musing to himself.

"I can see that too," Lerner said.

"… but I can't see what," Duncan said, and his voice was all ponder and wondering. Which was not quite usual for him. "Runes."

"Fucking Spellman," Lerner swore, spitting little flecks of the saliva he barely produced out of his mouth. "That screen has caused us more problems since we've gotten here than any ten fuv'quava or thirty eich'yurn. So help me, if anyone drops a dime on him, I will give them a full-on human kiss on any part of their anatomy they want."

Duncan just gave him the look, the one with the raised eyebrow. It was most of an expression, anyway.

Lerner turned away, fuming. It should have been easy, tracking down Spellman. It wasn't like they hadn't tried; the bastard had sold that Sygraath Gideon some highly objectionable shit. The sort of stuff that broke every single law of the Pact with room left over to break 'em again. But he'd also figured out how to dip some conjurings into the deep waters of the internet, and somehow every time Lerner or Duncan—or even Hendricks, when they'd tried to get him to do it for them—performed a search for the bastard, his website flashed nothing but taunting messages in old gril'vech. Which was insulting in and of itself, really, since the fucking gril'vech were a dirty, dirty people that were fully deserving of their special place in hell.

"I can't see anything after the hit," Duncan pronounced, and he almost sounded sad.

Lerner's annoyance flashed a little hotter. "Oh, no, another one of the seven billion people on this world has met a tragic end. Whatever will we do?" He snorted. "Oh, right, somehow carry on living like every other person in history."

Duncan was staring at the bloodstain, looking fucking solemn. "This man was the only one of them specifically like himself. No one else will ever be the same."

Lerner felt his jaw drop slightly. "Did you just ... pontificate?"

Duncan turned his head slowly to look at Lerner. "If each of them is individual, and different, then that makes them special. Special means unique, worthy of preservation."

Lerner sucked in a breath that would ultimately do nothing but circulate in his essence before he let it back out. He took it anyway. "So grab a jar of formaldehyde and get to preserving. Where is this soft-hearted Duncan coming from? You're beginning to alarm me with your thoughts on humans, and I've pondered just about every angle I can in this life and the next."

"I just see ... something special is all," Duncan said. "Something worthy of upholding and protecting."

Lerner felt a grudging, partial agreement to that. "Well, we've got protecting and upholding to do, that's for sure." But at least part of it was protecting his own ass, Lerner reflected, because an OOC who didn't do his job ended up in a much warmer climate. Lerner was about to mention that to Duncan, but he dismissed it as a waste of that breath he'd just taken. Besides, it was easier to just stand here and listen to the faint hum in the night of ... something?

Lerner frowned and jerked upright. What the hell was that?

***

"You want my wife to go to a whorehouse with you," Arch said, staring at Hendricks, who was standing in his living room. Erin had dropped him off on the way to her patrol. Apparently she'd known why he was coming over—which was to ask this very thing. Arch made a mental note to have a word with Erin on his next shift—and to try very hard not to make it a swear word.

"When you say it like that," Hendricks said, standing in the middle of the living room, shrinking inside his big black drover coat and cowboy hat, "it sounds ..." His voice trailed off.

"Wildly inappropriate?" Arch asked. He cast a look over at Alison, who was watching the proceedings with muted interest. She did pretty much everything with muted interest lately, at least since that blow-up they'd had after the dam. Actually, before that, even. The fight after the dam was just a short moment where things had seemed to be different.

Although what she'd done to him in the car earlier had been a pretty big departure from the norm of late, too.

"I was gonna just stay simple and go with 'bad,'" Hendricks said, "but if you want to get specific, I think we could add 'awkward' and 'illegal' to the billing."

"What does this gain us?" Arch asked. "Other than a possible solicitation charge for the two of you?" Arch's expression deepened to genuine vexation. "Also, how do you even know that Starling—Lucia—whatever—will accept both of you as ... clients?" He said the word with a genuine distaste, though he was trying desperately not to be overly judgmental.

"Just a hunch," Hendricks said, glancing at Alison and smiling tightly.

"And if she says, 'No way in Hades'?" Arch asked.

"We'll tell her Alison is there to watch," Hendricks said.

Arch knew he blanched at that. Knew it, and could do nothing about it. The whole discussion sent an uncomfortable spasm up his spine. The thought of his wife with anyone else—woman, man or anything in between—was enough to cause discomfort. The thought of putting her in a position where she might get arrested for it, well, that was—

"I'll do it," Alison said languidly, like it was of no more import than switching the wash to the dryer.

"Why?" Arch asked with a blessed fire from on high.

"I want to meet this Starling," Alison said, and she shifted her attention to look at him. He could see her eyes prodding at him, gauging his reaction. "She saved your life, too, after all."

"We don't even know if this is Starling," Arch said weakly. He could feel the conversation spinning out of his control, that he was losing the argument. He hadn't even known he was in an argument, he had just figured he'd batter Hendricks over the head with how dumb the idea was for a few minutes before turning him loose the way a dog finally lets go of a bone.

"And we never will if we don't chase this rabbit down her hole," Hendricks said with a grin that disappeared after a moment. "I should probably avoid hole-related metaphors until we're done with this mission."

"It's not a mission," Arch said. "It's not an anything. You're trying to have a conversation with a lady of the evening about something that she has already assured me she has no knowledge of."

"You believe her?" Hendricks said. "Erin says this Lucia is the spitting image of Starling. Said she was in the car with her at the dam and suddenly our red-headed Clark Kent disappears and Super Starling swoops in to help save the day."

"I don't like it," Arch said, crossing his arms against his chest. He flexed his pectorals against his arm.

"Relax," Hendricks said. "Nothing's gonna happen."

Arch just looked at him like he was dumb. "You're taking my wife to a brothel where some red-headed mystery lady with super powers resides in her mild-mannered secret identity as a hooker. Yeah, there's no potential for that to go awry at all."

"When you put it like that," Hendricks said, almost sarcastic. Then he turned to Alison. "Shall we go pay for a sex act that's still unlawful in Tennessee?"

Alison frowned at him. "What act are you talking about?"

Hendricks looked like he was going answer bluntly, but Arch caught his eye and the cowboy withered a little. "Uh ... um, well, the uh ... oral kind."

"That's not illegal here," Alison said calmly.

"What?" Hendricks had that squinched-face frown like he was caught by surprise. "Erin told me it was."

"Well, she's wrong," Alison said, getting up. Arch watched her as she made her way toward the bedroom. "Arch would never let me give him head if it was illegal." She paused at the door and looked back. "Ask him. I just did it earlier tonight, in fact, in the patrol car." She disappeared into the bedroom.

Arch felt his face squeeze tight for some reason. Some real obvious reason. But all he could do was look down at his shoes.

***

Erin had gotten a call about a disturbance over near the park on Creek Boulevard. She was the only one on patrol tonight, though Fries and Reines were supposed to be hanging close to a radio in case she needed an assist. It was getting near midnight, though, and nothing had come in so far that would require her full attention, much less the assistance of another deputy.

She'd had to get out of the car for this one. Rafton Park overlooked the Caledonia River, and she could see it up ahead, sparkles moving over the water from the moon overhead and the street lamps that lined the walkways of the park. Still, she had that big damned Maglite in her hand and at the ready. She wondered if she'd feel less jumpy if she'd been doing this a week earlier and decided that, absent the knowledge of the existence of demons, this still would be a creepy-ass way to spend the witching hour, knowing how many people had died of mysterious and horrible causes in Midian this week.

She spared a thought for Lerner and Duncan and wondered if they'd found anything at the site of Tim Connor's unfortunate end. Probably not. After all, what clue was there in blood splatters?

The wind whispered to her as she walked, boots squishing in the damp grass. The park was stretched out in front of her, the streetlamps flickering overhead like someone at the power company was refusing to give them the juice they needed to run properly. That wasn't technically her problem, but it would be if they went out.

The smell of the river, the faint sulfuric scent of the paper mill to the east hung in the air. Erin rolled her flashlight beam over the picnic area. She heard a rustle, and her beam fell upon a cat hissing from behind a toppled trash can.

"Geez, kitty," she muttered as the cat screeched and bolted into a nearby bush with a rustle of branches. "Give a girl a heart attack, why don't you?"

She could hear the thudding of her heart, thumping in her ears as she stared at the empty picnic area. She felt an annoyed need to chastise herself, like she'd done something wrong. It was true, having a gun in her hand would make her feel better during this search, but it would also be damnably against regulations to pull her weapon just because she was in a park at night and had an eerie feeling.

The law made no exception for Midian, Tennessee, being the current draw of the underworld, after all.

She thought about thumbing her radio mike, calling in and telling dispatch—the sheriff's wife was occupying her glorious former day job at the moment—that there was nothing here. She stopped herself before she did, though. "One last look around," Erin muttered under her breath. It wouldn't hurt to take a look at the path down by the river.

She felt a chill as she even dared to think that. She'd seen enough horror movies to know that those were famous last words in a situation like this.

Shrugging off the sudden sense of goose bumps that made their way up her arms, Erin started toward the river. She looked up just in time to see clouds rolling in to cover the moon. Ominous.

***

Hendricks let Alison drive, mainly because he didn't have a car and didn't want to rely on Arch to be involved in this errand, which he so clearly opposed. They went along in silence, Alison's little four-door coupe doing little better than rattling as they rolled through the Midian streets. It all looked sorta similar to Hendricks, though he supposed the town was far from cookie cutter like the newer planned developments he'd seen in suburban neighborhoods. It was just that all the houses in this part of town looked so … old. That gave them a uniform look in his eyes, even though there was a wide variety in what they actually looked like.

"So," he said, trying to cut the silence.

She glanced over at him from the wheel. She was a cool customer, this one. Hendricks was betting she was a real pro at the silent treatment. Probably even better at the riot act, when she was of a mind to read it. "Oh, are we talking now?" she asked.

That one caught Hendricks by surprise. "Were we … not … at some point?"

"Just figured you were more of the silent type," Alison said, turning her attention back to the road ahead. She was keeping the car easing along at the speed limit, which was pretty low here in town. "Spending years on your lonesome hunting demons."

Hendricks nodded along to that. "I was a loner for a long time. Didn't mean I was anti-social, though. I'd talk with other demon hunters some." He paused to think about that. "Every once in a while, anyway."

"But you're not anti-social?" she asked, like it didn't matter a whit to her.

"Just had a mission was all," Hendricks said. Now he was feeling a little tension. "Something to get accomplished."

"What was that?" she asked.

"I had it in my mind to kill a lot of demons," Hendricks said, and now he was staring straight ahead, too, the dark night broken by the headlights of her car, luminescence seeking out the darkness and destroying it for mere seconds as they passed.

"Well, now you have," she said. "Right?"

"Yeah, I've killed a lot of them," he agreed. He had. Hundreds. Probably a thousand or more by now, all told.

"But you're not done yet?"

That one halted him again. "No, not really," he said. "See, demon hunters are the line when it comes to a town like this—"

"Keep the demons on one side and the good folk on the other?" she asked. She still had a dull voice like nothing she was saying mattered. Maybe it didn't—to her. "Doesn't seem like you're doing a very good job around here, all these people dying."

"I'm the only demon hunter in town here," Hendricks said. "Usually there's a lot more of us."

"Right," she said, like she was just repeating something she already knew. "Because now there are eighteen hotspots instead of one."

"Yeah," he said. "Did Arch tell you—"

"He told me everything," she said, cutting him off, but not harshly. "Just assume he told me everything. I'll let you know if you start talking about something he might have missed."

"So he talked about Starling, about Hollywood, about Gideon—"

"Yes, yes and yes." She didn't give any hint of emotion about any of these.

Hendricks sat there for a second before deciding to go fishing. "What do you think about Gideon?"

She blinked a little at that. "He was a pretty twisted little fucker."

Hendricks did a little blinking himself. "That he was."

***

Erin started to hear a sound she couldn't shake. Faint, like buzzing bees in the far distance. She used to go to concerts and she listened to her iPod with the music way up, so she'd heard more than a little ringing in her ears from time to time. This was a lot like that, like the volume just cut out on one ear and was replaced by something that almost hummed.

She turned toward the noise and felt her face scrunch as she tried to focus in on it with all her senses. It was coming from the path down along the Caledonia, a noise in the distance. She could see the lights down the path for a spell and then realized that past a certain point, they just stopped.

Had they always been like that? She wasn't sure, hadn't spent much time down by the river since she was in high school. It was a decent bicycle path on a spring or summer day, or a good place to walk and talk. Hell of a view of the Caledonia. She glanced up at the clouds now covering the sky and reflected it wasn't a terrible place for a moonlit stroll, either, if there was moonlight.

One of the lights in the distance winked out. She blinked, trying to decide if she'd really seen it do that. There had been one there a minute ago, hadn't there? She rubbed her eyes with her free hand, and then she could swear there was another lamp missing, like they were impinging closer and closer to her, like the path was gradually losing all light ...

It took one more light to blink out before she realized it was not her imagination. Something was taking out the lights on the trail, one by one. The buzzing noise was getting louder, an unearthly sound. Were there demonic bees? She wondered this as she backed up off the path back up the slope a few degrees. The wet grass beneath her feet was slick, and she felt a bead of sweat in the warm summer night, starting to slide down her temple.

To hell with regulations. She pulled her gun and kept it at her side, wishing like hell she'd gotten Arch to part with that consecrated switchblade Hendricks had loaned him. She hadn't pressed on any of that, though, not really considering that they were coming up with more and more people who wanted to fight the demons coming to Midian, but they had a severe bottleneck when it came to making sure they had people equipped to fight said demons.

That wasn't technically Hendricks's problem. But she had a feeling it was about to be hers in less than a minute.

Whatever was coming, it was moving fast. Another light went down, and ten seconds later, another. The buzzing noise was louder now, more mechanical, and it almost sounded like she could hear the low grinding of metal on metal as it came. It didn't sound like a car or like a train, but it was devilishly loud, raising in pitch and intensity on a regular cycle as it ebbed and flowed in a circular pattern of wicked sound.

Erin stumbled as she backed off the path. She pointed the gun toward the darkness encroaching upon her. It was only a few hundred feet away now and the buzzing was a low roar, like the devil's own servants were coming at her in a swarm. The darkness was near total, and the only movement she could see in the light that was left was pure-black motion in the night, like she was watching earthworms writhe in the shadows. She could see the movement but that was all, shapes against the faint backdrop of the river.

She hurried backward, still aiming down the barrel of her pistol. It wouldn't do any good, but if they surged at her she might be able to at least back them off, hold them at bay. She thumbed her mike and then stopped herself; calling in Fries or Reines or even Reeve would just get them killed.

She needed Hendricks or Arch.

Another light popped—and this time she was close enough to see it happen. Sparks rained down and guttered out as they fell like fireworks dropping out of the sky. Before they'd died out, they'd done nothing but shed light on motion, giving her only the briefest glimpse of red eyes in the dark, moving fast toward her.

Only one lamp left.

Erin lost her footing on the slippery grass just as she pulled her cell phone out. Whether it was the wet grass or an uneven patch of ground or just simple clumsiness in her fear, she didn't know. Her ass hit the soft dirt, and she cried out more from fear than because it hurt. She almost felt like she was sinking into the ground, like something had grabbed her and was pulling at her, groping her.

Then the last light went out, covering her in darkness.

***

Hendricks stood on the porch, Alison next to him, a single light shining down on them from a gothic-looking sconce to the side of the door. He was waiting and realized his breath had caught in his chest. Nerves, most likely. He couldn't recall ever having been to a brothel before, not ever. He wasn't really looking forward to it, and he kept his hand outside his coat, running over the rough outer skin. It felt like canvas, rough and stiff, but it was treated cotton. Treated with what? He had never bothered to find out.

"You shouldn't have worn that," Alison said, not even looking at him.

"What, this?" He tugged on the drover coat. "Why not?"

She gave him a look that was bathed in patronization. "It's summer in Tennessee and you're wearing a full-length duster with a cowboy hat. I can't imagine anywhere outside of Montana where that wouldn't stick out, but I think it's going to be especially obvious in a whorehouse."

Hendricks started to open his mouth to argue that with her but stopped as he heard the lock slide back on the door. "Brothel," he muttered under his breath. "Don't antagonize the madam."

When the door opened, a woman with black hair and green eyes stood before them wearing a silken gown that revealed a surprising amount of—to Hendricks, at least, and he'd seen some wild shit over the years—cleavage. He saw at least the top of her dark nipples, and it might have been more like half. "Darlings," she said in a deep, throaty voice. "What can I do for you?"

Hendricks resisted the urge to tell her she could do damned well anything she pleased. She had a look about her—late thirties but still smoking hot. Probably trying all she could to fight off the effects of age and possibly hard living. The makeup was a little thicker than he liked, but she was undeniably still a beautiful lady underneath the extra layers of plaster there to hide the wrinkles.

"We're here to see Lucia," Alison answered before Hendricks could say something—in the words of Arch—wildly inappropriate. Nothing of that sort would even have been on his mind, but Erin had left him pretty damned frustrated and more than a little stiff in the crotch after what had seemed like a promising start to the night. Based on her attitude when she left for the rest of her patrol, he didn't hold out much hope for later, either. Hot and cold, the two of them.

"Oh?" the lady asked, not sounding like it was anything but a rhetorical question. "For business or pleasure?"

Hendricks looked sidelong at Alison, who still looked dulled. "We kinda figured it'd be both."

"Come in, come in," the woman said, waving them forward as she stepped aside to let them pass. "My name is Melina Cherry." She looked Alison up and down as she walked by, Hendricks noted as he waited on the porch for her to go first. "Will you be participating or just watching, my dear?"

"I don't know yet," Alison said, and she added just enough of a flutter to her voice to make it sound like she was a little nervous. "I guess I'm just not sure what I'm comfortable with."

"Oh, sweetie," Melina said, rubbing a hand over her shoulder. "Lucia will do everything she can to set you at ease. Just let her know what you want from her, and she'll find a way to accommodate you. She's very good with couples."

Hendricks exchanged another look with Alison, this one much less certain. He was beginning to feel the edges of his comfort zone in the execution of this plan, and they were approaching rapidly. For the first time, he was beginning to wonder if taking another man's wife to a whorehouse was really all that great of an idea.

"Lucia!" Melina called out, and clapped her hands as if she were summoning a dog. That drew a frown from Hendricks at the mere symbolism. Though it wasn't his place to say anything.

"You have a lovely home," Alison said, her sweet Southern accent drawling along as she said every word of it.

"Why, thank you," Melina said, every bit as sweetly back to her. "What is your name, dear?"

"Alison," she said. "This is Hendricks."

"Oh?" Melina said as a knockout redhead entered from a parlor that was curtained off just to the side of the foyer they were standing in. She brushed through the red velvet partition with a slow grace that wasn't diminished one bit by the fact that Hendricks had seen her beating the ass off a cow demon in the middle of a field not that long ago.

She didn't look exactly like Starling, but the differences were subtle. Hendricks could see the eyes on this girl, could see them clearly, and they were a deep green, like the madam's. This Lucia was wearing make-up, enough to accent her natural beauty, but not overdone like Melina Cherry's. She didn't have age lines to hide, not yet anyway. She wore a gown, full length, black cloth that damn near shimmered. Hendricks wondered if she was overdressed, just sitting in the back waiting to see if a customer would show up. Or maybe she put it on the minute she heard a knock on the door. Either way, the effect was not bad. Not bad at all.

But she wasn't Starling. He could tell by the eyes. And it wasn't just the color, either.

This girl had a soft look around the eyes. It wasn't that she hadn't seen shit—she plainly had. But she maybe hadn't seen the hardest, meanest parts of it. Insulated somehow from the worst of humanity, or else it just hadn't gotten to her the way it infected some. He'd seen someone who'd been burned up inside by evil before; they had a wary look about them, always expecting someone to hit 'em, no matter where they were or who they were with.

She didn't carry that world-weariness. Starling didn't either, but her gaze was always on something, on everything. She watched attentively.

This girl only had eyes for Alison and Hendricks, and she was young—he'd never been able to pin down Starling's age exactly, because her eyes threw everything off—this girl was probably twenty-two at most. Maybe younger.

And somehow, she still looked just a little wide-eyed. A little innocent.

"Hello," Lucia said, and Hendricks was shocked to realize he was already thinking of her as Lucia, not Starling.

***

The buzzing noise was a frenzy now, a parade of some hellish sound in front of her. Erin was struggling against the strangely sodden ground and its grip on her. Coldly, rationally, she knew that the ground wasn't pulling at her, that it was just her fighting against it to try and get back to her feet, but in the dark and in the moment she still had that clawing feeling like everything was reaching out for her.

There was a smell in the air, the scent of sulfur. Flashes of red, like rubies catching a reflection, were there in front of her as something moved in the darkness along the path. She faintly heard the shatter of glass as the next light down the path away from her broke. She could see the sparks shower in her peripheral vision, but her eyes were firmly anchored straight ahead.

She might have had an easier time getting up if she hadn't had her gun pointed at the writhing darkness in front of her. That was her assessment, anyway, that little voice in the back of her head that was being shouted down by the screaming, *What the fuck?!* fear bouncing around in her brain as she finally pushed up to one knee. She'd dropped the flashlight and it had rolled away, pointing upslope back toward the park instead of down toward the path, where it might have given her some idea of what was currently scaring the living hell out of her.

The buzzing reached a crescendo, and she heard it move a little closer to her, like it was coming up the slope. She was only a few feet off the path at best. It was close, so close. Something buzzed by only inches away from her, less than a foot. She heard a ticking noise and felt a blast of wind in its wake that caused the sleeve of her uniform to flap in the breeze. She jerked it back out of instinct, like she was afraid a car was going to take it off if she left it hanging out there.

This was no car, though. It sounded so eerie, like a swarm of creatures from hell was passing right by, and she couldn't move, couldn't breathe, the stink of sulfur stuck in her throat and nose.

The buzzing started to lower in volume, and Erin knelt there on one knee, paralyzed, her gun hand shaking as the sound started to subside. No more gusts of wind passed her, no more strange, scary chattering. The buzzing faded, like the demonic bees had moved down the trail. The angry noises, the ticking, the feeling that something was moving over the ground like a plague of locusts beneath her, all of it was gone.

She finally took a breath and lunged toward the flashlight, still pointing upslope. She grasped it in a dirty hand and pointed it back toward the path, beam lighting the black asphalt below to reveal—

Nothing.

She had just about caught her breath when something touched her shoulder from behind and she screamed, spinning and pointing the gun into the midsection of a figure behind her. The flashlight's beam caught his face just before she pulled the trigger, and she stopped a hair's breadth from riddling him with bullets. "Jesus!" she cried.

"Not exactly," Lerner said, looking a little pained. Duncan appeared in his wake, a little more solicitous. "What the hell just happened here?"

***

"Well, this is awkward." Hendricks spoke the words out loud, not even bothering to filter them because they were exactly what he was thinking, and they damned sure fit the situation. He and Alison were standing in the little room upstairs that was just down the hall from the one still cordoned off with police tape. Not that he'd eyeballed it as he went past.

Lucia was shutting the door, and she was doing it slowly. While she did, he had a marvelous view of her back, and her ass was a thing of beauty, he had to concede. The curves of it were just visible at the top of the gown's skirt. Erin's was nice as well, but Lucia had some muscular firmness going on that Erin's didn't. Not that he was complaining.

"Let me make you more comfortable," Lucia said as she turned from the door. He could tell it was a persona she was putting on, but the persona was nothing like the hollow, robotic feeling he got from Starling. Lucia was a little clumsy with it, but it was still seductive in its way. He wasn't feeling it, but that likely had more to do with the third wheel in the room with him than any failings on her part.

"I don't know that you can," Hendricks said, standing stiff—in more ways than one he realized with surprise and folded his coat closed. He caught Alison eyeing him and suspected she knew. There was also a waver in Lucia's voice; that was the main thing that gave her away. He felt his interest subside and a little shame came to him for thinking of her this way. She was paid to be interested; she wasn't *actually* interested, and with that realization, he felt his own interest dissolve.

"Let me try," Lucia said and swept close to him. She had a nice fragrance, but it wasn't doing anything for Hendricks now that he'd been reminded what she was. He'd had a little trouble remembering what he was here to do for a moment, and that embarrassed him even more.

"It's okay," Hendricks said, and took a step back as she placed a hand on his chest. "I don't ... um ..."

"What's the matter, baby?" Lucia murmured and shot a look toward Alison. "You want to watch us first?"

"Not gonna happen," Alison said.

A flicker of uncertainty crossed Lucia's pale face as she turned her attention back to Hendricks, and he realized it was because he was the one she was more comfortable trying to sweet-talk. "You're still pretty new at this, aren't you?" His brain didn't feel much of a filter in the stark clarity of that moment, and he just let it tumble right out. "The whole seduction thing? A little inexperienced?"

He caught a hint of embarrassment in the eyes, like she was stung he'd figured that out, and she went scarlet in the cheeks. "Let me show you what I'm not inexperienced at."

"Where's Starling?" Alison said, cutting through all the crap and turning both Hendricks and Lucia's head toward her in a hot second. "We're here to see Starling, not have an orgy."

Lucia's jaw dropped a little, then she managed to scoop it back up and close it. "Who ... is Starling?" She just wasn't convincing enough. The naivety did her in, and Hendricks exchanged a look with Alison that told him she read it the same as him.

"You've at least heard the name before," Hendricks said, moving his head to look her in the eye. Her focus was split between him and Alison, watching them both like they were gonna bum rush her any minute. "That much is obvious."

"I don't know what you're talking about." Her voice wavered.

"I don't quite believe you," Hendricks said.

"I don't know what you're talking about," Lucia said, but the cadence changed midway through her words and her eyes shifted constantly. "I think we should either get to the business at hand or you should leave—"

"Okay," Alison said.

"Yeah, we'll go," Hendricks said. "We don't want any trouble."

"I meant you should sleep with her," Alison said.

Hendricks sent her the most raised eyebrow look of *What the fuck?* he could manage. She shrugged in response. "I am not ... no." He shook his head.

"Then we should leave," Alison said. "Kind of a shame, though; I thought maybe she'd feel a little more truthful after you tickled her for a bit."

"How did you even marry Arch?" Hendricks asked in horror as he made for the door. He left Lucia standing in the middle of the room. "You know—reserved guy, quiet, really religious, probably not into suggesting sex with hookers—"

"It's not like I would have hung around and watched," Alison said, sounding vaguely offended. "I just thought maybe if you talked to her privately—"

"Yeah, really privately," Hendricks said as he reached for the door handle, glaring back at her the entire time. "Like, in flagrante delicto, with my privates talking directly to hers, apparently—" There was a flash of something and the faint mood lighting in the room went darker by about ten shades. "What the—?"

"Lafayette Hendricks," the cool voice reached him. He looked back at Lucia, standing in the middle of the room. It only took a couple seconds for him to realize that Lucia was gone, really gone. It was the eyes, of course. They were a whole different shade now, something different than they'd been before. And the innocence was gone, whatever of it there had been. "I heard you were looking for me."

He stood there with the door slightly cracked and shut it back gently. Alison was standing there, watching too, just a step from the door herself. "Well, what do you know," she said.

Hendricks had to agree with that assessment. "Hello, Starling."

***

"What the hell are you doing here?" Erin asked, still trying to catch her breath after Lerner scared the shit out of her.

"I asked you first," Lerner said, annoying the fuck out of her. "What the hell was that?"

"I don't know," Erin said, shaking her head. "It broke all the lights as it came down the path. Sounding like … I don't even know, like a swarm of demonic bees or a giant devil worm."

Lerner raised an eyebrow at her. "Demonic bees, huh? Well, I can assure you that's not a thing."

Duncan spoke. "Blurr'ashaa."

Lerner rolled his eyes. "Okay, other than blurr'ashaa, which this probably is not, since they tend to stay in Asia and Africa, there are no demonic bees." He gave Duncan the stink eye. "Besides, blurr'ashaa don't break lights as they pass."

"True," Duncan said. He looked at Erin, and he seemed concerned. "You all right?"

"Other than shitting my pants in fear and nearly shooting Dicky Lerner here, yeah," Erin said, holstering her gun, "I'm fine."

"I *should* change my name to Dicky," Lerner mused aloud. "It fits. Richard Lerner, Esquire."

"You're not a lawyer," Erin said, eyeing him with a level of irritability that was falling slowly, replaced by a weak sense of gratitude.

"That you know of," Lerner said with a wide grin. "Admit it, it would explain a lot if I was."

"Uh oh," Duncan said, and Erin noticed a glazed look in his eyes.

"Relax, I'm not changing my name to Dicky," Lerner said. "It was just a joke."

"No, there's—" Duncan started to speak, but a scream—faint but bloodcurdling—cut him off from down the path.

In the direction the swarm—the thing—had gone.

"Shit!" Erin said out loud, and she took off without really thinking about it. She drew her pistol as she ran, and saw Lerner and Duncan blast past her at a pace that made them look like superheroes or something as they tore down the path. They disappeared into the darkness without a whisper, without a sound, save for their dress shoes hitting the asphalt ahead. Erin was tempted to tell them to wait up, but it wouldn't really do to have to shout for the demons to come back and protect her. She was a deputy sheriff of Calhoun County, for fuck's sake.

And she was running alone on a path infested by demons of a kind she couldn't even identify.

She sped up.

Her breath came in short gasps, legs pounding against the trail. Trees covered this part of the path, obscuring the glow of the moon where it turned the clouds a silvery-white. The river made its noise off to her side, and she could not hear the buzzing, not now.

The sulfur smell was still there, though. Lingering, like they'd left a trail of it. Like slugs.

Her flashlight beam bounced as she ran, illuminating the asphalt. She slowed as the flashlight started to show figures ahead in the dark, catching the first hint of something other than a blank path in front of her. One of them moved and the light caught the eyes, lighting them up red like an exposure on those pictures Erin had seen from her childhood. It took only another second for her to realize it was Duncan, looking back at her in the night.

He was kneeling, and after another moment Lerner appeared just down the trail from him. He was standing, arms folded, a look of disgust on his features.

"What is it?" Erin asked with a sense of growing dread. She slowed to a walk, as though she knew it was something bad without waiting for the answer. Her mind was telling her to stay back, to get away.

"See for yourself," Lerner said. He didn't look happy about this. Not that he ever looked happy, really.

Erin edged closer, taking the slow walk. The beam bounced with her every step. She caught the shine just under Duncan's leg where he squatted, the dark liquid betraying a red tinge as it reflected her light.

Blood.

It only took a few more steps to see what Duncan was huddled over. Another figure, mangled and missing limbs. This one looked like it had been dragged along the path, skin missing and flayed to expose part of the skeleton. The blood dribbled out here and there as she stood over it.

"Sweet Jesus," she said, and thumbed her mike. "Dispatch, this is eighteen. Send a coroner van to Rafton Park." She paused, and felt a little wave of nausea sweep over her. "And you might want to wake the sheriff, because we've got another one."

4.

Arch awoke to the sound of his ringing phone. He hadn't thought he was going to be able to sleep, what with Hendricks and Alison having gone to the brothel. He figured he'd lay awake in bed and toss for a spell until he'd finally get up and pace for a while. Apparently that hadn't happened, though, because he was deep in a state of dreamland when he heard the phone's jagged tones.

He'd nearly swept everything off the nightstand in his bid to silence it before realizing exactly what it was. When he answered, he knew his voice was full of grog. "Hello?"

It took him a minute to interpret everything the voice on the other end of the line was saying—static and the natural fuzziness of his own train of thought keeping him from understanding right away. It even took him a minute to realize it was Erin, not Hendricks or Alison, who was calling him. And another few seconds for everything she was saying to register.

By the time he was fully awake, he was already moving toward the closet where his uniform waited. He had a feeling it was going to be another one of those days.

Of course, every day had been one of those since the demons had come to town, but that was not a thought that reassured him.

***

Starling stared at Hendricks. Hendricks stared right back at her. He couldn't tell if it was the mood lighting in the whorehouse or if it was just something about her eyes, but he couldn't tell what the hell color they were. He stared at her, ghostly white, in the middle of the room, trying to decide what to say, and then Alison went and solved that problem for him.

"What the hell are you?" Alison asked.

Starling cocked her head at Alison, and Hendricks just watched, wondering if she was going to snap at her, attack, continue to stare or maybe just answer truthfully.

"I am a matter of no concern," Starling said, a little too quickly.

"You're concerning us more than a little," Hendricks said. That was truthful. Nobody liked an unsolved mystery.

She turned right around to stare at him with those eyes, and Hendricks felt a little shudder. "This form is necessary to communicate with you. That is all that matters."

"So you're not Lucia," Hendricks said. Like he hadn't already known that. "Who and what are you?"

"Irrelevant," Starling said.

"Then what is relevant?" Alison asked, cutting right through the bullshit.

"I am here to help," Starling said. Hendricks couldn't shake the feeling that this was the truth, though he didn't know why. "To help you save this town from the destruction that is coming."

"How do you know what's coming?" Hendricks asked, getting right back on point himself. "How do you know what's happening here?"

Starling did not say anything for a long moment. "Irrelevant. Do you want the help or not?"

Hendricks kept himself from answering while he tried to consider the branching path that this conversation was taking. She had saved his life already—twice at least, by his count. "I could use some help," he said finally. "But I could also use some answers."

"Here is an answer for you," Starling said, and her voice had this echoing, otherworldly quality for a moment. "Destruction is coming to this town again—"

"Again?" Hendricks muttered. "Is this a daily thing now?"

"—and you will once more have to stop it." She kept on talking like he hadn't just smarted off.

"That's delightfully vague," he said. "Got any kind of other warnings, like, 'sometime in the future you'll experience a headache'?"

She cocked her head at him. "It is all the warning I have. The future is cloudy, and those aiming for the destruction of this place have taken care to cover their movements and activities."

"Right," Hendricks said and looked toward Alison. "Sounds like she's bound by the same vision problems as Duncan. Runes get in your eyes."

"There are other forces at work to cloud the future of this place," she said, and again her voice turned different. "There is more going on here than you know."

"Which is why we were hoping you might answer some questions," Hendricks said. "You know, in the interest of blowing away some of that fog we're laboring under."

"I have no answers for you," Starling said, voice back to nearly normal—but not quite like Lucia's. "The path you must walk is covered in darkness because to allow you to see farther might corrupt your actions today."

"Corrupt them?" Hendricks dropped his head, looked at her in slight disbelief as he rolled his eyes upward to keep looking at her. "That's a peculiar choice of words. How would my actions get corrupted?"

"Darkness falls," Starling said. Hendricks didn't care for the poetic sound of it. "And blackens all that it touches. Staring into the future would allow you to see the darkness in its infinite and unfolding form. No man can look upon that and remain untouched by it."

Hendricks frowned. "Wait … you're saying what's coming is so bad that I'll … what? Give up because I'm overwhelmed at the thought of it?"

Starling merely stared at him. "It is not for me to say."

"And that's what's going to destroy us now?" Alison said. She still sounded like she was curiously uninvolved in anything going on around them, but Hendricks thought he caught a flicker of interest from her at this. "This unfolding darkness?"

"What comes now is merely another harbinger—just as Ygrusibas was, just as the Sygraath was." Her eyes flickered, as though there were light somewhere within them. "What is yet to come is that which I speak of—and that which will surely herald the end of days."

"Great," Hendricks said, nodding. "So even if we beat whatever is coming at us now, the thing that's coming somewhere down the line is so horrible I'll take one look at it and shrug my damned shoulders to give up. Marvelous." He shook his head in sheerest irritation. "Listen, lady, I don't think you know me—"

"I know you, Lafayette Hendricks," Starling said.

"Then you know I'm motivated," he said, just a little hotly. "You think some demon spawn—some ultimate evil—is going get me to throw in the towel and quit? Lady, if you really believe that, I don't think you know me. Not at all. I've fought a war—"

"This will be unlike anything you have ever seen," Starling said. "Unlike anything any living human has seen."

"I—" Hendricks started.

"Go to your husband," Starling said, shifting her attention to Alison. "Another threat looms that requires your attention." With that, the lighting dimmed for a second and Starling was shrouded in a sudden shadow. When it passed, she shook her head.

"What the hell was that?" Lucia asked, her voice back to normal, eyes a glimmering green. Her hand came up to her face and rubbed her forehead.

"Grim," Hendricks said after a moment's thought. He looked at Alison, and she looked back at him with enough of a look that he knew she'd at least heard it all with him. "Really fucking grim."

***

Erin was just standing by the body on the path, waiting. She'd thought about going back to the car for crime scene tape, but Reeve would be here in a few minutes, so why leave the body? Not like there was a high chance of someone coming along and messing with it—

Wait, no, scratch that. If Erin really dug deep and examined it, a week ago she would have said it would have been impossible for this body to even be here. This was Calhoun County, Tennessee, dammit, and so boring that the high school kids didn't even bother to hang around on Saturday nights.

No, the idea that someone would even leave a body here was unlikely. The fact that this had already happened meant anything else she thought of as inconceivable was now fair game. So she had to stay by the body, lest some corpse-eating demon come along and destroy the evidence.

Evidence of what, she wasn't even sure.

"Dear Jesus," came a voice from behind her, and she turned, hand already on her pistol. She hadn't heard him coming up the walk, but it was Reeve, sure as shit. He'd gotten there faster than she'd thought he would, and she was suddenly thankful Lerner and Duncan had gone on down the path to try and track the—whatever the hell caused this—to where it was going. Trying to explain their presence to Reeve would have been about as easy as trying to explain the appeal of kale.

"Looks a lot like what happened to Connor," she said as he came out of the darkness. He wasn't carrying a flashlight, which she thought of as odd until she realized the moon had come out from behind its cloud. The river was visible once more, and she had a pretty clear view of everything around her. She'd just been too caught up in her own thoughts to notice. An experienced woodsman like Reeve probably didn't even think about needing a flashlight since he was following a path.

"It's the middle of the goddamned woods," Reeve said, and she could tell he was in a snit. Not that she blamed him. "How the fuck—" He looked around him like something was going to come barreling out at him at any second. "Dammit, I guess it's big enough to get a car down here." He looked around. "Maybe a Smart Car or a golf cart or a Prius or something."

"I think I could fit my Honda down here," Erin said.

"Dammit, son of a bitch," Reeve said, and his hand came up to his forehead so fast he knocked his hat off. "So now we've some fucker that seems to enjoy running people over so bad that he's willing to go off road to do it. Son of a whore." His face was partially shaded by the moonlight, but the flash of anger was unmistakable. "I wonder if it's the same bastard as the one who caused that pileup? Some sick fuck with a fascination for killing with cars ..." His voice drifted off.

Erin just stared at him. It wasn't like she could tell him that Gideon was dead, that this was something new. Presumably something new. Gideon had seemed to explode in the reservoir behind the Tallakeet Dam, after all. That had killed him.

Hadn't it?

Yeah, surely. Besides, this was petty shit for Gideon. He had planned to drown the whole town after he'd gotten to the point where he was killing en masse with things like the pileup. Doing onesie twosie would have been a step back for him at this point. No, this had to be something new, she was sure of it. Not sure enough that she didn't make a note to ask Lerner and Duncan to confirm Gideon was good and dead next time she spoke with them, but close.

Reeve was just standing in silence, hand on his face, obscuring his mouth. "Uh, sir?" she asked, staring at him. "You all right?"

Reeve didn't take more than a second to turn on her and his look was all *Are you fucking stupid?* "No, I am most assuredly not all-goddamned-right. Is that a fucking joke, Erin?"

"I don't know," she murmured, not really sure what else to say. She just felt bad for him, felt bad that he was so in the dark. She couldn't even imagine what he was thinking at this point. All hell breaking loose had officially kicked off here in Midian, and he was the quarterback for the opposing team. Poor bastard didn't even know the game had begun.

"You don't know," Reeve repeated, staring at her with a cold fury she knew was not born out of what she had said, not really. "Well, here's what I know. I live in a town that is my whole world. Calhoun County is my place. I've lived here my whole life, I've worked here since I was barely a kid and could first start working, and I'm likely to die here, God willing, in another forty years when I'm old and grey—" He ran a hand over the smooth top of his head. "Well, old at least. These people—I've known them either my whole life or theirs. They're my people, and when I took that oath to be sworn in as sheriff, I wasn't just pledging to uphold the law. I was pledging to protect them, Erin." Nicholas Reeve had a serious bent, and she saw emotions in the man right now that cut through her usual image of him. He normally had two states: joking and irritable.

This one felt more like … helpless.

"I'm failing," Reeve said, and he shook his head. "I'm failing them in record numbers. Record, as in this is a fucking record to have this many people die in a year, let alone two weeks. Record as in we hadn't had a murder here since … shit, I don't even know when. I'm supposed to protect this town, protect these people, who I have known for so long. And I … am … failing." He let out a long breath and turned his head to the side. "I have failed. I don't even know what to do anymore, other than call in the state police."

She felt a strange quiver in her belly. It hadn't really hit her on that level. Sure, some of the deaths had felt personal, but the horror was almost covered over immediately by all the things she had going on with Hendricks. With all the things she'd learned from Hendricks. She'd felt like she'd become a part of something in the last few days, and maybe it was cushioning the blow of all the stuff that had come down on them lately.

After all, she'd lived here her whole life, too, and it wasn't like she didn't know these people who were turning up dead.

Murdered.

She started to say something, started to try and express how she felt about all that—a messy jumble of feelings that had been covered over by something new and exciting with Hendricks—and with the purpose—but she halted before she got a single word out. What could she even say? She didn't know how he felt, not really. She was here, but she didn't feel responsible. Not with demons on the loose. That was beyond man. Beyond police.

So instead she sighed, trying to make it sound sympathetic, and stood in silence while Reeve shook his head as he stood over the corpse, and they waited that way.

***

Lauren Darlington had gotten the call in the middle of the night and had considered—just for a brief, happy moment—of telling Nicholas Reeve to go fuck himself with something sharp. She'd thought about it, but the thought had passed relatively quickly. Well, the intention to do it had passed relatively quickly, anyway.

The thought remained, along with at least some vestige of the sentiment.

What was she going to be able to do, anyway? Forensic pathology was out; it wasn't even close to a specialty for her. Post-mortem wasn't something she'd be able to perform right there in Rafton Park anyway, even if she were qualified to perform an autopsy. She was a doctor, dammit, like McCoy used to say on Star Trek, but not the kind that Sheriff Reeve needed, at least not now. The best she'd be able to do was stand over the corpse, touch her fingers to the wrist and say, "He's dead, Jim."

Which Reeve already damned well knew before calling her.

"Why couldn't he ask Doughtry or McClellan to do this?" she muttered under her breath as the wheel resisted the turn she made into Rafton Park. Two big, wooden posts held a white sign with all the pertinent info on the park, including the fact that it closed after sundown. Probably to prevent people from being—oh, say—murdered in it after dark. Mark that sign as a failure. "Oh, right, because they're the serious, long-term country doctors that service this hell-burg. Let's drag in the rookie who works in Chattanooga instead! She's probably too new and weak-willed to tell us to go fuck ourselves." She was working up to it, though, that she was pretty sure of.

She pulled into the parking lot and killed the ignition next to a cop car that had its blue and red lights flashing. It didn't do much to light the night, surprisingly, though she could see the path down by the river thanks to the illumination of the headlights. Lauren chewed her lip and thought about how smart it might have been to bring a flashlight as she opened up her door and stood there, listening as the river burbled in the distance. "Oh, that's right, I'm not that smart. Which explains why I'm standing here in the middle of the fucking night."

She had none of that sleepy feeling that she should have had at this time of the morning. It was gone, replaced by that foreboding sense of nastiness that came from knowing she was about to inspect a corpse for signs of … well, anything that her unpracticed eye could discern.

Lauren started down the slope toward the path, feeling her tennis shoes slip a little until she got her balance. The moon glowed overhead, and the night air carried just a little chill. It actually wasn't a bad place for a walk, even in the darkness; but she would rather have just been able to come down here to walk or jog without having to worry about stopping to examine a bloody chunk of meat that had once breathed and walked and jogged itself.

She followed the path to the left as it entered the trees. She'd done a fair amount of jogging here when she could get away to do it. Seemed a lot less lately than it had been before. Wasn't becoming an attending physician supposed to be easier than her residency? Didn't feel that way.

She could hear voices ahead in the night, at least one of them raised. She looked and saw a flashlight moving around, figures moving in the moonlight. She hadn't counted cop cars, but it looked like there were more than a few on scene. In Chattanooga, this kind of shit wouldn't have gotten a doctor to come out. They brought the bodies to the hospital; they didn't summon the doctor out to the body.

Then again, this sort of shit—hit and runs—happened in Chattanooga a little more frequently than they did in Midian. Still, two in one day? Weird. Beyond weird, really. Or beyond coincidence, at least.

"Hello, doctor," Sheriff Reeve said as she approached. There was another deputy there, a blond girl who really did look like a girl. Early twenties at best, Lauren figured. Maybe younger. She had that look, too, watching everything Lauren did as she approached. Cop look. She'd seen it in the ER more than a few times.

"Sheriff," Lauren said, not bothering to conceal her irritation. If he noticed it, he didn't respond. Which sort of made sense; the man looked a little out of sorts to her eyes, and she didn't even know him all that well.

"We've got another one," he said, sparing not a moment in informing her of not only the obvious, but of something he'd already told her before.

"So I see." Lauren held herself to civility. She still wanted to rail at his ass for getting her out of bed to come down here like this, but she really had no one to blame but herself for agreeing to it. One good "fuck off," and he'd never trouble her again, she suspected.

But he wasn't on the list. Damn him.

The female deputy illuminated the body for her with one of those big Maglites. Lauren didn't like 'em, thought they looked like the sort of thing a Cro-Magnon would use to knock a woman over the skull with before dragging her back to his cave. "Over here," the deputy said.

The light skittered along the ground just briefly, enough to catch a couple of dark red reflections that might have been water if one didn't look too closely. Lauren suspected they weren't, though, and she tried to take care in stepping over to the body. "Am I destroying a crime scene or something just by trampling here?"

The sheriff's hesitation was damning in and of itself. "I don't know how much of a crime scene we've got here," he said. Not exactly the vote of confidence she was looking for. But then again, why would the sheriff of Calhoun County know how to set up a crime scene anyway? At least for something like this, he wouldn't.

The deputy brought the beam around so Lauren could see where she was stepping. A few isolated drops of blood were scattered along the path and she avoided landing her shoes in them—for more than one reason. "Thanks," she told the short, blond lady. Did she know the deputy? Probably not; even if they had gone to the same school, they had to easily be ten years apart. She did look a little familiar, though.

"Not a problem," the deputy said. "You're Lauren Darlington, aren't you?"

Lauren felt a brush of irritation and looked over at the face hidden behind the flashlight's beam. The deputy lowered it so she could see a little more of the shadowed features. The deputy had soft ones, a little nose, blond hair that didn't make it far past her neck, and she wasn't all that tall, either. "Yeah. And you are?"

"Erin Harris," the deputy said.

That triggered a little bit of a revelation for Lauren. "Rick Harris's little sister?"

"Yeah," Erin said, and not much more.

Lauren had known her brother, had gone to school with him. He was all right; he hadn't made the list, either, him or his other two brothers that she knew of. She vaguely recalled Erin now, but only barely. When she graduated high school, this Erin must have been something like eight years old. "How is Rick?"

"Good," Erin said. "He's in management up near Cleveland—Ohio, not Tennessee. Helps run a factory up there."

"Made it out, huh?" Lauren idly mused, leaning over the body. "Good for him. So few of our class did."

"Made it out of where?" The deputy—Erin—asked her. Lauren didn't even look up or bother to answer, because the blond girl clearly got it a second later. "Oh." Yeah. Out of Midian. So few of their class got out of Midian. It was like the world's largest flytrap, and once it got you caught, you never got out.

Like this poor bastard, whoever he was. She stared at the body, and it took her a second to realize it might—maybe—have been female. There was a lot of stuff wrong with it, but she could see the long hair now. It was hard to tell, what with swaths of the scalp torn loose and folded over themselves.

"Well?" Sheriff Reeve asked. "What do you think?"

Lauren didn't even bother to stop herself, assuming she even would have had the willpower to if she wasn't half-asleep. "This man is dead, Jim." She paused. "Or ... this woman is. Hard to say."

"If they're dead?" Deputy Harris asked.

"No, that's for sure. I was talking about the victim's gender, though I suppose it'd be easy to tell if I were motivated to disturb the body enough to try and remove the pants," Lauren said. "I assume you probably don't want to know badly enough to do that, though."

"I suppose not," Reeve said. "Good Lord, though, identifying this poor bastard—"

"I'm not sorry I don't have to deal with it," Lauren said, a little more bluntly than she might have if this were taking place at midday. She sighed and realized that she should probably throttle back a little on the bitchiness. It's not like Reeve wanted to be here, either. She glanced at him. Hell, he didn't even look like he fully realized where he was.

It wasn't that warm, yet Reeve had sweat running down his forehead that glinted in the moonlight. She might have assumed it was tears if it had been below the eyes, but it wasn't. If she had his job, with the body count piling up lately, she would almost certainly have shed a few tears, even absent the fact that she knew indirectly or directly every person who'd died in the shitty events of the last week. She'd already had to take time off work to go to Kim Hauser's funeral.

"Any idea—any clue—what might have done this?" Lauren heard Erin Harris ask her, but she wasn't turned where she could see the female deputy. Still, there was something about the way she asked, a tremor of something in her voice, that was different than the sheriff's state of shock. It wasn't something Lauren could quite put her finger on, but she'd dealt with enough fake smiles and feigned "Oh, bless your hearts" over the years to be able to detect a little bullshit when it was being applied directly.

This wasn't quite that, but it had the faint ring of it. She glanced at Reeve, but he was far beyond noticing. Hell, maybe she really was just a little put off by the whole thing. She was ... what? Nineteen? Probably hadn't seen a whole lot of dead bodies.

"I don't know," Lauren said, a little guarded. "This isn't exactly my specialty. My gut says trauma did it. Blood loss or cardiac arrest in the aftermath of being smashed. As for what hit them? Not a clue." She stood, putting her hands by her side. She hadn't brought any gloves, which didn't matter because she didn't want to disturb the corpse in any case.

Lauren stared down at the body and then shook her head. Stuff like this happened at her work, not her home, and she'd been very careful to keep a bubble separating those two things. It was for Molly, she'd always said, and having the added benefit of the drive meant she could work farther away. But really, it was for Molly in the sense that things like she saw in the ER in Chattanooga didn't happen here in Midian. Murders, rapes, hit-and-runs ... they *didn't* happen here. Minor mischief, sure. Some assholes that beat their wives or girlfriends, yes. Drug use, for certain, and tons of it lately.

But this? This happened in her other world. Not in Midian. Not until now.

Lauren turned away from the body, feeling a certain rush to her head from the thoughts surrounding it. She turned and caught movement coming up the path. It took her only a moment to see the shadow emerging from the dark.

Archibald Stan.

"Looks like I didn't miss much yet," Stan said as he came up the path, looking smug and irritating in his deputy uniform. He always looked smug and irritating to her, though. Always had. Even before the uniform. "Miss Darlington," he said, and she could tell how much effort he was putting into making it sound polite.

"Doctor," she said. "*Doctor* Darlington, thanks."

You bastard, she didn't say.

***

Lerner was chugging down the trail, Duncan behind him. They couldn't hear it anymore, the sound of the thing—whatever the hell it was—somewhere far ahead. This wasn't all that surprising to Lerner, because they'd given the killer a hell of a head start, and demons weren't renowned for standing still when they'd murdered a human. Unless they were planning to make a stand, or planning to eat it, or just generally be a complete and total nuisance.

No, that didn't happen all that often. Flagrant violations like that would tend to bring the Office of Occultic Concordance down pretty hard, and no demon stood still for that. None.

"Get any sense of how much farther we're going to have to run?" Lerner asked. It wasn't like he was winded, though he could hear his body and it sure sounded like he was. "I only ask because this shell of mine gets wheezier the farther we go."

"You can control that if you put your mind to it," Duncan said, not even breaking a sweat. Not that he broke a real sweat, ever. He wasn't wheezing, either.

"Yeah, but that'd require me to actually put my mind to it," Lerner said, hiding his irritation with Duncan and his total lack of exertion, "and I have other things on it at the moment."

"Such as?" Duncan asked coolly. Lerner was a little surprised; Duncan wasn't the type to ask.

"Such as what's doing this shit for one," Lerner said. "Such as what we're going to do when we catch it. Such as how sweet it would be to find the essence behind that fucking screen Spellman and crack them open slow, after forcing them to drink some marstap solution—" He couldn't stop himself from smiling at that. Marstap solution burned the shit out of an essence. No demon wanted to go anywhere near it, but he'd gladly procure a few dozen bottles if he could turn some loose on the bastard that was making his life a hell of its own lately.

"Not exactly your deepest thoughts," Duncan said.

"But some damned fun ones," Lerner said. Especially the last one.

The moon was hanging high overhead, and the steady sound of their feet along the asphalt path was starting to grate on Lerner. Running was not fun, not for him, and he had a hard time imagining any human could enjoy it either, what with their muscles and joints and all the other stuff that got to experience the jarring pain of the up and down leg motions. Why did humans enjoy exerting themselves? he wondered. Was it all down to those curious endorphins they got afterward? He'd read they got those after sex, too, which sounded a lot more interesting than running to him.

"You've got that look on your face again," Duncan warned him.

"I'm keeping my thoughts to myself," Lerner said. Duncan just griped about everything fun. "You're what the humans call a mother hen about this shit. Or a wet rag."

If Duncan had a reply, he kept it to himself. "I'm still not sensing anything."

"So they're just gone? Or *it* is. I guess it could be an it."

"Seems like." Duncan slowed and Lerner adjusted his speed along with his partner. The breeze shifted the trees above, making a rattling noise that Lerner did not care for. Not in this situation, anyway. "The path forks up ahead, too."

Lerner looked and found it did, indeed, fork. One way looked like it was a dirt path, the other the continuation of the asphalt one, winding right to follow the path of the river. What did they call it? The Caledonia, that's right. Like Scotland. Lerner had been to Scotland before, a long time ago. Which probably meant it was due for a hotspot at some point in the next twenty years or so. That'd be nice. He'd kind of liked the taste of haggis last time he'd been there.

"Look at this," Duncan said, and Lerner finally came to a stop just where the path forked. He smiled. Something was forked, all right. He wandered up to Duncan, feeling the quiet singing of his essence inside his shell. A run like that would have put some humans in the hospital. Lerner had done some study on body types, and it was always interesting to him—

"Focus," Duncan said, interrupting his thought.

"What am I looking for?" Lerner gazed into the dark but didn't see anything save for a trail.

"I don't know," Duncan said. "We don't even know if the—the whatever—if it came this way."

Lerner sighed. This town was such a bust for him. Where was an easier assignment when he needed one? There were eighteen hotspots, and almost certainly every single one of them was in less peril than this town. Why couldn't the office have sent him to one of those? Somewhere pleasant, maybe. Like Ecuador. Or barren, like the one in the Atacama Desert in Chile. That one was probably a nice, easy ride, just keeping an eye on some chu'tuaka to make sure they didn't burrow too deep into the earth and cause quakes. "I don't see anything but tire tracks. Little ones." He snorted. "So unless you think our demons were riding on bicycles …"

Duncan stared into the darkness, and he did it for long enough that Lerner took notice. "No, I don't think they're bicyclists," Duncan finally said, and then lapsed into another uncomfortable silence. When he spoke again, Lerner could almost hear the misery. "This town's really going to fall, isn't it?"

"It's just a few isolated incidents," Lerner said, brushing it off. He realized on some level he was really just telling Duncan what he needed to hear, but still, he did it. "Nothing big enough and bad enough to wipe it off the map has shown up yet. Just a bunch of small-timers with big damned ambitions. Bugs with plans to take over the world can't be taken too seriously."

Duncan glanced back at him. "That last one got pretty close."

"To taking over the world, nah," Lerner said, brushing him off. "A Sygraath gone crazy is not exactly the doom of mankind, and it's not the herald of anything other than a town experiencing a hotspot. Demons do crazy things at hotspots. It's a law of nature, like coeds taking their tops off at spring break." He paused and stared straight at Duncan, concentrated on speaking to the essence within the shell. "It'll be all right." He said it. He tried to send exactly that feeling, in exactly that way, directly to Duncan—the real Duncan, inside the shell.

Then he spent a long time wondering if Duncan knew he was lying.

***

Mick slept in a trailer with a couple other guys from the carnival. They were human, but that didn't bother him. He'd lived among humans for longer than he could remember, after all, and that was fine. The food was good—if a little greasy—and they had a kind of tight-knit companionship. Mick didn't feel any concern he'd be found out, because he could blend better than most kinds of demons. He never reverted to his true form, could eat human food and excrete human waste. In fact, the only time he was ever exposed—really exposed— was when he needed to get laid. And really, not until a few weeks afterward, when the pregnancy tests started coming up positive. That, he supposed, was going to be a little different this time, what with technological and communication advances. It was a brave new world. And now he would be open to exposure, unless somehow the whole thing stayed underground.

Fortunately, this was rare. Rare, and filled with joy.

He could always feel it coming on. It had been building for months, the sense of urgent need. He'd thought maybe he could keep it bottled through the last few cities that they were in, and he had. He was looking for a really isolated place to dump his load, because doing it in a major city was just too exposed. He tried to play by the rules as best he could, keep things under wraps so the Office of Occultic Concordance didn't come shit on him.

But it wasn't like you could hide a whole town going down in flames.

Ideally he'd have preferred to keep going a little longer. Somewhere even more isolated than this place would be a lot better, but in the modern world it was hard to find isolated anymore. He'd watched the world change, watched the web that tied the country together get tighter and tighter, and he'd worried. In the 1980s, Hobbs Green had been small enough that it could be cordoned off and just vanish.

Now, though, it was a different story, wasn't it? Back then, he'd watched the news reports every chance he'd gotten, hoping not to see a broadcast centering on how a whole small town had gotten pregnant after a carnival came to town. And he hadn't seen it, which was a beautiful thing. With only three networks and a bunch of newspapers that didn't want to cover news of the weird, he had been safe. Not even the scandal rags had reported on Hobbs Green.

Now, though, it was twenty-four-hour news, and more networks than he could count. If that wasn't enough, there were blogs and internet sites, Twitter feeds and other shit he'd only heard talked about. Lots more chances of word getting out. Which would only be a concern if it got latched onto and spread far and wide.

Maybe it'd just fade away, though. Most people still didn't want news of the weird. They wanted to live their lives on an even keel, sure of their place in the world and in the order of things. Which worked for Mick, because his place in the world was a different one than everyone else's, and his view of the order of things was far afield from most others.

Every once in a while he wondered if in keeping things under wraps, in burying his secrets of the years, he'd been the lucky beneficiary of some help. It didn't seem too farfetched to him that there was someone pulling the strings at those networks back in the olden days, someone whose job it was to keep things like Hobbs Green from disrupting the ordinary view of the world.

He didn't like to dwell on that too much, though. Mostly he just liked to get his job done, enjoy the company of the humans around him, and sit back to wait for the build of his essence to start pushing at him.

He could feel it coming on, too. He'd already latched onto that Molly girl he'd seen earlier. He could tell she was going to be the one for him. She had just the right mix of rebellion and anger and curiosity. It was a perfect fit.

Of course he'd probably have to leave this carnival behind after this time. Maybe get a job somewhere steady for once. He'd have thirty years to settle himself somewhere before he'd need to start moving again. That was enough time to live a life. A human life, anyway.

Mick thought back to that Molly again. Yeah, she wasn't bad. He liked knees. That would have made him weird, he guessed, based on his conversations with the guys in the trailer. They always talked about girls. He'd been around enough guys talking about girls that he knew what to say—tits, ass, oh, yeah, she was a smooth one when I got up in there—but he knew what he liked. Knees.

He didn't labor under any illusions of trying to blend in when he didn't have to. He was different. His view of the world was different. The other guys, they might have left babies behind, changed a life or two along the way at most. Mick left behind destruction in his wake. And he was as okay with that being the price of getting off as the guys in the trailer were with their cost.

In fact, he couldn't wait to do it again. Soon.

5.

Arch yawned a big fat yawn as he stood in the crusted, muddy ruts of Old Man MacGruder's driveway. Dawn was breaking overhead, and the sky was already a gentle blue. The last few days of dry, hot weather had completely eliminated any trace of the torrential rains. Arch hadn't never really seen anything like that before, at least not that quick—but then, he hadn't seen a rain like had come recently, either, and wondered if all this was the product of the hotspot.

He pushed at the ridge of the giant tire tread that his shoe rested on. It flaked and crumbled with a little effort, like a segment of wall falling down into the middle of the track. It didn't do much to entertain him, but he didn't need much at this point. He'd been standing around in the park all night, and it'd worn him to the point where he was about ready to be cursing.

Well, maybe not that much.

Alison was standing across from him and so was Erin, with Hendricks off to the side. All of them but Alison had jumbo cups of coffee in front of them. Hendricks and Erin were just exchanging glances, furtive—and a little cooler than yesterday, if Arch wasn't mistaken.

"What was up with Lauren Darlington, Arch?" Erin's question cut over the quiet hum of the crickets just over in the meadow. Some bird was chirping nearby, too, and they shut up as she asked the question.

"No idea," Arch said. The good Dr. Darlington had given him the stink-eye when he walked up to the crime scene, then said something about how she had to go home and sleep—which, even probably being true, had sounded like an excuse to everyone, including

Reeve—and took off like she was about to go for a run in the opposite direction. "She's always been a mite cold to me."

"She seemed fine until you showed up," Erin said, and he could tell she was musing on it. "Then she clammed up fast and took off. Sounded a lot ruder to you than she did talking to me, too."

Arch just shrugged. "She seems to have a problem with me, but I'll be dogged if I know what it is."

"Maybe she's a racist," Hendricks said, sounding utterly unconcerned. "Do we need to wait for the demon brothers, or should we get this show on the road?"

"You tell me," Arch said, eyeing the cowboy coolly. He switched his gaze over to Alison, who was still operating a few degrees south of normal. This was not usual for her, but then again, neither were demons and all manner of other trouble.

"They do seem awfully interested in Starling," Hendricks said, and he looked like he was chewing it over. "Maybe a little too interested."

"They might be able to give us some insight," Alison said, still sedate. "They know this world better than we do."

"And it might just be that they'll take whatever we tell them and run somewhere bad with it," Arch said. He still didn't trust Lerner and Duncan, not really. They may have been handy up on Tallakeet Dam, but that didn't mean they were anything other than self-serving. Or demonkind-serving. One of those.

"Do what?" Hendricks's face was crumpled in confusion. "You think they'll take the basics of this—which is, by the way, not much—Lucia turned into Starling when we confronted her—and do what with it? Kill her?"

"Maybe," Arch said. "We don't know what Starling is. Seems to me like she's on the other side."

Hendricks rolled his eyes. "Like an angel or something?"

Arch had a little trouble digesting that. "Maybe. I don't know. Hollywood told me they don't get involved anymore. Not that he was a sterling source of information, but I'm not sure why he would lie."

"Because he was a piece of shit?" Hendricks suggested. "I have a hard time buying Starling as an angel."

"Do you even believe in angels?" Arch asked, still eyeing him.

"I believe there could be creatures that call themselves angels," Hendricks said. "But if they exist, they're like demons to me—just some other, different form of life. Might as well be aliens for all I care. There's nothing mystical about them, and the idea they would serve some all-mighty protector and master and creator of human life is such bullshit I can't even find the words to say—"

"Got it," Arch said, more than a little sour. He was used to the cowboy's sour attitude toward the Almighty, but he still didn't love to listen to the man sermonize about it. Probably any more than Hendricks would have enjoyed hearing him sermonize about his beliefs.

Hendricks just rolled his eyes. "So, now you know. Starling and Lucia are one and the same, at least as a matter of physical form. The hooker seems to disappear when Starling is on the premises, though, and acted like she didn't know what happened when she came back."

"That's just weird," Erin said.

"Weirder than demons rampaging through your town?" Hendricks grinned at her as he said it. Arch wondered if she found it charming.

"No," Erin said. By the way that she said it, he knew she did not.

"There was another thing," Alison said, and for the first time in a while, she looked a little more animated. "Starling gave us a warning..."

Arch listened. Listened to every word. Even in the early morning summer heat, it gave him a chill.

***

Lerner pulled into the driveway of the farm that the humans used as a meeting place, sighing as he turned in. Duncan hadn't spoken to him since the fork in the path, and they'd had a long walk back to the car after that, so that had been a lot of silence. He wasn't mad, Lerner could tell, just had his mind on other things. Normally, that would have been fine, but Lerner was running short on things he was willing to keep to himself. Still, he kept his quiet. Painful as it was.

The town car bumped in the ruts as he took her down the driveway to the farm. He could see the two cop cars ahead, and another car—probably Deputy Stan's wife's car, since he doubted the cowboy had a vehicle to his name—and eased up behind them. It looked like the humans had all fallen silent. Lerner was a little bit of an observer of human nature, and nobody in this group looked remotely happy. At least, that was his professional opinion.

"Don't everybody get all excited and greet us at once," Lerner said as he stepped out of the car. Duncan was as subdued as the rest of this group, which was annoying in its own right.

"Did you find anything?" Deputy Harris spoke first. She looked the least down of all these people. For fuck's sake, were they all that depressed about a couple people getting splattered? Humans were weird. He glanced at Duncan and saw a long face there too. Maybe not just humans.

"Not really," Duncan answered, breaking his several-hour silence. Lerner just raised an eyebrow at him. "Path came to a split, and all we saw were bicycle tracks."

"Which makes sense, since it's a bicycle path as well as a walking path," Deputy Stan said. "Hard to believe some demon thing that made as much noise as Erin described didn't leave a trail."

"Unless it was flying off the ground," Hendricks said. Lerner thought the cowboy looked like he was thinking deeply.

"You run into a lot of flying demons, cowboy?" Lerner asked with a grin. He was just messing with the cowboy; of course there were demons that could fly. But that close to the ground? That would just be a weird choice. Especially given the noise the thing had made.

"A couple, yeah," Hendricks said, staring him down. The cowboy had found his spine. Lerner liked that, too. When they'd first met, he'd just sort of folded on a few things Lerner had tweaked him about, and that kind of shit got old fast. A mark who doesn't know he's a mark was not as much fun as pulling something over on someone who was aware it was coming. That was a challenge.

"This feels pointless," Mrs. Stan said, stopping Lerner before he could try to twist the cowboy around again. "No one really knows what this thing is, what's causing it." Lerner watched her. She had a deeply serious look about her. From what he'd seen so far, when she spoke, she tended to be either wise or frivolous. Not a lot of in between. "We're just sitting here jabbering about it and guessing."

"It only comes at night," Hendricks said. "That's when the two incidents have happened."

"The two splatterings, I think you mean," Deputy Harris mumbled under her breath.

"That makes it sound like diarrhea," Mrs. Stan opined. Frivolous again.

"That's not exactly a huge reveal, kid," Lerner said. "Most of our kind prefers to operate in the dark, especially if they're doing the kind of things that kill humans. They're like you people in that regard."

They lapsed into silence. Lerner could sense the frustration brewing under the surface. He couldn't say he didn't feel it like the rest of them, though it wasn't exactly the same. His frustration wasn't because he couldn't catch some creepo demon that had only killed a couple people so far; his was more rooted in the general progression of the town's degeneration. "Downward spiral," Lerner said, drawing every eye to him.

"What?" Deputy Stan asked.

"He's talking about the slow fall of the town," Duncan said before Lerner could compose an answer. He was only so slow in responding because he was trying to find a tactful way to broach the subject. "The more demonic incidents that openly occur, the more socially acceptable it becomes to our kind to do these things—and worse."

There was a pause. "You're saying that as more bad shit happens," this from Deputy Harris—she seemed like a smart cookie to Lerner— "the more demons think it's okay to openly massacre humans?"

"Our society thrives on rules and order," Lerner said, and even he was subdued on this one.

"A society where you can order human meat in most major cities," Deputy Stan said.

"That's a little underground," Lerner said. "They're not openly slaughtering humans in the streets. It's kind of like modern-day America, right? There's crime—burglaries, armed robberies, murders. There's organized crime, where they set out to profit from things that are illegal. But none of this is socially acceptable in mainstream society. How many of you regularly hang out with murderers and rapists?" He glanced at the two cops. "When you're off the job, I mean."

"We don't tend to get many of them around here even when we're on the job," Arch said.

"Because it's not socially acceptable," Lerner said. "You can't walk out onto the street and murder someone without expecting a societal response—some sort of societal response. It's the same thing in the demon world." He paused. "Except in hotspots."

"So that's where demons go to blow off some steam?" Deputy Harris asked. "It's like their version of the bar?"

"I'd say it's more like their version of a no man's land," Lerner said. "OOCs are in charge of enforcing demon law. Of keeping the lid on the things our people would do unfettered, things that would expose us to mainstream human society. But when it comes to a hotspot ... it's like our version of...I dunno, pick a spot on the globe filled with chaos and apathy."

"Washington, DC?" Alison said.

Lerner felt himself grimace and didn't have to wonder why. "We try, okay? We try and police those spots, but once the shit starts to roll down the hill, if it gains enough mass, there ain't no stopping it from wiping out everything below."

"Downward spiral," Deputy Stan said. "And that's how entire towns disappear off the map."

"You got it," Lerner said. "The problem here isn't just that things are progressing fast, either." He looked around the little circle of faces. "That happens sometimes, especially when a town is remote enough that we can't get to it en masse quickly enough. No ... here it's a worse problem."

"Yay, a worse problem," Deputy Harris said. "Well, don't keep us in suspense. What's the worse problem? Because we could use not only some bad news right now, but some *worse* news."

"Let me guess," Hendricks said. "With eighteen hotspots flaring at the current moment, you can only cover so much ground."

Lerner tilted his head slightly. "The cowboy gets it in one. The Office of Occultic Concordance ... is officially out of manpower." He paused then sighed. "Well, demon power."

***

When the alarm went off at six a.m., Laura wanted to hit it, so she did. When it went off again at six-fifteen, she smacked it hard enough to leave a bruise on her hand.

At six-thirty, even in her fog of sleep, she knew she couldn't ignore it anymore.

The sharp, delicious smell of coffee greeted her as she opened her bedroom door. It was the same door she'd been opening her entire life, the same bed she'd been sleeping in since she was a kid. As she yawned, she reflected that it felt like she'd been living the same day a lot lately. Work, home, Molly, work, repeat. It wasn't quite a grind. It was more like a good sanding.

She thumped her palm against the bannister as she descended the stairs. Her mom was already sitting at the kitchen table with the newspaper spread out in front of her. Molly was there, too, her soft brown hair twirled around and a tip of it stuck in her mouth. Lauren hated that habit in principle, but in practice, it'd been cute ever since Molly started doing it at roughly the age of three, when her hair had finally gotten long enough.

"Morning," Lauren pronounced, and she could hear the drag in her words, the tiredness. She felt every ounce of the middle-of-the-night awakening, and the irritation of running into Archibald Fucking Stan at the crime scene was predictably a sour note as well.

"Did you leave in the middle of the night?" Vera asked. She did not look up from her paper.

"Yeah," Lauren said, pulling a coffee mug that said "World's Greatest Mom" from the cupboard. It was her mother's, not hers. She stuck it under the coffee maker and grabbed one of the single-serve cups. "Sheriff Reeve called again."

"Oh, no," her mother said, voice dripping with that small-town sense of worry that was absent in all but the most empathetic people Lauren had met in the thriving metropolis of Chattanooga. It was a lot easier to have a "Shit happens, shrug it off" attitude when you didn't personally know the people who died tragically. "Who was it?"

"No idea," Lauren said, taking her first sip of coffee. She swished it around in her mouth, tasting the glorious flavor of the dark beans as it circled down the back of her throat the way she imagined liquid leaving through a drain. She'd need to keep it coming today. "It wasn't a body that was in great condition for identifying, it was dark, and I was just there to …" She paused. "I don't have a clue why I was there."

"Somebody else died?" Molly asked, looking up from her homework. The little knot of chewed hair had saliva dripping from it, which was decidedly un-cute.

"Yeah, Midian is turning into a real Sunnydale, California, lately," Lauren quipped. She paused. "You should be careful, just in case."

"This is just awful," Vera said. "I ain't never heard of nothing like this in all the born days of my life."

Lauren rolled her eyes at the "all the born days of my life" bit. She'd traveled a little bit in the last few years, and she hadn't heard anyone else, anywhere, say anything like that. It was uniquely Tennesseean. Still, her mother had a point. "It has been a little grim here lately." To say the least.

"You think it's the same person causing all this mess?" Vera asked. Lauren would have been willing to bet that her mother had had this conversation before, probably every day for the last week, with all her friends. Fortunately, Lauren hadn't been around to hear it. She viewed her mother through the lens of having known her for all her life, and her motivations were as plain to Lauren as the dime-sized blemish on her mother's cheek. She had these conversations because she got something out of them, some little delight in the misery being discussed, some small reinforcement and social joy out of having something delightfully negative to talk about. When it wasn't something as big as this, it was the small things, like how so-and-so's husband had stepped out on her. It was always "stepped out on" instead of fucked around, which would be how Lauren would have said it. Another generational difference.

"I have no idea," Lauren said, not wanting to get drawn into her mother's dramatic mess. It was a conversation that could last decades when it was a matter of insignificance like a cheating husband; she didn't even want to think about how long a conversation could go on with the grist for it being the shit that had been going down in Midian lately. She had to get to work, anyway.

Lauren blinked some of the sleep out of her eyes and looked over at Molly, whose head was back down. "Is that your math homework?"

Molly did not look up, which was telling. "I'm almost done."

"Why didn't you finish it last night?" Lauren asked. It was a valid question, but the minute it came out, she had a feeling it wasn't going to be taken well by her daughter.

Molly's eyes came up flaring, widened as her lips became a thin, hard line. "I fell asleep, okay? I fell asleep early, that's all." Super defensive.

Lauren just stood there, coffee cup in hand, the steam swirling off the liquid. She had a pretty good bullshit detector, and it was squealing at her just now. "Did you?"

Molly did that teenage thing where she grunted, sighed like she was being put upon, and nudged the cover of her math book closed. "I don't have time for this, Mom." She slid her chair out and scooped up her books and paper, carefully settling her homework into the page she'd been working on. Lauren could see the algebra from where she was standing; it was only half done by her reckoning. "I've gotta go." Molly shrugged into her backpack and motored out the door with her math book in hand before Lauren could come up with a reply.

"She was lying, you know," Vera said, not looking up from where she was flipping the page of her paper.

"I caught that, yeah," Lauren said, staring down the hall to the front door that had just been slammed shut. Now just what the hell was she supposed to do about this?

***

Hendricks was in the passenger seat, rolling along with Erin at the wheel. They'd split shortly after Lerner's grim-ass pronouncement. It was on his mind more than a little because it dovetailed with his own experience. Plus, it went right along with Starling's scary-ass prophecy. He glanced over at Erin. She hadn't said a word to him, which was— well, it wasn't fine, that was for damned sure. He was tired enough to not want to delve into it, though, having only gotten a few hours of sleep on Arch and Alison's couch before Mrs. Stan had shaken him awake to meet with Arch and Erin as they came off their emergency shift.

All in all, it had not been a good night. He thought about voicing these thoughts to Erin, but she was clammed up, jaw tight. He figured she was still pissed about the whole Starling visit, but didn't know quite how to approach that particular minefield. He decided on the direct approach, limbs be damned. "You still mad because I went to a whorehouse?"

She turned to look at him sidelong with eyes that would have burned the skin off of Superman. "No, I'm totally fine with you visiting a whorehouse. Hell, do it every night. Send me postcards, or better yet, take some video footage of yourself in the act so we can watch it and get all sexed up together."

"'Sexed up together'?" He let out a low guffaw that probably didn't help his standing any. "You know damned well I didn't do anything untoward in that place."

There was only a grudging hint that he might have been right in her reply. "I don't know that you didn't." She wavered just a little.

"Don't get me wrong, Alison suggested I should," Hendricks said, letting himself crack a grin, "but somehow I resisted the lure of a possible STD and the cold embrace of a woman with multiple personalities. Can't imagine why. Maybe it had something to do with the fact that she can turn her entire disposition on a dime." He glanced at Erin, who was now looking a little less hostile. "Kinda like that, yeah."

"You're not helping your case any here, Marine."

"Sorry," Hendricks said, genuinely contrite. "Look, we needed answers. Shit is weird around this place, way weirder and more hostile than any hotspot I've been to before. We're stumbling blind in the dark here. Someone has the potential to shine a light for us, I'm inclined to go a little out of the way for the illumination. Even if it means I gotta go somewhere I don't really care to go." He meant every word of it, and hoped like hell she could hear it from him. "And I hope you believe me when I tell you that it wasn't a place I truly cared to go."

"I believe you," Erin said after a long pause, "but that doesn't mean I'm happy about it."

"Well, there's a long list of things I'm not happy about," Hendricks said. "Starting with demons being a real thing and ending with several people making some pretty shit predictions about your hometown's chances of survival." He shook his head. "Starling said that whatever was coming was so bad it'd be likely to make me give up. Me! I've been fighting this war for five years, and she thinks I'd just throw in the towel and bail town, I guess. Maybe she doesn't know so much as she thinks she does—"

"Can we not talk about her for a while?" Erin's voice was quiet, but it cut across him nonetheless.

"Yeah, sure," Hendricks said and waited a minute or two. "What do you want to talk about?"

"Nothing, right now," Erin said, and she shot him a slow, only halfhearted smile. "I don't think I want to talk at all at the moment." Hendricks just nodded, ready to fall back into silence. "But," she said, "I can think of something we can do when we get back to my place that doesn't require a word to be said."

Hendricks felt the slow creep of the smile across his face. He'd forgotten what it felt like when things were new, were exciting, still intoxicating and fresh. He thought about responding with a "Yes" or a "Yes, ma'am!" but realized that silence just said it best.

***

Mick was out on the square, just waiting. The sun was already creeping up, like it did in summer. Not as bad as it got up north, where it could be out at five in the morning, but it was up now and getting hot already. The businesses were alive all around him, some diner with a sign that said "Surrey's" was a buzz of activity, little bees coming in and out with coffee cups and such on their way to face the day.

Mick liked the small towns. They weren't as crazy as a big city got, weren't as much of a hive. Here there was some room to breathe. Some room to think.

And you didn't have to work too hard to stalk someone in a small town because there weren't too many places they could go.

The girl named Molly passed into the square about a half hour after Mick sat down on the bench to wait for her. He didn't know for a fact she'd come through, but he suspected she would. He knew the school was a couple blocks away, and if she'd come through last night, odds were she would pass through again. She took no notice of him—not of anything, really, because her head was down and she was hurrying along in her own little world.

Mick took off after her at a trot. More like a jog to a human, where it would look like he wasn't trying too hard—just a little. It wouldn't do to break into a full-on demon sprint and scare the shit out of the locals by tear-assing after a young girl like he was some kind of stalker. Even though he kind of was.

He slowed to a faster walk as he caught up to her. She was skimming the edge of the square, still caught up in her own head and letting her feet walk for her on a path she probably walked every day. He watched her long, dark hair bob and sway as she walked. She had a little bit of a duck-footed thing going on, turning out the toes at a forty-five degree angle with every step. Mick liked that; it was cute, too. He could tell he had a little infatuation going for this girl.

Plus, she was wearing a skirt, and he could see her knees.

He reluctantly came alongside, matching his pace to hers, and waited for her to notice him. It only took a few seconds before she looked up and he totally blasted the little world she'd been inhabiting. Her jaw dropped a little before she recovered and pulled it back up. She went from shock to annoyance fast, too.

"Good morning, Molly," he said with a hint of a smile that he hoped was infuriating. She was already a little irritated, maybe adding a little more would bump it over into the charmed category? At least that's what he thought.

"Good morning, Mick," she replied, letting it drip with sarcasm. "Are you following me around now?"

"Maybe I'm sleeping in the square," he said, still trying for charm. He thought he could pull it off. He used to be able to. "In which case, it's rude to step into someone's home and not say hello." That one took her off balance, and he could see the desire to make a smartass reply tempered by the hesitation she felt in wondering if he was genuinely homeless. He felt a little hilarity at preying on her natural decency this way. A little. "I'm just kidding. I was here to go to the diner and saw you crossing. I'm not homeless. I'm in town with the carnival."

"So, you kind of are homeless." Whew, now she was irritable and unrestrained. "In that you don't have a permanent home."

"I guess you're right," he said. Juveniles were so … juvenile. But innocent. And that was a prize in and of itself. "But I wasn't sleeping in the square. Not that I've got anything against it, I've just got a nice trailer—"

"You're a real leaf on the wind," she said.

"Watch how I— GURRRRRRK!" he said, shooting her a smile.

She couldn't help it; she smiled too. "You a fan of *Serenity*?"

"I like all kinds of movies," Mick said. He really did. They took him away—not that he needed to get away because he liked his life. But it was nice to see other things, other places that he couldn't go.

"It's a nice retreat for a while." No need for her to think he was anything other than a noble drifter suffering his way through life. Women still liked angst, didn't they? He'd heard that somewhere. Angst and brooding.

"Yeah, well, this isn't a romcom," she said. "You're not cute and charming, about to sweep me off my feet. I'm not lovelorn and craving a man's attention." She stopped and turned, letting him get a little ahead of her. "You're only in town for a few days, right?"

"Yeah," he said, a little guarded. This was different. She was way more jaded than he would have expected. He could still feel the innocence, but it was definitely behind a wall. He hesitated, trying to figure out which track to take. "Listen, I just wanted to say hi, maybe … get to know you a little—"

"In the biblical sense?" she asked. Holy shit, was she blunt.

"Ah, well, look," Mick said, trying to think fast. This had not happened before. "I'd be lying if I said you didn't interest me in that way, because let's face it—I'm a teenager, and I think about sex all the time." Neither of those was true, though he was thinking about sex all the time right now. "But that doesn't mean that I have shady ulterior motives. That I'm just following you around like a dog, trying to figure out how to hump your leg—"

"Gross, but possibly accurate," Molly said, her eyebrows lifted and lips pursed. "I don't know you."

"Nobody knows anybody when they first meet," Mick said and chanced the smile, but faintly this time. Too big would be sleazy. Subtlety was the key with this girl. Everything needed to be subtle, because she was a major overanalyzer. "I get that maybe you want to write me off already, save yourself some time by fitting me into some neat little box, 'Oh, he's a user, I've heard of this before—'" he watched her blanch just slightly and knew he'd hit home—she didn't have any real experience with a user, "but you don't know me, as you just pointed out. I could be a perfectly nice person. I could be the nicest person you've ever met, but you'd never know because you're making a snap judgment based on what you think I am." He paused, trying to give a little effect. He was really having to work for this one. "You know what they call that, when you make a decision about someone based on a snap judgment? It's called—"

"Yes, thank you," she said, eyes almost closed. He sighed a little within. Back in the game. And all it took was preying on this poor girl's deep desire not to appear prejudiced against anyone at all, ever, for any reason. An open mind was a wonderful thing to lay waste to. "Fine. I don't know where you think this will get you, but—"

"Go out with me," Mick said. She wasn't going to be a one-shot, that was for sure. Not an easy conquest like the others. This might take some work, because her wide, innocent eyes had been tempered with something—some tales from some sour source poured onto the lenses to turn the rose-colored glasses into shit-colored ones. "Just a dinner at a diner, something to give us a chance to talk. Find common ground."

"And what do you plan to do on this common ground?" Molly asked. Now the jadedness was back—a little.

"I want you to like me," Mick said, adopting an aura of frankness that was as false as his purported age. "I want you to like me so you'll hang out with me again. So I can have someone to talk to who smells nice." He smiled. "I sleep in a trailer with five other guys who all work the carnival, and we have a portable shower that doesn't get used that much by anyone but me..." He shrugged ruefully.

"Oh, God, lovely," Molly had a look of genuine disgust. "Yes, thank you for that horrifying glimpse into carnival life."

"I promise I use it at least once a week, whether I need it or not," Mick said, grinning.

Her disgust broke into a smile that wrinkled her nose. It still had a little distaste in it, but less. "That's a sad story. You want me to bring my violin on this date you're proposing?"

"Just bring yourself," Mick said. "Save the violin for some other time." He smiled. "Whaddya say?" He made it sound like he was a Brooklyn kid with the accent. It gave him that strange and unusual sensation, like he had brought something foreign into this girl's little world. He wondered if she felt the same about it.

She got a look like she was rolling it around in her head. "All right," she said after a moment, and with more than a little reluctance. "A date. Only one. And in a well-lit, supervised environment. The diner here in town, after school—in broad daylight." She eyed him. "If you think you can get out of work for that."

"Hell yeah, I can get out of work for that," Mick said with a grin. Maybe this wouldn't be so hard after all. "What time should I meet you?"

6.

Lerner was lying on the bed at the hotel, staring up at the popcorn ceiling. He didn't know why it was called that, because it didn't look like popcorn to him. It looked like boogers in white snot, like he'd seen blown out of a guy's nose one time after the guy had died. Those were red from the blood, but still. Boogers in snot, that was what popcorn ceilings looked like to him. Probably didn't have a very alluring ring to human ears to call them booger-in-snot ceilings, though.

What was it with people desiring to make things sound pretty? Life was tough and short for these humans. Why all the pleasantries? Why all the social niceties? Why not just get down to the business at hand, even if it was cold and brutal and short? Sometimes things needed to be said, and fast. Given how short their lifespans were, Lerner would have figured humans would prefer getting to the point. But, no, they talked around it, going for nice and pleasant rather than getting it over with. The whole thing was boggling to him. But it wasn't the only thing.

"Hiding," Duncan murmured from the other bed. Neither of them really slept, they just would lie down for a while when they weren't doing something. Paperwork was finished for the day, so they were both lying down and staring up. Lerner might have asked Duncan what he thought of the popcorn ceiling name but he was clearly in the middle of some thought of his own.

"Who's hiding?" Lerner asked, less out of any genuine interest and more out of the faint politeness that Duncan expected. He was getting soft after over a century on Earth.

"This thing, whatever it is," Duncan said, still staring up. "It's only attacked at night, and it's so loud and obvious that it'd be noticed during the day. Which means it's hiding somewhere during daylight hours." He reached up and tapped on the wooden frame of the bed, absently. "So where is this thing hiding?"

"Fuck," Lerner said. "It could be anywhere. I know they call this a small town, but it ain't that small. Plus the hotspot seems to extend out into the county, which ain't exactly a trivial thing to search either."

Duncan was quiet for a minute. "You ever wonder what governs the range of a hotspot?"

Lerner didn't answer at first. These were the first questions that led down a road he didn't want to tread. "No."

"Okay, then." Duncan was quiet for about an hour after that, and he spoke again as if they'd never stopped talking. "Do you think it fears daylight?"

"Could just fear the attention daylight brings," Lerner said. "It might be wearing its game face all the time, or it might just be shaped in a way that it could never pass for human." There were enough of those kinds of things still out there to give the Office a fucking headache or ten. Dispatching them all was the widely suggested solution among the OOCs in the field, but the head office had yet to go for it.

"Something big, maybe," Duncan said, still lost in thought.

"If the little blond deputy is to be believed, it sounded big," Lerner said.

"Why do you do that?" Duncan asked, and turned to look at him. "You know their names."

Lerner grunted. "Of course I do."

"Why not call them by them?"

"Have you been out of our world so long you don't even think about how names carry power anymore?" Lerner asked, more than a little crabby. Duncan was in the process of going native, no doubt about it. The question of whether that was going to be a problem was an open one, though. It could be benign.

"No," Duncan said softly. "I guess I don't think about it much anymore." He fell silent for a while longer. "Where would it hide?" he asked when he broke the silence again.

"I don't know," Lerner said with a sigh he felt down to his essence. "Let's ask ..." he hesitated, "... Arch and Erin. They know the area, after all." He ignored the fuck out of Duncan's expression.

***

Arch didn't like the silence anymore. He thought he'd have broken through it by now, gotten over how it hung in the air of their apartment like the drywall dust still hanging in the old one from when the demons had destroyed everything. He wasn't used to it, though, not by a mile. By several miles, actually.

After years of dating and years of marriage, Arch was coming to a difficult conclusion.

He didn't know his wife nearly as well as he thought he did, but she knew him up, down, forwards and backwards.

He felt that stubbornness cling, though, that desire not to be the one to break his silence. He'd felt it dissolve after Tallakeet, at least until he'd found out she'd been the one firing the shots up there. Then it was back with a fury, back with a vengeance, even though his brain was calling him a hypocrite and worse for resenting her not saying anything to him. He'd been keeping his own secrets, after all, keeping to himself what he'd been doing with Hendricks at night. It was easier unsaid, easier to keep to himself the way that demon hunting made him feel—

Arch glanced over at Alison. She was sitting coolly on the sofa, looking for all the world like she was just thinking things over. And she probably was, but what she was thinking over was a complete mystery to him. Every move she made to break down the wall between them was matched by some other thing she did or he did that put it right back up.

The worst part of it was, he wasn't sure he had it in him to work on breaking it down himself.

He was just starting to say something, working up to it, when his phone rang. He glanced at it, thought about ignoring it, and then picked it up and answered. He knew it was Lerner before he did so. "Hello?"

"Got a bare hint of an idea, Deputy," Lerner said, getting right into it. Arch didn't mind that at all, especially right now. "Where would something hide around here?"

Arch didn't roll his eyes, though he thought about it. Not like the demon would have caught it over the phone. "Could be anywhere. How big you thinking this thing is?"

"Bigger than a breadbox but smaller than a corinth'al'eshan," Lerner's voice came back from across the phone. Arch waited for him to translate for him. "Big enough you'd notice it. Car size or bigger, probably."

"Any garage in town," Arch said, "if we care to guess it's killed a family or taken over a house somehow. We got a few unoccupied warehouses on the outskirts. Maybe some of the bigger caves in the area—"

"Any of them run through town?" Lerner asked.

Arch glanced over at Alison; she was watching him. "I'm not exactly a spelunker, but I've heard the ones under the town are small. Too small for anything car-sized."

"Any house in town," Lerner said, the sound of his teeth grinding coming through the phone's receiver. It got on Arch's nerves. "Well, we can't search every house."

No kidding, Arch didn't say. "It'd help if we had a little more to go on."

"Wait 'til tonight, maybe you will," Lerner said, and he sounded positively nasty about it. "Not sure you want to wait for the next body to show up, though."

Arch sure as heck didn't. He had a thought. "This thing likes darkness, right?"

"Seems to."

That had to be worth something to his mind. "So it's hiding somewhere dark, it stands to reason."

"Which is why I asked you about caves," Lerner said. He sounded a little faint and tinny on the other end of the phone.

Arch started to say something else but stopped when Alison started to move. She went over to one of the boxes that hadn't been unpacked yet and started to rummage around. He watched her idly for a moment, watched her bend over in those jeans, working to get something free from the box. It took her a few seconds, and Arch had just about mustered his thought back when she came out with a map. She carried it over to the table and spread it out. "Just a second," he said to Lerner.

"Tim Connor got run over here," Alison said, pointing to the little map square for Berg Street. The map she had was a small, local one. The interstate neatly bisected it, and the whole thing looked like it had been torn out of a bigger atlas for the entire state. "And then last night's kill happened ... here ..." she pointed to Rafton Park, the big, blue snaking curve of the Caledonia River running right next to where her finger landed. "If this thing needed to get back to where it was going before sunup—"

Arch frowned and leaned over, clutching the phone close to his ear. It took a second for him to realize there wasn't even the sound of breathing on the other side. "You still there?"

"Yeah," Lerner said. "Just listening to your clever lady spell it out."

"You can hear that?" Arch asked.

"Whatever it was, it was going in this direction when it hit Tim Connor," Alison said, pointing northwest. "Berg Street runs nearly out of town in that direction ..."

"It was going roughly the same direction when it made its attack last night," Arch said, running his finger along the Caledonia's line where the path remained unmarked on the map. "Trail splits about here ..." He fell silent in contemplation. "Either way, it goes north or northwest."

Alison looked up at him, a knowing look in her eyes. "Whatever this thing is, it's up there during the day."

"Up where?" Lerner asked on the other end of the line.

"Only one thing of interest to the northwest," Arch said, clutching the phone tight to his face. That wasn't exactly true, but there was only one thing that dominated the landscape in that direction, one central thing to which all else was subject thanks to basic topography.

"Ohhhh," Lerner said, getting it at last. "You mean that big damned mountain."

"Mount Horeb," Arch said, nodding, though he knew the demon couldn't see it over the phone. "Whatever this thing is, it's hiding somewhere up in the wilderness around the mountain."

***

Erin was caught up in that sweet, sweet feeling of afterglow. That's what she'd heard it called, and she tended to agree with it because her whole skin felt flushed and wonderful, in a state of total relaxation. She was still getting control of her breathing, though, but in a good way, like she'd just gotten done with a run or something.

Hendricks was already nodding off next to her, his cowboy hat hanging off the edge of the nightstand. The sun was shining outside, it was the middle of the day now, and she didn't have to be anywhere until later tonight. It was a good feeling, the cheap cotton sheets she'd bought at Wal-Mart pressed tight to her skin, laying just across her belly. She felt sweaty and sticky but those were problems for later, not now.

A thought occurred to her, and she voiced it out loud. "How long do you think this is gonna last?" She didn't really mean it to be a downer question, but she knew the moment she said it, it sure as hell was.

"The hotspot?" Hendricks murmured sleepily. "Weeks. Months, maybe. Less than a year."

"I didn't mean the hotspot," Erin said. She'd felt the rush of insecurity and just asked the question. Now she realized she'd just burned an opportunity to back out of putting it out there. Oops.

Hendricks stirred slightly, and she wondered how much of the afterglow he was feeling. She'd heard guys were sleepier afterward, and that was born out by her experience. Especially after a day and night like they'd had, there was no reason to expect he'd want to be awake afterward. "Well ..." Hendricks said, and she could just hear the hesitation drip off.

"Once this is over with, you'll be on your way, right?" She reached down and pulled the sheet up to cover her chest. Why was she even asking this? They'd known each other for like a week. She'd just been looking at him as a fresh, fun lay, to break the monotony when they'd hopped into bed together. This was a serious topic, even for her.

"I guess," Hendricks said, and the tension filled his voice. "I mean, I don't know. You might end up on your way, too, if all this grimdark crap about the end coming to Midian turns out to be true."

She felt a trickle of fear run down into her belly, and she gripped the sheet tighter, rubbing the low-threadcount sheets between her fingers. "I don't know. What happens when a town ... goes down like that?"

Hendricks was silent, and she tried not to look at him, as though that would make it all go away. "Different every time, I've heard. Depends on what kind of demon does the job, really. Sometimes it's like rival gangs come in and just drive the residents out. Other times ... they get eaten." He rolled over to her. "It's not like it happens a lot, okay?" His voice still carried that hint of tiredness, though she could tell he was trying to be reassuring. "It's rare, even for hotspots."

"But Lerner says we're heading that way." Her voice sounded empty, even to her. It was a big deal, wasn't it? Losing an entire town? How could some place, with people, with families, with homes and businesses and life just vanish? Just disappear without a word, without a trace? "How come no one ever notices these places are missing?" she asked.

"I don't know," Hendricks said, subdued, and she could tell he was awake now, fully. "It's a mystery to me. Government cover-up, maybe? I'm not really sure. The one time I saw it coming, there just wasn't a word breathed about it anywhere except in the dark corners of the 'net most people don't take seriously." He shifted in the bed. "Or so I've heard. I don't exactly spend a lot of time online myself, you know."

He seemed like he'd be more at home navigating a giant spider web than the world wide one, she realized. His face was scratchy with a day's worth of stubble, but she kissed him anyway, just rolled over and kissed him. She felt his chest hair against her bare skin, and it felt good. The warmth was reassuring, the touch was sweaty and sticky and just as sweet as what they'd done a few minutes ago. She felt the compulsion for reassurance but kicked herself for feeling it at the same time. Like every nineteen-year-old should just face up to the idea their entire hometown could get wiped off the planet. Totally normal.

He was running delicate fingers over her cheekbones and tracing the lines left by the salty tears she didn't even know she was crying when the phone started to buzz on the nightstand. She looked at him for just a moment, frozen in that pause in time where she knew she was going to have to move, to leave his embrace behind, but didn't want to.

Then she answered the phone. "Hello?"

"Hey, it's Arch," came the deep voice on the other end of the line.
"Hey," she said, restraining a sniffle. "What's up?"

***

Lauren had gotten done with work early, thankfully, and drove home down the blistering interstate under a sweltering sun. Her car's AC had gone out yesterday sometime, and she hadn't noticed it until this morning. It was another item on her "To Do" list that she really didn't have time for, but Tennessee summer wasn't near to done, unfortunately, even though it was almost September. Too much shit to do, too little time to cram it all in there.

She pulled into the driveway and threw the car into park with a little more aggression than she normally would have. It had been a crap day, a busy day, with a steady influx of patients. Some of them died, most of them lived, and because of her bleary-eyed state, all of them were running together in her mind at this point.

She slammed the door and started up the walk to the white house. She never parked in the garage because her mother's car took up most of it and the rest was junk still left over from when they'd cleaned out the house after her daddy died. Hell, there were probably still baby clothes in there from when Molly was a newborn, stacked in with the transistor radios and other shit her father had collected.

She could hear the violin going upstairs through the window as her key hit the lock. Molly was practicing, practicing like she did every day. Lauren felt a spike of frustration. Molly was a good student, a good kid overall. Seeing her do her math homework this morning was strange because usually there was no need to ride her about getting schoolwork done. She was on that shit, serious about it. Way more serious than other kids. She acted more like an adult than her peers, that was for certain.

But finishing her math homework first thing in the morning? That wasn't just a departure from the norm; it was a full on jump from the train tracks when the train wasn't even heading toward its normal destination. It was bizarre, that's what it was, and to have it come along with a bullshit excuse of "I fell asleep," gave it all the more urgency to Lauren. Something was happening there.

Nothing good.

She opened the door and closed it swiftly behind her, as though there were some way she could keep a fly from following her in. She couldn't, and she knew that, but she tried anyway. She could practically hear one of them buzzing faintly in her ear even now.

"You're home early," her mother remarked as she entered the kitchen. It opened up on the family room, and *Let's Make a Deal!* was playing on the TV in front of Vera.

"Really?" Lauren asked as she set her purse on the counter. "Because it feels like I was gone for about a year."

"One of those days, huh?"

"You said it," Lauren agreed. She paused, holding onto the strap of her bag. "Have you talked to Molly about—"

"No," her mother said, not taking her eyes off the TV. Wayne Brady was about to offer someone a deal, Lauren was sure. Clearly more important than worrying about your granddaughter. "That's your responsibility, dear."

"Yeah," Lauren said under her breath. "You know, I work—"

"No doubt," her mother said with that little slathering of false sympathy she did so well, "and so hard, too, going to college and medical school and doing your residency. All that after being a teenage mother." She tilted her head around. "I been holding the bag here for you for sixteen years, and I believe I am done now. You're an attending physician, what you always wanted, and now it's time, before your daughter leaves for college, for you to do the last mile of the parenting."

Lauren just stood there with her mouth slightly open as her mother turned back to the TV. She was somewhere between shock and outrage, but she wasn't quite sure where she landed on the scale. "I've been here, okay? It's not like I left you with her and disappeared, I was here for birthdays and Christmases, and in the evenings wherever I could—"

They false sympathy came out again. It probably sounded real to people who hadn't lived with her mother for thirty-two years. "Oh, I know, dear, every chance you could. But you didn't get that many chances with your school and work and residency demands. Now it's on you." She still didn't even turn around, watching Wayne Brady count out hundred dollar bills.

Lauren could feel the seething set in. But what was she going to say? Medical school wasn't easy—or cheap. College hadn't been, either, not to get her pre-med reqs out of the way. It was time intensive, becoming a doctor, and the oddball shifts and all the demands had been leading up to this moment. She could look back and see the trade-offs now, but at the time they'd been just as natural as could be. You didn't pour this many years into achieving a goal to get into the middle of it and seriously considering walking away. That would be a ton of sunk time and effort that had no payoff.

A waste.

She thought back now, about Molly, the sixteen years. It was time she'd enjoyed, but it had been tiring. It was the little moments that she remembered, not the daily stuff. That kiss before bedtime that had caught her in the eye, the birthday party where she'd spun her around in front of the piñata a few times before she missed and started to cry.

Lauren sighed, and it was a sigh of weariness and one of desperation. "This parenting thing ain't easy," she said as she headed toward the stairs.

"You said it, darling, not me," her mother replied as someone made a deal.

***

Lerner didn't mind cutting down on the rest period. It was pretty unnecessary for them anyway, and he always felt like it was time wasted. Sure, they skipped it regularly when they had something brewing, but when they were rudderless, it was a regular thing. They spent a lot of time rudderless, though. Home office was like that; pointed you in the general direction and then let you walk a ways. He was used to it, so it didn't frustrate him anymore. New arrivals into the Office tended to be pretty ecstatic about getting out of the confines of the underworld, so the heavy hand of all the attention landed on them.

Lerner wondered how many newbies the office was handling right now? He guessed a lot. Would have bet on it, actually, though he hadn't been to the home office in quite some time.

"A whole mountain is a lot of ground to cover," Duncan said from beside him. Didn't even have his eyes closed; Lerner could tell he was getting out of the habit of even bothering to look around with his essence anymore. This Spellman had really fucked the whole system up.

"Less than we had this morning," Lerner said, feeling a little more chipper. Progress was progress, even on this dinky shit case. Without it to focus on, they might as well go door-to-door looking for trouble, or sit by a police scanner and wait for trouble to crackle over the radio. The damned runes made them blind in this town, since everyone with half a brain or a connection to a connection had them. Gossipy fucks. Demons really were just one giant social circle, the stupid underworld. They'd be lucky to catch a meth dealer at this point.

"Where would it hide on the mountain?" Lerner could tell Duncan was just thinking out loud.

"Supposed to be abandoned mines up there," Lerner said. "Coal and shit. Or some of the deeper pockets of woods, maybe. Hunting cabins. Could be anywhere, really." Duncan nodded along; Lerner knew he knew all this. But then again, Lerner didn't mind speaking it aloud because it was better than being told to shut up for pontificating some obscure point of human behavior.

They were heading up a back road toward the mountain. It was visible in the distance, just a low slope on the horizon. It wasn't anything like the Rockies, that was for damned sure, or Alaska—which was the Rockies too, wasn't it? Lerner didn't know, all he knew was he'd been both places, and to Canada, and even seen some of the Himalayas once on a flyover. Tennessee's Smoky Mountains were nothing so dramatic as that. They were practically foothills by comparison—but they were still mountains.

He didn't know the exact elevation of Mount Horeb, but he knew he was a lot happier driving it than climbing the damned thing. Besides, the whole thing was covered in trees all the way up, looking like some monster with a bowed back rising out of the earth. Lerner clicked his tongue in his mouth. Where was this motherfucker hiding?

***

Lauren paused at the door, hesitating before she knocked. The sound of violin music filled the air, not a single sour note. Lauren was no expert, but she could hear that her daughter wasn't quite like a concert violinist. She was pretty proficient, though. She listened through the door, waiting to see if Molly missed a note, and held back from knocking.

It wasn't like she didn't want to see Molly, but the thought of picking up the conversation where they'd left off when she'd stormed out this morning wasn't exactly appealing. It was a lot easier to let her mother handle the duties associated with being the bad guy, while she could just swoop in and be the good guy in the limited amount of time she usually had with her daughter.

The thought that those days were over was cause for a little more joy to be robbed from her life. Stressful job, a sheriff who considered her his personal mortician, and now this? Ugh. Double ugh. Triple-quad-quintuple ugh. She knocked.

"Come in," Molly said, as the sound of the bow running over the strings came to a stop. It wasn't one of those scratchy, abrupt stops, either, it was a graceful stop at the end of a note, not like when the needle came off a record mid-song.

Lauren entered the room, pausing at the threshold. There was still a lot of pink in here, though she doubted it was much to do with her daughter's taste. The room had been pink since she was a little girl, and it hadn't ever been repainted. Who would have done it? She was too busy, Molly was too disinterested, and her mother had left that sort of stuff up to her dad before he died. As a result, the few posters her daughter had put up had a pink background. The place smelled nice, though, the result of a vanilla-scented candle burning on the dresser.

"Hey, kiddo," Lauren said. She shifted to lean on the frame of the door with her shoulder and crossed one foot behind the other. She was still wearing her scrubs.

Molly was sitting on the desk chair. Light shone in on her across the old wood floor. "Hey," she answered without enthusiasm, the violin still stuck under her chin, bow in hand but away from the instrument.

Lauren stood there for a minute pondering her angle of attack. She didn't want it to be an attack, but she knew—knew for sure—that Molly was going to see it that way no matter how she put this. How could she not? "Did you finish your homework?" She asked it low and slow, lowering her head to stare at her own feet and the floor as she did it.

"The homework from this morning? Yeah," Molly said, and Lauren looked back up. She was still holding the bow, ready to get back to her practice. "Turned it in at school, of course."

"I meant your homework for tomorrow," Lauren said, and she bobbed her head up to look at Molly while she said it, but only with great effort. It was so damned uncomfortable.

"No," Molly said, and her voice seemed suddenly strangely husky. "I'll get it after I finish my practice."

Lauren felt another one of those sighs coming on, the one that told her she was tired and that she damned sure didn't want to do what she was about to have to do. "I think you need to do it now."

Molly stared at her, probably fifty/fifty on dumbstruck and annoyed. "I'm running a straight-A average. Are you sure you want to question my process?"

"Way to sound like a corporate employee," Lauren said. "But since you brought it up, call this a management initiative from your mother to try and keep you from having to do your algebra in a rush as you run out the door."

"I got it done fine," Molly said, and her brow had descended, eyes turned dark with fury.

"I'm sure you did," Lauren said, trying to figure out how to broach the other gaping subject just sitting there in the middle of the room. "But the real question is why you didn't get it done before that—"

"I told you, I fell asleep." Molly's voice crackled with teenage anger. Lauren started to wonder if she'd sounded like this at sixteen, but she didn't have to think it over very hard. She knew she had.

"I'm not gone so much that I don't know when you're lying." Lauren just laid it out there, quiet, trying to avoid the path that would set her off. Doubtful that this would do it, but it was worth a try.

"You think I'm—?" Molly's eyes flickered. They still held that resentment, but there was a flash of uncertainty. "Whatever. I got my homework done, turned in, and my grades are sound. I don't know why you're bitching at me."

"I'm not 'bitching' at you," Lauren said—but she was, wasn't she? Same shit her mother would do to her, that passive aggressive thing where she'd latch on to something unrelated to what she really wanted to talk about—which was the reason she was lying about not finishing the homework. Lauren remembered sixteen like it was yesterday—hell, it practically was—and there was always a reason for her to do it, too. "Who's the boy?"

Molly just stared at her but didn't adjust quite quickly enough. "What boy?" she asked, a second too slow.

Lauren laughed, light, near-toneless. "God, I wonder if it was this obvious to my mom when I was lying?" Of course it was; she'd almost always figured it out.

Molly made a half-grunt, half-seething sound. "I have to practice. And then I have homework to do." She made the dagger eyes, the ones that Lauren had made at her mother.

"I'm going to check your homework later," Lauren said. "Leave it out for me, okay?"

The eyeroll was prodigious. "Fine." It was definitely not fine.

"Okay, then," Lauren said, and started to leave her daughter's room.

"Close the door behind you!" Molly called, a little more snot in her tone than was really needed. Lauren did and stood out there, just waiting, listening as the tone of the violin picked up.

It was late afternoon, the sun was still high in the sky, and she could feel the tension wracking her. What to do? Normally she might have tried to squeeze in a run by the Caledonia River, but since she'd seen that body at Rafton Park, she had no desire to go anywhere near there. Or town, for that matter, since Tim Connor had gotten run over on a jog of his own.

No, she needed air but not danger. Those places were right here in town, along with whoever the hell was being so damned vicious as to run people down. Lauren wanted somewhere a little more isolated, a little more removed from what was going on in Midian. There was the road up on Mount Horeb that she'd run a few times. Maybe she'd try that.

***

Arch could see Erin's Crown Victoria behind him—the sheriff's own car, he still thought of it—easing up the curved road leading up Mount Horeb. It wasn't like they'd planned to travel in a convoy, but once they were out of town she was a little heavy on the pedal and he was light, so it was natural she'd catch up to him eventually, he supposed. Besides, they weren't going all that much farther.

"Where do you think this thing is?" Alison asked from next to him. She was pretty quiet, thinking it over on the way up. "Hiding in one of the old mines by day, slouching down to Midian by night?"

"Could be," Arch said. "It'd be tough to comb all those old mining tunnels, though. Best we check up and down the main roads first, see if there's any sign of anything amiss. Maybe look at driveways for a sign of ..." He let his voice drift off. "Well, I don't know what we'd been looking for a sign of."

"Mmmm," Alison said, and he could tell she was lost in thought again. She was pretty smart, his wife, valedictorian of her class and all. Sometimes he forgot how smart she was because she didn't always come out with the deepest thoughts. She put her mind to something, she could usually do something with it, though he wasn't sure exactly how far she'd get with demons hiding somewhere on the mountain. "Locals," she said.

"What?" Arch asked, holding the wheel tight around a curve, the vinyl steering wheel smooth against his fingers.

"Erin said this thing made noise. Loud noise. When it came past her." They passed a mailbox on the right, and Alison flicked her wrist to indicate it as it shot by. "Some of the locals might have heard it, especially if it's following a path or a road."

"Well, shoot," Arch said, blinking in surprise. He hadn't come near to thinking of that.

***

Erin eased off the gas and pulled into the overlook as Arch guided the Explorer off the road in front of her. She had been expecting him to drive slow, but he was past slow and into granny territory. She bit off another complaint, let it die on her lips, and just took the Crown Vic in to park behind him and the town car already waiting for them. The overlook was on a curve, and down below the whole Caledonia River Valley was laid out, with other smaller mountains and foothills providing the rise that fenced it all in.

"Here we are," she said, stating the obvious to Hendricks, who was already reaching for the door. They hadn't talked much on the way up the mountain, because there wasn't much to say. Plus, she could feel her own fatigue setting in, and she knew he was dealing with more than a little of his own. She'd already picked up on the fact that when Hendricks got tired, he got cranky and sullen. It wasn't subtle, either, though he seemed pretty pleasant overall right now. She attributed that to the idea that they were maybe close to something on getting this demon.

"Evening," Arch said as Erin got out of the Crown Vic. The overlook was a nice view, all green valleys and a nice picturesque scene of Midian lining the valley floor. It was a fun drive, usually, a real scenic thing to do on a Sunday morning, maybe meander on up to the Mulberry Lodge near the peak of the mountain, such as it was. Nice restaurant, nice place for prime rib. It had the added bonus of a hell of a view, so it tended to cater to a little higher-end crowd. She'd been there a couple times with her folks back in the olden days, celebrating special events, before her brothers had left town.

"So what now?" Hendricks asked, and Erin could hear the cranky and sullen starting to come out.

"Alison had an idea," Arch said as Lerner and Duncan came shuffling over. "Erin said this thing was loud; maybe someone who lives up here might have heard it."

"Good point," Lerner said in that Boston accent. He wasn't acting like a dick at the moment for some reason, and Erin wondered what it was. "We could split up, canvas the area a little."

"Closer to the bottom of the hill, the better," Erin said. "We know this thing probably came toward the mountain, but it may not be up the mountain. It could have veered off before it got here."

"It could have," Arch agreed. "Could have gone to the far side over the pass to the north. Probably didn't go easterly, because there are other roads that would have made more sense to take out of town if it meant to go that direction—"

"Maybe this thing doesn't know your town that well," Hendricks said.

"Maybe," Arch conceded. "But this assumption we got is all we've got to go on, so we might as well—"

"Work it, yeah," Hendricks said, sounding a little resigned to her ears. "Probably best if the cops knock on the doors, right?"

"It'd make more sense than having Lerner and Duncan flashing their badges," Erin said with a half-smile. She gave them a frown. "Do you even have badges?"

Lerner pulled something out of his jacket and flipped it down; it wasn't something she could easily read, but she got the sense it was important and that he was very official, whatever it said. "We have something close," he said with a grin. "It'll work well enough to get us answers if we knock on a door."

"Maybe we should split up," Hendricks said then paused. "Wait …" He almost sounded like he was slurring his words. "Never mind, that's a plot from a horror movie."

"It's still daylight," Erin said. "That means we're fine, right?"

"No telling," Lerner said. "Teams of two would be my recommendation. At least one of us law enforcement types to balance out you two civilians." He gestured vaguely to Hendricks and Alison. "I'd also really recommend that you don't put me, Duncan or cowboy together."

Erin felt an insufferable smile coming on. "What's the matter? You two having marital tension?"

Lerner grinned. "Well, we've been not sleeping together for about a hundred years, sweetheart, so there is that. But I was suggesting you split us up just so because the three of us are the only ones carrying something full length that can handle killing a demon." He waved a hand faintly at Arch. "No offense to your safety knife, but that thing is gonna be about as effective as a toothpick for poking at something that moves as fast as this thing supposedly does."

"None taken," Arch said. "All right, how about—"

"How about I go with Duncan?" Alison said. Erin felt a little surge of surprise at that one.

"I'll ride with the blond deputy," Lerner said, and Erin's surprise increased, mingling with irritation. Her annoyance increased as well as he headed toward her patrol car without even waiting for her to say yea or nay. "I guess that leaves you boys as the dynamic duo." His eyes flicked from Arch to Hendricks.

"I guess it does," Hendricks said, shrugging as he headed for Arch's Explorer. Erin started to say something to him, but Lerner stepped up to the door Hendricks had left open before she had time to come up with something that expressed what she was feeling. She just watched the cowboy go, the black outline of his drover coat nearly touching the gravel and dirt of the overlook as he disappeared around the back of the Explorer.

"I have a feeling you and I are going to get along just great," Lerner said with that toothy, dickish smile. Did he know how fucking annoying she found him?

"Yeah, we go together like Rikki Tikki Tavi and Nagaina," she said.

"I like you already," Lerner said as she got into the car. "That's such a great film. A classic."

Erin slammed the door harder than she ever had before. They might even have heard it down in Midian.

***

"This is called canvassing," Arch said as Hendricks considered tuning the man out. He was already bleary-eyed, and the intro to basics of police work was about as boring as any of the ten thousand procedural shows he saw on the rare occasions he'd turn on the TV in his hotel rooms.

"Yeah, thanks for that basic instruction," Hendricks said, noting the quick flash of annoyance on Arch's face. "Think I've heard that somewhere before. Seems like the thing to do is for you to knock and me to sit in the car with the window open, since—hopefully—we're not going to accidentally stumble onto the actual demon we're looking for in the course of this canvassing thing."

"You never know what you're gonna find when you knock on doors," Arch said, and Hendricks could see the tension in the man. "Could be anything."

Hendricks could feel the annoyance building. "Tell me about it."

"Mountain folk get a bit peculiar at times," Arch said. Hendricks was already bored of the lecture. "Most of them are normal enough, but every once and a while you get a real weird one. Anti-social types. Maybe even a little angry at the authorities, if you catch my meaning."

"Yeah, sure, hostile," Hendricks said with a yawn. "I realize that's probably a foreign concept to you," Arch said, giving Hendricks a little angry side-eye.

"You ever hear of Ramadi?" Hendricks waited, but there wasn't even a hint of recognition in Arch's face when he looked over. "It was a town in Iraq where there were insurgents hiding. We—the Marines—had to go busting down the doors to houses. It was fucking shitstorm, too, a real Charlie Foxtrot." Hendricks looked out the window.

He could hear the gears grinding for Arch, and when the policeman spoke, it was a lot quieter, a lot less irritable and with a mountain of humility. "What happened?"

Hendricks shrugged. He was too drained to put much into it; not that he had much to put into it anyway. "I was nineteen. We go busting down doors, sometimes I'm on point. Thing is, the guy who's on point? Something like two out of three of them go home in a coffin, family gets the American flag to display on their mantle. We didn't even get to use our fancy scopes and shit. We just short-stocked the rifle, lined our pointer fingers up with the barrel and BANG. Point and shoot. Pink mist splashing the walls. It was a goddamned clusterfuck. So, yeah, I've knocked on a few hostile doors in my time, even before I started finding demons on the other side." He sniffed, irritation causing his face to twitch. "Hell, I prefer the demons to some fifteen-year-old fuckstick with an AK-47 that thinks he's doing God's own work. At least I don't have to feel guilty about what I do to the demons."

Arch was hesitating, and Hendricks could hear it. "You feel guilty about what you did over there?"

"Hell, no," Hendricks said, staring at the greenery passing by out his window as they wended their way down the mountain road. "It was us versus them. I don't care what you've heard, we didn't fight over there because of orders or CO's or for some fucking butterbars—that's a junior lieutenant that doesn't know his ass from an M203—trying to get a goddamned medal." He turned to look at Arch. "We fought for the guys in our squad. If I'm blowing through the fatal front—that's the three feet around a door, which you gotta clear in a goddamned big hurry—I'm doing it because of the guys with me. My buddies. It's us versus them, and anyone who ain't with us gets a bullet in them if they raise so much as a finger that looks like a pistol barrel." He turned back toward the window. "That's why it doesn't bother me, having Lerner and Duncan with us. Because they're with us, not them."

"For now," Arch said.

"For now," Hendricks agreed. "But be honest. Those guys are working on the side of order against chaos. You think they're gonna go switching sides when all we're getting promised is chaos in the forecast?"

"I don't know," Arch said, guiding the Explorer into a slow turn. "I don't have any idea what they're about—really—and we ain't got a lot of time to dig into it right now." He made a face. "Help is help in this situation. I guess we need all of that we can get."

"We do indeed," Hendricks said and came within about a millimeter of asking Arch if he thought his wife was going to be a help or not. He didn't, though, because he could've felt the tension between the two of them even if he hadn't known Arch for a little while now.

***

"So what do you think this is?" Erin asked, waiting to see what Lerner said. She figured now that she had him alone, maybe she'd get the straight dope, the rumors and shit he didn't feel compelled to share with a larger group.

"Fuck if I know," Lerner said. "Don't get me wrong, I've seen a few bodies get the shit beaten out of them, flung for a distance like these two have been, but it never quite looked like this. I mean, this shit isn't like a beating. This is the sort of thing you'd swear was vehicular homicide if you didn't already smell demons slinking about in the streets."

"You said 'slinking,'" Erin said, glancing over at him. He was cool as a cucumber, just sitting back like he didn't care. "You don't like your own kind?"

"I don't like trouble," Lerner said, not looking at her. She didn't mind; she didn't like his grin anyway. "Every one of the ones that's drawn to a hotspot is trouble, lots of them with a capital T. It's the nature of my job to deal with trouble, but much like a prison guard, I don't have a lot of love for the inmates."

"You run across a lot of the same shit?"

"There's a lot of variety in the demon world," Lerner said, still pretty close to neutral—and not like a douche. "Hell, you should remember, you grabbed your boyfriend's demon guide. Thick book, right?"

"Like a Bible or an encyclopedia," she said.

"It probably doesn't even cover close to everything," Lerner said, putting his hands up behind his head and leaning back into the seat rest. She worried his slick hair would get grease on the upholstery, but she didn't say anything, just ticked another box against him. "There's a lot of different kinds of demons out there. We number as many as the stars in the skies."

She thought that sounded vaguely familiar but didn't know from where exactly. "So how do you tell what you're dealing with?"

"The thing you gotta understand," Lerner said, and he finally turned his head to face her, lecturing like he was some professor and she was some fresh-faced student just out of high school, who didn't know the world was going to fuck her for all it was worth, "is that most of the kinds in that book your boyfriend has are extinct or nearly extinct. They may have been prolific back in the day, but there was a war between man and demon, and demonkind got its collective ass kicked real hearty. Lots of species died off or came near enough to it as not to matter. The ones that survived learned to adapt and go underground. Stay out of human sight, keep things quiet, let them forget about our kind. Those are the ones that are still walking, still feeding and living their lives. Maybe they were fruitful and multiplied, who knows—"

"Don't you know?" she asked. "Weren't you there?"

"Hah!" He barked a laugh. "Good one, kid, but I've only been on earth for about a century. This was thousands of years ago. Point is, the demons you see today are mostly integrated into human society. The troublemakers are the ones that travel around, look for the places of upheaval—hotspots—and thrive on the chaos there. They come to a town like this, where you probably had more than a few demons living already, all peaceful and normal, and they stir the pot. They come and whatever they touch gets tainted. Corrupted, I guess you could say." Lerner's expression turned dark. "Just like a good man might live his whole life decent and gentle in a place where he's safe and secure. But you put that same man in a lawless waste where he's gotta steal and kill to survive, and you get a whole different animal. See, these wanderers, these agents of chaos—they come to a hotspot when it flares, and they start breaking down society. Dead bodies in the streets. Some family gets turned into dinner. Worse things happen. Point is—that lawful demon who's just been living his life, suddenly he's wondering why he's bothering. He's strong—stronger than a human. Maybe he's got a taste for flesh, wants something his neighbor has—so he takes it. Because he saw someone else do it. Because he can. Because all the things that told him how normal it was to just be one of the people, they start to evaporate." Lerner tapped the window with his fingertips, and Erin saw him leave oily residue on them. "See, the process of corruption leaves marks behind. Leaves spots. Dirt. The things that were once clean and pretty get ugly fast." He held up his hand, then used his sleeve to wipe the fingerprints, leaving a smudge behind. "But just like this, it doesn't come off so easily." His smile was gone. "Sometimes it never goes away."

***

Alison watched Duncan steer the car around the slope. They were set to tackle the middle of the road, between the overlook and the bottom of Mount Horeb. It had been quiet in the cab so far; she could tell the demon liked silence. So did she. But there were some questions that just needed to be answered.

"So," she started, "what's it like being a demon?"

When Duncan looked over at her, she just smiled. She could tell he didn't know what the hell to say.

***

Lauren stood at the overlook up the side of Mount Horeb looking out on the town. It always made her feel tiny, like she was a nothing and a nobody being here. Midian looked pretty small itself, but not as small as she felt staring down at it. She stretched her hamstrings, felt the pull and the pressure as she did so, leaning against her car.

Molly. Molly was on her mind now. She'd left work behind, and now all she could think about was Molly and whatever she was getting into. Probably nothing good.

But maybe not. She was pretty responsible, wasn't she? She wasn't the kind to just get crazy—

Oh, wait. Neither was Lauren herself, but that had changed when Molly's dad came into the picture. Charming son of a bitch. Lying, charming son of a bitch. Lying, charming, deadbeat son of a bitch. Not that she was still irritated at him or anything. A little help might have been nice, though.

She shuffled back and forth, preparing herself mentally. She'd run down the side of the mountain road before, and fortunately it had a lot more shoulder than the average road. She'd need to be safe on the tight turns, maybe move a little closer to the edge, but she should be fine. It was a pretty safe place to run, after all, low traffic, and fortunately a decent distance from Midian, what with all that had happened down there of late.

She grabbed her water bottle and took a last squirt for hydration before she headed down the mountain. She'd need to turn back before she got very tired, because the trip back up was going to be the real killer.

***

Erin knocked on the door of Chauncey Watson's house with the back of her hand. It was a solid wood door in a solid wood house, an A-frame monstrosity that looked out over the valley. Hell of a view, probably go for a hell of a cost nowadays, but Chauncey Watson had been living here forever. Or at least since she'd been a girl.

Erin could hear the motion inside the house and glanced back to the car. Lerner was just waiting in the passenger seat, watching the whole process with a measure of disinterest. This was the third door she'd knocked on, and Lerner hadn't showed any more interest in house number one or number two.

Erin stood there, baking in the damned heat, feeling the sweat pour down from her scalp. It was tracking lines down the back of her neck and across her forehead. She would swear to it that noon was nothing compared to the late part of the day, when the heat settled in on the valley before sundown and shit just got sweltering. It made her back itch, and she longed for the cool air conditioning in the car.

The door cracked open and a magnified eye peeked out at her through a glass thick enough it could have been cut off the bottom of a Mason jar. Chauncey Watson stared out at her, the half of his face that was exposed telling her that he was looking at her like she was a specimen for dissection or something. "Erin?" he asked. "Erin Harris?"

"Hey, Chauncey," Erin said. She'd known him a little here and there, just like she knew a lot of the town folk. Chauncey Watson worked at a big engineering concern near to Cleveland just down the interstate, doing something with numbers or schematics or some such shit that she didn't pretend to understand. She'd known him from his work volunteering for the engineering club when she was in high school. As far as she knew, it might have been his only human contact with people other than when he'd shop for groceries once a week. He'd always been sweet to her, at least for the year she was in the club. Always said hello to her when he'd run into her in town, too.

Chauncey pushed the door open all the way, and she just about took a step back from habit. The man was standing there in nothing but his boxers, tanned, sunken chest and skinny body distracting only slightly from those 40x magnification glasses he wore on his head. They really were magnification lenses, too, not real glasses, because no one's damned eyes were that fucking big normally, were they?

"Whatchoo doing up here on Mount Horeb, Erin?" His voice was high and meandering. He glanced at her clothing. "Oh, I s'pose it's Deputy Harris now. I always thought you'd have been a good mechanical engineer, you know, but—"

"Chauncey," she said, interrupting him gently, "I'm awfully sorry to bother you, but I got a question."

"Oh?" He stood there, his sunken chest heaving up and down with the effort of keeping him breathing. The man didn't look like he ate even one meal a day, and his expression was what she'd called gentle befuddlement. "What can I do for you?"

She started to say something then stopped, trying to decide if she should mention his state of undress. She decided it was better to skip it. "Did I catch you in the middle of something?"

"I was just painting a miniature army," he said, still staring at her through magnifying glasses. "They're gonna be my fourth army this month, getting ready for a tournament up in Knoxville next weekend. Those dadgummed boys from Johnson City—last year's champs—they ain't gonna know what hit 'em." He laughed, a loud, high sound, then blinked, and fumbled for the magnifying glasses on his head, tearing them off self-consciously. "Sorry," he said. "I forget they're on, sometimes. I wear 'em so much in the evenings, you know, cuz I'm working on my armies. Damn, that's embarrassing."

She glanced downward at his skinny, hairy legs, exposed from the crotch on down. "Yep." She looked back up at him and he watched her earnestly, without a trace of self-consciousness. "I can see how that might be a little ... uncomfortable. Listen, I'm investigating a noise disturbance up here—"

"Oh, you talking about that eerie-ass noise that comes rumbling down the mountain in the early evening and early morning?" Chauncey leaned forward, mouth slightly agape. He was definitely interested in what she was saying.

"You've heard it?" Erin asked, feeling a chill. The last two houses hadn't.

"Shoor 'nuff," he said. "Every night for the last three. Rolls through just as dusk is coming on—we get dusk a little earlier here than y'all do, being in the shadow on this side of the mountain and whatnot. Noise comes rumbling in, then passes back up just 'afore daybreak."

She listened to him with increasing interest. "Chauncey ... did you happen to see what it was that made the noise?"

"You know, I actually did not," Chauncey said with mild disappointment, as though he'd forgotten a can of tuna he'd paid for at the grocery store. "Last two times I tried I was too slow, only saw a little of it as it went 'round the curve over yonder." He gestured toward the downward slope where the road wended just past the trees at the perimeter of his property. "I'm just not as light on my feet as I used to be. Anyway, looked like a black cloud moving down the mountain, all different parts going at once."

"Was it big?" she asked, taking a breath.

"Fair big, I s'pose," he said. "Wide, more like. Flat, not high off the road, from what I could see. Hell, it was all shadows but looked like a mass just sweeping on down. Coulda been anything. I was running through my brain trying to figure it out, but coming up dry. Saw some ... something like a reflection from it, but uh ... I don't know. Figured maybe it was one of them big ol' groups of running people going from coast to coast like they did in that one movie with that feller had the slow mind—"

"*Forrest Gump?*" Erin stared at him in mild disbelief.

"Course that don't account for the noise ..." Chauncey was now in a world of his own, not even looking at her. "I believe it sounded like a buzzing, like bees or something, but different. You know, I really don't have the first idea what that is. I should set up on the road tonight and maybe take some pictures—"

"Chauncey," she cut him off. "You really shouldn't. Whatever this is, it's killed two people so far."

"Killed 'em?" Chauncey's jaw dropped open, his skinny mouth falling open to reveal perfect, shining teeth. "Holy shit. You know, nobody ever tells me nothing, all alone up here on the mountain. Oughta include that sort of stuff in that Emergency Broadcast System, cuz that is news you need to know! What if I'd gone out there tonight and got myself killed, too?" He leaned in toward her, eyes wild. "How'd they die, you don't mind me asking?"

"Looks like they got run over by something," Erin said, and she shot a furtive look back to Lerner, still in the car, before turning back to Chauncey.

"Well, now that don't make no kind of sense at all," he said, and she could tell his engineer's mind was brainstorming out loud. "Whatever that was, it was moving way too low to be a car of any kind. In fact, it was kinda like ... oh." Chauncey straightened, and his mouth formed a perfect O with his last word. "That's what it was."

"What?" Erin stared at him. His eyes were far away, looking past her to the road. "What was it, Chauncey?" She waited, but his mind was still adrift. "What the hell was it?"

***

Arch opened the car door and got back in, feeling the cool air conditioning hit him in the face as he sunk down in the seat. It was danged warm, way too danged warm, and he'd had just about enough of summer by now. The rains that had come a few days earlier, as ugly as they'd gotten, sure had been a nice cooldown for the town. If it weren't for the whole flooding problem, he'd gladly have had them back right about now. He glanced at the dry dust in the driveway he was parked in. Looked like the ground might be grateful, too.

"Any luck?" Hendricks asked. The cowboy was still wearing his full-length drover coat, that black nightmare that made him look like some sort of cross between Batman and the Lone Ranger. Arch had seen a couple kids in town laugh at Hendricks's getup behind his back, but he didn't feel compelled to share this with the man.

"Not as such, no," Arch said. "People have heard a noise, but they got no clue what it came from. Some don't even rightly know when it came through. Sounded a little like a train to this last couple." He'd been viewed with a little surprise, maybe a little suspicion, at the first house. Things like that happened sometimes when the police came to call unexpectedly on a door out here. But at the second house he'd been invited in for crumb cake and coffee, which he'd had to decline. Being a football hero in Midian had its perks, that was certain.

This house had about been a bust. Older couple, didn't even seem to realize that their house was across the valley from train tracks. They'd been nice enough, though, in spite of not inviting him in for crumb cake.

"Damn," Hendricks said as Arch put the car into gear. He backed into a turnaround in the driveway and aimed the car down the rutted gravel driveway back toward the road. "I suppose it might make some sense, though; this house is set back awfully far from the road."

"Land's a little flatter here, closer to the bottom of the mountain," Arch said. "Got themselves a nice parcel where they could build back a ways."

"More than those last couple houses, anyway," Hendricks said. "Maybe we should leapfrog to the next house over, or the one after. There's a spur up the way, I noticed—"

"Old mining road," Arch said, nodding. "I hadn't ruled out that this thing could be coming from up there. Not sure we want to go poking down that way until we're sure." The thing was gated, actually, and as they'd passed he'd looked carefully; it didn't seem to have been disturbed in a half century, though it was hard to tell, he supposed. "Might be some exposed shafts out there."

"You make it sound like a bathhouse," Hendricks said with a grin.

Arch felt the frown come automatically. "Is everything a dirty joke to you?"

Hendricks just kept grinning infuriatingly. "I got a dirty enough mind to find something naughty in just about anything, yeah. It's a talent."

Arch turned away before rolling his eyes. "It's an unsavory habit. Like swearing."

"What is the problem with swearing for you, anyway?" Hendricks asked. Arch gave him enough of a look to see he was being genuine, not mocking. "I mean, I can understand goddamn—"

"The Third Commandment would be my problem with that one, yes," Arch said, a little irritated. Did he have to do that in front of him, always?

"But what about the rest of it?" Hendricks said, leaning back in his seat and tipping his hat. "Where in the Bible does it say you can't let loose with a 'fucking shit' or a 'son of a whore' every now and again?"

"Philippians 4:8," Arch said, giving him an annoyed look.

"You'll have to forgive me," Hendricks said, looking unimpressed. "My knowledge of the Bible is a few years out of date. And also fairly unimportant to me in the scheme of things."

Arch stifled a sigh of frustration. "It's a letter from the Apostle Paul to the Philippians, in which he tells them to dwell on that which is pure and good." Arch drummed his fingers on the steering wheel. "The idea being that if you're constantly dwelling on the impure, your mind is not where it is supposed to be in order to be a good servant of the Lord."

Hendricks had his mouth slightly open, and Arch just waited for the jibe. It never came. "Okay, then," Hendricks said, but he didn't sneer. He just waited. "So … where does it talk about getting blow jobs?"

Arch did roll his eyes at that one, after slamming the brakes so he could turn to Hendricks and give him the full attention for this. "She's my wife, and she and I can do anything—"

"Wait, wait, wait," Hendricks said. The car was halted just a few yards from the road. The end of the driveway was nestled between two big trees, and the entire property line was shielded from view of the road by a line of woods no more than twenty or thirty feet deep. Just enough to obstruct the mountain road from the house.

Arch paused, still ready to unload on Hendricks for his disrespect. "What?" he asked, not bothering to conceal the anger in his voice.

"Do you hear that?" Hendricks asked, holding a single finger aloft, pointing to the ceiling, as though something was coming from above.

"Hear what?" Arch said with purest irritation. But as he sat there in the silence, he realized he could hear it too. A faint, buzzing sound, growing louder as it came down the mountain road ahead.

***

Lauren was making good time down the mountain, but she could tell she was feeling the first strains of fatigue. This was the easy part, she told herself. The downhill run. Turning back, that was bound to be a cast-iron bitch.

The sun was setting, and the orange glow didn't quite reach her over the peak of Mount Horeb. It was over there somewhere, to be sure, but she couldn't see it from here, not on this side of the mountain, and that meant she was going to be running in the dark in an hour or two.

Reluctantly, she slowed, pulling to a stop in front of an old mailbox that said "Cooper" on the side in faded white letters. She was sweating prodigiously, feeling the burn in her legs from not doing this for a few days and now pulling this shit on her body on a damned mountain. She'd feel it tomorrow, but if she could just get a little further along, it'd be all good because at least she'd get the endorphin rush. Runner's high. She loved that feeling; it kept her doing this even though the amount of time she had for it was nearly nil.

She was just hooking around when she realized there was a noise over the sound of her heavy breathing. Something ... buzzing. Something loud. She looked back up the mountain but saw nothing. The road made a sharp turn around a bend to the left just a hundred yards ahead, and everything past that was well out of her sight. A steep cliff's edge to her left blocked the one side of the road, and the shoulder only extended a few feet to her right. The yard of the Cooper house—she didn't know who that was, some out-of-towner's cabin in all likelihood—came to an end just ahead. She followed along the road, listening to the sound.

Whatever it was—probably a semi with engine trouble—it sounded bad. A little ominous, too, but ... bad. Like someone's car was not having a good day. Like it had smashed into a train and was clacking as it rolled down the mountain.

She shrugged it off and started back up, and watched the shoulder narrow to her right, then fall off into a sheer cliff face. Something about that unnerved her, too, but she didn't pay it much heed because it was the mountain, and she still had a few feet of shoulder to dive to if someone hugged the lane a little too hard.

The noise grew louder. More persistent. Now it was hissing, descending from above, the mountain road's S-curve wending up to her left to ride a sheer cliff face a hundred feet high. She could hear it up there, that awful sound, that unearthly buzzing, with just a little screech mixed in. She thought she heard something else, too, like tires squealing on pavement.

What the hell made that kind of noise?

She scuffed her shoe a little and mentally kicked herself. Paying attention to the road was important, lest she stumble and find herself with a bloodied knee. Or worse.

The noise was louder now, starting to drown out the sound of the birds on the mountain, the crickets in the grass. She realized a little late that she hadn't actually heard any birds or crickets in quite some time and tried to remember if she'd heard them at all on her run.

It had been quiet the whole time, eerily so, save for a couple cars that passed her by.

What the hell was going on here? What was that sound?

The buzzing grew to a crescendo, and she knew whatever it was, it was just around the next bend in the road. Her pace slowed automatically, as though her head was telling her to back off, to keep away from the corner.

Then she saw it. And only one thing came to mind.

"Oh, fuck."

7.

They moved down the mountain like shadows at high speed, catching Hendricks's eye through the windshield. He was peering through the trees at the end of the driveway, standing like upright posts on a football field, like he was staring through about to kick a field goal.

This wasn't a goddamned field goal, though. This wasn't a football game. This was—

It was—

"What the fuck?" he whispered under his breath.

They moved through that gap between the trees like dark clouds rolling past on the road. They were fast, damned fast, but the wheels were visible, just barely, in the dusky twilight.

"Is that …?" Arch just let his voice trail off.

"You have got to be fucking shitting me," Hendricks said, just staring at the things swirling across. The buzzing was hell on his ears. "It really is, isn't it?"

Arch didn't sound surprised when he finally spoke up. "I always hated those sons of guns, but I never thought of them as real demons."

Hendricks just stared straight ahead as the last of them passed the driveway and rolled down the hill. When he spoke it was in complete and utter disgust. "Bicyclists.

"Demon fucking bicyclists."

***

Alison had half considered hanging out the window as Duncan steered the car down the mountain behind the demons. On bikes. Demons on bikes. She thought about it, and dismissed the idea as stupid, because trying to fire a .50 out a window while the vehicle was in motion sounded like a recipe for 1) deafness as the crack of the rifle echoed in the town car like God's own thunder sent down from heaven and 2) a really sore shoulder coupled with some poor shooting. For all those reasons and more, she was just watching instead, watching the swarm of bicyclists move down the mountain at a speed that wasn't possible for human beings.

She turned her head as tires squealed behind her and saw Arch's Explorer burst out onto the road. The sirens weren't wailing, but he had his lights on. Duncan took barely any note of it; he just kept his cool and took the town car into a sharp curve at over sixty miles per hour. Alison just held on and mentally added on another reason why she didn't want to chance shooting out the window. "What now?" she asked and waited for the expert's answer.

***

"What the hell are we gonna do now?" Hendricks asked.

Arch ignored him for a minute because he had no idea at all other than chasing the demons down. "I thought you were the expert demon hunter."

Hendricks just sat there for a second. "Maybe I am, maybe I'm not, but I can promise you I've never dealt with a pack of demon bicyclists before. I'm still just trying to get a handle on this situation. I mean, they killed two people just by hitting them with a bike?"

Arch had to concede it sounded funny, but those demons were moving awfully fast down the mountain. "They're stronger and faster, makes sense they could pedal a bike faster. Look at 'em get on down the road."

"I wouldn't want to get hit by them, I guess," Hendricks conceded. "But ... there's gotta be like fifty of them, how are we supposed to—" The sound of a ringing phone filled the air.

"Hello?" Arch said, terse, holding the phone with one hand to his ear while he followed Duncan's town car into a tight turn with the other.

"It's demons on bicycles!" Erin shouted at him from the other end of the line.

"Figured that out for ourselves," Arch said, and he heard the tires squeal underneath him.

"How?" Erin asked.

"Cuz I'm looking at them right now, like a big ol' swarm of people who are serious about their physical fitness and enjoying nature. We're not far below the overlook—get down here. We're in pursuit." He hung up without waiting for an answer. "So ... how do you kill a swarm of bothersome flies?" He glanced over at Hendricks, waiting to see if the cowboy knew the answer.

Hendricks just smiled. "One at a time."

***

Arch's Explorer gunned past the town car on Alison's side. Arch glanced over at her only briefly as he shot past on a short straightaway. She could see Hendricks already out of his seat, sword out of its scabbard. He was leaning out the window.

"Shit," she whispered, and unfastened her seatbelt so she could get to the rifle in the backseat. "Looks like we're really gonna do this."

Arch tried to keep the car somewhat steady as they came up on the pack. There could be fifty, a hundred of them in there; it was hard to tell. It wasn't that they weren't wearing helmets and bicycle shirts and pants, because they were. It was just that every single one of them was black as the night itself. The bikes were all painted black too, save for a couple. Arch caught a glimpse of a couple reflectors still wired to the spokes of one bike, spinning a circle as the light caught it; pretty much all the rest lacked them.

"Well, this looks like a safety hazard," Hendricks said, mirroring Arch's own thoughts. "Don't they know you're supposed to wear bright clothing when you're cycling at night?"

"Apparently not," Arch said as he slowed to cope with a steep, hard right S-curve. "Which is too bad, because if you do that, it's nobody's fault but yours when you get hit by a car."

He gunned the engine and closed the last ten feet between him and the back of pack. He edged up enough to let Hendricks hang out the window, and watched as the cowboy extended his sword to poke—just poke—the last guy in line. With a blast of black flames that consumed the demon's dark clothing, the bike fell to the ground and filled the air with the sound of screeching metal.

***

"I think they've noticed us now," Duncan said as he swerved to avoid the bicycle clattering on the road. Alison braced herself as the car shook, veering right as Hendricks killed another demon ahead. The others were looking back, and the buzzing was somehow louder now.

"What is that?" Alison asked.

"Looks like a bunch of vembra'nonn on bicycles," Duncan said. "Light-shelled demons, like speed. Usually they're drawn to doing stuff like hanging on the bottom of airplanes or riding in the back of pickup trucks going at high velocity. I did catch a rumor about a group into extreme sports a couple years back; hang-gliding, base-jumping, skydiving, that sort of thing. Can't say I've heard of bicycling ones before, but ..." He shrugged as Alison flipped the latches to the gun case.

"Can you keep us steady?" she asked as she pulled the ear protection out of the case first and draped the muffs over the sides of her neck. She grabbed the glasses, too. Safety first, especially when it came to dodging a .50 cal shell hitting you in the eye. That would probably cause blindness.

"I can try," Duncan said, and she could hear the strain in the demon's voice.

Alison stuck the magazine in the Barrett rifle, then turned awkwardly, trying to bring the oversized thing around without smacking the barrel into the windshield. It wasn't easy; the rifle was awfully big.

"That thing is like a cannon," Duncan said matter-of-factly. "You might be able to kill a vembra'nonn with one of those."

"I thought guns didn't kill demons?" Alison asked. She was distracted for only a second then chambered a round. *Focus.*

"Not most of them, no," Duncan said. "But these are light shells. Most demons have hard shells. Kinda like bone density in people, I guess. It's rare, but sometimes you get these guys with a big essence and in order to fit it all in, they have to shrink the amount of shell—"

"Huh," Alison said, and hit the automatic window. She swung the rifle barrel out as the wind whipped her in the face. She draped the heavy shoulder pad against her and stuck the butt of the gun hard against it. "Let's see what we can do, then."

"You might want to—" Duncan started to say something, but Alison slipped the ear protection on and focused on her target. There was a demon at the far back right that fell into her sights. She led him a little bit and fired.

"There's your wife!" Hendricks called as a deafening rifle blast echoed down the mountain. He was hanging out the window, probably in one of the less safe moments of his life, even compared to Iraq—this one was going to stick out in his memory—and the wind was blowing at him. He took off the cowboy hat and tossed it back through the window into the floorboard. No point losing it, after all. It had sentimental value.

"I believe she just killed one of them!" Arch shouted back at him. Hendricks could barely hear him over the rush of the wind blowing his hair. Hendricks looked over and saw a bike rattling and skating down the road, no sign of a demon on or near it.

"What the fuck?" Hendricks muttered. "With a gun?" Arch had steered him closer to the peloton of these bicycling demons, and they were all looking back at him now. They had the whole inhuman eyes thing going too, their demon faces out on display. It was not pretty, either. They were a wave of black, a nasty little pack of demons rolling on along. "Hey there, hell on wheels!" He jabbed his sword into another one that tried to swerve to avoid him.

"Get in here for a second!" Arch called at him. Hendricks slipped back inside as Arch eased off the speed and they drifted back as the road turned right in a lazy curve.

Hendricks sat there, waiting expectantly, watching the peloton ahead, the bicyclists' black helms bobbing up and down as they sped up their pedaling. A few of them were still looking back, hissing at the Explorer. "What now?" he asked finally.

"This." Arch gunned the engine as the road straightened. Hendricks could hear the whine as he accelerated down the slope. The speedometer rushed from fifty to eighty in about two seconds, and Hendricks felt a compelling need to reach for the oh-shit bar as the Explorer shot down the hill.

Arch steered them straight as Hendricks fumbled for his seat belt. He clicked it in place just as Arch ran them into the rear wheels of six bikes at the back of the group. The impact was immediate, black suited freaks falling sideways, flying over handlebars. He watched black flames crawl over the skin of at least two of them from their impact against the hard asphalt. One of them in the center was launched up and onto the hood of the Explorer.

Hendricks reacted before he even realized what he was doing, leaning hard against his seatbelt to snake out the window with his sword. He saw the tip pierce the cheek of the demon and appear within the gaping mouth. A black flame welled up inside and swallowed the thing whole in a matter of seconds. "Fucking A!" Hendricks said, grinning at Arch. "That's how we do this shit."

***

"Those who live in glass houses should not throw stones," Duncan was shouting over the muffles on her ears, "and demons without hard shells shouldn't be riding bicycles at high speed!"

Alison just ignored him and led another demon. The crack of the rifle was followed by the sight of her target dissolving into black flames straight from the bowels of hell. She drew a bead on another.

***

"What the fuck is this?" Lerner asked from the passenger seat. Erin felt she agreed with his sentiment, bicycles and a few bicyclists littering the road in front of them. "Seriously? Demons on bikes? Have they no brains?" He paused. "No, scratch that, they definitely don't have brains. Have they no sense?"

"Of style, you mean?" Erin asked, steering around a black-clad bicyclist who was recovering from a wreck in the middle of the road. She wanted to put a dent in the fender of the sheriff's cruiser like she wanted a firm kick to the square center of her ass. She caught Lerner looking at her out of the corner of her eye. "Bicycle pants look dumb."

"Bet they're comfortable, though," Lerner muttered. She ignored him and swerved around a demon, who shook his fist angrily at them.

"Should we stop and deal with these?" Erin asked.

"Better keep on," Lerner said. "I'm guessing there's a whole lot more ahead. Probably better to focus on the core rather than the dregs."

***

Hendricks unfastened his seat belt again. Arch had played bold at first, but after that last bicyclist he'd run over had left the handlebars scraping under the car with a gawdawful clunk, he'd gotten a little less bold. Hendricks couldn't blame him; it wasn't like it was even his car. He'd have to explain the damage to the sheriff. Hendricks got the feeling he was kind of a ball buster.

"We're steamrolling them," Arch said.

"More like Cleveland Steamer-ing them," Hendricks said as he started to lean out the window again.

"What's—?" Arch asked, but Hendricks lost it in the roar of the wind as he stuck his upper body out.

There had to be at least thirty more of them, and they were starting to scatter again. Their first response to the shit rolling down the mountain with them had been to pedal faster, but they were more prepared for a city where they could outrun foot pursuit rather than being stuck on a mountain road with cars bearing down on them.

That cannon blast fired again, Alison Stan lighting up another rider. Hendricks watched a bicycle drop to the road on the far side of the peloton, the rider already evaporated like water on a hot day. They may have done some damage, but there were still a shitload of bicyclists.

He leaned a little further out the window, ready to deliver a love tap to the nearest. He did it, the bike dropped, the rider fell, already covered over in the flames of hell, but he only saw the motion in his peripheral vision at the last second.

The demon slammed into him from his right. He realized too late that the bastard must have been hiding in the shadow of the car's bumper, just waiting for a chance to do something.

And he'd done something all right. Judging by the fire in Hendricks's side, he'd broken at least one rib. Maybe more.

Worse than that, he still had a grip on Hendricks, and Hendricks could see the dark malice in the bastard's eyes as he prepared to hit him again.

***

"Uh oh!" Duncan yelled, but it sounded like a whisper to Alison under the muffs. She hadn't been paying attention to Arch's side of the peloton, instead trying to deal with thinning the herd on the other side. She saw the demon riding in the wake of the police cruiser just before he made his move. Black spandex thundered up the side as Arch put the brakes on for a turn. Hendricks was hanging out the window and the demon hit him hard. Duncan blanched in the driver's seat from the impact.

It didn't look pretty, that was for sure. Worse than that, the demon had positioned himself perfectly—lined up just between her and Hendricks. She didn't even bother to try; even if she could have shot him, she'd at least clip Hendricks in the process.

***

"Well, well, look at this here clusterfuck," Lerner drawled as Erin got them on a straightaway and hit the accelerator. She could see the next turn ahead, but for now she had the Crown Vic up above one hundred miles per hour, and she was screaming down the mountain. She figured she had about another ten seconds tops before she'd have to apply the brakes with everything she had, but that would buy a little time for them to catch up to the battle unfolding down the mountain.

"There sure are a lot of them," Erin said as she started to hit the brakes. "How the hell are we supposed to kill them all?"

"I'm surprised you're worried about that right now," Lerner said coolly. "I figured you'd be concerned about your boyfriend."

Erin glanced at him, then looked ahead. Sure enough, Arch's car had a black-coated figure hanging out the window, and one of the bicycling demons was—

—was—

—was on him.

Hanging on to him. Dragging him out of the car? Eating him right there? Erin couldn't see.

She stomped the accelerator into the turn and took it fast. When the tires started to skid, she saw Lerner clutch his oh-shit bar, which concerned her. But not enough to hit the brakes.

***

Arch saw the thing hit Hendricks just a little too late. He hadn't been watching his rearview, which hadn't seemed like a mistake until that demon came out of nowhere behind him and showed him how wrong he was. Now the cowboy was out there at its mercy, feet still hanging in, sword pointing the wrong way, and getting manhandled in a close encounter by something that was a lot stronger than him.

Arch had a sense of where Hendricks's balance was, and it was failing fast. He did have his legs locked in good, could probably hang them up under the dash if need be—

Arch jerked the wheel to the right and heard the resounding thunk of the bicycle's frame hitting his passenger door. He heard it skid after that, screaming metal meeting the pavement, and almost took a breath until he saw the demon still hanging onto Hendricks, dragging him out the window as he clutched on to the cowboy.

***

Erin roared past Duncan's black town car like it was out for a Sunday drive. She didn't know if he was going slow because they were afraid to get in there and mix it up or if it was because Alison was a better shot at a distance, but she didn't care. She cut them off like a Nascar pro and slipped in behind Arch's Explorer like she was about to start drafting.

"Take the wheel!" she said to Lerner. He didn't need to be told twice.

She hit the window control and had her pistol drawn as she leaned out. This was going to be a motherfucker of a shot, and she was still leaning hard on the accelerator. She had always hated math, but she figured just by judgment she had about five seconds to pull this off before she was going to have to hit the brakes for the next corner, and the curve would screw up what she had in mind.

She drew down, staring over the white sights of her Glock, holding it out one-handed. She didn't get to the range as much as she would have liked, which would have worried her if she had more time to think about it. She didn't, though, and so instead she pushed hard on the accelerator to bring her closer. Less distance made it harder to miss.

She drew a bead on the demon holding Hendricks. She aimed for middle back, because he had Hendricks good above the waist, and looked like he was sinking his teeth into—

She fired, the obnoxiously loud burst of the gun muted amid the squeal of tires and roar of engines. It was like the time she'd gotten tickets to sit in the sixth row at Talladega, the roar of the race loud enough to drown out the end of the world if it came.

She watched the demon fall, dissolving in black flame as he disappeared under her front end. The bump of the body under the Crown Vic was horrendous, like she'd run over a cinder block. She would have sworn the entire suspension went with him as he blew out under the right rear tire, and the shock knocked her pistol out of her hand. The impact jarred her, and she hit her armpit on the door, then bounced back and caught her left shoulder against the back of the window's frame.

It hurt; like fire, like hell. It took her a second to recover from it to realize that Lerner was screaming at her, but by then it was too late. They were going eighty when she stomped the brakes, but there was a hairpin turn up ahead.

The tires were still screaming when they went into the flip off the side of the road.

8.

Alison saw the sheriff's car squeal into the turn. Duncan had already backed them off and slowed them down for the curve. Arch had done the same but pulled hard right to take the Explorer into a near ninety-degree turn. He'd made it, just barely, and the smell of burned rubber and clouds of black smoke from tires were everywhere in the air. Alison couldn't see very well, but she knew the trajectory that the sheriff's car had been on, and knew that things had gone very, very wrong when it didn't emerge from the cloud of tire smoke on the other side.

***

Lerner had a bird's-eye view for the car going over the edge of the cliff. It wasn't the sort of thing he'd been looking forward to when the day began, but it was the sort of shit one had to deal with when engaged in the high-stakes thrill ride that was demon hunting. He was holding that oh-so-helpfully-named oh-shit bar as the car rolled the first time. He kept his grip as they went into the second, and third, and fourth.

Not having bones to break or skin to lacerate certainly helped. The lack of nerves to send screaming signals to the brain he didn't have was also a plus. The airbag managed to hit him squarely in the nose, but it was fairly useless at stopping his movement because it deployed forward and they were not moving forward at all.

He watched the whole thing with a sense of interest that he normally reserved for PBS documentaries. The windshield shattered on the second roll, breaking into tiny pebbles of glass. Lerner had seen glass break before, and it came out in long, sharp shards that would make a fine weapon to cut a human being if need be. Not that he'd thought about it.

These were pebbles, though, safety glass broken into tiny pieces that wouldn't do much of anything unless they hit you full in the eyes. There was some bouncing around in the cabin, but most of it fell out on the third roll. He realized—a little surprised—that the passenger window next to him had exploded at some point, and he hadn't even noticed it.

The roof caved on the fifth roll, sinking down a good three inches and turning the cloth-lined ceiling of the cabin into a crinkled mess. He could see the bare metal peeking through next to the shattered windshield, and the sun visors had completely broken free of their harnesses and were whipping about.

After the sixth roll there was a moment of peace. If he'd been human, Lerner would have take a breath. Actually, if he'd been human, he'd probably have been properly fucked, being good and dead from the impacts of the damned car rolling down the hill.

The moment of peace didn't last, though. There was a feeling of weightlessness that accompanied it as the car turned once more in the air. Slowly. Painfully slowly.

He saw movement out of his window and turned his head to look. He could see the ground just below, racing up toward him. For a moment he had a perfect view of it—another road, little pebbles ground up in once-black asphalt that had turned grey with the ministrations of time.

Ah, yes, time. One of Lerner's favorite things to ponder.

He wanted to think deep thoughts about it, but the sight of the ground racing at him replaced all the possibilities with one and only one.

Is my time up?

***

Lauren Darlington had seen the bicyclists coming around the steep S curve, all in black and not looking like any group of bicyclists she'd ever seen. The helmets, the bike outfits, everything was black. *This cycling team is brought to you by the color ebony, dark as the night itself.*

What was missing what the sense that they were in any way human beneath all that surface shit.

She saw red eyes—red eyes, glowing ones, looking at her. She had a long run across empty pavement to a sheer cliff face on her left and nothing but a long-ass drop to her right, and those things were bearing down on her a hundred yards ahead.

Nowhere to run, nowhere to hide.

She caught the sense of malice even as far back as she was. What the hell were these things? They were pedaling fast, too, faster than she'd ever seen a bicyclist go. Was it just the mountain, aiding in their downward motion?

What the fuck was going on here?

Her gut was telling her to jump, to chance the face of the cliff and the drop below, telling her to go for it. That wasn't normal, was it? Rational, analytical thought was intruding in. It was a weird dichotomy, but she was used to it. It was like the part of her that came out in an emergency room situation was watching her now, running down what was happening in slow motion and telling her non-rational mind to shut the fuck up, sit down, and ride this out.

And she was all ready to jump over the edge of the cliff when the car came crashing down the hill.

***

Hendricks knew a fuck lot was wrong as he gradually reeled himself back in to Arch's cruiser. He was hurting up and down, could feel the blood running down his neck. He'd felt that fucking demon bite him and knew nothing good would come of it. His right arm had gotten wrenched and trapped first thing, pulled clear out of the fucking socket so he couldn't do a goddamned thing with it. It was right there, screaming at him along with his ribs.

His left arm was more or less okay, though; that was a plus. Or it had been until he'd heard the squeal of tires behind him. He'd known something had happened with the demon to make it let go, but he was in a little too much pain to figure it out until he was back in the seat. Arch was screaming at him about as loud as the pain in his own head, and it took a minute for him to decode what the fuck was going on.

***

"Shit shit shit shit shit," Duncan said. Alison had the muffs off by now, but every word that the demon was saying was still low enough that she had to check to make sure they were off. They were in a hard turn now, the S-curve that Erin had missed, and the demons were threading around right down the hill toward where the Crown Vic had run off. Alison just held her breath.

"Oh, Lerner, you bastard," Duncan said, and Alison glanced over at him. The only thing she felt at the moment was a sense of wicked gratitude that Arch hadn't been in the car that went over.

***

The car hit the road and it was like an explosion of metal and glass. Lauren covered her face and looked away, felt something sting her on her bare legs. After a half-second she turned back to look, unable to keep down for long, and she saw the car settled on its roof. It was sitting in the middle of the road.

Holy fucking shit, holy fucking God! her mind screamed at her. *What the fuck what the fuck?!*

Then the analytical took over again. The bicyclists were still coming, like a black sea surging down the hill. Like a cloud descending to cover her.

She knew what they were. Could feel it. Could feel death coming.

Her legs stung as she came up off the ground—when had she fallen? She ran—that was what she was here to do, wasn't it? Why the hell did it hurt so much? She ran for the car and squatted down behind the hood where it had come to land, facing down the mountain road like it was going to slide the rest of the way to the bottom.

It didn't slide, though. It just sat there, like a rock in the middle of the crashing tides, and she sheltered under it as a horrific buzzing noise rose around her and the bicyclists in black swarmed down the hill on both sides of her like hell was riding behind them.

***

Lerner never lost consciousness, because he didn't do that sort of thing. He could hear the buzzing start just after he got his bearings upon landing. There was a sense that something was wrong, a sort of veiled sensation that his equilibrium was off, but he attributed that to having gone over a cliff in a car.

The air was filled with the smell of oil, and a ticka-ticka-ticka noise came from the engine, like it was cooling off after a long car trip instead of being one hundred and eighty degrees from its correct positioning on the horizontal plane. Lerner was hanging by his seat belt, suit crumpled and ripped in places.

The buzzing came and he recognized it. He knew it was coming down the hill, and he felt a rush of anger over that peculiar sense of something being terribly wrong.

And yet he did not give a fuck.

He pressed the release on his seatbelt and caught himself on the shoulder as he landed. He saw feet crouching under the place where the front of the hood rested only an inch or two from the pavement. He wondered who they were, but did not give much of a fuck about that, either.

Lerner emerged, pulling himself out of the window as the first bicycles were going by on his side of the car. They did not bother to steer around him because they did not see him, pushing his way out through the crumpled, misshapen passenger window. The damned thing was like a fucked-up rhombus from all the impacts, and it made it more difficult to get his slightly saggy shell through. He realized, quite absurdly, that it was as though the wreckage of the car were giving birth to him, letting him slide and wriggle out into the world like one of those miniature humans.

He was halfway out when he realized that they'd start to run him over soon. He would have thought of it sooner, but he attributed his scatterbrained-ness to the fall, putting aside for a moment that impacts like that wouldn't have any real effect on his thought process unless his shell was cracked.

He jerked the baton free of his shredded jacket and deployed it into the front spokes of the next bike that passed him. He felt himself smile automatically as the flimsy spokes tore against the hell-forged metal and sent the rider flying through the air. He saw the landing, a burst of black flame disappearing around a figure who had just lawn-darted head first into the fading asphalt of the mountain road.

Lerner saw another bike swerve to miss him after seeing what their compatriot had just been through. He thought it was a bad move on their part, avoiding the body of the one inflicting the harm to their little collective in order to swerve around. He proved it was a bad move to the unthinking demon who had done it, too, by using his legs to propel himself off the side of the car and wedging the deployed baton in the front wheel of that bike. There was a scream before that one hit the ground and evaporated.

Lerner pulled himself to his feet, glancing down to see his suit completely ripped across the front. His bland chest was partially displayed from below the right nipple down to his slightly protruding belly. He ignored this and slammed the baton into the face of a passing biker who burst into dark flame in the air before leaving a brimstone stink lingering around Lerner.

He heard the shouts, the cries of "OOC!" and watched the bikers that remained in the peloton scramble to go the other way around the car. Seeking safety.

He lit up three more that cruised his way. Each tried to make small moves to stop him—hitting him with a hand as they passed, clipping him with the bike, and the last even tried to hit him dead on. Every one ended in a black cloud of flames, but the last did manage to knock him over as the bastard burned up.

Lerner lay there on his back, the sound of the buzzing bicyclists receding in his ears. That feeling of something wrong—something fucked up—was still hanging on. He didn't want to get up, didn't want to move, just wanted to lie there and wait for Duncan. He felt a cringe come on involuntarily and knew that was bad news. That meant the shell was telling him something.

Something bad.

He let his hand fall to the place where his shirt had been ripped and ran a finger down the length of his body. He found it just above where the pelvis would have been on a human, a little ridge so insignificant that a human wouldn't even have called it a scratch.

But he wasn't human. And he knew it for what it was.

A crack in his shell.

***

Arch took them around the corner slower, the fear of all manner of badness put into him now. His concern was assuaged slightly by the fact that Alison was just behind him, he could see her as he glanced in the rearview. Still, he had a sick, swimming feeling in his stomach, like it was in the kind of free-fall Erin's cruiser had just experienced.

He glanced at Hendricks. He'd intended to look for just a moment before turning back to the road. Instead he ended up staring.

The cowboy was in rough shape, with a hand held up to his neck and blood rushing between the fingers. His lip was bloodied, and he was holding his body at a peculiar angle. There was a jagged cut along his eyebrow, too, though Arch wasn't exactly sure where that had come from. All told, the poor guy was clutching himself like he was hurt in a dozen different places. For all Arch knew, he was.

"This is gonna be a problem," Arch said, trying to think ahead. "I gotta call it in."

"Do it," Hendricks said, his voice muffled as he seemed to try and keep his mouth clenched as tight as possible. "Erin ..." His words drifted off.

Arch paused, and stared at the mike on his car. He clenched his jaw and picked it up, wondering exactly how deep the trouble was going to run on this one.

***

Lauren came out from her little pocket at the front of the cop car like she was a groundhog coming out of her hole on February 2nd. Tentative didn't even come close to covering it. She poked her head out first, making sure there weren't any other bikers streaming down the hill toward her.

There weren't.

The sound of the engine and the burning scent that filled the air around her worked with her already fast-beating heart to give her a sense of numbness and a nausea-inducing taste in her mouth. She thought she was going to puke, to chuck hard right there staring at the broken and beaten frame of the cop car. There were torn branches lodged in the fuel lines and transmission, all speckled throughout the undercarriage like the damn thing had been feathered in them.

Lauren took a deep breath in disbelief, then another. She could hear sirens up the hill but she didn't look up there. Not yet. First she saw a guy in a ripped suit lying on the ground to her left, just lying there, hand moving like he was poking at his hip.

Her training kicked in and overcame the desire to just sit there and stare, openmouthed, at the shit that had unfolded before her. She hurried over to him, still dimly aware that there was pain in her legs. She hit her knees at his side and snapped her fingers in his face. "Sir, can you hear me?"

"I can hear you just fine," he said in a Yankee accent. Sounded like he was from Bahs-ton. "I can also see you."

"How many fingers am I holding up?" she asked, throwing up a peace sign in his face.

"Two," he grunted. "I'm fine, my back just hurts a little. Check on the girl in the driver's seat."

She whipped her head around to look in the window of the car. Sure enough, there was someone hanging there, limp, in front of the wheel. Thin arms dangled down lifelessly, along with longish hair that she could tell was blond in the last fading light of day. "Is that Deputy Harris?" she asked.

"Fuck, all you people really do know each other here," Bahs-ton said. "Yeah, that's her. You might want to go check on her. I just barely got her seatbelt fastened around her in time."

Lauren started to get to her feet, ready to head around the car to do just that, but a police cruiser SUV came screeching to a halt just in front of her a second later, and out stepped Archibald Fucking Stan.

***

Alison got out of the car as soon as Duncan brought it to a stop and threw it into park. They'd seen a figure in a suit lying splayed out on the ground before Arch's Explorer had blocked their view. Even without being able to see much in the way of a reaction on Duncan's fairly impassive face, she could sense the temperature change in the town car. And it wasn't a favorable one.

Duncan, for his part, bolted without even bothering to stop the ignition or pull out his keys. He was in a state, that's how her mother would have described it. Seemed like it fit pretty well.

Alison watched Arch as he got out of the car, watched Duncan fly past him like he was running in an all-out demon sprint, cooking down the hill like he was on a skateboard or was one of the bicyclists. She just needed to make sure Arch was all right, and then she had a job of her own to take care of.

She knew he was all right by the way he stood there at the door, staring over it at whatever was happening past his car. Still, she watched him for a second. Looked at the wrinkles of his uniform, thought about how it needed a washing and an ironing later. Someone had to do it.

Then she hefted her rifle and went around the front of the car to use the hood as a rest. She figured she wouldn't have to wait but a minute or two.

***

"How is she?" Hendricks asked, shuffling his way out of his seat only with great difficulty. There was a dark-haired woman with running shorts and bloody knees between him and the overturned cruiser, and he wasn't entirely sure he could make it to her without tipping over.

"I—" The woman had a look on her face that was none too pleased. Hendricks didn't know her well enough to speculate whether that was because of the bloody knees, the fact that there was an upturned car sitting in the middle of the road next to her, or because that was just her personality. Something about the lines around her eyes told him it was the last one, though.

"Lauren," Arch said, calling her by name. Hendricks made a note of that through the fog of pain. Made of a note of it that was promptly balled up and thrown away as his ribs flared at him, pissed that he had the audacity to get out of the damned car. He fell straight to the pavement, and he couldn't even rip a hand away from his chest to cushion his fall, which hurt like someone had dropped a semi-trailer on his side.

***

Arch watched Hendricks fall and was torn about what to do next. He knew Erin was in the upside-down Crown Vic, but that car was so trashed he was having a hard time imagining her surviving. The fall was at least a hundred feet down a mountainside, and that wasn't the sort of crash resistance that the NTSB tended to rate on, he suspected.

"What the fuck is going on here?" Lauren said, and she made a move for him. She ran for Hendricks, and he watched her struggle as she went. She was tottering on weak legs, and blood was running down from both knees like she'd taken a hit from something.

"Hard to explain," Arch said as something whizzed past his door, buffeting him with the breeze. It took a second for him to realize it was Duncan, and he was beside Lerner before Arch could say anything at all about it.

***

Lauren dropped down to triage the guy in the black coat and was again dimly aware of pain somewhere in her knees. That was the thing about triage, though—you needed to assess what was the worst so you could work on it. This guy looked like he'd been fucked up good. Whatever had happened to her legs was minor by comparison. She still needed a little better read on the guy in the middle of the road, but Deputy Harris was in desperate need of some assessment.

Even though Lauren suspected she was dead.

"Where are you feeling pain?" she asked the guy in the coat. His hair was all mussed and flattened back, like he'd been wearing a hat. She wondered what kind of hat would even go with this getup. Then he moved, and she saw the pistol holstered at his waist. She flinched back a notch.

"What?" he asked, shifting and then grunting in pain. He followed her eyes to the gun on his belt. "I'm riding with a sheriff's deputy. Do the math on that."

"You're law enforcement," she said and then leaned in closer to check on him again. She still felt her body grow stiff from the unease of being near to him. Lauren had a few cardinal rules, and avoiding guns was one of them. She glanced at Arch Stan. Figured that asshole would end up carrying one for a living. It just made him easier to dislike.

"Where does it hurt?" she asked the black-coated guy again.

"Ribs are broken," he said, rattling it off between cringes. "Got a superficial lac on my neck, but it's bleeding like a fucker. Some other minor shit. What about Erin?"

Lauren looked over at the upturned cop car. "Keep pressure on your neck wound, and try not to move. If you've got broken ribs, you've probably got other internal injuries."

"I'm fine," Black Coat said. "Go." He waved her off with a bloody hand that he removed from his neck for just a second. She got a look at the wound he was covering; the blood was already starting to crust on it.

"Paramedics are on the way," Arch finally said. She would have deemed him less than useless, but he was saying it from a prone position as he was wriggling his way into the passenger side of the overturned car. She could hear him, but he was muffled.

Lauren was ready to tear a strip out of him, but he'd gone the long way around to get to Harris, really. She came around the car at a jog, dropped down at the driver's side window and saw the blond deputy still hanging there. She gently poked for the carotid pulse and felt the thrum of it. Harris's chest was heaving up and down in gentle time, but she was straining, probably because she was upside down. Some open wound from somewhere on her body were causing long streaks of blood to run down her face and into her hair. There was a steady drip to the crumpled roof of the car as Lauren rested her hand on the underside of the—

A sound like thunder but louder and more violent caused Lauren to jerk, smacking the back of her neck on the door. Little pieces of shattered glass fell out of the door and down into her shirt. One of them caught on the back of her sports bra before it shook out. "Goddammit," she said, and caught Arch Stan's eye under the hanging deputy. "The fuck was that?"

"Gunshot," he replied.

"What the fuck is going on here?" Lauren asked.

"Don't you need to get her down?" he asked.

"I can't," Lauren said, not bothering to be polite. "She could have a neck injury. Moving her could be fatal, or it might mean she never walks again."

"She's bleeding awful heavy," he said.

"I noticed that, too," she mumbled, one step from ignoring his helpful words. "Do I need to worry about that gunfire? Because you don't seem too alarmed by it." Lauren was one step away from freaking out on him, but since he wasn't exactly running to deal with it, she assumed he knew what he was doing. Though it did make her question her sanity.

"That's our covering fire," Arch said. "Still got some … bad guys … coming down the mountain."

She looked up at him, only mildly incredulous. "Are the bad guys you're talking about those assholes on the bicycles?"

"One and the same," Arch said. "They're the ones who killed Tim Connor and that other … person." She wondered if that corpse had been identified yet and realized he'd just given her the answer as he knew it.

"So you're up here on the mountain trying to stop them?" she asked. "And they what? Resisted arrest?"

She didn't need to be a psychologist to tell he was pissed. "You could say that."

***

Arch was lying. It wasn't coming natural, either, so he tried to let Lauren Darlington fill in as many of the blanks herself and just work around that. So far he wasn't having to get too out on a limb. The problem wasn't with her, though, it was with what was following her.

And what was following her was Sheriff Reeve, at some point.

"She's got … her abdomen," Lauren said stiffly. Arch couldn't tell if she was being so short with him because of the situation or just because she was short with him all the time. He didn't have much cause to run across her, but when they had she had made it abundantly clear she didn't want anything to do with him. Arch was fine with that; would have preferred to avoid her himself—because of how she acted, not because he had any personal grudge against the woman—but lately it hadn't been real easy. "Put pressure here."

Arch was not in an easy position to maintain. His frame was long and not exactly small, but he'd managed to crawl up in the front seat of the Sheriff's Crown Victoria by shimmying in on his back like a mechanic changing oil. His chest was pinned under the center console and he didn't have much mobility in his arms. "Need me to do what?"

"Put your fucking hands right here!" she shouted at him, and it echoed in the car. He didn't flinch away, though, because it was like trash talk on a football field to him. No big deal. Heck, the louder she got, the cooler he tended to get in response. It was just his way.

He put his hands up there where she pointed, and he could see a dark blood spot on Erin's khakis. Lauren had been able to get up a little higher and pull it down, but he couldn't see over the ridge her clothing made hanging down. "You're gonna have to guide my hands, I can't see."

"Superman's got no x-ray vision, huh?" she snapped, and he wondered again how much of that was the situation. She grabbed his hands roughly and pushed them onto Erin's belly. He could feel the wetness, and something sticking out of her skin, something metal maybe? He wondered what it was. "Now hold there," she said.

"Yes ma'am," he replied, as another of Alison's big gunshots echoed down the mountain. He didn't even flinch.

***

Alison took a breath and let it out slow. How many of these demons had they left behind? She waited until three of them had come around the curve and started to open up on them. She didn't know whether they had ill intentions or not, but she knew she wasn't going to give them a chance either way. It was possible they would have just pedaled on by the crash scene, but she didn't live her life staking on possibilities and she didn't much plan on letting her husband's life hang in the balance, either.

She dropped the last one with a double shot. Missed the first time, hit the second. She wasn't exactly a dead shot with the rifle, but she was getting better. Shooting was a perishable skill, and while she was good, handling a .50 was a whole different league of shooting.

But she knew—had known all along—what it took to just hobble these things, and she didn't feel like hunting bear with a squirtgun. That was why she'd chosen the Barrett, the prize of her father's gun collection, rather than something a little more manageable, like, say, a .223.

She stayed down, rifle still resting on the hood of the car. She knew the sheriff and paramedics had to be close by. It wasn't like Midian was that far away. But it didn't matter now, things were about to come out in the open in a big way, and she knew—

"We gotta get out of here," Hendricks said, and she jerked her head around to see him standing a few feet distant, still clutching his side. He wasn't standing straight, either, but leaning against the back of the Explorer like he was about to keel over any second.

"Pretty sure leaving the scene isn't going to win us any points," Alison said, and turned back to her scope. She kept an eye on the road. Didn't they teach this guy anything in the Army? "Probably get us and Arch in a mess."

"We're already in a mess," Hendricks said. Alison kept looking through the scope, popping back up to make sure she wasn't missing anything in her field of vision. Three bikes remained up the road a ways, upturned and fallen where their masters had burned up. "Getting caught here with Lerner and Duncan isn't going to make it any better."

"There's a witness," Alison said, evenly, "in case you missed it. Even if we were to leave, I doubt she's inclined to just forget about us being here. That's likely to cause Arch and Erin more trouble than it's worth. Even if Erin's trouble might take a while to settle, if ever."

"What the fuck is that supposed to mean?" He sounded ornery, and she wondered if it was from the pain or from her half-assed way of saying his girlfriend might die.

"It means what you probably think it means," she said.

She could practically hear him stuffing a response deep inside. When he came back at her again, it was with a thin veneer of civility. "What do you think is about to happen here?" he asked. "Shit is going down. We're all going to get questioned, and when our answers don't match up—and they eventually won't, because unless we tell the truth, which will land us in a crazy house, the effort of getting just the four of us to lie like fucking dogs is going to tangle us real quick. Which means we either get Lerner and Duncan in the car and get the fuck out of here to leave Arch to come up with the lies on his own, unimpeded, or we all wrap a big fat fucking stone around each of our necks and jump in the water with him."

Alison froze and pulled her eye off the scope to survey the road. There weren't more than three, were there? She couldn't recall. She'd been viewing the world through the scope when Arch had hit the bastards with his Explorer and turned them aflip, so while she'd seen the bikes and riders fall, she hadn't had the best view to count them. If there were any left, they were being damned crafty, though. "We can't leave Arch to do that. He's terrible at lying."

She could feel Hendricks easing up behind her, but she didn't turn, she just kept her eyes on the curve, waiting to see if one more of these dumb, life-sucking, black-hearted demons emerged. "Either he lies terribly on his own, or we all drown in this trying to do it better than him." She didn't look back at him as he spoke. "By himself, he's got enough credibility with the sheriff he might make it out of this. With us …" She could hear his voice turn nearly dead. "Well, you ever see a man try to swim carrying four dead weights on his back?"

***

Lerner could hear the conversation even before they were coming. Sirens in the distance were getting louder, too. He was looking up into the round face of Duncan and it was all grimness. Having a crack wasn't necessarily the end of the world, but it wasn't sunshine and fucking lollipops, either. He knew it, Duncan knew it, and what would need to happen next was hanging over both of them.

"We need to go with them," Lerner pronounced.

"I know," Duncan said.

"Glad we're in agreement," Lerner said and steeled himself. This part was not going to be easy. "Help me up, you sad sack bastard."

Duncan reached down and did just that, slowly, getting him onto his feet over the course of about thirty seconds of levering. Lerner could hear Alison and Hendricks coming, could hear the lady rattling the rifle over her shoulder as she moved. She already had the case in the back of the town car, so at least there was that.

"Arch?" Lerner called as Duncan steadied him, wrapping Lerner's arm around his shoulder. It was pretty important that Lerner didn't move that hip—hell, that whole side of his body—for the immediate future, until they could figure things out. "We've got to pursue the suspect." He laid it on thick, throwing out the agent-y words like he was playing a role. It was second nature to him after watching episodes of CSI and shit.

"Where do you think you're going?" This from the lady with the bloody knees. She didn't emerge from the car, but he could hear her, and she sounded pretty damned unhappy.

"Lean on me," Lerner said, and Duncan deposited him against the upturned Crown Vic for support. "Flash her the badge." Duncan nodded. Lerner probably didn't need to say it; Duncan knew what had to happen here to try and make it stick. He disappeared around the car, and Lerner could hear him squatting and pulling out his badge to show her. All she'd need to do was look at it and it'd make Arch's story a little stronger—whatever that story ended up being. "We are federal agents in pursuit of the suspects that caused Deputy Harris's accident and are responsible for multiple homicides here in Midian and elsewhere." He kept laying it on thick, like he was using the verbal equivalent of a shovel. He couldn't see the lady he was speaking to, but as long as she took one look at Duncan's badge, she'd get the impression that he was a federal agent. As for the rest of the story? Hopefully just the impression would make it hold together, but this wasn't exactly an exact science, was it?

"We gotta go," Hendricks said, and Lerner looked over at him. Alison had the rifle over her one shoulder and was trying to support Hendricks with the other. "Over the—"

"Shut up," Lerner said. "Duncan, we good to go?"

"We're good," Duncan said, emerging from behind the upturned wreck. He scrambled around to get his grip on Lerner again. Lerner could feel it, the crack, and he kept that side of his body still and let Duncan take up the weight for him. He waved his right hand at the town car, and Hendricks started toward it with Alison following in his wake to help catch him if he pitched over.

Lerner was betting on it happening, but he hoped the cowboy would at least have the decency to wait until they were in the car before he dropped. Otherwise, it was gonna hamper the hell out of their getaway. And those sirens in the distance were not all that distant anymore.

***

Lauren saw the guy's badge, just for a second, long enough to know that they were federal. The other guy threw it all at her pretty quick, the guy with the hip injury. She couldn't see him while he was talking, but he sounded like he was in a hurry to get after the bicyclists. She didn't have a lot of attention to give, what with trying to save Deputy Harris's life with nothing more than her clothes and her own hands to do it.

She'd found a new problem, too, and it was giving her fits. Harris's knee was all manner of fucked up, probably from hitting the underside of the dash. Lauren was lacking in bandages and couldn't send Arch to his cruiser for the first aid kit lest Harris bleed to death from the wound he was keeping pressure on, so she made the next most reasonable request. "Take your shirt off," she told him.

He looked up at her from where he was lying on his back, reaching up to hold her insides in. "For bandages, right?"

"No, because I really want to admire your fucking awesome gym body," she snapped. "Yes, for bandages."

He looked like maybe he wanted to say something back to her on that, but he stifled it. Good. She didn't need any of his shit today, anyway. He just pulled a hand down and went to work taking his uniform top off. Once he got the second button down, it was obvious he was wearing an undershirt anyway, the fucking prude.

***

Hendricks made it to the car and got in before he slumped against the window. He even waited until the door was closed to do it, falling over against the passenger window like he was going to take a nap. He wasn't, though, he was just in so much pain he couldn't hold himself up anymore. He let a loud grunt, like he trying to hold in the world's biggest fart, and he laughed a little at that thought, which hurt even fucking more.

Alison slid into the driver's seat next to him, and he heard Lerner and Duncan squeeze into the back somehow. He turned his head a little and glimpsed Lerner's long legs butting up against the door immediately behind him. Based on the angle, he guessed the poor bastard was sitting in a pretty fucked-up manner. He didn't have a clue how Duncan would get in there, either.

"Drive," Duncan said from somewhere behind Alison. That wasn't even a direction Hendricks could bend at the moment.

"Your shell casings," Hendricks mumbled as the thought occurred to him.

"They're gonna have to stay," Duncan said from the backseat. Lerner had gone quiet, which was distinctly unlike him. Could he have passed out, too?

Hendricks heard the roar of the town car's ignition, and Alison took it into a gentle three-point turn before she gunned it up the slope of the mountain. She wasn't taking it easy, and she drove the first curve with a grace that told him she might maybe have done this before.

"Slow it down!" Duncan ordered from the back seat. He was quiet for a second. "We've got wounded here." Hendricks had to agree with that, on every level. Then the pain he'd been pushing down caught up with him on a curve, and he really agreed with it, strongly, with everything in him as it came bursting out in a scream that followed him into the blessed blackness of unconsciousness.

9.

Arch was standing off to the side when they loaded Erin into the ambulance. His part was done, he figured, the paramedics tending to her along with Lauren—Dr. Darlington. He was just standing there, night coming on mingled with the smell of the burned rubber tires still lingering in the air and the engine of the overturned police car still making a ticking sound as it drained or something.

The paramedics were talking some gobbledygook, all medical terminology that Arch didn't fully understand about IV's and such. Lauren was making her presence known, and Arch caught the paramedics giving each other looks that said they weren't as impressed as they were clearly supposed to be.

There were other personnel on scene now—Reeve was here, milling around, looking at the crash and all the mess that had come from it. He hadn't said much once he'd heard the phrase "Federal agents in pursuit." Arch hadn't gotten too in-depth with it yet, and now he was just standing off to the side, staring at the paramedics loading Erin into the ambulance. He'd retrieved a spare shirt from the Explorer, an old t-shirt he kept in a gym bag, and was standing there with it clashing against his khaki uniform pants, feeling like this was the last place on earth he belonged.

She was a real mess, Erin was. Her face was bloody, though how much of it was from anything on her face was an open question. She hadn't regained consciousness the entire time, and from the doctor's offhand comments on the matter, that was either to be expected or a really bad sign. Hard to say which.

"We need to take her to Red Cedar in Chattanooga," Lauren said, and her word sounded like the final one on the matter.

"Ma'am, SkyRidge is closer—" One of the paramedics made the mistake of speaking up.

"I know Red Cedar," Lauren said, and that one had the cut of finality as well. "You will take us there, right now." The paramedic took it a lot better than Arch would have, shutting the back doors to the ambulance as Dr. Darlington climbed in with him. Arch got the feeling that there was going to be more to it than that, but his part was over with. The flashing red lights on the top of the ambulance glared in the night as it started down the mountain road. It weaved between the two other police cruisers, the volunteer fire engine and the wrecker parked below, and Arch watched it disappear slowly into the night, brake lights flaring one last time before it rounded a bend.

There were a thousand noises around him—conversations, firemen doing things he didn't have any idea about, Ed Fries trying to examine the scene for whatever clues he could come up with. Arch was aware of them, but not one of them made an impact, stuck. His mind was like Teflon, slippery, not absorbing a thing beyond that ambulance heading down the mountain road and a growing discomfort for what was coming. It let out its first wail now that it was out of sight, a piercing sound that cut through the conversation and all else like the sounding of a horn or like a train passing through on a quiet night.

"Arch," Sheriff Reeve said, jerking his attention back to the man. His face was lined in shadow on one side, and the red light of the nearby fire engine gave the other half an otherworldly tinge. Arch could feel the world drawing in like the night was constricting to envelope him. "What the hell happened here?

***

When Hendricks woke up, he was in a dark room that smelled like faint perfume, the kind that made him think of old ladies. Not quite nursing home old, but old, not something he'd ever smelled in a bar or dancing close to a pretty young thing. It was heavy and sweet, almost cloying, something that brought to mind blue-haired grannies and fuzzy sweaters and other stuff he couldn't readily attribute to any clear memory of his own.

There was something else underlying that smell, too, something heavier and deeper, like grease and something frying. Maybe dinner, once upon a time. Hendricks peered into the darkness as he came to realize his eyes were open. There was only a faint bit of light in the room, shining through some blinds just above his head. Thin lines of white light made him think it was either a fluorescent or the blinds were doing a magnificent job of holding back sunlight. He doubted it was the latter, even though he was having a hard time figuring out how long he'd been out.

He swallowed and found his mouth dry and sticky. Smacking his lips together brought new pain from his face where he'd been struck. This had happened before, but damn if he hadn't gotten his shit kicked more times than he could count since coming to this small town. Before, demon hunting had been a hazardous occupation but not one that was quite as much of a bloodsport as it had turned into lately. He'd gone for fringe demons, causing trouble and nesting. He didn't even see the fringe demons in this town; there were too damned many main-eventers. Big threats, big chaos, and apparently all in town for the convention from hell. This hadn't been how a hotspot worked, at least not the ones he'd been to.

This was something new.

"You awake?" Alison's voice cut in through the dark, causing him to shift his head to look at where her voice had come from. He was rewarded with the dormant pain in his side flaring back to glorious, horrible life and reminding him that his ribs were fucked, fucked and fucked again. No lube, with a desert-dry cooch.

"I'm awake." Every breath brought pain, every one of them, and pain brought with it a desire to breathe, which caused more pain and made him want to scream a stream of curses into the air around him.

With that, a light clicked on, a lamp next to the bed he was lying in came to life, showing Alison Stan's hair hanging in long, stringy strands on both sides of her face. She looked thin and tired, like the night had taken its toll on her as well. She pulled her hand away from the lamp and he caught a glimpse of black smudges on her fingers from where she'd been firing the rifle.

"Where are we?" he asked.

"My parents' house," she replied without emotion. He was getting used to that from her. He tried to remember when he'd first met her.

She hadn't been lifeless then; she'd been ready to tear Arch a new asshole. He hadn't seen that side of her lately; she'd been pretty inscrutable. He wouldn't have wanted to play Texas hold 'em against her the way she was now, and he wondered what could cause that kind of change in a person.

"We're here alone?" Hendricks asked, just keeping himself still for a moment. He didn't even want to think about moving, though he knew that was coming.

"No," she said, just as sedate as ever.

"They don't care you brought a wounded guy in a cowboy hat home with you?" he asked, shifting in bed.

"You don't have your hat," she said simply, just as lifeless.

Hendricks froze. "Still, injured guy in a black coat who's not your husband. Gotta raise a few questions."

"My daddy's home," she said. "Momma's in Atlanta overnight. My brother's downstairs, but I don't think he's been up to find out you're here."

"Oh, yeah?" Hendricks ran a hand—the one not on the side where he had the broken ribs—over his face, rubbing at it and finding a couple of places north of his eyes where he had bruises. "What is he, twelve?"

"Twenty-three," she said. "Got done with college, moved back home because he couldn't find work."

"Must be rough," he said, not really feeling all that sympathetic. Leaving home at eighteen had left him pretty cold to these stories he'd heard, though he knew people ooh'd and talked about how sad it was. He felt something else turn him colder. "How's Erin?"

"Don't know," Alison said. There was a measurable drag on her words, like even she was feeling the weight now. "I haven't heard from Arch."

"She was in bad shape," Hendricks said, thinking out loud. He hadn't seen her, but that kind of crash … he'd heard a little of what that lady doctor had said on the scene after she'd left him. Erin had still been alive when they'd left—which had been a damned cowardly thing for him to do, he realized in retrospect. He hadn't been thinking clearly the whole time after the crash, after that demon did his part to put the hurting on him.

She'd saved him. She'd maybe gotten herself killed to do it, but she'd saved him.

Maybe.

He forced himself up, causing more than a little pain in the process. Alison just watched him, a hint of alarm behind those dull eyes. "What are you doing?"

"We gotta go," he said.

"Go where?" she asked.

He stared at the door, looked at it forlornly, knowing that he was about to have to do something that would damned sure piss off someone he didn't want to piss off—if they found out about it. "We have to go see someone."

"We don't even know which hospital she went to," Alison said, low and kind of comforting. "Or if she's—"

"I know, and we're not going there—yet." Hendricks straightened himself up and got his feet over the edge of the bed. "We need to go talk to someone. Need to go get something." He moved slowly, hoping the small moves would keep him from drawing screaming pain from any one of his countless injuries. "It's for Erin." *And for me,* he didn't say.

Alison just looked at him, and he could tell she was sizing him up, figuring out if he was delusional. "Where are we going?" He liked how she just sort of got on board for the plan.

"We need to go see Wren Spellman," Hendricks said, shifting again so he could put both feet on the ground. This he did without causing too much pain, again. He knew at least some was coming, and he was readying himself for it. He'd have to force his way through, because this—this was too important to even think about waiting on.

"That guy that Lerner is always bitching about?" Alison asked, and he caught a faint furrowing of lines in her brow. "The one who's selling all these demons runes so they can hide from him and Duncan?"

"One and the same," Hendricks said, and he started to stand. Alison was up on her feet in a hot second and helped him. "We need to go see him, and now. Then we need to figure out where Erin is and get to her immediately."

"Why?" Alison asked. "What can this Spellman do for her that's so important?"

Hendricks steadied himself and felt the pain start the minute he tried to take his first step. Alison had an arm slipped around his, but she wasn't giving much support. She probably couldn't, because he was damned heavy. It didn't matter; he could have walked to Spellman's house in the country right now if he had to. "Save her life," Hendricks said. "Spellman can save her life."

***

Lerner was lying still on the bed in the hotel room. Duncan was nearby, on his own bed. Not lying down, though. He was sitting up, staring at Lerner like the black flames were going to consume him at any moment. That motel smell was hanging in the air. It lived there, after all, something like a sense that the place had been scrubbed but that some dirt each guest left behind was going to linger, forever, in the smell. It was a weird thing, but it was true of every motel Lerner had ever stayed in.

Duncan was like a stone. Like a stone sitting on the bed, absorbing all the energy in the room. More like a black hole, Lerner supposed. It sounded better, given what Lerner knew about astronomy. It had gone on far, far too long. Better to call it out than let it fester. "Stop being so damned grim," he said.

"You've got a crack," Duncan said tonelessly.

"I know I've got a crack," Lerner said, "because I'm the one with the crack. This is not the end." *Necessarily*, he didn't add.

"But neither is it good," Duncan said. "It's not like you have a body that heals itself."

That was true, Lerner had to concede. Once cracked, you were always going to be at a higher risk of breaking open, and that only led one place. And it was not a good place. "I'm not busted open just yet," he said. "Maybe we can epoxy me closed."

"Epoxy?" Duncan asked, a note of disbelief in the way he said.

"Something," Lerner said. "You know, I watch these medical shows—"

"I don't think you can epoxy a shell."

"I don't think it's ever been tried," Lerner said. "It's above my hip, in an area that doesn't flex much—"

"And if it flexes just once and breaks the epoxy hold, you're dragged back to hell in a wash of flame."

"Which might happen anyway," Lerner said. "Better than sitting here for the rest of eternity, staring at the ceiling and watching Dr. Phil during the long-ass days."

Duncan was quiet for a bit after that. "You could always try and prevail on the home office—"

"I think we both know how that would go," Lerner said. It wasn't the sort of thing one asked for. It was the sort of thing you wrote a report about and hoped they didn't notice. Which was probably a faint hope, in any case. It wasn't like nobody read those things. They read every one and you hoped they got the right impression out of them.

Duncan was quiet again. "Epoxy?"

"Go to the store and pick some out," Lerner said.

"I let Alison keep the car, remember?" Duncan asked.

Shit. Lerner had forgotten. "What, are your legs cracked? You can't walk to the store? Rogerson's or whatever it's called? I've seen it on the highway that runs through town."

Duncan kind of paused. "I don't want to leave you alone."

Lerner chuckled. "Believe me, I'm not going anywhere 'til you get back. And I ain't moving, either. So hurry, will you?" He fumbled with a hand outstretched toward the nightstand. "I get tired of Dr. Phil pretty fast, and I suspect this motel has a low limit on the number of channels."

***

Lauren felt the bump as the ambulance turned onto the interstate. The sound of the engine accelerating was muted, probably because of good insulation in the back cabin. The paramedic was keeping a decent eye on things, so Lauren just sat back in the jump seat watching Deputy Harris's vitals. She didn't know the girl very well but that didn't matter. She was from Midian and she wasn't on the list; that was enough to keep Lauren fighting hard for her.

Like it would have made any difference if it had even been Arch Stan on the gurney. She'd still be here, still trying to keep him alive, too. That ass.

The monitors beeped and beeped and beeped, a steady rhythm indicating the deputy's pulse and oxygen were still in the acceptable range—for now. Lauren had her doubts how long that would last. Harris almost certainly needed surgery, but she needed to stabilize first. They had her head wrapped up in a collar to prevent spinal damage because that shit would put a kink in the rest of the girl's life. And she really was still just a girl, Lauren thought, still a teenager, right? Right. Whole life potentially still in front of her.

"Lucky thing there was only one person in the sheriff's car," the paramedic said, breaking Lauren out of her thoughts.

"There wasn't," she said, still looking at the monitor. Wait, what? There was another person in there, wasn't there? Shit, how did she forget that? "There was a federal agent in the car with her. And some other guy got hurt riding with the other deputy." Had she seriously gotten so focused on Harris that she'd forgotten she'd treated two other patients at the scene? And they'd both left, against medical advice—and any sane thinking. Both of them, gone. She hadn't even realized it. Where the fuck was the common-sense emergency room doctor on that one?

The paramedic let a low whistle. "Guess they were lucky if they both walked away, huh?"

She didn't respond. The guy in the black coat had barely been able to walk. The federal agent had been lying on the ground, unable to move when she first examined him. But they'd both gotten up and left the scene to pursue the fugitives? The suspects?

But they hadn't even gone the same direction as the bicyclists, had they? She hadn't heard them pull their car around the wreck, had she? Could she have been so focused and tuned out to her surroundings that she missed that, too?

What the fuck?

She wanted to give it more thought, try and hash her way to a reason for that supreme level of incompetence on her part, but the monitors started beeping to indicate that Deputy Harris's heart rate was crashing, and suddenly she didn't have an ounce of thought to devote to that mystery anymore.

***

Reeve had listened to Arch's story without interrupting him, not once. Arch was trying to decide if that was a very good thing or a very bad thing, and he hadn't really landed on which yet. The old Reeve, the one he'd known before demons started showing up in Calhoun County and wreaking havoc, would have reacted one way, and it was a fairly predictable way.

This new Reeve just stood before him, almost impassive, watching Arch stone-faced as he spun a tale of two federal agents who had asked him and Erin for help, then led them in a chase down a mountain against bicyclists on the run for reasons that hadn't been elaborated on by the agents—save for to point the finger at them for at least some of the deaths in Midian. Arch wasn't proud of it, but at least his lies were mostly truthful. He was really just leaving a lot out of his story, that was all.

Because a lie of omission wasn't a lie—except for that whole part of it that was plainly stating it was a lie.

"Well," Reeve said once Arch had finished. And then he stopped, just stopped like "Well" was all he had to say on the matter.

It did not sound good to Arch. Not at all.

Reeve just stared at him for a minute and then drifted back toward Fries's car, which was how he'd gotten to the scene. Arch spared a glance back at his Explorer, and it looked like it had been through the mill. The ringer, too. Dings and damage to the bumpers and huge scratch on the left side where something had ripped it up. Not as bad as the sheriff's own car, which was being winched up onto the back of the tow truck after being righted. The roof of it alone looked like aluminum foil that had been crumpled off the top of a casserole dish.

Arch just sat there, watching the car and stealing a look at Reeve every now and again. The sheriff had eased into the front seat of the cruiser and was on the radio. Arch could see his lips moving, but couldn't hear a word of what was being said.

And that concerned him more than a little.

***

Mick had been waiting at the Surrey Diner for Molly for an hour after she'd promised to show up. It wasn't exactly a tough thing for him to do, since he didn't have anywhere else to go. He was just hanging there, drinking free coffee refills and getting the increasingly unpleasant looks from the waitress for doing it.

She'd started out real friendly, but that had faded as the hour wore on, and the "sugars" and "huns" had been dropped about half an hour ago. He figured she'd rather let him sit here all night than get unpleasant enough to kick his ass out, but you just never knew, did you? Plus, the proprietor was giving him a look from behind the counter. Like there weren't a hundred other seats in the place unoccupied by paying customers, he had to worry about the one guy drinking his coffee.

But when Molly walked in, every increasingly ugly word from the waitress and every suspicious glare from the owner had been worth it. He'd thought about leaving, maybe giving up on this town and waiting to fill his need until the next one, but dammit, he didn't want to. This place had the right feel, and being a hotspot it was bound to get a little warmer than a normal place, right?

Right. This was the town.

And, he reflected as he caught a glimpse of her knees under a skirt that reached almost low enough to cover them—this was the girl.

"Hey," he said as she sidled up. She had a look like she'd maybe dressed up a little, changed what she was wearing since he'd seen her this morning, but she'd gone just as casual so he couldn't be sure. It was probably a tactic, trying to gussy up without looking like she was trying. He was pretty sure she was trying, though, at least a little. That was a good sign.

"Hey," she replied. She was playing it cool, though; he knew that much from watching humans for as long as he had. She was taking this seriously. Probably because she hadn't been on many actual dates.

"How was school?" he asked, offhand, like he was more curious than he really was. How interesting could the answer be, after all? Math class was super neat, factoring polynomials is the best! He would have bet on her answer before he got it, and he was not surprised when it came.

"Okay, I guess," she said, shrugging her shoulders like it was no big deal. Which it wasn't. After all, that was a daily grind for her. "Just another day, really." Playing it cool.

"Sure," Mick said, shrugging his shoulders a little, too. "I was just curious because—well, you know."

She flickered with a little bit of annoyance. Of course she didn't know. He knew she didn't know. But he was playing it cool too, and she didn't have a clue he was doing it on purpose. "No, I don't. What?"

"I was just wondering because I'm not in school anymore," Mick said. "Never really went to a regular one, so I'm just ... wondering what it's like?"

"Really?" There was a hint of earnestness in her answer, and he could tell he'd broken through the first brick of that wall of cynicism she carried for her own defense.

"Yeah," Mick said, like it was nothing. It was nothing to him; he didn't care. But for however long it took her to answer, he was going to pretend it was the most interesting damned thing in the world to him.

"It was ... a normal day," Molly said, a little less guarded this time. "We only have six classes a day, see, and I start with algebra ..."

Mick nodded as she went, trying to follow along. Sure, it was boring as shit, but it would be worth it if he could just get through that wall that surrounded her—and into her damned panties.

***

Hendricks felt like he was taking forever getting down the hall. In rough terms, he probably was taking forever. He could feel himself dragging, the material of his coat scuffing against the white-painted wall. Alison stood off a few inches from him, hovering, ready to try and catch him if he fell. It was a laughable idea in his mind, since he weighed far, far too much for her to help without toppling over.

"Ali?" came a smooth voice from ahead of them. The hallway looked like it was extending, growing as he shuffled down it. Hadn't it only been twenty feet earlier? Now it looked like a hundred. Two hundred. Shit, it was still growing.

"Right here, Daddy," Alison said, and Hendricks watched her take her eyes off of him. He tried even harder not to stumble at that moment. As though she weren't hovering enough as it was, he sensed that if he keeled over now she'd never let him go unwatched. He just needed to get to Spellman, post-haste, get this pain and these wounds taken care of. He shifted his neck to look at her and the demon bite screamed at him, hard enough to make him fall against the wall an inch or so. It didn't quite light his ribs afire again, but close. It took him a minute to control his breathing.

There were pictures on the wall that rattled as he shifted against it, his arm knocking against a wooden frame. "Urgh," Hendricks murmured, keeping it down.

"Is your friend all right?" came that voice again—smooth, like an announcer on the radio. A voice you could trust to sell you a used car or a water filter.

"I'm fine," Hendricks managed to get out before Alison could answer for him.

"All appearances to the contrary, son," the voice came again, and Hendricks managed to get his head up enough to see the guy this time. He was tall, powerful-looking, looked to be in his sixties. Not a guy Hendricks would have cared to get into a scrape with, if he could have avoided it. "You look like you could use a doctor. Or a drink."

"I need something, that's for sure," Hendricks said and tried to straighten up. It didn't go so well, and he found himself still against the wall a few seconds later, no better off than before. "You might be right. I should get to the car. That'll … I need to …"

"To get to the doctor, yes," Alison said. "Daddy, can you help him?"

"Certainly," Alison's father said, shuffling closer to him. He was damned big; not quite Arch's size, Hendricks thought, but maybe close. Hard to tell at this distance and without Arch here for comparison. "What happened?" he asked as he placed Hendricks's good side of undamaged ribs against his, wrapping Hendricks's left arm around his shoulder.

"Bar fight," Hendricks lied. It wasn't so far off; he had been in a bar fight a few days earlier.

"Huh," the man said. "What's your name, son?"

"Lafayette Hendricks, sir," Hendricks replied.

"Well, Lafayette Hendricks, I'm Bill Longholt." He could feel the scrutiny. "Army?"

"Heh," Hendricks said, feeling a little lightheaded. "No. Marine."

"Oh, you're one of those," Longholt said. "I was Army."

"I'm sorry for you," Hendricks said, unable to avoid the needle jab. "You know what Army stands for? Ain't Ready for Marines Yet."

He felt a sudden, sharp pain as Longholt readjusted his position, causing his side to jar, just a little, pressing his wrecked ribs together.

"Oh, I'm sorry, Marine," Longholt said, not sounding contrite at all. "Thought I was losing my grip on you there for a second. You know what Marine stands for? My Ass Really Is Navy Equipment."

The hallway swam around Hendricks, and he could see a white door up ahead. "Lordy."

"Say, is that a bite on your neck?" Longholt asked him.

"My girlfriend got a little rough last night," Hendricks said, vision swimming. Did that even make sense?

"Daddy, he needs a doctor," Alison said from somewhere in the periphery of his vision. It was dark in the hall, and growing darker by the second, swirling motes of blackness crawling around in his eyes.

"Right you are, dear," Longholt said, and Hendricks felt his legs drag forward in motion. "Bar fights and a girlfriend who bites you so hard, your hicky bleeds. That does sound about like the Marines I knew."

There was sound and motion in the corner of Hendricks's eye, and suddenly there was a newcomer there. All Hendricks could tell about him was that he was a white guy with dark hair, and he was shorter than Hendricks, even in his crumpled-up state.

"What the hell happened to the dimestore cowboy?" the guy asked.

"Fuck off, Brian," Alison said, stronger than Hendricks had ever heard her speak before, and they just kept on going, out the door.

***

The waitress at the Surrey Diner had gotten miraculously friendlier when Molly showed up. The "huns" and "sugars" made a sudden return, and the coffee refills came a lot quicker. The owner's glare softened, too.

The boring fucking stories portion of the evening had commenced as well, but there was a price for everything, right? A tradeoff, Mick figured.

It'd be worth it.

***

Lauren didn't panic in crisis situations. She had that detached part of her brain, the part that saw everything from a distance, that evaluated coldly and without emotion, and that part always worked overtime during these moments. It was training, beaten into her head through long practice just as sure as if it were a nail hammered into a board through repetition. She'd had a moment when she was a kid—before she'd had a kid of her own—when she'd seen a friend damned near lose a toe in a bike chain. Panic had taken over, and she'd tried to help her friend yank it out. Hysterics, crying, screaming—from both of them—and an emergency room visit later, she'd been stuck in the waiting room feeling like an impotent failure. That was probably the catalyst moment for her, looking back. She never wanted to feel that panicked and out of control again.

And she hadn't, except for when she'd fallen in love with Molly's father. But that was panic and loss of control of a different kind, when she'd realized she couldn't hold on to the sonofabitch. Now she realized that there wasn't much worth holding onto in him, but her teenage self had seen it differently and always would.

She did what she had to do. Stabilized the pulse, got the deputy breathing again. The beeping of the heart rate in the background was steady, repetitive, maddening. Like it should be.

Lauren sat back, took a breath. "Don't check out on me yet, Deputy," she said, staring down at the face of Erin Harris, the massive bruises on the girl's cheekbones just starting to appear. This was going to be some surgery, she suspected, and she was glad—not for the first time—that it wasn't her specialty. The ambulance bumped, the sirens still blaring as the shot down the interstate toward Red Cedar. Pretty soon they'd get her there, get her triaged. That's where Lauren's responsibility would end, and it couldn't come soon enough for her.

***

"Turn here," Hendricks said as they reached an old, overgrown driveway. There were gravel tracks that perfectly mirrored tire placement, and a big wedge of green in the middle of the path where grass stood tall. It made the place look like no one had driven up to it in a while, though Hendricks was pretty sure that was all illusion and bullshit.

He was sitting in the passenger seat, just about ready to pull a bullet out of his .45 so he could bite down on it to stifle the pain. He'd never tried it, but the thought of chomping down on something seemed like a nice idea at the moment. Anything, if it might help ease the pain. He would have sworn something in him was about to break if he wasn't already sure something had.

"That was your brother, right?" he asked, trusting the words would make their way out of his mouth and find Alison wherever she was sitting—in the driver's seat, probably, about two thousand miles or an arm's length away. Same difference at this point, since he didn't want to move his arm. Or anything else.

"Yeah," she said tersely, and Hendricks wrote off that line of inquiry for later. Family was a touchy topic for lots of folks; he couldn't see it being much of an issue for Alison, though. For crying out loud, her dad had offered to accompany them to the hospital. Seemed like a nice guy, got along with his daughter.

There was a farmhouse ahead, and the sight of it jolted Hendricks back to the here and now. It looked like any other farmhouse to Hendricks's eyes. His attention was a little scattered at the moment, just enough to give Alison the directions he'd had in his mind but not enough to pay attention to every detail along the way. Or even most of the details. She was from here, he figured, she could pay attention. Or that was how he justified it to himself as he squinted his eyes shut through ninety percent of the trip and focused mostly on not whimpering.

He opened his eyes and tried to take a harder look at the farmhouse. Didn't happen. He'd bitten his own tongue at some point during the journey, blood filling his mouth, and frankly, it was the least of his hurts. He was sunk down in the leather seat.

"We're here," Alison said, like he hadn't noticed the car bump to a stop. It was the bump that did it, sent him wailing in his own head. He'd gotten off the bed somehow, but dammit, a car ride on an uneven country road had just about fucking done him in. How did that happen?

Hendricks tried to open the door and failed on his first attempt. Just couldn't get it pushed open, and it closed back. Not completely, though, that little annoying click telling him the door was still partially open. He tried again and failed, not able to use his strength to throw it open and not able to lean far enough to get it clear of the fucking latching mechanism.

This was pathetic, even by his somewhat weakened estimation.

"Wait just a second," Alison said, and he heard her get out.

Fuck waiting. He wasn't going to be that much of a pussy. He pushed hard and nearly tumbled out. When he opened his eyes, the car door was still only open about six inches. But at least he hadn't hurt himself in the process. Victory.

Then Alison tugged at the door and he felt a thundering agony run down his side as she pulled at him in a way that his body DID NOT FUCKING LIKE AT ALL and he spent the next thirty seconds—or maybe ten years—trying to keep from cursing at her in every possible way, starting with the words that were least polite, then moving to the ones that were most polite. If there was such a *cunt motherfucking sonofabitch ass hell damn* thing.

"Maybe you should let me go in and talk to this Spellman," Alison said as he sat there, eyes rolling back in his head from the feeling oh *sonofafuck* the feeling.

"Just help me up," Hendricks said, but he was not sure he meant it wholeheartedly.

***

"Arch, why don't you get on out of here?" Reeve said. Said, not asked. It had sounded like asking, but Arch knew it wasn't, could tell it from fifty paces. They'd finished winching up the sheriff's car now, the tow truck driver—Sam Allen, Arch could see from here—about to take it down the mountain and to his body shop. Arch had his doubts there'd be much they could do to fix it, but if anyone could, Sam could.

"Sure thing," Arch answered, light on the enthusiasm. "Anywhere you want me to go in particular?"

Reeve just stared at him, bald head catching the reflection of the flashing red lights of his patrol car. "Why don't you just head on home for now?" And then he got back into his car, not a word of explanation further.

***

Hendricks burst into the farmhouse barely supported by Alison, ignoring the room to his immediate left. Alison partially blocked his view, anyway, which was good, because he could smell the fetid scent of animal and human waste from the creatures in cages. He could almost taste it, like something had crawled up his nose before it lost the fight for life, leaving behind nothing more than a rotting corpse, with all the waste and shit that came out after.

He'd never really been in a place like this, but he knew what a deal with the devil looked like, and when you were ready to make one it was best to avoid looking right in the fucker's eyes.

"Well, well," said a man in a Han jacket with a full head of hair that was grey around the edges. He had a relaxed bearing, holding his fingers together in a sort of steeple configuration as he stared down the hallway at Hendricks and Alison. Dark floorboards shone with fresh wax, and the Pine-Sol scent almost—almost—covered up the smell from the room to their left. "If it isn't Corporal Hendricks. And Alison Longholt Stan." The man bowed. "Such a pleasure to have you both here in my humble shop."

"This is a farmhouse," Alison said with aplomb, but sounding to Hendricks's ears like she really believed it.

"Well, the outside certainly is," Spellman said with a little bow.

"I'm not a corporal anymore," Hendricks said, unable to hold himself upright and not even fucking bothering. "Nice touch, though, knowing that."

"Indeed," Spellman said. "As you know, I'm in a customer service business, and the more you know about your customers, the better you can service them. I pride myself on being in tune with my clientele and knowing their needs."

Hendricks looked at the empty bastard with one eye. He missed his hat; it was always more effective to survey someone from underneath it, because the brim did a great job framing the face. "What is your customer-centric focus telling you about what I need?"

A line of wrinkles folded on Spellman's forehead. "I have just the thing for what ails you." From out of the sleeve of his jacket came a vial. "What do you get for the man who has it all? Well, everything except ribs that are intact, and skin that's not seeping blood from a vembra'nonn bite, anyway." He pointed, keeping the vial safely in his other hand, in view but not in reach. "Those bites can cause some complications, by the way. I'd clean it out when you get a chance. In fact, if you'd like, I have a medical kit I'd be willing to throw in for—"

"Spare me," Hendricks said. "How much for the drink?"

"Well, as you know, the first one was free," Spellman said with a little twinkle. "But this one won't cost you much."

"Cost us much what?" Alison asked. "Gold? Silver?"

"I deal in the coin of the realm, whatever realm I'm in," Spellman said. "That said, my IRA is not in tangible assets at present, so I'll just take cash. U.S. Dollars," he amended. "Say … two hundred."

"Cheaper than a hospital stay," Hendricks muttered and fumbled in his coat, causing Alison to sway with his motion and damned near lose him.

"Come, have a seat," Spellman said, beckoning them forward. "I'll have a look at that neck while you drink up." He waited, and as Hendricks staggered his way forward, the man slipped the vial in his palm. "You'll probably have an easier time reaching your wallet once you've had a sip or two."

"No cow bladder this time?" Hendricks felt just a little bit of the burn of pride as he looked at the man—no, this wasn't a man. He looked into the eyes, looked right into them, and he could see only a little something there. That didn't stop him from pulling the stopper on the vial and chugging it back.

10.

Arch followed the wrecker back into town, providing an unasked-for police escort the whole way. He had his reasons, but Sam Allen didn't need to know them, not straightaway. Darkness had fallen on Midian, maybe not just metaphorically, either. He tried to sift through things in his head, making the mental rounds on all the things that had happened and everything they'd learned. Erin was out of commission, Lerner was waylaid—he still wasn't clear on how that had happened—Hendricks looked like he'd gotten put out of the fight for a while.

That left him, Duncan and maybe Alison on defense, all versus a whole mess of bicyclists for whom the Tour de France looked like an easy win. No blood doping needed, unless it involved drinking said blood. He put a vision of Hendricks's neck, dripping scarlet, out of his mind. Vampires on bikes.

Unprompted thumps and clacks from the Explorer entered his consciousness every now and again. They were not normal sounds but something produced when the vehicle had run over those accursed bicyclists. He suspected he'd need to get it checked out at some point, but this was not the moment.

Sam guided the tow truck through the gate of his yard and Arch followed, the Explorer's undercarriage protesting as he bumped up over the curb and left the paved road behind. Glowing yellow lights every hundred feet or so illuminated a corrugated metal building that looked like it was at least fifty percent rust. And that might have been optimistic. The yellow lights cast cone-shaped illumination on a few entry portals—garage doors and a standard one for people to walk through—shedding the kind of light that told Arch that Sam Allen hadn't made way in his budget for those newfangled CFLs just yet.

Sam stopped the wrecker and backed it up. Mountains of flattened and beat-up cars littered the yard. It truly was a junkyard, and he had a maze of the wrecks out back, Arch knew. He'd come to Sam's a few times to pull salvage off destroyed vehicles. It was cheaper getting a hubcap from Sam than ordering it through one of the auto shops in town, and everyone knew it. Alison might not have known it, come to think of it, but then he'd had to get the hubcap for her, so she was covered, he supposed.

Sam was winching the sheriff's car down from the back of the truck when Arch caught up with him. The red tail lights of the big tow truck glowed, casting Sam's unshaven, three-four day scruff in a light not unlike that which Reeve had been in when Arch had seen him. That caused a moment of disquiet, thinking about that particular landmine, still lying in his path undetonated.

"What can I do for you, Arch?" Sam asked, glancing up at him as he approached. "I don't reckon you followed me back here just to make sure I got home safely."

Arch didn't bother splitting into a grin for him, but the man had figured that much out. "Police property in the trunk, Sam. I can't just leave it to get smashed."

Sam blinked at him, lines around his squinting, folding like the middle of an accordion. "Arch, this trunk is all beat to shit, if you'll pardon my French. I don't think you're gonna be able to open it with a key."

"I can't leave it in there, Sam," Arch said. "Sheriff stored his long guns in the back."

Sam scratched his face, giving it a thought. "Got a pry bar. You might could work it loose if you were willing to put some elbow grease into it."

Arch let out the hint of a smile. "That'd be mighty helpful, Sam." He watched the man nod and make his way slowly back to the cab. It wouldn't do to just let what was in the trunk of the car get lost, not when Arch had an idea of how they might make use of it. Waste not, want not.

***

"You look much better already," Spellman opined, the sorry fucker.

Hendricks could hear the sounds from the room down the hall now, the rattle of cages. Deal with the devil nearly done, he was about ready to start looking someone in the face. He gave a moment's thought to the absurdity of using the phrase metaphorically and moved on.

"Your color is much improved," Spellman continued.

Hendricks tore his eyes away from the empty skin that was Spellman and looked Alison in the face. She was sitting next to him at a finely appointed dining room table that would have looked a few degrees out of place in an actual farmhouse. It was a little too swank, a little too polished, a little too unused. He doubted a fork or a knife had ever been set upon the surface of this smooth monstrosity. The whole room had that feel about it, all appearance, with no sense that anyone actually lived here.

"You do look almost alive now," Alison told him in that flat, antidepressant tone of hers.

"Thanks." He swept his gaze back to Wren Spellman, trying not to look him in the eyes and taking in the salt and pepper sideburns instead. "I need another round before I go."

Spellman was hovering, his—its?—hands a few inches from Hendricks's head. He did have a medical kit, Hendricks noticed, wondering where the hell that had come from. It was open in one palm, and he had a nice piece of gauze pinched between his fingers. It reeked of rubbing alcohol, even though Hendricks hadn't seen him open a bottle nor dip the gauze in it. "This is going to sting, so you might want to prepare yourself."

"I've had wounds cleaned before, thanks," Hendricks said through gritted teeth, already preparing himself for the pain.

"I wasn't talking about the wound cleaning," Spellman said, pressing the swab to Hendricks's neck. It burned only a little, surprisingly. Probably the effects of the drug already working on him. "I was talking about the fact that I can't sell you another round of the medicine you just took."

Hendricks felt himself give a comically exaggerated blink. He could feel the cool, mentholated burn of the swab on the skin of his neck, dabbing away the crust of blood as Spellman's hands worked with precision to clean whatever was left of the wound. "Beg pardon?" he asked. "What, are you out of the stuff?"

"No, I'm quite well stocked," Spellman said coolly, and it took all Hendricks could manage not to jerk around and start battering the smug fucker with a fist. "I just can't sell you another vial knowing what you plan to do with it."

Hendricks lost his battle with restraint, and the chair flipped over behind him as he came to his feet. He had a few inches on Spellman, the empty bastard, and he drew himself up to his full height as he stared down at the Screen, looking for something behind the eyes. "Say that again."

"I can't sell you any more of the compound in question," Spellman said with a shrug, like it was just a fact of life. "You see, you intend to use it on Deputy Harris, a noble—no, really, *laudable* goal." His face fell, the tics of emotion following along with his speech. "The problem is, Deputy Harris is in the hospital at this very moment, fighting for her life. Doctors are working on her. X-rays are being taken, magnetic resonance imaging is being done—all the wonders of the human medical world are being applied to her." Spellman's hands were clean now, not a hint of bloody gauze anywhere in sight. "So if you were to walk into her room and administer some of my compound to her, you would produce a verifiable medical miracle. You'd practically bring her back from the dead." Spellman's face went dead. "I can't have that, no matter intimidating you look, all puffed up like that."

"I don't really do much puffing," Hendricks said, "or huffing. Pretty much skip straight to blowing your house down."

"Ah, yes, my house," Spellman said with a light shrug. "It'd be a shame if you did that. I wouldn't be able to help you any more if you did. And I'd have to go through the trouble of pulling up stakes, of finding a new storefront. A very messy headache would entail. Of course there'd be the matter of revenge, too—"

"Are you threatening me?" Hendricks said, and it was only through sheer will he didn't seize the man by his Han jacket and smear him all over his too-fancy table.

"No more than you're threatening me," Spellman said, face inscrutable. "No, I can't sell you the compound you want. But … perhaps there is something I can do for you."

Hendricks hadn't reached for his sword yet, but damn if he hadn't wanted to. "Go on," he said, once he got his jaw to stop locking up from anger. It took a moment.

***

Lauren didn't push the gurney because she didn't really need to, but she was right there with the paramedics as they did, riding it right through into the Red Cedar ER. She saw Doctor Burnham as they came in, knew he'd been on duty tonight but decided to divert here anyway. Still sort of young, married, but fooled around with any woman he could sink his dick in. She'd heard from two of the nurses that every time he fucked he made a "The doctor is in!" proclamation when he got his tip wet. She hadn't been interested in him before that, and afterward it had put him on the DNF list forever.

"Gimme the bullet," Burnham said as she slid in alongside the gurney into the trauma room.

"MVA, possible skull fracture," Lauren said, noting that Burnham didn't even say a word about her being in the ambulance, like her picking up a shift and coming through the door in runner's clothes was a perfectly normal occurrence. She ran through the rest of the vitals on memory, not really paying attention. She was eyeing Deputy Harris's face again; the poor girl ... she just ...

"So, Lauren," Burnham said as he got to work, "what the hell are you doing here?"

She ignored the twitch of a nerve at the corner of her mouth. "I'm not here, Chase," she said, calling him by his first name. If he wanted to get familiar, it was a two-way street. "I'm a product of your overactive imagination." She pulled the latex gloves from her hands one by one, letting them snap as they were removed. "You got this?"

Burnham only spared her a glance as he started to assess his patient. His patient. Not hers anymore. "I got it." Dipshit he may be, but Burnham was a decent doc. If he said he had it, he had it.

"Great," Lauren said, and looked down, remembering that faint pain in her knees probably meant she needed sutures. "Because this doctor is *out*." She pushed through the swinging doors before Burnham could say anything to that. She paused in the white tile hallway, looking down the path straight ahead, staring off into the far distance of the corridor. "Good luck, Deputy," she said, and started toward the locker room. After she cleaned up she'd have to find a ride back to Midian. And Molly.

Oh, Molly.

***

"I'd like to see you again," Mick said. He'd done it right, he knew it. Her face was all aglow, the overhead lamp hanging above them, the skies dark outside the window, lights of the square the sole guard against the blossoming night. The proprietor of the café was the only one left, and he was giving Mick the eye again. Not a good look. Every time he passed near, though, he was all smiles for Molly.

Molly's face was flushed, and she had a good look to her, at least to Mick. She'd had fun. He'd made her laugh. That seemed important, making her laugh. Those pale cheeks pink with the laughter, like she'd brushed them with a rose, leaving traces of the color behind on her snowy skin as they passed. "I'd like that," Molly said, her lips fighting not to turn up in the corners.

Oh, yeah. Mick had this one. It was almost in the bag. "How about coming to the carnival tomorrow night? I've got the evening off, and I could show you around." He just tossed it out there. Like bait. Waited for her to go for it.

She stared at him soberly, looked down for just a second. Thinking it over, he figured. "All right," she said finally.

"Want me to pick you up at your house?" he asked. Fishing again.

Her eyes darted to the proprietor. "No," she said, hushed. "Not unless you *don't* want me to go with you."

He nodded like he was some kind of sage. "Parents. I get it."

"Just a mom," Molly said. The cheeks weren't quite as red now. "She used to be cool, but lately she's just … ugh. Anyway. Meet me here? In the square? Say around sundown?"

"Sundown, tomorrow, here," Mick said, spelling it out. He forced a smile. "Sounds good. I think you'll like the carnival. I might be able to show you some things you haven't seen before."

She didn't answer in words, just a slight nod, and a partial smile that hid a subtle enthusiasm. Oh yeah. Mick knew he had this. Right in the damned bag.

CORRUPTED

***

"How long do you think it'll take to work?" Hendricks asked, staring at the banana bag skeptically. He'd already paid, figuring something was better than nothing. He gave it a squeeze, and the clear liquid seemed to glimmer with the motion, like there was something hidden inside it.

"It'll begin working immediately," Spellman said. "It just won't have as sudden of an effect as what you've taken. This is a watered-down version of the compound. Slow burn instead of ... raging forest fire." He shrugged. "It's an imperfect metaphor. The point is, it will begin to heal her as soon as you manage to trade this for her present IV."

"Great," Hendricks said, and started to leave. He didn't wait to see if Alison was at his side, just turned on his boot and felt the slip of the ornate rug underfoot.

"A word of caution," Spellman said, and Hendricks turned back to look at him. Alison was behind him, between him and Spellman, just watching the screen where she'd entered the hall outside the archway to the dining room. "Even if you administer the dose, she may not recover in time."

Hendricks felt that rampant desire to grab the man by his jacket again, to smash his head through the glass curio cabinet on the side of the dining room. To ventilate his skin, just a little, to let the essence run out. "Clarify, please." He said it with restraint.

"You might want to settle down, just a little," Spellman said. "That threatening mien may work all manner of wonder when you're out in your role as demon hunter, but it does so little good for your complexion in this light."

Hendricks took a step and stopped when Spellman held out a hand. "I've given you the best I can; what I mean to say is that your ... lover? Paramour? Fling? She's in a terrible condition, putting it mildly. She may die regardless. I want to warn you, because I'd hate to have you angry at me because of some perceived failure on my part. So I'm giving you the product warning." He moved his hands as if he were indicating a marquee of some sort: "Warning: you need to get it to her in the next couple hours to have a chance, and even then...this may not save her life."

"Then give me the one that does," Hendricks said in a low growl.

"I'm afraid I can't do that," Spellman said. He wasn't quite gleeful, but he was way, way too close to it for Hendricks's taste.

"Then I'm afraid you're about to feel the embrace of the warm summer air in your innards," Hendricks said, and started for his sword, pushing aside the rough fabric of his coat.

Spellman laughed, looking skyward. "I don't think you quite understand what you're up against here, but putting that aside—even if you could somehow compel me to part with the potion ... what makes you think you could get your poor, unconscious lady friend to drink it?" He stared back at Hendricks, who had a hand on his sword's hilt. "You need something that works intravenously."

"I'm about to give you something that works intravenously," Hendricks said and made to draw his sword.

The lights darkened and the fixtures rattled, and Spellman's eyes went red. "I'm not a garden variety demon, and I think you'll find that my bite is worse than any vembra'nonn."

"Hendricks," Alison said warningly.

Hendricks kept his eyes locked on Spellman but didn't draw his sword. He realized that the lights had not flickered, had not dimmed; there was some sort of darkness in the room, a pervasive aura of blackness that seemed to be pushing against Hendricks, wrapping his chest, squeezing him. He struggled for breath like he was in a bear hug. "You know, I've got a couple friends that would just love to know where you are."

Spellman made a sound like a squeal, but lower and more violent, like a breath hissing out of a balloon with vibrato. It made his ears ache. "I wouldn't go confusing any OOCs in your acquaintance with friends. I suspect there won't be too many days until it's driven home to you in agonizingly obvious ways that those ... things ... are not on your side." Spellman's eyes faded. "Besides, they couldn't find me if they wanted to. My invitation is open to you and only you." Spellman paused. "Well, you and one other member of your ... entourage. Your ... association? Your ..."

"Watch," Hendricks said. "My watch."

"However you like it," Spellman said with a flowery bow. "Are we now settled in all the matters of discussion between us?"

Hendricks kept his gaze on the screen, his hot, resentful eyes the only expression of the gut-level emotion churning in his belly. He wanted to throttle this motherfucker, put his face against the tread of a tire and peel out until the skin—or shell—was all gone. He was fairly sure that Spellman could see all this as he looked into those mildly glowing red eyes, but that smile never dimmed. "We're settled, all right."

"Then I look forward to seeing you again when we have further commerce to conduct," Spellman said with that trace of a smile. "Good day, Corporal." He smiled more broadly at Alison. "Mrs. Stan."

Hendricks didn't turn away from the bastard, just kept his left hand cupped around the IV bag, right on the sword hilt, letting his fingers play on the leather that wrapped it. He gestured for Alison to get moving, and she did, not taking her eyes off of Spellman either. "Yeah," Hendricks said. "I'm sure I'll be walking through your door again real soon."

"I'm sure you will, too," Spellman said without a trace of irony.

Hendricks let the door close behind him, avoiding a last look at that room by the entry as though his life depended on it. The deal was done, but he felt less than satisfied. That was how a deal with a devil went, didn't it? Feeling like you got fucked, but your pants were still on?

As the door closed behind him, shutting out that smell, those sounds, and giving him the curious sense that a gateway was shutting to something like another world, he was left standing on the porch of a farmhouse next to Alison, staring out at the messed up town car that they'd taken from Lerner and Duncan.

"Now what?" Alison asked.

As if he knew. Other than getting the IV bag to Erin, he had nothing. "This," he said, waving the banana bag, the liquid within catching the light and sparkling as he waved it in front of her face. "This and ... hell, I don't know. Find those bicycling bastards somehow."

"You think they're just gonna stick around and let us run them over again?" Alison asked. She didn't look all that impressed with his plan.

"Seems like they came out of it hurting less than we did," Hendricks said, a little stiffly. He could feel his pride burning, still, from the confrontation with Spellman. It was sticking in his craw something fierce that he'd backed down. Hendricks hated backing down. The only thing he hated worse was losing, and he'd gotten a real good sense that losing was approaching on the horizon if he kept sailing toward Spellman.

"In the sense that there are probably still forty of them left to the four of us, yes," she said. "But we killed a lot of them. And I don't think they're going to flee town just because we ran a few of them down. Unless that's usually how it works with these hotspots?"

Hendricks felt his eyelids flutter at her a few times. She had a damned annoying point. "No. That's not usually how it works. Demons don't typically flee hotspots. I don't know how these vembra'nonn work, but ... no. With things going like they are around here, they'll probably stick around for a while yet."

"Your flock of vembra'nonn are irrelevant, Lafayette Hendricks," came a voice out of the darkness. He spun to see her there, under the porch light, pale as a fresh Wisconsin snowfall, her red hair blazing behind her and those dark eyes threatening to out-blacken the night sky. "There is a greater danger approaching this town than some kamikaze cyclists."

"Well, hello, Starling," Hendricks said with as much aplomb as he could gather to him on the short notice afforded by her appearance. "Is it the end of the world again already?"

"You mock, but it comes nonetheless," Starling said, and Hendricks would have sworn the shadows around her eyes moved in a way that the light shining on her face couldn't have supported. "And soon—only a day away."

11.

Alison stood there, under the porch light, staring at the redhead. She felt it build inside, that pressure, the need, and then she could hold it back no longer. She let out a long, cackling laugh that split the night, echoing over the flat grass surrounding the farmhouse, corralled by the trees that edged the horizon, barely visible as sentries against the surrounding night. It was a good laugh, a hearty one, and when it drew the frown from Hendricks and the cool look of surprise from Starling, she found she still couldn't quite get it under control, the wracking hilarity bubbling up from within like its origin was somewhere in her toes.

She was doubled over, feeling the pull and tug of muscles warring over her direction. Consciously, she wanted to be upright again, but the humor—God, the sheer humor of it!—pulled her earthward. Why was it so funny to her? Even as she laughed, she knew it wasn't really *that* funny.

"Care to share the joke with the rest of the class?" Hendricks asked. He looked odd without his cowboy hat, his brown hair pointing in every direction, matted down in front where the Stetson had pushed it flat and spiked in back where his stint on his back at her parents' house had given him a wicked case of bed head. This, too, gave her an inescapable bout of giggles, adding right to what was already a losing battle with mirth.

"It's funny because she's a redhead, and she said—" Alison felt her lips stretch, her belly feeling that slow ache from the hilarity of it all. "Like Little Orphan Annie, because she's a redhead and 'only a day away'... Never mind." She drew herself upright again. "It was probably one of those things you can only appreciate in the moment."

"I do not understand," Starling said, staring coldly at her.

"I figured the meaning behind that one might go sailing over your head," Alison replied. Why would a super-powered hooker know the words? "It was just ..." She sniffled a little, her nose running in the night from the laughter of the moment. She could look back on it now with the appropriate perspective; it wasn't that funny, but everything else was just too crazy for it not to have made a strange, hilarious diversion.

"There is a threat at hand," Starling said.

"Is this the one that's gonna cause me to lose all hope?" Hendricks asked. He didn't sound too impressed to Alison. "Because I can't keep track of all these scary things anymore."

Starling just kept those dark eyes nailed on him. Alison didn't like that look, it was just a little too appraising for her taste. "This is the next of your trials."

"I don't really go in for trials," Hendricks said with a low sigh. He was walking upright now, like a real boy and everything. Already a far cry from the shattered mess that had required her help just to get into the house a few minutes earlier. "I'm just a demon hunter. Trials mean someone's putting me through something I don't care to go through. I just fight."

"You will experience trials," Starling said, like that was the last word on the matter. "You will be tested."

"This conversation is doing a mighty fine job of that," Hendricks said.

"The town is in danger," Starling said, like it was some kind of conclusion. Alison just watched her, feeling a little like a kid while her parents were arguing, talking adult stuff in serious tones.

"This town is always in trouble," Hendricks said with a sigh. He was recovered enough to drop that wall of anger that had cropped up when Spellman had been telling him how it was. Alison had watched that, too, wondering if the cowboy was going to push the man. (Was Spellman a man? The OOCs kept calling him a screen, whatever that was.) She hadn't cared for the odds, but she also had a contingency plan in case things had snaked in a downward direction on that one. She eased her hand onto it now, a slapjack she had ready to hammer Hendricks on the head if he got stupid again. She was not signed up to die if the cowboy got a sudden case of the moronic.

"And it is in trouble again," Starling said.

"I saw this episode last week," Alison said, "and the week before."

"The threat is new," Starling said.

"Please tell me it's the bicyclists," Hendricks said.

"It is not the Night Riders," Starling said. "Their threat is isolated, restricted only to those who cross their path."

"The … 'Night Riders'?" Hendricks asked, dully. "Do they call themselves that or is that your name for them?"

"It is their own designation," Starling said. Alison realized she sounded a little like a robot from science fiction movie.

Hendricks let loose a long cackle. Not quite the belly laugh she'd experienced, but a fair guffaw that had him bending at the knees a little. "Man. The 'Night Riders'. What's their leader's name? KITT?"

"His name is unpronounceable with your tongue," Starling continued, as if she hadn't just been laughed at, "but he likes to call himself Michael."

Alison felt herself snicker a little at that one, and she was joined by Hendricks, who shot her a look, the bridge of his nose crinkled with laughter. "Fan of the 'Hoff, huh?"

"Probably from Germany," Alison cracked.

"They are most recently from Germany, yes," Starling said flatly, sending Alison into a deeper laugh. Hendricks, alongside her, howled with laughter. "How did you know?" The redhead had her face cocked to one side, analyzing the situation. Still robotic.

"Lucky guess," Hendricks said, shaking his head as he straightened. "All right, so these Night Riders are pulping people all over Midian, but they're not the world-ending threat that will shake my belief in everything. Fine, then. What is?"

"I cannot give you the answer," she said.

"Of course not, because that would be far, far too easy," Hendricks said, throwing up his hands. His black coat sleeves fell to mid-wrist, revealing dried blood in the dark hairs of his arms. Alison wondered where that had come from. "What can you tell me, lady of mystery—and the night?"

"The fate of Midian is tied to another town, long buried in the past," Starling said, the words flowing like they weren't coming from a human voice and throat, but from somewhere deep inside the creature that was Lucia on her off days. "This place is a nexus, a summoning ground for all the darkness that calls forth the true believers."

"Believers in what?" Alison ventured to ask. She did not get an answer. She got ignored.

"Some come by what appears to be chance," Starling said. "But there is no chance. It is calculation. Forces move in the shadows that conspire to bring ruin to Midian, to hasten its fall, its demise, knowing what that will bring."

"God, let it bring pizza," Hendricks said, shaking his head. When Alison gave him a questioning look, he just shrugged and said, "I'm hungry." Turning back to Starling, he asked, "Any chance you can tell us what will happen if Midian falls?"

"The world will end," Starling said simply, like it was nothing. Like a natural consequence, like a math problem. A plus B equals the end of the world. No big.

"Midian falls, the world dies," Hendricks said, and by now he was so jaded, so worn, possibly disbelieving—Alison couldn't quite get the read on him—that he got matter-of-fact about it, too. "Got it. And you're some sort of benevolent hooker angel, sent to help us even the score."

"I am Starling," she said, like that answered that.

"Cool," Hendricks said in a tone that suggested it was anything but. "All right, well, I get the sense you've just about reached the limit of what you're going to share, so … spit it out." He waited, and the redhead said nothing. "Well, go on, give us the last little bit of the puzzle we need to start stumbling around in the dark to solve your little mystery game."

Starling just stared at him. "You will need to go to Hobbs Green, Alabama, in order to understand what comes to Midian."

Hendricks blinked. Alison noted it like she'd note a butterfly floating by as a catastrophic storm destroyed everything she cared about. "Hobbs Green," she breathed.

"Well, that's a little more than we usually get from the mystery box," Hendricks said.

She heard him at a distance, ten thousand miles away from the vision of carnage that was flashing through her mind. She could see the smoke and fire, all lit up in her head, black ash in clouds and fallen on the ground in every direction in her mind. She could taste it, see the black specks falling on her suntanned skin, see it smear when she touched it to brush it away. It was memory, it was real, it was bile rushing up from her stomach and doubling her over again in a way that was nothing like what she'd felt moments earlier—

She fell to her knees and exploded in a gush of vomit, her stomach hurling everything out in a wave of sudden and uncontrolled nausea. The yellow liquid splattered on the white porch and splashed like a bucket poured everywhere. The acidic smell washed over her, the awful taste of that stringy, empty, viscous liquid that was heaving out of the back of her throat overcame her.

"Holy shit!" Hendricks said, and she watched his boots dance backward, thumping on the porch floorboards as she made her mess.

A few more heaves and she was empty; she hadn't had much to begin with, but she finished as abruptly as she began, trying to hold in the last little bit of fluid and keep herself from dumping her entire stomach out there in the half-light of the porch. She sat there for a brief second before the self-consciousness came rushing in, and she become keenly aware of Hendricks staring down at her, his messy hair framing his rough, unshaven face. His lips were slightly parted, both eyebrows keening skyward as he asked his question with his expression rather than his mouth. *What the hell?*

"Sorry," she said, brushing the dot-like splatters on her hand away on her worn blouse. She never liked this one anyway, and it had blood on it now. "We gotta go."

"What?" Hendricks asked, and his head whiplashed around, searching for something that wasn't there. "Where the hell did Starling go?"

"Back to the whorehouse, probably," Alison said, shaking her head as she fought to her feet. She fumbled in her pocket, brushing past the slapjack, and came up with her cell phone. She had it dialed before she even got to the car and was speaking as she was climbing into the dinged-up mess of the Lincoln. "Arch? We need to meet," she said, putting the key in the ignition and starting the thing before Hendricks was even in. He was a step or two slow, and she was tempted to throw it in reverse before he was even in the car. He took a second too long to gather his drover coat around him and she hit the gas, sending the car backward down the drive and whipping around in an empty space in the yard, closing the door on Hendricks's side handlessly, prompting a yelp from him. He fumbled for his seatbelt as he watched her with cautious, wide eyes. "Call Lerner and Duncan," she said and then just hung up on her husband as she gunned the town car's engine, sending a cloud of dust billowing behind them as she raced down the farmhouse's driveway.

***

Lerner was just staring up at the ceiling. He was still trying to figure out the popcorn thing, but only because he wasn't in a mood to watch TV. Something about the peril hanging around his immortal essence didn't entice him to want to laugh with nerdy humans on that Big Bang show or get overly involved in the drama surrounding a cooking contest.

Duncan was in the next bed over, freshly returned. The epoxy had been applied, and now it was a waiting game. Waiting to see if it held, if it would do any good. His money was still on "maybe."

"Want to talk?" Duncan asked. None of the lights were on; they were sitting there in the dark, the only illumination the occasional set of headlamps from passing cars that would drag slowly from one side of the room to the other, shifting the shadows as they passed.

"You never want to talk," Lerner said, more offhand than he meant. That was bad. If Duncan was willing to talk, and he'd seen the crack while he was applying the epoxy …

"But we could," Duncan said. It had the air of an easy suggestion, something put out without effort or care. No problem, let's just chitchat while we wait for you to do the demon equivalent of spontaneous combustion.

"Anything to break the sense of misery, huh?" Lerner said. He cracked a smile then frowned, not wanting to do anything associated with the word "crack."

"It's not that bad," Duncan said. Only someone who hadn't known him for a century could fail to catch all the subtle nuance in the way it was said. "It's not the—"

"End of the world?" Lerner asked. He felt his lips push hard against one another, puckering with emotion he didn't normally feel. It was a sense of anger, sure—and that he felt all the time. But there was something else there, too, something deeper. "You remember that one time, in Oklahoma …?" He didn't even bother to finish the thought.

"With the shopping mall," Duncan said, picking it up with their easy shorthand.

"And the lady with those massive clogs!" Lerner said, feeling himself chuckle, just a little, his shell's natural reaction to that levity. "Her feet were the size of hams, all shoved into those things—"

"Was she a dancer, you think?" Duncan asked.

"Maybe in her youth," Lerner said, "about two hundred extra pounds before we met her. The heels on those things must have been industrial grade to keep from breaking until they did." They both lapsed into silence. "You remember that sound she made? When she died? When that … chis'thago tore her throat out?" He spoke soberly, the levity all faded. "I think about that sound sometimes." He stared at the ceiling. "She was trying to say something, you know, staring up at us, the only 'living' witnesses to her death, that clog busted on her fat foot, twitching as she lay there dying."

"It was a gruesome thing," Duncan said.

"We've seen worse," Lerner said, a little huskily. "But that noise! That noise she made. It was like …" He played it back in his head, that wail. "It was like pleading, but without the words." He pressed his puckered lips together and found them dry. He didn't really need water, but for some reason just now the fact that his lips were parched bothered the hell out of him. "I think about that sound. That pleading sound. Like it was her way of saying, 'I only want a few more minutes, please, please, just a few more minutes.' Bargaining. Hoping for just a little more."

Duncan was quiet for a moment. "That was a long time ago."

"I know," Lerner said. He felt the stir. "I know." He shifted his head just long enough to look at Duncan. "I just want a few more minutes." He could feel the hint of a plea as it formed on his lips.

"You've got time—" Duncan said, not looking at him.

"I really don't," Lerner said, and Duncan turned his head so quickly Lerner thought it might snap off. He was off the bed in a roll and next to Lerner in a hot second. Demon speed. It almost wasn't fast enough.

"The epoxy—" Duncan said, and he tore his eyes from Lerner's face down to where the wound was. Lerner couldn't see it, but he could feel it, sucking away like it was a sinkhole, dragging in the skin around it— "Oh, shit," was all that Duncan said.

"I just wanted a few more minutes," Lerner said, and he felt that sinking feeling run all the way through him. A hundred years—the best hundred years he could have imagined, out of the pits, out of the fires, out of the—

He watched Duncan's wordless face as black flames filled his vision in all directions, dragging him back to the waiting hell. Duncan's eyes were the last thing he saw before he left—wide, weary, and infected with that human sentimentality that Lerner had spent the last century resisting with everything he had. As the flames ate him up, he wished—oh, how he wished!—that he had just let go as Duncan had, because the place that he would be going now would have been just the same, but at least he would have felt—

12.

They met out on MacGruder's farm like usual, Arch kicking the dirt while he waited. Hendricks looked calm, his cowboy hat retrieved from Arch's car, his face a twisted knot of thoughts that had yet to bleed. He squeezed the banana bag of IV solution in his hand, not too hard, cupped it like it was a softball or a soft fruit, aware it was there and fiddling nervously but not harshly with it.

Arch, for his part, was sick of kicking the dirt. He had taken to studying Alison's staid face in glimpses here and there. She had a little something hanging on the corner of her mouth, and she hadn't made to kiss him. He knew they were on a strange road, a rough path maybe, but that wasn't like her. He could catch a whiff here and there, though, when the wind shifted, and had a suspicion kissing was not something he would have wanted to do even if she'd been amenable.

A dog howled in the distance, a couple plots of land down the road. He'd stirred the dust as he'd shot down it to the meet-up, hammering his way out of town as soon as he'd gotten Alison's call. It sounded urgent; he'd hurried up and now he was waiting, waiting with the other two. Three of the six they'd had the other day when they'd been here, just waiting to see when Lerner and Duncan would show up.

Arch's uniform clung to him like it was midday and the sun was hanging overhead instead of a half-moon with a vague crescent casting silver light on the clouds that had it surrounded.

"Did you get ahold of Lerner?" Hendricks asked, finally, breaking that awful nervous silence. Arch didn't care for it, for once. He had a feeling—just a hint—that he was going to get some of that from the sheriff for a while. He was supposed to be on shift right now, but he'd heard not a word directed toward him on the radio all night. That was the sheriff's wife on dispatch, after all, and maybe a suggestion of her husband's current sentiment filtering through.

Or maybe he was reading too much into it. "Got Duncan," Arch said. "Said he's on his way."

Hendricks nodded. "How'd he sound?"

Arch pondered that; it didn't quite compute. "Like Duncan, I reckon."

"Huh," Hendricks said. "I wonder how Lerner is doing."

"Not good when we left him," Alison said.

"He had a crack in him?" Arch asked. It had sounded a most peculiar thing to have, something positively bizarre—but no good at all.

"Don't we all?" Hendricks said with a smirk.

"If he's cracked, does that mean he'll break open?" Alison asked. She said it a kind of wandering voice that he recognized as fatigued.

"If he does, he'll burn like the rest of them," Hendricks said, but Arch caught the ring of uncertainty in the way he said it.

"You sure?" Arch asked.

"Think I heard 'em say it before," Hendricks said with a shrug. "They're demons, right? Break 'em open like a piñata and that black fire swallows 'em back to hell. Rules of the game."

"Yeah," Arch said a little sourly, "and the others rules of the game include the idea that guns don't kill demons, right?"

Arch could see the cowboy's jaw tighten in advance of his answer. "Just because I've been in this game for longer than the rest of you, don't assume I know everything." Hendricks folded his arms in front of him, gingerly moving to avoid damage to the banana bag. "Though I have to admit, the learning curve had leveled out considerably until I got here. Things are happening in this town I hadn't even heard of before."

"What's the new deal?" Arch asked, figuring he might as well pry while they waited. Who knew how punctual a demon was? They could be here until the dawn.

"Starling paid us a visit," Hendricks said, moving his hands to expose the IV pouch again. "While we were picking this up for Erin."

Arch felt his face twist involuntarily. "What did she have to say?"

"Nothing good, as per usual," Hendricks said. "Promised us the end of the town is in the offing. Suggested it would lead to the end of the world if Midian goes down."

"That's a new wrinkle," Arch said, but he could see by a flicker on Hendricks's face that it might not have been all that new. "She give any hints on how it's gonna happen?"

"Name of a town," Hendricks said, glancing over at Alison. "Hobbs Green, Alabama. Ring any bells?"

Arch felt the frown crease his forehead. "Not for me. Why?"

"Because—" Hendricks started to say, but he was cut off by the sound of something laboring along the road. A thin, ticking sound, repetitive, like spokes on a wheel— "Holy shit, is that a bicycle?"

Arch had his gun pulled, low rest, facing down the driveway before he saw the figure on the bike in the half-light. He took aim, and saw Alison out of the corner of his eye already going for the town car's trunk while Hendricks matched his aim with his own .45.

"Cool your boots, gents," the figure on the bike said, emerging into the moonlit night, his lime-colored suit bleached of its color in the placid light.

"Duncan, what the fuck?" Hendricks asked, not lowering the barrel of his 1911. He didn't look too happy in Arch's view; then again, when Arch sifted the jumble in his chest, somewhere below that hammering heart was a flash of anger of his own at the demon. "A bike? Now? Of all times?"

"You have my car," Duncan said, bringing the bicycle to a stop with a skid on the dirt driveway. "Walking would have taken longer, and stealing a car would have drawn more attention, so ..." He shrugged, near-emotionless, though Arch saw a flash in his eyes. "You call, and I appear."

"You could have asked for a ride, man," Hendricks said, still not holstering his gun. Arch dropped the barrel of his, and watched Alison slam the trunk of the town car, the sound reverberating over them. The cowboy was fixated on the shiny metal frame of the bicycle, his eyes anchored on it like they'd caught on a hook.

It was an old bike, not exactly modern standard. Duncan stood there, astride the thing. "Where's Lerner?" Arch asked. "He on bed rest?"

"He's gone," Duncan said, a pronouncement with no more enthusiasm or note than if he'd declared the night dark. True, and boring.

"Gone where?" Hendricks said, still a little sizzle in his reply.

Duncan just shrugged a lime-suited shoulder. "Fires of hell. Stygian depths. Home office. Whatever you want to call it."

Alison spoke first. "Jesus." He didn't even give her a hard look for taking the Lord's name in vain on that one.

"Quite the opposite, toots," Duncan said in a reasonable approximation of Lerner's accent.

"Is he gone for good?" Hendricks asked. "I mean, can you come back from that?"

Duncan did not blanch, just stared flatly ahead. "No. No, they don't let you come back from that. Being an OOC is like parole; you get broken here, you get dropped back to the … well, let's just say you don't want to go back." His lips turned into a thin line. "Lerner didn't want to go back."

"Fuck," Hendricks said, shaking his head as the brim of his hat hid his face in shadow. "Fuck, fuck, fuck."

"Eloquent and accurate," Duncan said.

"We're down another ally," Arch said, dully, not quite sure what else to say.

"We need to get this to Erin," Hendricks said, holding up the banana bag. "Need to get it to her now."

Arch stared at it, glinting in the moonlight, and thought he saw something else in the liquid, something he couldn't see when he squinted closer at it.

"Where did you get that?" Duncan asked, with the closest thing to feeling he'd exhibited since he'd arrived.

Hendricks waited a full five seconds before answering. "You know where I got it."

Duncan let a pregnant pause hang before he replied. "You're looking fit compared to when last I saw you."

"I'm a real physical specimen," Hendricks said, and Arch caught the interplay between the two of them, not a clue of what any of it meant.

"Don't drink any more of that stuff," Duncan said, and he turned his head away from the cowboy, like he was done. Just done. "But you should get that to Harris right away."

Arch blinked. "I can probably do it, I guess." He reached out for the bag and Hendricks handed it off to him. It was a little cool to the touch, springy plastic wrapped around liquid, and it sloshed as he took it in hand. "What's this other thing you're into? Nob Green or whatever it is?"

"Heh," Hendricks said. "Hobbs Green. And you should ask your woman about that, because I get the sense she knows more than she's saying."

Arch dragged his eyes around to Alison, who was staring into space like she hadn't heard. "You know something about this place Starling mentioned?"

"Starling?" Duncan asked. "That redhead? She show up again?"

"Cryptic warning and all," Hendricks said. "Town's gonna be destroyed, world's gonna end."

"Is that all?" Duncan asked with a shrug. "I thought it was serious since you called me in the middle of the night."

"The world we're currently resting our shoes on coming to an end doesn't strike you as serious?" Arch asked.

"I was joking," Duncan said, still inscrutable. "It's probably important to keep it spinning. How is it ending, and what does that have to do with the town?"

"That's the 'cryptic' part of the warning," Hendricks said. "She gave us that Hobbs Green thing as a bonus, like it was some sort of blueprint for how things are going to go."

"What did you do to this bitch to make her hate you so bad?" Duncan said, and his voice scratched as he said it, dragging Arch's head back around from the uncharacteristic nature of what was said. Duncan was mild. Duncan was polite. Now Duncan was swearing and tossing in something like that?

"Hell if I know," Hendricks said, raising his shoulders up in a shrug, like he could just drop all the weight off them.

"She said you had to go through trials." Alison spoke up at last, a thin thread of a voice in a chorus of louder, deeper ones. Everyone heard her, though.

"Trials?" Duncan's eyes narrowed. He was thinking something, that much was obvious, but exactly what was going through his head was as much a mystery to Arch as it was ... probably at any other time. "It's never simple," the demon muttered.

"What's never simple?" Hendricks asked, the cowboy tilting his head toward Duncan like he was waiting for collected wisdom to spray out and hit him in the face. Arch had a sense that he was about to be disappointed.

"Nothing. Nothing is ever simple," Duncan said, shaking his head. "We got a flock of vembra'nonn tearing through town on bikes and now something about to end the world. I long for the days of an ychoraba dispute."

"What's an ychoraba dispute?" Alison asked.

"Family quarrel," Duncan answered. "But they're all sex partners in addition to being related."

"How the fuck is that simple?" Hendricks asked.

"They're partially human, and they're inbred, so their intelligence is low," Duncan said, almost sighing. "Ergo, they're ..." He just laid it out there and waited for them to stumble into it like a landmine.

"Simple," Arch said. "Classy joke." Duncan nodded his head but didn't smile. "So what do we do about these bikers and the end of the world?"

"I want the bikers," Duncan said tightly.

"That's what she said," Alison tossed in.

"You want the world to end?" Hendricks asked, ignoring her and directing his inquiry to the demon.

"No," Duncan said. Not quite as tightly.

"We need to make like the doctors and do triage," Hendricks said, sweeping his gaze over all of them. "I don't like these bloody messes that the Tour de Midian is leaving, but I like the thought of the whole town being flattened or destroyed even less, especially if it triggers the end of the world somehow." He glanced at everyone but Arch, and for just a second Arch got the sense the cowboy really was holding something back. "I want to beat their bicycle-pants-wearing-asses too, but I've done the whole vengeance thing, and I'm over it." Arch sensed he was not over it. At all. "We have priorities here."

"You may be over it, but I'm not," Duncan said simply. "Set your own priorities, and I'll set mine." He started to shift his weight to ride off.

"Hold up a second, Duncan," Arch said, stalling for time, hoping a brilliant idea would descend from heaven just before the demon rode off with a quarter of their remaining strength. Probably more. "I don't think you're gonna get your revenge on the bikers if the world comes to an end." It sounded lame even to his ears, though it had that ring of truth to it.

Duncan halted, the front handlebars angled up the driveway toward the road. "Go on."

"Well," Arch said, trying to spin the wheels a little faster, "do you think these things are gonna leave town?"

Duncan stared at him evenly. "Unlikely. They don't have much reason to."

"Even with everything we did to them?" Arch asked. The mess up on Mount Horeb would have scared away any criminal with even a tenth of a functioning intelligence. Only a real fool liked to do their odious deeds in the presence of those who would catch them.

"Where else would they go?" Duncan asked, like it was an answer in and of itself.

"I dunno," Hendricks said, droll, "any one of the other eighteen hotspots currently running?"

"Something is going on here," Duncan said. "Something home office either doesn't know or isn't telling me. This place is getting the draw. Eighteen hotspots, there should be a more even distribution of chaos. But things are gravitating here for some reason." He chewed his lip like it was invincible, tearing into it with a savagery that made Arch want to take a step back from him, in case he started crackling with black flames. "No, they're not going to leave. Find a new place to hide, probably. Leave ... I don't think so. You'll be scraping up their victims for a while yet, deputy." He placed a peculiar, needling emphasis on that last word, looking at Arch as he said it.

Arch didn't care for it, but he didn't want to lose sight of his objective, either. Keeping a player from storming out of the locker room when they were already behind on the scoreboard was more important than replying to the cheap goad. "So they can wait just a bit for us to deal with them."

Duncan moved his head forty-five degrees, clicking like a machine, turning to focus on Hendricks. "You sure want to let this pass to the back burner? After what they did to your girl?"

Hendricks's jaw looked ready to sprain, like the bone was going to break and come shooting right out of the skin he was pressing his teeth together so hard. "I don't *want* to," he said when he finally managed to pry his lips apart. "But there are bigger things going on here than a bunch of shitheads who have a hard-on to get their morning ride in. Let's settle this 'end of the world' business first." His jaw muscles worked in obvious ways under his skin. "Then we'll make hood ornaments out of the rest of these fuckers."

Duncan just stared at him for a long moment. "Sounds like a plan," he said at last, and Arch could feel the sense of relief wash over him, even as he fumbled a little nervously with the IV bag.

***

"You wanna talk about it?" her mother's voice had the maddening edge of reason to it, like she was making clear sense, but Lauren wanted no part of reason, nor sense. They were on the way home from the hospital and Lauren just wanted to go to bed. To forget this day had happened, to forget what she'd seen up on the mountain, and go on about her life like that buzzing swarm of bicyclists had never descended that road and made her feel … something. Desperate.

Afraid.

Yeah, that was it.

"No, I don't want to talk about it," Lauren said, keeping her eyes straight ahead. Dusk was long past, and it was closer to midnight now. Her relaxing run had turned into a several-hour clusterfuck, an inadvertent return to work when she least wanted to be there. She'd had plans, dammit, plans that didn't involve ministering to the medical emergencies that seemed to revolve around Nicholas-goddamned-Reeve and his entire department.

Still … there was something about the whole thing that picked at her, itched in her brain. Those agents. The guy in the black coat. The wreck.

The bicyclists. What the hell had been so damned fearsome about a bunch of men dressed like they were out for an evening ride? What was it about that buzzing, that noise that had made her want to leap off a sheer cliff face, casting aside every thin fiber of reason that remained with her?

"You sure?" Vera asked again. Persistent.

"I'm sure," she said as the car's headlights swept around a turn onto their street. The row of white houses was settled under a dark sky, the green grass swallowed up by the night and given color again by their headlights as they passed each house in turn.

"Suit yourself," her mother said, like it was her loss for not wanting to delve into the details of watching a young—damned young—sheriff's deputy fighting for her life. That had been a hell of a thing, watching the car come tumbling down the mountain. And the fact that she'd felt driven to hide behind it as those cyclists came roaring down around her—

Lauren felt her face crease in a frown. Why had she felt compelled to hide from men on bicycles? Everything was so damned muddled—

The car's headlights swept along in a turn as they pulled into the driveway, and all thoughts of bodies, deputies, blood and jumping a cliff flew right out of her head as the lamps illuminated a figure hanging off the trellis that ran up the front of the house, furtive, deer-in-the-headlights look in those big eyes that Lauren had known from the time she was a baby, nursing out of a bottle.

"What. The. Fuck," Lauren said succinctly as she watched Molly freeze on the trellis, hanging motionless for just a moment before dropping the three feet back to the ground, giving up on her climb.

She hit the ground with a thump that was all in Lauren's head. She could hear it in her mind, the sound a reverberating bass hit like the hammering of a drum. A damned furious drum, beating over and over with each heartbeat. "Stop the car," she told her mother.

"Well, I was just gonna park it under the carport anyway, but since you asked so nicely." She threw it in park and Lauren felt the shudder of the transmission shifting into place, that slight drop as the car steadied out. She could feel her mother's eyes burning on her, boring into the side of her head as she stared at her own daughter out in the headlights. "Well, go on. Make a scene on the front lawn, wake the neighbors."

"I'm not gonna—" she shot a furious look at her mother.

"Well, you damned well should," her mother threw back, common sense. "If anything warrants, this is it. You just caught your daughter out well past midnight. When are you gonna start acting like her momma instead of a slightly disinterested commentator on her life? 'Oh, looks like she might have done a bad one here; let's she what she does next.' Maybe it'll be coming home pregnant at sixteen, because *that* won't make her life harder at all—"

"Oh, just shut up!" Lauren said, throwing the car door open. She felt her long black hair spill over her shoulders, stirred by the breeze soughing its way down the street. "What are you doing?" she asked, keeping it calm. Calmer than she wanted to be. Not wild enough for a YouTube video, anyhow.

"Hey," Molly said, the practiced, sheepish look. She'd done it since she was a kid. Probably because it worked. So innocent, oh yes, couldn't possibly have done anything wrong. "I, uh … guess I'm kinda busted, huh?"

"That's one word for it," Lauren said. "Busted." She was still calm, determined not to throw a white trash scene here on the front lawn, a hissy fit of epic proportions. "'Fucked' would be another."

Molly's sheet-white face reddened and changed into a sneer. "What?"

"I said you're fucked." Lauren closed the car door gently as she heard the motor die. "Screwed. Nailed. Boned. I can go on, if you want, there's really no shortage of euphemisms to cover how shafted you are, kid."

"It's nice how they all tie right to the same act," Molly said, and she folded her arms and looked away. Down the street and into the dark, like she was gonna run for it. Her body showed no sign of tension; just the opposite, in fact. She was braced for the tirade she seemed sure was coming.

"It seemed appropriate, what with you sneaking back into your window at this hour," Lauren said, meeting her with folded arms of her own. She was in scrubs, her running clothes a write-off with all the blood on them. It was like she could still smell it right now, though. "Or were you just somewhere innocent, whiling away the dull hours after curfew?"

"I don't technically have a curfew," Molly said with a sideways, smug smile. "You probably should have set one, huh?"

"It hadn't really been necessary until now," Lauren said, hearing her voice rise on that last point. "My honor roll student daughter was always responsible enough that I didn't manage her life in the micro—"

"Or the macro," Molly said under her breath, stepping Lauren's irritation to eleven.

"I figured you were so good at doing what was expected of you that you didn't need a warden," Lauren said.

"Who are you kidding? Grandma Vera was the warden," Molly said. "You weren't even on the parole board."

"I like how we went from a sex metaphor to prison ones," Lauren said. "I'm pretty sure you can see where the natural progression is gonna take this next."

"Yeah, it's an episode of *Orange is the New Black* around here," Molly shot back. "Are we done yet?"

"Oh, you're done," Lauren said. "You are. Done."

"Okay," Molly said, uncaring. She snugged her arms tight around her. "Then I'm going to bed." She started forward, eyes rolling automatically and giving Lauren a few feet of berth as she passed.

"You're grounded for a month," Lauren said.

"Fine," Molly said, but her voice had changed. "Whatever." She disappeared under the carport.

"It amazes me how she can say 'whatever' in the same tone I use for 'Bless your heart,'" Vera said, still leaning on the open door of her car.

"And the same way the rest of us say 'fuck you,'" Lauren replied, staring under the carport after her daughter.

"Mmm," her mother said. "It was a multipurpose expression from a gentler age."

Lauren just stood, staring straight ahead as she heard the door to the house slam. "Do you think this is gonna make any difference?"

Her mother eased up by her side, a presence she could feel as the wind blew a little cooler. "Did it for you any of the times I did the same?"

Lauren just stared. "No."

"Well, then probably not," her mother said, and patted her on the arm reassuringly. "But bless your heart for trying."

Lauren felt the nasty frown take over as she watched her mother shuffle inside without a backward look. "Bless your heart, too," she muttered, but it didn't sound nearly as sweet when she said it.

***

"Take I-75 south to Chattanooga," Alison said from the back seat. "Then it's I-59 into Alabama, I think."

"Oh, you think so?" Hendricks asked, a little mocking, into the town car's warm air. He was a little jumpy in the front seat, holding the steering wheel. Duncan had waved him to the driver's side and gotten in the passenger door, leaving Hendricks—the only one in the car without a valid driver's license—to take the wheel. Alison had gone for the back seat like it just made sense. It did make an odd amount of sense to Hendricks, kind of a weird instinctual thing, but he could no more explain why it made sense than he could explain why a redheaded hooker seemed to know the answers to questions no living person should.

"Yes," Alison replied, but she wasn't snippy about it. He caught a glimpse of her in the rearview, messing around with that honey blond hair she had hanging all about. She was still holding something back. He knew it and she knew he knew it, but she was just hanging onto it. Woman's prerogative, he supposed, not quite sure how to approach it just yet.

The car made the turn onto the interstate real smooth. It hadn't been that long since Hendricks had driven, but he was a little rusty. The last time he'd driven on a regular basis, his vehicle of choice had been a Humvee. Before that, it had been a pickup truck back in Wisconsin. Every now and again, he wondered idly what had happened to that truck.

"So we're riding into danger," Duncan said, "but we don't know what kind."

"Sounds like a happy day, don't it?" Hendricks asked, not taking his eyes off the road.

"As joyous as any occasion can be," Duncan replied, and Hendricks was not quite sure if he was being facetious. "What's the deal with this town?" That question was directed to the back seat.

"What makes you think I know anything about it?" Alison asked, almost innocent. Almost.

Hendricks caught Duncan pointing a finger at him. "He suggested you did."

Hendricks kept his hands on the wheel, resisted the urge to throw them off to make a gesture to protest his innocence. "Starling suggested it, I'm just passing it along to the committee for consideration."

Alison stared down at her lap, Hendricks could see that much in the rearview. "I've been there before. The town's wrecked, all right."

"Define 'wrecked,'" Duncan said.

"Burned," Alison said. "Filled with creatures of the sort you deal with for your job."

"Ah ha!" Hendricks crowed. "You knew about demons before I even came to town!"

"Of course I knew about demons before you came to town," Alison said flatly. "I knew what they were when they came busting through the door of my apartment. I couldn't believe they were there, but I knew what they were. Do you think it's a normal reaction to follow your husband around with a big bore rifle when you think he's just been attacked by psychopathic meth dealers?"

"No." Hendricks cast a weary eye into the mirror, receiving nothing in return. She was still looking down, and her voice was consequently muffled. "But I'm not sure it's a normal reaction to tote a .50 around in response to demons, either."

"But a smart one," Duncan said sagely.

"You knew about these things, you got into the fight, and you were just gonna ... what? Keep it quiet?" Hendricks asked. "Follow Arch around and provide covering fire as needed?"

"Somethin' like that," Alison said, still muffled.

"Why didn't you tell him you knew?" Duncan asked.

"Why is how I conduct my marriage any of your business?" Her voice was sharp.

"Maybe let's focus on what matters here," Hendricks said. "What about Hobbs Green? What are we gonna find there?"

"A burned-up town," Alison said. The shrug was implied in her tone. "There was a survivor last time I was there, but this was years ago. Kinda doubt she'll still be lurking around. Not exactly the friendly type, either."

"What was she doing there then?" Duncan asked.

"Living life," Alison said, "such as it was. I didn't really get a chance to talk to her. Got a good idea of what she had surrounding her—demons and such. Left before it got too messy."

"She have a nice standard of living?" Hendricks asked, sending a smirk at Duncan, who did not respond. "Parking her flag in a demon-torched town?"

"Do you?" Alison sent right back at him. "Hopping from cheap motel to cheap motel?"

Hendricks felt a little zing as that one grazed him. "Sometimes I upgrade to a flophouse."

"Here's the question that's been nettling me since we met, demon hunter," Alison stopped focusing on her lap and leaned forward to place her hands on the back of the front seat. "Are you really in Midian to save the town? Or do you just want to kill demons?"

"What kind of question is that?" Hendricks brushed it off, looking at Duncan with a "Can-you-believe-this-shit?" look.

"Probably a serious one," Duncan said.

Hendricks felt that one scrape him harder than the comment about his living arrangements. "What the hell are you here for, Mr. Demon? To keep the status quo so as not to disrupt the market price for human meat?"

"Wouldn't want the price of hindquarter to go too high," Duncan said. "Some poor huagh'tii in the Kentucky backwoods might not be able to afford to feed its litter."

"And you ask me if I'm here to save the town?" Hendricks asked, turning his head slightly to look at Alison.

She just stared back, cool. "He's a demon. I know what to expect from him, I think."

"I wonder if you do," Hendricks said, guiding the car through the night. He could see Arch's headlights behind him and hoped the deputy was enjoying his nice, quiet drive.

13.

Arch pulled into the hospital parking lot forty-five minutes later. He stopped the car and just sat there after he'd pulled the keys from the ignition, feeling the weight of the married key and fob between his fingers as he stared up at the lighted windows of the Red Cedar Medical Center. A hospital by any other name, he figured.

The nurses all saw his uniform, and it activated that extra solicitousness that came with the vague and insubstantial threat of arrest. Or maybe it was just a desire to help those who protected society. Whatever the case, Arch was directed to Erin's room with little trouble. He had figured she might be in surgery but she wasn't; she'd been stuck in a private room off the ICU all by herself, with monitors adding their subtle beeps to indicate she was, indeed, still alive.

The wheeze of the machine helping her breathe was as regular as the beeping, and she had tubes running every which way to and from her. It wasn't hard to find the IV tree, nor replace the bag subtly and quickly; a simple snap of the plastic fasteners put the new one on and let him pull the old one off. It was easy, even for a layman like Arch. He stepped into the bathroom and drained the old bag by squeezing it into the toilet, then washed it off and wiped it down before dropping it into the trashcan and covering it with paper towels. Better safe than sorry.

He heard movement outside, and the hammering in his ears made him worry for a split second about the danger of a heart attack. He was done, the job was finished, and all that was left was escape. He had felt surprisingly little emotion throughout the process, not equating the thing lying out there with tubes running in and out of it with Erin Harris, the bright, vivacious deputy who had thoughts and feelings and ambitions, and who had spent enough nights in Fast Freddie's to qualify for a frequent flyer card, if they'd had such a thing.

Looking in the bathroom mirror, Arch took a moment to compose himself. His face was drenched in sweat, whether from the hot, late summer night or the stress of the deception inherent in his mission, he couldn't say. He wiped his dark brow with a paper towel and watched it fall into the metal trashcan, adding another shovelful to the grave of the old IV bag. He took a breath and heard it, a strangled moan from his own throat that made him sound like he'd exerted himself running a marathon or something.

He pulled open the door to the room and saw Nicholas Reeve waiting for him there. His thudding heart became a booming one, and he hoped he controlled his reaction better than he felt like he had.

"Arch," Reeve said to him. The sheriff was turned away from him, giving him his left shoulder and only a half glance as he remained facing toward Erin's bed.

"Sheriff," Arch said, a little formally, and with his voice a little high to his own ears. "You just checking in on her, too?"

"Figured somebody ought to," Reeve said. "Her momma and daddy are out of town, trying to catch a flight back from Sacramento or some such place. Of course, her brothers are all gone, too, away in various corners of the map. Sounds like they'll be a while getting here, if at all."

"Huh," Arch said in muted acknowledgment. If it'd been him in the bed instead of Erin, he imagined only his in-laws would be around for it. Them and Alison and Reeve.

"How long you been here?" Reeve asked. His head was slightly bowed, like he was in prayer, and he did not look at Arch as he spoke.

"Few minutes," Arch said. "Not long at all. She going in to surgery?"

"I guess they stitched up all they could stitch up," Reeve said. "They did a ..." Even without turning, Arch could see Reeve's brow crumple as he tried to recall, "some sort of ... well, they pumped fluid into her belly, and it came out not bloody, which is good. So now she's just got a lot of exterior wounds and some broken bones and a head injury to beat the band." The sheriff made a slight slurping noise as he licked his lips. "Even without the threat of internal injuries, I guess she's running against the odds here."

Arch felt his eyes inadvertently creep toward the IV bag he'd just hung. "Doesn't sound too promising."

"No," Reeve said, "it doesn't."

Arch waited for an accusation, for elaboration, for anything. It did not come. He shuffled away from the bathroom door, heading for the other side of Erin's hospital bed. The main lights were off, only a dim incandescent overhead bulb was shining on the scene. He could see the shadows on her face, on Reeve's face, from the solitary light. The sheriff's brow, in particular, still looked lined like something had dug trenches across it, shadowed in a darkness so deep he could not see how far down they went. "About what happened—"

"You don't want to start swimming across that particular river at the moment, Arch," the sheriff said, clipping him off.

Arch waited, mouth slightly agape, his bottom teeth testing his lip. He fought off the urge to bite in nervousness. "Pardon me?"

Reeve's eyes lifted off the near-lifeless body on the bed and searched him. "Rule number one when you're in a deep hole is stop digging your ass deeper and put down the shovel."

Arch swallowed, he hoped unnoticeably. "I don't understand."

"You sure you want to take that tack?" Reeve asked. He still held himself amazingly still, almost inscrutable.

"What tack?" Arch asked, holding back that ounce of defiance he felt surging through him at the challenge.

"All right, then," Reeve said, lowering his eyes and nodding like it was some inevitability. "If that's the way you want to play it."

"Play what?" Arch felt himself grow warmer. The shadows in the room grew longer with every lie, creeping around him as the room seemed to contract in his view.

"I put a lot of faith in you, Arch," Reeve said, averting his gaze and letting it fall on the TV hanging off the wall at the foot of the bed. The screen was black.

"I know that, sir."

"I've known you for a long time, son," Reeve said, laying it on thick with the "son," even though he wasn't looking at Arch. "So here's what I see. I've got a deputy I've backed to the hilt, one I thought was an honest man. Now every other thing he tells me is a lie." Reeve's eyes flashed and they found Arch, coming off the darkened TV screen like a boxer coming out of the corner at the dinging of the bell. "Don't even try and argue it. You're an awful goddamned liar, though I think with the practice you're getting, you might just be proficient at it before too much longer."

"What exactly are you accusing me of?" Arch heard his own voice, level steady, dead inside.

"I'm not gonna peel this particular onion just yet," Reeve went on. "But I will tell you this—if she dies, I will dig so deep into this incident that you won't be able to hide in China. I will come after you, Arch. With everything I have." Reeve still stared at him, combative. "You better pray she lives."

"I already was," Arch said, too stunned to be defiant. He felt the burgeoning desire to club the man, to hit him right in the jaw solidly, to let the wrath take over. To throw it in his face what was being done, what he'd done. But he held it all back, and heard his voice get quieter. "I don't know what you think I did—"

"I don't know what you did or didn't do," Reeve said, and his eyes were once more nowhere near Arch. "Maybe this time it is exactly as you say. Maybe federal agents did drag you two into something deep, something that ended with my car and my deputy flying over a mountain cliff. If so, then this is incredibly tragic timing." His eyes flashed. "But that don't take away from the lies, Arch. A whole damned mountain of them by themselves, one you could just about fall down yourself at this point."

Arch just stared at him, a ringing in his ears telling him that it was time to flee, time to run, not time to fight. He put a foot ahead of the other and walked away from the bed with its occupant, scarcely paying attention to that slow beeping, that sound of the respirator wheezing its breaths into Erin Harris.

"I've seen good cops go corrupt before, Arch," Reeve said as Arch was nearly out the door. The fluorescent hallway was like an oasis of light, an escape from the shrouding, crippling darkness he felt was surrounding him. "You know what another word for corruption is?" Arch didn't turn, but he heard the hard edge in Reeve's voice. "Rot. And there's a hell of a lot of rotten things going on Midian lately."

Arch did not look back. He shuffled into the light of the hallway, out of the dooming darkness, and felt no better as he made his way slowly back to his car.

***

They stopped at a waffle place south of Chattanooga near daybreak. Near as Hendricks could tell, the main draw was that it was open twenty-four hours a day. The aged, yellow tables might have started out as white or they might have been meant to match the sign, but either way they were a product of an older restaurant, designed long ago and probably in need of an update.

Hendricks shuffled in behind Duncan, who had remained pretty well mum about any need for food. Hendricks reckoned he didn't have a need for it, but that didn't matter. Hendricks needed a bite, and now, so when Alison had suggested the waffle place, he'd jumped. It smelled pretty decent in the joint, too, that aroma of something good cooking.

Alison slid in to the middle of her side of the booth and Duncan moved all the way over on his, leaving Hendricks with the conclusion he was going to be sitting next to the demon. When he brought it up with a quizzical look, Alison just shrugged. "I'm married," she said, like it explained everything.

"I went to a whorehouse with you," Hendricks said with a certain smugness. Of course the waitress showed up right then.

She got a load of his cowboy hat and the drover coat, taking it all in with a once-over before moving on to Duncan. The demon had switched it up, and his suit looked purple in the restaurant's light. Hendricks felt himself hold his breath, then swept his gaze across to Alison, who was in jeans with a tight-fitting t-shirt with the name of—presumably—a band called Naked Prozac. Hendricks wondered, just idly, if that was in fact a band, and decided that if not, then the meaning was best left very, very unclear.

"So," the waitress said in an drawl, "is the circus in town?" She said it with great amusement, as though it were not an all-night restaurant at four in the goddamned morning and weird shit didn't happen all the time. She had the look of a woman who had been on her feet for a long time and was taking her boredom out in the form of smartassery. Hendricks could empathize.

"Carnival, actually," Alison said. She had her menu up and was thumbing through it. "But we're not with them."

"Y'all might be the most unlikely travel companions I've ever seen," the waitress said. She looked to be near forty, just a couple of visible streaks of grey in her dyed brown hair, just a couple of wrinkles starting to escape the thick patchwork of concealer. Her name badge proclaimed her to be Marian. Marian, queen of the waffle place just across the Alabama line, that's how Hendricks thought of her. "You fresh off the rodeo circuit, darlin'?" This she addressed the Hendricks, just the corner of her mouth turned up.

"I'm a Texas Ranger, actually," he lied.

She made a low laugh, letting her eyes drift to Duncan. "And you?"

"Bureau of Alcohol, Tobacco and Firearms," Duncan said without missing a beat.

Marian turned to Alison without missing a beat. "I suppose you're FBI?"

"Health Inspector," Alison said. "How are the burgers?"

Marian showed the first sign of suspicion. "Friendly advice, dear." She leaned forward. "Our graveyard shift cook tonight is a little new, so you might want to stick with the waffles. Let him get trained up with somebody else."

"I'll take waffles," Hendricks said.

"Waffles," Alison said.

"I'll have a burger," Duncan said. "He's gotta learn sometime," the demon added with a shrug.

"Suit yourself," Marian said and gathered up their menus. "Drinks?"

"Coffee," Hendricks said.

"Same," Alison said.

"Water," Duncan replied.

Hendricks shot him a look that was at least seventy percent frown.

"You just dare to be different there, darlin'," Marian said, giving them a last nod before she walked away, the weary motions of a woman who was only an hour or so from the end of her shift. When she got back around the counter she paused about two feet from the short order cook who was standing in front of the stove, the entire kitchen visible to everyone in the restaurant. The guy looked young, pimply and nervous, and the nervousness didn't get any better when the waitress started yelling the order at him in some sort of code phrases less than two feet from his ear.

"Well, that's a little odd," Duncan observed.

Hendricks just stared. "Is that a local thing or Southern thing?" He shifted his gaze to Alison and felt Duncan do the same.

"I dunno," she said with a shrug, her chest's movement causing the band name on her shirt to fold to read 'Nad Prac.' If Hendricks had been in a laughing mood, that might have done it.

***

Mick had come shuffling in a couple hours before dawn, especially cognizant of the fact that most of his fellows were already in bed. He tried to be quiet, tried to tiptoe and shut the door near-silently. He was patient and he had excellent muscle control—mainly because he didn't have any muscles, which made things easier. When he got to his bunk, however, both of those things were rendered pointless by the squeak of his mattress springs.

He made the vault quickly after the first squeak, settling as fast as he could. He was on the upper bunk and hadn't ever complained about it; three double-decker bunks in the trailer with five occupants, someone had to take the high beds. Mick didn't mind, though he doubted his entry tonight was going to make his buddy Rex on the bunk below him very happy.

He listened to the squeak fade under the gentle snores of Troy a couple beds down and Michael in between them. The aroma of feet and body odor was a little strong in the room, but it didn't trouble him much.

"How'd it go?" came the hushed whisper of Rex from below. He didn't have that slick sleepiness in his voice; Mick could hear the keen interest of a man who'd maybe been waiting up.

"Good," Mick replied, just as hushed. Didn't want to wake the others, after all.

"I saw you with her on the square earlier," Rex said, still whispering, hissing into the night like a snake. "Pretty little thing. How was she?"

"Dunno," Mick said, pulling his thin sheet across his body more out of habit than need. It was hotter than fuck in the trailer, like the humid swamp air had rolled up from Florida and taken up residence in the room, never to leave. "I'll find out tomorrow."

"Hot damn," Rex said, and there came a noise of him re-settling himself. "I'll root for you, boy. Get yourself in there and get some of that young pussy."

Rex was a dirty old man by Mick's reckoning. Not that he was older than Mick, but he had to be going on fifty. He stared at the young women walking around the carnival like they were filet mignon and he was a starving man. He was big around the middle, too, and Mick imagined his fat belly on a thin girl like Molly, sloshing around as he plowed in and out of her. Mick was vaguely aware that it was the sort of image that might cause disgust in others with human sensibilities. For him it was of no more interest than a math problem; quickly there, perused, and discarded once solved.

He heard Rex's breathing get a little more labored, heard the sheets move underneath him. Mick was used to this, too, living in a bunk room with four other men; their conversation was at end. He rolled over and didn't pay much attention to the sound of Rex taking matters into his hands. For Mick, this was even less of a thought worthy of consideration.

He focused his attention on Molly as the sound of Rex's breathing came to a head below him. Tomorrow night—tonight, technically—would see the end of the tale. Relief, sweet and long sought, would be coming soon. It had been a long, long time.

He listened to Rex finish with disinterest—it had been less than a minute by his reckoning—and drifted off to sleep as the pervert below him lurched off into a satisfied stupor of his own.

Tomorrow.

14.

Dawn had broken a while ago, rays of light shining from the forest on every edge of the horizon. Pine needles and the scent of something smoking in the far off distance filled Alison's nose as she stood before a rusted out, ten-foot-high chain link fence. NO TRESPASSING and KEEP OUT signs were posted at regular intervals. There was no gate built into the thing, and the road had been broken up, removed a half mile before they'd reached this point. It had been a trek based on memory—her memory—and the directions she'd gotten texted to her cell phone.

"This fence has seen better days," Hendricks commented, surveying the thing with hands on hips.

"How long do you suppose it's been here?" Duncan asked.

"Twenty years, maybe?" Alison said, not really sure. "Maybe more. It was here the last time I came. Looked a little weathered then."

"You cross it that time?" Hendricks asked.

"Of course," she replied, and took a step forward. She hesitated, staring at the barbed wire across the top. She reached into her jacket pocket and pulled out the little wire cutter she'd carried, clicking it together experimentally.

"Let me handle it," Duncan said, and extended his hand. She gave it to him and he was off, scaling the fence like it was no more difficult than the walk had been on Hendricks.

"You look nervous," Hendricks said, sidling up to her as they watched the suit-clad demon pause at the top of the fence, the sound of the cutters being applied to the barbed wire filling the air with a hearty click that echoed in the early morning.

"I don't have my rifle," Alison replied. Carrying the obscenely heavy Barrett over uneven ground on her shoulder hadn't been a proposition she'd been excited about. Then again, she wasn't excited about facing whatever was waiting inside without it, either. "You probably don't understand; you still have your sword and pistol, after all." She had a pistol as well, a Glock she'd borrowed from her daddy at the same time she'd gotten the Barrett, but she was under no illusions about what it was: a holdout weapon, no more. It wouldn't do much more than make a demon flinch back, if that.

"Believe me," Hendricks said with a sly grin, "as a Marine I know how important a rifle can be to a person."

"Okay, start climbing," Duncan said, looking back down at them. He dropped the wire cutters to the ground and they bounced an inch or two before coming to rest in a patch of weathered, near-white grass.

Hendricks just stared at them, lost in thought, before shifting his gaze to the two-foot gap in the wire at the top of the ten-foot fence. "Why didn't we just have him cut a couple foot square out of the middle of the fence?"

***

Arch was up early because sleep didn't come. He'd waited for a while, hoping it would, but unlike last night when Hendricks and Alison had gone to the brothel, it hadn't bothered to creep up on him. It hadn't shown up at all, just stood him up and left him staring at the glowing red clock face, the puckered ceiling and the empty space in the bed next to him in turn. There was only so much of that he could take, so he rose at five-thirty and showered, dressing in his uniform. There was a peculiar certainty that clung to him, even after the confrontation he'd had with Reeve the night before, and it was centered on the idea that Erin would wake up and exonerate him. All the bad feelings and that cloud of suspicion that hovered over him in Reeve's eyes would just be blown away like a cloud hanging over Mount Horeb on a windy day. That was the hope he labored under, anyhow.

And it lasted until he walked into the sheriff's station that morning and talked to Ed Fries.

"Mornin', Arch," Fries called out as he entered the near-empty room. Fries sat behind the desk munching on a McMuffin. The portly deputy ate often, which was no surprise. Hash browns spilled out of his paper bag onto the desk next to him, leaving a greasy sheen on the dirty, nicked wood top.

"Mornin', Ed," Arch returned the salutation as he passed through the counter's gate. The air conditioner was cranking full strength, blowing lukewarm air out of the vent above Arch as he crossed over to Fries. "What are you up to?"

"Holdin' down the fort," Fries said with a bite of his sandwich. His puffed cheeks moved in time like he was working on a full pack of bubble gum. "Took over for Mrs. Reeve a couple hours ago."

"So, you'll be the voice at the other end of the radio today," Arch said as he punched his timecard.

"Didn't know you were on duty," Fries said with a frown.

"Figured y'all could use all the help you could get," Arch said with a weak smile.

"I'd a thought so, too," Fries said, pausing from his eating. "Especially with that fresh body that just turned up on Lincoln Avenue this morning."

Arch felt the tingle before he'd finished processing the words. "Got another one?"

"Bloody smear on the pavement, yeah," Fries said, and his stubby fingers snatched a greasy hashbrown the diameter of a nickel off the desk and popped it in his mouth. Arch could hear it crunch, and he didn't know if it was Fries's eating habits or the thought of another murder that he hadn't even been called in on that caused his stomach to turn. He'd eaten lunch with Fries plenty of times before, though, and hadn't felt like this, so he supposed he had his answer. "What do you reckon is doing this?"

"I don't know." Arch shook his head.

"Well, you saw it up on the mountain, didn't you?" Fries pressed. Didn't stop eating to press, but he pressed.

"I don't know what I saw," Arch said. He shook his head again, and pulled his time card out of the repository and punched out. "Guess I'll head home."

"But you just got here," Fries said.

"Doesn't sound like the sheriff wants me in on this," Arch replied.

"Probably short on cash," Fries said sympathetically. "You close to overtime?"

"Nope," Arch said as he moved back through the swinging doors to the counter. "Pretty close to done, though, I think." He kept that part back until he was safely in the entry hall, with a bulletproof door between him and Fries.

***

Lauren planned the conversation in her head before it was to happen. She'd been planning it all night, in fact, in lieu of sleeping. Fatigue edged around her, swooping in and pecking at her like a carrion bird, but it had stubbornly refused to send in a big-ass predator to just finish the job and drag her carcass away to dreamland, so she'd let her mind race as she plotted out everything she wanted to say.

She'd run the gamut in these conversations from the stereotypical angry mother—"I'm worried about your safety, you lying little liar!"—to the solicitous and friendly mom—"You know I'm just concerned about your well-being…"—to the grossly inappropriate girlfriend-instead-of-mom approach—"So, how was he in bed?" The last one nearly made her vomit to even consider, so she'd settled on something between the first two. Something self-aware, something cool, something that would not set off all of Molly's parental proximity alarms, she hoped.

Also, something that would reassure her, as a mother, that the, "So, how was he in bed?" line was wholly unnecessary in this case. Because moms worry about that sort of thing, especially when their own experience has given them cause to worry.

Molly came down with slumped shoulders around the usual time. Lauren's efforts had been directed toward the stove for most of the morning—or at least the last few minutes—and she did not say anything as Molly entered the kitchen, waiting as her daughter poured a cup of coffee and with the first sip seemed to realize that something was out of the ordinary.

"What … the hell?" Molly asked.

"I'll take 'Things I said last night for $1,000, Alex,'" Lauren tossed out, with as much good humor as she could muster on no sleep. And with shit on her mind that wouldn't go away.

"What is this?" Molly asked, staring at her over the coffee mug, steam blurring her features slightly.

"It's called 'breakfast,'" Lauren said, stirring a skillet of eggs with a spatula while she took a quick glance at the timer. The toast was in the oven, and she figured another two minutes would see it done. "I don't blame you for not recognizing it, though, since we haven't really seen it 'round these here parts for a while."

Molly did not look amused. "I'm not hungry."

"Come on, kid," Lauren said, putting a note of pleading into her voice. "I know you generally like the sort of morning meal that comes wrapped in an aluminum package and has more preservatives in it than a freshly embalmed corpse." Molly blanched at that—maybe it was a little topical for the occasion. "But it's Saturday, you've got no school to run off to in a rush with homework in tow. I made fresh eggs."

"How fresh?" Molly asked, still looking either suspicious or put out. "Like ... farm fresh?"

Lauren paused before answering. "Like ... they might have been purchased at Rogerson's sometime in the last few months."

"I'll stick with the Pop-Tarts, I think."

"Oh, don't go organic-superior on me now, missy," Lauren said, pointing the spatula at her, "and especially not with your carb-infused, post-apocalyptic toaster pastry."

"Whatever," Molly said, nonplussed. She turned to leave.

"Who's the guy?" Lauren called after her. She saw her daughter's shoulders hunch just a little, and a slight slosh of coffee hit the linoleum.

Molly swore, quietly, mildly, under her breath but just loud enough that Lauren could hear it. She turned, and there was that look of half-guilt, half-wonderment. "You keep asking that. What guy?" Like she hadn't just given herself away.

"Come on," Lauren said, stepping away from the stove. "It's me. You're out of the house in the middle of the night, you think I don't know there's a guy involved somehow?"

Molly's brow arched down. "Projecting much?"

"Probably," Lauren said lightly, letting that one skate past. "I assume you're at least a little like me."

Molly's forehead was home to its very own thunderclouds. "I'm not ..." She sighed. "I'm not that much like you."

"Just a little," Lauren pressed. "So, what's his name?" She could feel the hesitation. "Come on. You had to have been seen with him in town. You know by noon your grandmother is going to have enough information on him to put out an arrest warrant to all fifty states and Interpol."

Molly made a disgusted noise, one that held just a hint of concession. She waited a minute then spoke. "Mick. His name is Mick."

"Ugh." Lauren did not even try to hide her distaste. "You cannot go out with a guy named Mick."

"Why not?" Molly asked, more than a little umbrage cracking through. Her coffee had stopped steaming, but she had just started, Lauren figured.

"Because you'd be 'Mick and Molly,' and that's just unacceptably cutesy." Lauren waited, burying the unease, letting a little smile— maddening, infuriating, she knew, and just a little too close to the edge of 'Mom trying too hard'—creep up. She just waited.

Molly's face softened, her shoulders slumped, and her head pitched forward. "Yes. How could I not have seen it before now? 'Mick and Molly.' I'll call the whole thing off immediately."

"As well you should," Lauren said with a smirk. "When are you seeing him again?" she asked, a hundred degrees cooler than she felt. If this Mick had been in front of her right now, she would have wedged the spatula firmly up his nose.

"I'm not," Molly said, a little too coolly herself. "I'm grounded, remember?"

Lauren took a slow, painful breath. Her lungs felt leaden, like someone had filled them full of air already. "When were you supposed to see him?"

"Tonight," Molly said. "At the Summer Lights Festival."

"I trust I don't know this Mick for a reason?" Lauren asked. "I mean, I don't recognize the name, so I'm assuming it's not just a nickname one of the boys at your school decided to adopt, like Razor, or Scooter, or—"

"Strangely, no one at my school goes by the name 'Razor' or 'Scooter,' though there is one who goes by the name 'Razor Scooter.'

He's about as cool as you'd expect someone with that nickname to be." That was Molly back on her feet, the fun, the snark all flowing out.

"Sounds like the equivalent of a skater when I was growing up," Lauren played along. "Totally gnarly dudes, those guys." She consciously softened her approach as she pushed a little more. "So ... Mick. I don't know him?"

"He works for the carnival," Molly said, just a little sheepish. "He's a really nice guy. He's leaving town after tonight."

Lauren felt her face go ashen inside, that sense that she'd stood up entirely too fast after sitting for a long while, but she kept the smile in place from her last joke. "Your grounding can start tomorrow morning, I think."

Molly took it without a sign, save for a little glint in her eyes and a little smile crawling up on her lips. She did walk with just a little more spring as she headed back toward the stairs. "Thanks, Mom."

"You're welcome," Lauren said, and then belatedly remembered the eggs on the stove. They were like pebbles in the pan. She sighed, then sighed again as she threw them into the garbage. The blackened toast followed a few minutes after.

***

Midmorning came and went without a sign of any sort of dwelling. Hendricks felt antsy, Alison looked just tired to his eyes, and Duncan walked on without a care in the world. Hendricks found himself envying the demon, even though he was hardly exhausted at this point. The drover coat was hot, though, with the summer weather in full effect. He could feel the sweat popping out everywhere, and his thighs were sticking together down below. A most uncomfortable sensation.

"How far?" he asked Alison. The smell of greenery in the air wasn't too bad. Pine, he figured. It wasn't as hot as Iraq, that was for damned sure. The humidity was a real bitch here, though.

"I don't know," Alison replied. She just looked worn down, and Hendricks found himself wondering how long it had been since she'd slept. He knew it'd been a while for him, too, but whether it was the waffle place's coffee or the vial of whatever Spellman had given him, he felt no urge to sleep. "A couple miles, maybe?"

"Memory a little faded?" Duncan asked. He seemed a bit too chipper.

"Like I said," Alison sniffed, her shoulders with a pronounced bow to them, "the last time I came here I was a kid. It was a long walk, I remember that much."

"Your daddy brought you here?" Hendricks asked. "Not just a Sunday drive, I presume."

"One of his friends had moved down here after medical school," Alison said. "They were close, talked all the time on the phone. One day he called and got an 'Out of Service' signal. He tried a few more times over the course of a year and finally decided to take matters into his own hands."

"Didn't call the state police, I guess," Hendricks said, taking an uneven step over a shrub that brushed his jeans. The cowboy boots were nice for a fight, but not particularly great for long walks. He could feel blisters forming. Ah, the sexy life of a demon hunter.

"He couldn't conceive of a scenario where he'd need to call the state police for this," Alison said. "So he drove down one day, just me and him. When we got to the fence, he figured it was some kind of mistake. Spent a half an hour looking at the map, then took us back up the road. Once he figured he was right, he decided to cross the fence." She exhaled softly. "I went with him."

"Trespassing?" Hendricks said with amusement.

"Yep, we were regular lawbreakers," she said without amusement.

"I'm getting the hints of that," Hendricks said. Didn't really believe it, though, not really, even with her nighttime sniping of late. "So what did you find?"

"I told you—"

"What did you really find?" Hendricks shook a finger at her. "No more of this woman of mystery crap. Starling's got that well and truly covered."

He watched her swallow, and almost pale in the faint sunlight. The clouds were hanging a little low, Hendricks thought. "We did find a survivor," Alison said. "Didn't really talk to her or anything, but we saw her. And there were creatures. Things."

"What kind of things?" Duncan asked before Hendricks could beat him to the punch.

"Demons, for sure," Alison said, "though we didn't really know that at the time. They chased us. Nearly got us."

"What stopped them?" Hendricks asked.

"My daddy goes heeled everywhere," Alison said simply, like that was an explanation.

"Heeled?" Duncan asked, his face exhibiting the first hint of curiosity. "Like ... in high heels? They were put off by his innate sexiness?"

"I think it means armed," Hendricks offered helpfully. "In Old West slang or something."

"He carries a pistol, yes," Alison said. "Everywhere he goes. He pulled his pistol and kept the things off of us while we ran. We saw someone as we hurried out of town. It's not like we were ready for a fight. But those things ... demons ... they kept on coming until we were well into the outskirts. Then it was like they had their chains pulled, and they peeled off of us to go back to town."

"Dogs?" Duncan asked. "They were like dogs?"

"Ran on all fours," Alison said without emotion. "Looked like hellhounds or something."

That one sent the OOC to puzzling, and he kept his silence. Hendricks wanted to interrupt him to ask about it, but figured he could wait just a little bit longer before he absolutely needed to know.

***

Lauren arrived at the hospital just a little bit earlier than she had to. The pall she'd felt the night before had more or less vanished, aided not by a burned breakfast that had all gone to waste but by the feeling of honesty and connection to Molly. Yeah, it sounded a little hippy-dippy even for her, but she'd take it. This was how she and her kid got along best; she trusted her to make good decisions.

And not fuck a carnie who was about to leave town.

Well, that part was implied.

Oh, God, was it implied? It needed to be plainly stated, she figured, and made a panicked mental note to have another conversation with her daughter when she got off shift that afternoon.

Still, it was with a mostly calm feeling that she rode the elevator up to the fourth floor so she could—person of conscience that she was—check on Deputy Harris before she started her shift in the ER.

She found the nursing staff absent from the station in the hallway, which was not exactly unusual. They didn't have a ton of patients to cover, and they were probably out checking around. She just checked the board behind the desk, saw that Harris was in room 412, and whistled her merry way into the room. She found the respirator still going, the heart monitor still beeping, and the poor deputy's color much improved.

Lauren grabbed the chart off the end of the bed by sheer habit. Checking the notes, she peered from what she was reading to what she was seeing. Heart rate was looking a lot nicer, and so was the pulse ox. That didn't necessarily mean anything by itself, but it was a good sign after the way the girl had looked when she'd been brought in.

Lauren almost made it out without seeing two things of note. Almost.

One was Sheriff Nicholas Reeve, asleep in the corner of the room with his hat down over his eyes. That made her tread quieter, afraid she'd wake him up. He would almost certainly want to talk about something, and she didn't really have time for that.

The second thing was the IV bag hanging from the tree. She almost made it past before something nagged at her and pulled her back. She stepped back and looked at it again, and it just jumped out at her.

There was no writing on the bag at all. Not a brand, not instructions, nothing.

"What the fuck …?" she said, so undone by the surprise she did not bother to keep her voice down.

"What the fuck what?" Sheriff Reeve repeated, hat coming down off his eyes, blinking the bleariness out.

She told him. The eyes went from bleary to hard in seconds flat, and Lauren had this feeling—just a hunch—that she was going to be late for her shift.

***

Time slowed to a crawl as Hendricks made his way through that half-forested plain that passed for Alabama countryside. It was hillier than he expected, but he kept good time. Alison looked more and more worn out as the time passed, however, and he started to feel sorry for her. "Maybe we should take a break," he suggested.

"I'm fine," she said. She was not quite wheezing, but it was evident from her gait that she was feeling the hike. She looked to be in reasonable shape, but Hendricks knew looks could be extremely deceiving. He'd met a few truly skinny people who were in just awful health, without enough cardio fitness to run across a driveway.

"Maybe just a little rest," Duncan said, giving him the eye. Hendricks could see the demon was observing the same phenomenon as he was, and wondered if the OOC was feeling a flash of sympathy. "No point in getting there if we're exhausted when we arrive."

"You planning on running when we arrive?" Hendricks smirked at that, though upon reflection he wasn't sure that was much of a reason to smirk, really. He felt himself rest a hand on his pistol grip, just to reassure himself the old 1911 was still there.

"Depends on what we're staring down," Duncan said. He lurked, walking slowly across the forested ground, the crunch of leaves under his dress shoes as Alison leaned against a tree. They hadn't brought water, which had been stupid on Hendricks's part. He'd been back in civilization so much of the time that the ordinary precautions of war had faded as he returned to a place where you could buy a water bottle in every store if you got thirsty. Sloppy.

"What do you think we're up against?" Hendricks asked. "Based on what she saw?"

"Hellhounds are a broad category," Duncan said, like he was just recalling it all right up, out of a memory bank or something. "They're not really dogs, most of them, just four-legged and propel themselves like one. Or near enough so as not to matter."

"You people come in all shapes and sizes," Hendricks said, leaning on the "you people." He remembered a little belatedly that Lerner had needled him about that just a few days earlier.

"There is a long history of hellhounds being set loose on earth," Duncan said in what sounded like agreement. "Not really sure what class they'd be, though. Some of them look more like beetles, and those are a real bastard to dispatch—"

"Why?" Alison asked.

"Hard shell," Duncan replied. "Low essence, low intelligence. Built like tanks, if tanks were low to the ground and moved like a cheetah."

"Abrams tank can get up to about fifty," Hendricks said for no reason he could point to. Except that he hated feeling out of his depth, and marching into some town that had been dropped off the map for probably very good reasons felt like the dumbest move he'd made lately. Which took doing. Why was he buying into this again?

Oh, right. Starling. If he really reflected on it, putting his faith in a girl who had as bad a problem with ambiguity as she did seemed like the dumbest move of all.

"It seem like it's getting … darker to you?" Alison's voice came out in a low wheeze, like air coming out of a balloon. It was a sneaky, squeaky noise, almost irritating.

Still … Hendricks looked into the sky and saw a dull grey cloud hanging overhead, wisps of its structure dark with only the vague sense that the sun might lurk somewhere beyond. "It's just that cloud."

"I remember it getting dark early last time I was here," Alison said, leaning against a tree with her shoulder. It didn't look like a strong one, and Hendricks surely wouldn't have trusted his weight to it. "Like midafternoon was black as night."

"Gets like that up north in the winter," Hendricks said mildly. "Back in Wisconsin it gets dark at four in the afternoon in December sometimes."

"It's not winter here," Alison replied, slumped slightly forward, hands resting on her—dammit, Hendricks noticed, though—shapely thighs. "It's still summer."

"Barely," Hendricks said.

"Sounds like an unnatural phenomenon anyway," Duncan said.

Hendricks frowned. "A cloud's an unnatural phenomenon? You've been living in the underworld for a little too long."

"*This* cloud is an unnatural phenomenon," Duncan said. "What she's describing … midday darkness? That's not normal. When you couple it with the idea that this town is a hotbed of some sort of demonic activity …" He just shook his head. "I'd say they're related."

"How do you not know about this place?" Hendricks asked. "If this town got wiped out, shouldn't that have registered on your OOC radar? Or does that not matter to your office?"

"Not my case, not my department," Duncan said with a lack of concern that Hendricks found to be the latest un-damned-settling thing in a whole line of them. "Like I told you; the Office of Occultic Concordance is not big on the info-sharing. I know what I see, and I'm told what I need to know."

"Any chance you boys gossip around the water cooler like normal working stiffs?" Alison asked, and Hendricks damned near applauded for her asking such a useful question. And for getting his mind off her thighs.

"We don't work with others very often, but yes," Duncan said. "That does seem like a constant. Still, never heard of this place nor anything about it."

"Well, that's pretty much fucking useless," Hendricks said, just shaking his head and turning back to Alison, who met his eyes without any reluctance. He didn't know whether to find that to be a problem yet or not, but she was still cool. "You want a few more minutes?"

"No," she said and shook her head just once before starting off into the woods. Her t-shirt was drenched with sweat down the back, the cloth almost blackened from wetness. It clung, and so did her jeans. Hendricks tried to put that thought out of his mind and focused instead on the branches of the trees around them. The light that once flooded in from a hot, shining sun grew dimmer and dimmer with each step they took until finally, Hendricks had to admit that there was something mighty damned unnatural going on around him.

***

Arch wasn't the type who was predisposed to sit around while there were things to be done. Another body somewhere out in the town was a stark reminder that there was work to be done and he pored over his map trying to puzzle it out. He thought it unlikely—but not impossible—that the bicyclists were still hiding out in the same place. He had that circled on the map, the mine where he figured they'd been up on Mount Horeb. Charging in there seemed like a darned, foolish course of action, so he was resolved not to undertake it unless he had to. He did have a different idea of how he might approach it if another day was to turn to dusk without the rest of his crew—that was the oddest way to think of them, as some sort of crew, like they were all in the mafia together—returning from Alabama.

Arch took to his feet again. He'd paced around the table in the kitchen, staring at the map over and over. Not even knowing where the latest crime had been committed was a liability to his investigation. But then, he couldn't exactly call and ask Ed Fries. That might look suspicious, and he needed more suspicion on him like Job had needed more torment.

Arch gave up the pacing and hit the couch. The soft material, like felt, hit his neck with a loving touch of comfort. It drew his mind to Alison, to that particular brand of relief she'd brought him just the other day. It was the strangest thing, being drawn into thoughts of that after seeing death up close and personal. It was as though a bony hand had reached out and tried to pluck one of their number, had clenched ivory fingers around Erin and ripped her out of their midst. Something about the whole thing had set his mental teakettle to boiling, bringing an unease he was finding it real hard to shake.

He ran rough fingers over beard stubble, letting out a hot breath that stank of coffee even to his own nose. That velvety sensation of the couch on the back of his neck rubbed at him like he wished Alison was. His eyes wandered to the kitchen counter; he'd started with a full pot of coffee just an hour ago—

Now it was empty, just the smell remaining. He'd downed the last cup and not even noticed how much he'd shotgunned into his system. He pulled his hand away from his face, waiting to see if it shook. It didn't, not a whit. A whole pot of coffee, a complete lack of sleep, some crazed events cracking their way through his life like a lobster getting broken out of its shell, and he was thinking about—

Arch wiped his mouth again, feeling a thin line of perspiration on the stubble of his upper lip. Maybe that was the caffeine. Or maybe that was the oddly placed, strangely rampant desire for Alison that he couldn't explain as anything other than grossly inappropriate. For a long time he'd felt out of sorts in his life, bizarrely longing for something else. It was a call he'd heard and ignored in favor of just doing his job, and now that he was in the middle of a mess outside his control ...

His hand didn't shake. Not at all.

For a man whose boss had turned on him, he felt strangely calm. Even stranger considering that whole pot of coffee he'd downed.

He stared at the wall for about another minute before he found himself standing again, stalking back to the map in the kitchen as he paced once more around the table, seeking perspective on a problem he knew he needed to solve. And the one he was considering didn't even involve Nicholas Reeve, not even tangentially. It was the beasts on the bikes that were all he could think of, them and them alone. He would find them, he would crush them, break them, send them back to Satan with relish and gusto—

Then he'd see his wife again, and maybe that inappropriate thirst he wanted to sate wouldn't feel quite so inappropriate with this problem out of the way.

***

Hendricks had to concede that things were becoming more and more ... unnatural as they progressed further. Once-fresh shoots of trees gave way to gnarled and ragged trunks that twisted unpredictably in ways that nature never intended. The skies darkened, the wispy grey clouds turning darker, until finally he could ignore it no more. "What the hell are we walking into?" he asked Duncan and Alison. "Mordor?"

Alison stared at him blankly, her breath ragged and heavy. "What? Where?" She sounded about ready to keel over, which did not bode well for any running they might have to do.

"One does not simply walk into Mordor," Duncan said, eliciting a grin from Hendricks and a shake of the head from Alison. "I love catching those movies whenever they're on cable."

"I have no idea what you people are talking about," Alison said.

"Come on." Hendricks waved his arm, beckoning them onward. Any sign of a road had long since disappeared, and Hendricks wondered who might be responsible for that particular bit of ominous work. Could some agency have come in here and plowed it up to discourage visitors? If so, what did they do to keep the supposed demons that were lurking at bay while they did it?

"Not far, now," Alison said, and Hendricks saw her bearing change. Her breathing went much shallower, like she had overcome her difficulty with it. He watched for a second then caught Duncan doing the same. The demon didn't betray much with his look, but it was enough to make Hendricks think he was on the same track. Alison's gait straightened, losing the lopsided limp she'd been harboring a minute earlier as though she had a stitch in her side.

Hendricks eased toward Duncan and whispered, "What the hell was that?" She had changed in seconds, no longer the weak, winded little princess.

Duncan just shrugged, not taking his eyes off of her. "Seems like we're being played with."

"But for a good reason," Alison said, and Hendricks stopped just in time to avoid plowing into her. She was right there, halted in the middle of their forward path. She was stiff, slightly hunched, her hand hovering at her side. She was tense, that much was obvious just from looking at the back of her jeans.

Hendricks dropped his hand to his side as well, opening the drover coat. He waited, hand near his belt, trying to decide which weapon to pull. The air was hot and humid, and he felt drenched and sticky, everything clinging to his skin.

"Son of a bitch," Duncan said, and the night started to close in around them—even though it was midday.

Hendricks listened. The chirp of crickets was strangely absent. So too was any other ambient noise. Gone was the familiar hum of the woods—the rustle of the leaves, the sound of silence or of distant cars. All that was missing, vanquished by the falling dark. He could no longer even hear Alison's breathing, save for the occasional low breath. Duncan made no sound at all.

There was almost a sound of buzzing in the distance, and Hendricks's first thought ran to the bicyclists. He drew his sword, a sound of metal on leather as it cleared the scabbard. The noise passed, though, and left him clenching his blade. Duncan had his hand filled with the baton, and now Alison had a subcompact pistol in hers—a Glock, he thought.

They stood arranged in a rough triangle, facing the perimeter of the woods. The clouds had become complete, and the sun's last rays had disappeared. There was only a hint of illumination—like red moonlight—shining down from above. It cast Alison's face in a strange pallor, her blond hair turned strawberry like someone had hit their brake lights right in front of her. It gave Duncan's suit an even more exotic look. Hendricks was left to wonder what he looked like by the fading, demonic light.

"My kingdom for a flashlight," Hendricks muttered, and he heard a click as one turned on.

Alison held one in her left hand, crossed under and supporting the pistol in her right. "Guess you Marines don't prepare for everything, huh?"

"That's the Boy Scouts," Hendricks said a little bitterly. "And I have a flashlight, but no one told me I'd need it."

There was another click, and suddenly a white beam streamed from where Duncan had stood moments earlier. "A gun and a sword on your belt, but you don't have room to carry a micro flashlight? They weigh ounces."

"I didn't know I'd need it." Hendricks repeated, more irritable the second time through.

"You're a demon hunter," Duncan said, and the beam started to move ahead, with a rustle in the leaves that echoed through the air around them. "Don't you have to go into dark places sometimes?"

"I try to travel light." Hendricks could feel the aggravation, like a heavy stone being dragged through his chest. It was painful, this galling little lesson. He followed behind the two of them, watched their silhouettes in the light of the beams as they danced along; Alison's swayed considerably as she walked, while Duncan's was as steady as though it were mounted on some moving frame. "But thanks for the reminder," Hendricks muttered under his breath.

The lack of noise was disquieting, and with every step forward, Hendricks became more aware of even the red light through the clouds fading away. He could hear his companions, could smell Alison's sweat, that scent of outdoor briskness and activity when he got close to her. He followed just behind her, wary of bumping her but even warier of getting too far away from the only people that kept him out of total darkness.

"Do you hear them?" Duncan asked. Hendricks stopped to listen closer, breath stuck in his throat. Give him a thousand demons head-on rather than one lurking in the darkness, that was his take. The overwhelming evil he could see versus the tiny little one he couldn't. It resonated in his head, in his heart, that feeling, and he chafed under it, wanting to throw caution aside and charge into the underbrush blindly to stab whatever was out there. Foolish but cathartic, he thought, with an emphasis on the foolish part. His superiors from his Marine Corps days would not have approved. Understood, but not approved.

"I don't hear anything," Alison said. "But I can feel them."

"They're watching," Duncan said. "Growing in numbers. Feels like they're working in a pack. Surrounding us, maybe, before they come in." He sniffed, and Hendricks wondered if he was actually breathing. "Or leading us."

"Where are we going?" Hendricks asked, absolutely rhetorical.

"Deeper," Alison said. Better than any answer he could conjure. Because really, no matter how you sliced it, that was true.

***

The day dragged like a dog wiping its butt on the carpet, and Arch gave up on the pacing after three hours. Looking at the map was a steady descent into madness, staring at gridpoints and coordinates until he went blind in both eyes. He felt the itch get progressively worse as time passed and his phone stayed silent. He wanted to call Alison, check in, but even if she'd been in a place to answer a phone, he knew what that could prompt. They were heading into the heart of trouble, into a place where a sudden noise could be a real detriment to your continued well-being. So he kept his hands off his phone, kept his eyes on the maps, and kept his feet moving until he could bear the weight of his uselessness no longer.

It was a simple craziness that came on, that cabin fever feeling. He'd ignored it for an hour, then another. By now, the utterly insane was sounding more and more intelligent. There was a cave on Mount Horeb. This much he knew. An old mine. Probably had contained the bicycling demons only a day earlier. Were they there now? Unlikely.

But his brain buzzed in circles around the hope that there was some sign of their flight still hidden in that darkness.

Of course all the reasonable reasons to not undertake this path were perfectly present and cogent in his mind. They could actually still be there. He could be walking into a trap laid by demons. He could be outnumbered and devoured, drawn and quartered or worse by soulless beasts from the very depths of the biblical hell that he had feared since childhood.

But every hour he stared at the four walls of his apartment was another hour where taking the initiative to go deep into the mine seemed like a better and better idea, even without a whit of backup.

His rational, logical mind argued again, then again, that was dumb beyond dumb. That this was the height of arrogance, it was Samson not listening to the warnings and seeing his strength ripped away with his hair. The forces of the Morning Star—and he fully believed with every bit of his heart that was who was at work here—would exult in every champion's fall, and his would surely be no exception.

But that part of his mind became quieter as the hours passed, and as he grabbed his keys and walked out the door, it lost to the part that suggested that even one more night going by without a read on where these things were hiding would result in yet more death. More chaos in the name of the one who reveled in these things. The thoughts were still there as he revved the engine and took the damaged Explorer onto the road, heading toward Mount Horeb once again, but he let himself think that self-sacrifice for the greater good was the one that was driving the car, and ignored that little part of him that said he was just losing his good sense and giving in to wrath.

***

Hendricks was way too close to Alison for his own good. He was practically up on her back now, in boner-stabbing distance, he might have called it in the Corps, nuts to butts, but he was a little too aware of the worsening situation to feel much like bonering right now. He was young, though, and sex was always—ALWAYS—in the back of his mind if it wasn't in the front, and even in a forest that was dark as hell's pits during midday, standing close enough to poke the wife of his friend, with his own recent lover lying in the hospital, yep, it was still there, even with a demon watching on, and it would have been to Hendricks's shame if he hadn't had those other worries to keep him from exploring it much. There'd be time for guilt later, he figured, maybe after the running and screaming and all hell had broken loose. He figured that was moments away based on the way his internal tension was ratcheting up, the heat just building under his coat like a furnace inside him had gotten stoked with fresh wood.

Wood. Heh. He wasn't too wary to appreciate that one, either. Wood.

"Gettin' hot," Duncan said, a clear statement that made Hendricks come out of his own head for a minute. He was sure that the feeling of warmth was from the coat, from the fact it was Alabama in summertime and the fact there was a pretty girl just in front of him. Sweaty, but pretty.

"Thought it was just me," Hendricks said.

"You ain't that good lookin', sweetheart," Alison said flatly, like she could read his mind and wanted to pour some cold water on him. Southern drawl, too.

"I meant—" He felt the frown rise. He kept the sword in one hand and grabbed the lapel of his coat with the other, flapping it like it was a valve he could turn to let some steam off. Jesus, it was getting hotter. "Never mind." There was no way to say it without coming off like a sour sonofabitch, anyway. "How's it getting hotter if the sun's behind the clouds?"

"Good question," Duncan replied, his gait completely unchanged from when they'd first started. For Hendricks, the chafing had started. He'd heard it called being galded, where the thighs start to stick together as you walk. It made him want to sashay sideways for a bit, but he knew he'd look ridiculous and have a bitch of a time keeping up, so he didn't. "I don't know," the demon conceded after a brief intermission, maybe to think it over. Hendricks didn't think that boded too well. It was like having the native guide on an expedition telling you that you were off the fucking map, in hostile territory. Like you wandered into North Korea or something. Oops. Bad luck. Sayonara—or however you said it in Korean.

Even his fucking feet hurt by this point, and his boots had been broken in long ago to the point where he could hump it for miles in them. Hendricks had had e-fucking-nough of this town, and they weren't even there yet. He bypassed the coat and went straight to his t-shirt collar, finding it completely drenched with sweat. He peeled it off his chest, making way for the heat to come rushing out. It didn't seem to help. God, if he could only take off his coat ...

He felt the trail of the drover touching the ground before he even realized it was. He looked down and saw his legs were buckling, and his first thought was that he was being such a damned pussy. This wasn't that far of a walk, and he wasn't in that bad a shape. Then his eyes flicked up, and saw Alison hobbling a little, too. Not like she'd been earlier, with the wheezing, but like the gravity had turned up. Her Naked Prozac t-shirt (what the hell was that band, anyway?) was completely soaked through now, looked black even in the beam light, and he saw her knees slightly folded.

"Shit," Duncan announced, and Hendricks just stopped.

Sweet fucking son of a fuck, it was stifling, the air growing hotter and hotter, like he'd stuck his whole body up next to a barbecue grill someone had opened on the hottest day of summer. The sun he couldn't see was shining down on him, the black coat absorbing every bit of it, and he felt the sweat just coursing from under his sleeves, making trails that tickled their way through every hair on his arm. His palm gripped his sword tighter and he felt the grip slip, the leather wanting to slide out of his grasp.

"Not a good ... sign," Hendricks said, barely getting it out. He wanted to open his mouth and pant like a fucking dog in hopes the heat building inside would just *Please Just Get The Fuck Out Already*. It was like a rubber suit had gotten wrapped around his whole body and he was sweating into it. He could barely take a breath without smelling that stifling sweat smell, that faint hint of fucking charcoal or ozone or something, Sweet Jesus, *something* that made his head tingle from the beads of water dripping down under the hat. He wanted to tear it aside and mop his brow with a canvas-hard sleeve, but he knew that wouldn't do it and—

"Holy fuck," Hendricks said as Alison hit a knee. She was breathing heavy again now, her hair completely and totally turned from straight and dry to a soaked, streaked mess of tangled blond turned dark with perspiration. He watched her fold and knew—just knew—that this wasn't the heat, even though *FOR FUCK'S SAKE WOULD SOMEONE PLEASE TURN DOWN THE*

GODDAMNED THERMOSTAT ON THE WORLD BECAUSE I WANT TO—

His free hand came up and ran across his face, smearing stinging salty liquid into his eyes, and he bumped his hat clean off even though he knew—HE KNEW—that it would not help at all. Shaking off the coat would similarly have no effect, but that was another thing that the distant corner of his brain whispered while his body told him to strip it all the fuck off and be rid of it, to jump naked in the nearest body of water, to drag Alison with him and get the poor girl some help because it was just out of control, this feeling that—

Ice cream on a summer's day, sherbet melting down the side of his face as he licked his way to the cone. That thought popped into Hendricks's head and it helped. That sweet, tangy tartness hidden in the first feel of chill that the lick brought.

He imagined his skin the time he'd done the polar plunge that time for charity in high school. Frigid cold water that sprang over his flesh as he jumped into the lake and felt his balls make a rapid and strategic retreat as his skin felt like it froze fucking over—

The air conditioner in that shithole base in Iraq working double overtime after they'd come off a five-day mission. It was like a cool bath standing in front of it, trying not to get into a shoving match with the dipshit next to you, all thought of you being brothers in arms forgotten while you were trying to just get a little more cold soaked up, like it was the only thing in the damned world, with that mechanical smell filtering out the desert outside—

Hendricks felt the will to crumble leave his legs. He was still sweating like a motherfucker but it was like the wool sweater he'd had pulled over him had been ripped off in one move. He could feel something pressing on him, like a wave of heat hanging out at arm's length, kept at a distance by his mind.

"You figure it out?" Duncan asked, not looking at him. The OOC was facing into the darkness, his flashlight beam dancing over the gnarled and twisted tree branches, illuminating blackened husks of things that might have born leaves and shoots once upon a time, but that was a long time ago, galaxy far away, all that jazz.

"Heat demon of some kind," Hendricks replied, and his sleeve drifted over his soaked upper lip. The salty taste dribbled onto his tongue. "It's pushing thoughts on us. Feelings."

"On you, yeah," Duncan said.

"You don't feel it?" Alison asked, and Hendricks thought that this time—for sure—she was truly breathless.

"I feel it, but it doesn't matter," Duncan replied, like a freezer of cool compared to their surroundings. "They ramped it up pretty fast, and that was dumb because then it was obvious to me. Still wouldn't have affected me like it hits you, but I'd have been less likely to notice if they hadn't trumpeted it like an invading army."

"The Mongol hordes of heat," Hendricks joked weakly, still feeling the heavy toll the flaming beasts had been trying to exact from him. "Think cold thoughts, Alison. Think of the times you were freezing your ass off."

"Can't," she said, and her head was slumped to the side.

"Whoa, whoa," Hendricks said, and stepped in closer to her. She pushed at his leg, trying to force him away because of the heat or because she had nothing else to do. "When was the last time you remember being cold?"

"Hunting season," she said after a minute. "In the woods. With Daddy. Years ago."

"Think about it," Hendricks said, not taking his eyes off the trees around them. Where were these fuckers? Wouldn't now be the time to strike? "What did it feel like?"

She let another heat-laden breath out as she answered, and it came up at Hendricks like someone had opened the barbecue again. "Felt ... like a blanket of chill settled over me. Like it wrapped me in a fall day, with a first snowfall a month still off, but the freezing feel on its way. Like I could see my breath frosting in front of me on the air, not steam and smoke. Like my lungs hurt from the cold when I walked home through the woods too fast and took a breath too deep. Like I could stick my tongue out and catch the air as it turned to ice on the tip."

She shuddered once, and he saw the tension leave her. She worked back to her feet at her own pace, and it took a minute. "I don't remember it being like this last time," she said once she was upright again. "Not like this."

"Likely whatever is here is getting stronger." Duncan had pulled closer to them now, making their triangle tight, his purple-tinted jacket just a finger's distance from Hendricks, who wanted to touch it, see if there was sweat beneath it at the small of the demon's back. He knew there wasn't, but after the assault on his senses he'd just weathered, he was curious. "Some of our kind can develop an affinity for a certain place; makes them more powerful the longer they're homesteaded there."

"Must be nice to have a place to hang your hat," Hendricks said as he picked his hat up off the ground. He brushed the dirt off the brim and settled it back on his head. It was still gawdawfully warm but not unmanageable. "How much farther—?"

He barely got it out before Alison's beam hit on something that didn't look like woods. It was too smoothly rounded, though it was still a little like a tree trunk, wood scorched and reaching skyward. She started moving first, a little more sure now, but less than she'd been before the warmth had tried to melt them down. The object came into clearer focus as they went, Hendricks fighting to get one foot in front of another, the world swaying around him like he'd crossed the whole damned desert on his faltering legs.

The scorched trunk of the thing became obvious when he got close. Little nails jutted out from it, blackened by time and heat, he supposed, but not unrecognizable. Alison's beam shot skyward and his gaze followed with it to the top, where the crossbeam was still attached, though the wires that had once been strung across it were long missing.

"Telephone pole," Hendricks said for all of them. He wanted to wipe his face again but held off. He pictured that ice cream cone again instead, and it helped some.

"Another one up ahead," Duncan observed. They were moving now, a train sprung to motion, Hendricks's steps coming erratically but coming, following Alison's lead, all thoughts of boner distance forgotten. Her smooth beam caught a straight line and Hendricks followed it, blackened edges emerging out of the dark.

"Building," Duncan pronounced, now leading the way. They were in line, and Hendricks did not dare look back for fear of a misstep while his head was turned, for fear of taking a tumble he could not recover from while lollygagging.

He followed them, feeling his consciousness on a lower level than usual. It was almost surreal. Then suddenly there was orange light again that had nothing to do with a sun in the sky that he could no longer see or believe in. His steps were staggering, one leg locked permanently to keep it from betraying him from the fatigue or the mind-fuck or whatever that was working on him.

"This way," Duncan said, threading them into a gap beside the scorched wall. There was another a few feet away, Hendricks realized, and as they drew between them he could see the fire marks staining the walls where heat had burned its way through the alley they walked. He could see the orange light at the end and knew that it was not a train. Trains didn't have orange lights, did they?

They stepped out of the end of the alley, Hendricks playing caboose (fucking trains again, why was that? He felt like he'd been run over by one, maybe). The orange light drowned out Alison's flashlight. Duncan's was already off, and Hendricks hadn't even noticed until now.

He stood there, and it took him a minute to realize he was leaning on Alison for support. She was leaning right back, and he could feel her softness pressed against him on the side. She moved, and he watched her leave a trail of sweat on his coat as she slid an inch back and he caught her, his sword hand wrapped around her shoulders. He transferred the weapon to his left hand and barely avoided dropping it from the slick, sweat-drenched hilt.

"Well, here we are," Duncan said as they stared out on what Hendricks figured had once been a town square not that dissimilar from what Midian had. There might even have been a statue on that pedestal in front of them at one point, that stone block base that just stood there in the middle of a black-dirt field, with a bonfire burning right in the middle of it.

The bonfire was a mile tall to Hendricks's eyes, and black smoke piped off it and mingled with the clouds, like they were coming down to take it up and blow it evenly around the four corners of the sky. He didn't see any wood in the bonfire, though, like it was burning without fuel, fire without source.

The first shape broke out of it without so much as a waver in the flames. The second followed, then a third. Low to the ground, walking on four legs, each step sending up a hiss that was audible even over the crackling of the flames, and Hendricks saw one of the paw prints turned to glass in the dirt, catching the refracted light of the fire as flaming devil dogs emerged from within one after another.

They had a sick, hungry look in their eyes that reminded Hendricks of a stray he'd gotten a little too close to one time, some element of desperation in those red pupils that he could see from halfway across the square. "Here it comes," he muttered, and waited, sword in hand, afraid to take another step.

But it didn't come, and the dogs formed a little path, a little chain on either side of the bonfire as they stacked up in a line, that black earth laid out like a red carpet between them. They turned and faced each other like a salute, and Hendricks didn't know whether to be impressed or just say fuck it and run. "Looks like someone tunneled a little too deep into the Mines of Moria," he said.

"Not big enough to be a Balrog," Duncan replied. "Though they've got the look, the fire and darkness thing going on."

"You people are nerds," was Alison's only comment on the matter.

The bonfire rippled again but taller this time. It belched a human shape out of the flames, a figure that looked impressively tall next to the four-legged flame beasts but not so big for a human. He could tell by the slightness that it was a woman, or a girl, and her steps were even more lopsided than his had been, like she'd been worn the fuck out and never replenished.

She made it all the way out to the street that ringed the square before she stopped, bare blackened feet perched on the edge of the curb, a river of broken asphalt between her and them. He looked in her eyes out of curiosity more than anything, and he didn't see the red fire there that the dogs had.

He saw a screaming fucking horror that stretched all the way from the top of the girl's bald head to the pit of her near-empty soul.

She just stood there and stared at them, the dogs flanking her on either side, a hearty dozen of them, presumably with a shit ton more in the fire if need be. Hendricks didn't love those odds, but he called out anyway.

"What's your name?" he asked. His voice sounded like he'd swallowed the bonfire all the way down, and it'd left nothing but scorched cracks from the back of his tongue to somewhere in his belly, where the fire had gone out completely and left nothing behind in its wake.

When she spoke, it was a crackling whisper, something that demanded attention, and every one of the demon dogs seemed to hush to make way for her speech. It was an awful quiet too, split by the voice of the thing—the girl? The woman?—they paid some sort of homage to, here in the wreckage of lives, of homes, of a whole town.

"My name is Mandy," she said, and it was not anything approaching human, the way she said it. Like she'd almost forgotten. "My name is Mandy." Like that meant anything to anyone.

15.

Lauren rode up Mount Horeb in silence, her mother driving and her in the passenger seat, again. It was tiresome, this co-op thing, but she hadn't had time to get her car before morning shift, and so she'd had to impose on her mom again. It was probably the least of the impositions she'd put on her in the last few years, though, so she didn't feel too fussed about it.

Besides, her head was a little too busy swirling with the tandem craziness of Molly and her carnie boyfriend and what Arch Stan had maybe done this morning. The former was personally important and of special interest, while the latter had been good for making her late for her shift and would possibly bear fruit in delivering a comeuppance to one righteous sonofabitch, smacking him down off his high fucking horse. And, she dared to hope, with all the trampling underfoot that might follow such an occurrence.

Lauren was so wrapped up in this fascinating yin/yang of karma—the Molly situation because of the parallels she could draw with her own teenage years, and the Arch Stan one because ... well ... because karma was a stinging, mean-spirited slut when crossed, apparently—that she barely noticed when her mother nudged the car to the side of the road behind her own, which sat waiting on the overlook, nothing but a thin layer of brown dust to indicate she'd left it there some twenty-four hours before.

"You're not going for another run, are you?" her mother asked, jolting Lauren back to the world.

"I'm in my scrubs," she said, indicating the blue garments in answer.

"So, that's a no?" her mother asked. "Because it seems to me I've seen you go out in what looked like a bra, and this is quite some improvement over that—"

"Ughhhhh," she let out in frustration and forced the door open. "It's called a sports bra, Mom—"

"—with your belly out there for the world to see like you were in a whorish bathing suit, and your bosoms all flopping around—"

"I'm a B cup, there's really not that much flopping, thanks."

"I just wanted to know if you'd be home for dinner," her mother said as Lauren stood there, one hand on the door and the other on the roof of the car, leaning over to look in at the grey-haired pronouncer of judgment on everything. "That's all."

"And maybe take a little zip or two at my wardrobe choices in the process," Lauren said, "because really, there's never a moment when you should waste an opportunity to point out the things I do that you disagree with."

"Oh, get over yourself," her mother said, putting the car back into gear. "I ain't got time in my day to point out all the things you do wrong." Lauren barely slammed the door in time to let her mother drive off, pulling around into a U-turn and lurching off down the mountain.

Lauren could feel her internal teakettle boiling and sighed to let off the steam. It was pointless to hold onto it, because even if she did just bottle it up all the way home, unleashing it like a factory whistle, blowing as she came in the door, her mother would just look up at her with that faintly amused smile—*Are you still on about that? But that was ages ago!* There was a statute of limitations on every unpleasant conversation, and it was always as short as her mother wanted it to be.

Fuck it, she said to herself. She got in her car and started the engine. She stared off the overlook, willing her irritation to be pushed off, because it would do her no good alive. One time, she goes jogging in a sports bra, gets reminded forever. All because that fucking biddy Genevieve Lane mentions to her mother than Albert Daniel—the old horn dog—was gawking at her. Not her fault that Albert Daniel hadn't gotten laid since protesters were chanting about how many babies LBJ had killed that day. Not her fault that the shithead would probably stroke off until he stroked out, the pudgy fuck. Her legs were all right, she guessed—guys had mentioned them before in bed as being good—but nothing else was worth writing home about, certainly not her sports bra. But Albert Daniel—*aww, fuck it.*

She blew the hostility out again as she drove. It was a process, a slow one, dealing with her mother's little sand spurs that she tossed with unerring accuracy. She could land 'em in the gap between the mental sock and shoe, and for the rest of the day they stung, no matter how much you dug at 'em. Lauren took another breath out, trying to steer back to something more productive. Back to the yin and yang of karma. Back to Molly …

… and Arch Stan …

… who was driving past her on the road up the mountain, still in his fucked-up, dented police Explorer, signaling to turn onto that abandoned road that the old mining company had left gated off.

She frowned. Reeve was gonna arrest the man, based on what she knew. It sounded inevitable. The only thing they were waiting on was lab results from that IV bag he'd apparently hung.

But he was driving his police cruiser up here on Mount Horeb?

She half expected him to hang a U-turn and come back down after her, like he could read what she'd been conspiring to do to him. She watched in the rearview, though, and his car disappeared down the road. She watched—and watched another few seconds, and then she hit the brakes. There was not another car in sight, and Arch Stan was still up there, still down that road somewhere.

She went through about three phases of thought in quick succession. The first was the extremely natural *Ah, well, fuck him, too* that she sensed came almost as much from her feelings about him as from the man himself—that bastard. The second was the deeper thought—the suspicion, the wondering *What the hell is he doing up here?*

The third came with a fresh breath of annoyance, and ended as she spun the car in a U of her own, heading back up the slope with full intention of following the bastard to see what exactly he was doing trespassing on the mining company's land. Maybe it'd give the sheriff even more reason to stick the karma Taser up his deputy's self-righteous ass.

***

Arch was in the dark. It had felt like the right thing to do. He'd plunged into that mine entrance at a run, slowing only as the darkness fell and he'd had to flick on his light and draw the switchblade. He wasn't counting on conventional threats, so the knife made sense. It wasn't like there was a high likelihood of a bear hiding up in here, after all.

He'd found the gate to the mine ajar. Well, a little more than ajar, actually; it'd been hanging off the hinges, open wide. Tracks for more bikes than he could rightly count were all over the ground in front of the entrance. It looked like the tunnel stretched down a ways, maybe to an elevator or something else. The gate at the front of the cave was a half-butted effort to keep teenagers out, Arch figured, the product of a company that had hit the bankruptcy skids and lost everything, even the consideration for others that might have caused them to spend their last dollars on a more substantial method of keeping out trespassers. But bankruptcy was bankruptcy, and you couldn't get blood out of a turnip. He eased down the tunnel, done with the running.

His light fell over dark rock, stone bereft of value. Supports lined the walls, designed to keep the world from falling in around him. There wasn't much to see—yet—but his eyes kept track of it all. The smell of cave air would have been a little dank, he figured, but for the opening behind him. He very carefully did not look back, knowing that the sight of sunlight would blind him for seconds, and Arch was now fully aware that even a second's blindness was far too long when one was dealing with demons.

He came to a carved split in the rocky tunnel about a hundred yards in and found himself faced with a choice of which way to go. The cool air crawled up his arms, causing his skin to tingle in a way he surely wouldn't have felt were he still standing out in the hot sun. Which way to go, that was the question. It didn't take him long to decide, because lingering about was surely a fast way to get himself made into a ripe target for ambush. He headed right, flashlight beam bouncing its way in front of him, revealing nothing but rock walls and the detritus left behind by a mining company on its way out.

The tunnels were wide; he couldn't reach from wall to wall if he'd tried. They were open channels bored into the earth, and the cut tracks on the ground indicated where the mining company had transported the minerals out of the earth with steam locomotive hauling cars. Arch minded his steps as he walked into the silence.

His footsteps echoed, but at such a low resonance that he wondered if they could be heard down the shaft. He slowed his pace, listening, but the sound of a faint dripping in the distance overcame the soft steps. He became aware of his own breathing, even though it was quiet.

His flashlight beam caught the first hint of something foreign in the rocky tunnel, and Arch stopped short. He stood there, the pale light stretching across the dusty tunnel floor until it found a lump, something cloth-like that reminded him of a cocoon. He stood there, hesitant to even move, waiting for something else to stir, as though the mere light could awaken something in the darkness.

He heard something and froze, that crash of fear like a cymbal in his head. He straightened, a pang of awareness running down to his stomach. He was vaguely aware that he'd frozen at the thought of some trouble and told himself that it was natural, that he needed to listen. He needed to know where it was coming from before he could deal with it.

Arch listened, listened hard, waiting for some subtle clue about its location. Was it a demon? A drip of water? The hand on the flashlight shook, and even the knowledge he'd fought a demon that breathed fire at him—on him—did nothing to bring him warmth as he stood there in the dark. It had been a bad idea to come here, he knew that now, not just in his mind, but his gut, which had told him just moments ago to charge into this. The beam shook on the cloth object in front of him, fooling him for just a second into thinking it was moving.

There was a quiet scrape of something and this, he knew for sure, came from behind him. His head snapped around, and he could see no hint of the entrance and the bright sky somewhere above. He could see nothing, not really, like he'd turned off the lights around him and stood in the dark. His hand sweated on the flashlight, felt it slickly in his palm, the ridges feeling almost ineffectual against the tangible proof of his nervousness—his fear.

He almost shouted "Hello!" but remembered himself. There was reassurance in that word, in hearing it echo, in hearing someone else repeat it back. But he kept it in, knowing that here in a mine that had so recently harbored demons, reassurance was not what he was likely to find.

Arch's eyes adjusted, and now he could see the faint light somewhere down the corridor. Outlines were visible, the dark of the mine broken just slightly by his flashlight's beam and the far-off promise of daylight somewhere around a curve in the distance.

His breath came slow, controlled as he drew it while measuring his fear with each exhalation. Nerves were a killer in a place like this. It was a mine, after all; demons weren't the only things in a place like this that made noise. Natural things could do it as well, like water seepage and bats.

Arch brought the flashlight around slowly, casting light over craggy walls and dark stone clefts, until it was shining back up the tunnel from whence he'd come. Coming here still seemed like a bad idea, he reflected as he turned the beam around, and as it fell on a face in the darkness he was struck from behind, a scream filling his ears as he hit the ground and the flashlight rolled out of his grasp, casting his whole world in flashes of light for a moment before it stopped.

***

"Mandy?" Hendricks asked, repeating it like he hadn't heard it. He stared at the girl, bald as Lex Luthor, her skin wrinkled like she'd been a sun worshipper her whole life, that leather handbag look to it. He was still leaning heavily on Alison and she on him, and it surprised him that they weren't both flat out on the ground because she sure as shit didn't look strong enough to bear his weight.

Duncan hummed a few bars of something, and Hendricks cocked his head over to the demon. "*Mandy*," Duncan said. "The Manilow song?"

Hendricks glanced at Alison, who shrugged. "Who the fuck is Manilow?"

"Kids these days," Duncan said. "Mandy ... what are you doing here?"

"I live here," came the ragged response from the fire lady.

Hendricks raised an eyebrow and surveyed the square again. He'd seen shittier shitholes but not too many. He'd broken down doors in Ramadi that looked more livable than this place—and that was after he and his boys had plowed through. "I'm a little surprised anyone lives here," Hendricks said, holding back the honesty—because it felt like it might firehose out, irritating that girl and her flaming devil dogs. And he didn't feel like fighting quite yet.

"Lots of people used to," Mandy said. She sounded a little hollow, a little high-noted mixed with some scratch, like she hadn't used her voice in a while.

"What happened to them?" Alison asked, and Hendricks gave her a frown. Didn't she already know?

"You were here before," Mandy said, staring at Alison with hollow eyes. They were taking it all in, those eyes, but Hendricks had a doubt that it was all making sense to the brain behind them. Mandy looked about eighty percent checked out, by his reckoning. The lights were on, maybe, and that was about it. "You came last time."

"I came last time," Alison agreed. "I saw you, from a distance, before we ran. But I didn't talk to you."

"No one talks to me," Mandy said.

"Better than hearing voices, I guess," Hendricks said. He regretted it as those empty eyes took him in for a minute.

"You look a little like him," Mandy said, and her bald head went to a forty-five degree angle as she surveyed him. "I think." She paused and put a burned finger up to her cracked lips; Hendricks could see the dried skin flaking off in a way that suggested to him that a whole fucking tube of Chap-Stick could not fix the dryness problems this lady had. "It's been so long since I've seen him."

Hendricks wondered how long they should indulge the crazy cat-lady—minus the cats. He landed on, "At least a little longer," when his eyes fell across the flaming dogs again. They were just waiting, like a command barked would send them leaping forward. Hendricks's eyes darted to his sword, then back to the dogs. Nope, not great odds. He did not favor them. Walking out would be a lot better. "Who is he?" he asked, trying to sound interested while he worked on a backup plan. None was forthcoming.

"He—" she snarled, "he's the one who—" She made a guttural noise in her throat that reminded Hendricks of a dog growling. He eyed the flame dogs and decided that nope, it was coming from her. He shot a sidelong glance at Duncan and noticed the demon was still taking it all in, not making a hostile move. The baton was still in his hand, though, which was either a good sign or a damned bad one.

Mandy made a new sound, now, a high, whining one, and it took Hendricks a second to realize what it was.

"She's crying," Alison said a second after he got it.

"You'd be crying, too, if you had what I had," Mandy said, turning those blank eyes on Alison again. "Did you ever have a man ... who took everything from you?" Her eyes fell to Hendricks. "Well? Did you?"

"I've never had a man, no," Hendricks replied, regretting his glibness as soon as he'd said it.

It seemed to fall right off Mandy, who focused back on Alison. "Have you?" Mandy asked.

"I have a man, yes," Alison replied, a little carefully to Hendricks's ears. He didn't have to try hard to wonder why; Mandy sounded a little on edge. Well, actually, she sounded like she was on the edge of the cliff standing on her tippy-toes and leaning over, trying to give the abyss a big damned smooch.

"Is this him?" Mandy nodded at Hendricks.

"No," Alison said.

"What about him?" Now Mandy sounded tired, as she laconically gestured at Duncan.

"Definitely not," Alison said, and Hendricks cracked a smile at that one. "My man's not here."

"I had a man once," Mandy said, and she'd settled back into a trance-like state where her eyes were fixed on the red-black sky. "He's gone now."

Hendricks's mouth spoke again before his brain could get a grip on that slippery weasel. "Can't imagine why; it's such a lovely town you have here."

She looked at him, but there was no flare of anger. Hendricks felt a jolt in his ribs from Alison, caught the look from Duncan that chided him for being a moron. "It wasn't always like this," Mandy said.

"I'd imagine with a name like Hobbs Green it might have been a little ... greener, at some point?" Hendricks asked. He got the elbow from Alison again, but this time he fired back a look of his own. He'd kept it diplomatic, dammit.

"It was green once," Mandy said. "Blue skies, too, I think?" She gazed at Alison with that broken look. "The skies were blue, weren't they?"

"Still are, elsewhere," Alison said cautiously. That was probably the safe way to say it, Hendricks figured. "Little different here, though."

"Yes," Mandy said, agreeing with a sorrowful aura. "Things are different here."

"What happened?" Duncan asked, and waited for her eyes to fall on him. "What happened to turn the skies dark and the ground black and ..." The demon just let his voice drift off.

"Why, the most joyous thing in the world, of course," Mandy said, again delivering this like it was self-evident. If nothing else, she was doing a marvelous job of convincing Hendricks that her motor would never again fire on all cylinders. And he had doubts she was ever a V8 to begin with. "I had a baby." Her hands fell to her stomach, and Hendricks noticed for the first time that what he had thought was black clothing was soot as the covering on her belly smeared and revealed more wrinkled flesh below.

"Holy shit, she's naked as the day she was born," Hendricks muttered under his breath. For whatever reason, Alison spared the elbow this time.

"Have you seen my baby?" Mandy asked, her voice off-note this time, some perverse mixture of joy and sorrow.

"Can't say I have," Hendricks replied, beating out the other two. "Where is ... they?" He switched gears mid-sentence and felt like a moron for the two seconds it took for him to remember he was in the ruins of a demon-burned Alabama town and not a grammar rodeo.

"Why, right here, of course," Mandy said and knelt. One of the fire dogs padded over to her, leaving scorched earth with every step. Hendricks saw similar paw prints of glass all over the square and realized that everywhere it tread, it left a mark. It made a gawdawful sound that was somewhere between a scream and a mewl, then it brought out a flaming tongue and ran it quickly over Mandy's cheek before settling lower, anchoring on her small breast. She fell backward as it did, falling on her ass with apparent glee as it suckled from her. The next closest dog came over to them then, not leaving a single glassy paw print as it did so but latching to the other side, rubbing against her with its flaming body and leaving a smear of black soot across her shoulder as it did so. The answer for how she got that fancy suit of ash clothing popped into Hendricks's head. The other dogs maintained their guard formation as the two front runners nursed, the flames of their bodies burning brighter as they did so.

"These are my babies," Mandy said, and Hendricks found the time to look over at Alison, her face two inches from his. The discomfort was unmistakeable, but she kept it shy of horror by a long margin. Mandy's hand ran over the fiery back of the one on her left breast. "But this one is the one I birthed myself."

Duncan beat Hendricks to the punch. "Who birthed the rest of them?"

"The other women of the town," Mandy said, smiling at her suckling pups. Hendricks found the way she was looking at them really fucking disturbing, and he thought he'd just about hit the peak when the acid-cum-spurting demon had burned his way through a hooker last week.

"Okay, Khaleesi," Hendricks said, and caught a funny look from Duncan. "Sometimes I stay in hotels that have HBO," he explained. Turning his attention back to Mandy, he tried to keep himself level. "What happened to the other women? The other ... mothers?"

"They weren't the mothers," Mandy said with a shake of her head as she scratched behind the ear of her favorite. "They were surrogates, wombs of convenience to hold my other babies, the ones my own womb couldn't hold." Now her crackling voice just sounded like some fucked up mix of innocent and sinister. Hendricks was not taking bets on which of those descriptions was leading in that race, either.

"Where did the babies come from?" Duncan asked. "Who was the father?"

Mandy's dead eyes flared. "He was a demon from hell."

"Yeah, I think that's pretty obvious to all of us at this point," Hendricks said. No elbow this time, either. "But ... uh ... did this demon from hell have a name?"

"His name was Mick." Her hand slid along the neck of her dog.

"I see," Duncan said, taking it all in. "Was he Irish?"

"Jesus," Hendricks said, "you really were around in the eighteen hundreds, weren't you, you racist."

"All you skin puppets look the same to me," Duncan replied. "Where did this ... Mick ... come from?"

"He came to town with the carnival," Mandy said, her voice taking on a dreamlike quality. "He showed me things ..."

"Like his cock," Hendricks muttered under his breath.

"... things I'd never seen before ..." Mandy went on. "Made me feel things ... I couldn't have imagined ..."

"Like her hymen bursting, I'd guess," Alison added. Hendricks approved.

"... and he lied to me, made me give it all to him. Then the carnival left, and he left, and I was left behind with ... my baby," Mandy finished, rubbing the flame dog again. "My babies," she amended.

"So he worked for the carnival," Hendricks mused. He blinked for a second. "What the hell is the moral of this story? Don't fuck a lying carnie?"

"All men are scum who just want to get laid?" Alison suggested, looking at him with a point harder than the elbow to his ribs had been.

"You humans are all idiots," Duncan added, playing the game.

"He made me special, you know," Mandy said.

Hendricks let a wary eye drift over the dozen dogs of fire he could see. "Looks like he made a lot of girls 'special' before he left town."

"No," she said, shaking her head. "He was only ever with me. The others—they—they could feel it because he was with me. Felt him with them even though they didn't touch him, didn't love him like I did."

Hendricks tried to sift through that, coming up with nothing. "What the fuck is she talking about?" he asked Duncan under his breath. It was almost a stage whisper.

"Sounds like something I've heard rumors of but never run across," Duncan said. "Ancient name; a species that doesn't really walk the earth anymore. It takes a ... partner," he nodded toward Mandy, "and any women with a fertile womb within a certain distance get hit by this ... I dunno, thrall? They get a dose of highly narcotic, erotic, spiritual essence hurled at them. It takes their root in their reproductive organs and, uh ..." He waved at the dogs. "Nine months later ..."

"He ..." Alison's voice sounded strong, then faded away before exploding out again, "he does a *MASS GROUP SEXUAL MIND ASSAULT?!*"

Duncan just stood there, like he was trying to evaluate his answer before speaking it aloud. "That's as good a descriptor as any, but if you want to be technically accurate, you'd need to add in something about essence or soul to the rape charge."

"This is fucked," Hendricks pronounced. "This guy is coming to Midian?"

"Carnival," Alison said. "The Summer Lights Festival is in town. He's probably already there."

"Yep," Hendricks said. "Fucked." He turned his attention back to Mandy. "You said he, uh ... you know ... did his thing with you ... the night before he left town?"

"Yes," Mandy said.

"If that's a pattern," Hendricks said, "and who knows if it actually is, then when does the carnival leave town?"

"Tonight's the last night," Alison said.

"Shit, fuck, damn," Hendricks said. "What the hell time is it?"

"About time we left," Duncan said, shooting a gaze at Mandy. "If we're allowed to." For this he raised his voice.

"I would let you leave," Mandy said, rubbing the neck of her fire dog, patting it like a master taking care of their pet. "But my babies ... they're hungry. There hasn't been a real meal here in a long time ... and they can't just nurse, you know? They're getting a little old for that ..."

"Yeah, most of us stopped using the nipple to nurse a long ways back," Hendricks said.

"Kinda figured we were about to go headlong into that snag," Duncan said. He clutched his baton and set his feet defensively. Hendricks gently detached himself from Alison, trying to stand on his own two feet. He wobbled a little. To his surprise, she took their uncoupling better than he had.

Hendricks hoisted the sword in front of him. "Just once, I want to go somewhere that doesn't suck, where the people and demons aren't trying to kill me." He realized, truthfully, that this desire was surprisingly soul-deep, something he'd never before said out loud.

"This is not your day," Duncan said.

"Tomorrow's not looking so good for that, either," Alison chimed in. She had her pistol drawn and was tracking the nearest flame dog, looking down her weapon's sights at it.

"Well, here's hoping the day after, then," Hendricks said, as the first of the fiery beasts leapt at him, and all hell came crashing down around his ears.

16.

John Watkins had been coming to Melina Cherry's brothel since he was eighteen years old. He'd been a fan of the lady herself for the longest time, because not only did she know how to run the place, she knew how to run his shaft. She'd tickled his cock in more ways than he could count, finding new methods of wringing old pleasures out of his dick all the time. John was thirty-six now, and it didn't bother him at all that Melina had gotten up there in the years. She still knew how to run his cock.

But ever since this redhead had shown up, his loyalty had wavered. "It's all right, baby," Melina had assured him the first time he'd gone to bed with red, just like the other times she'd passed him off to the blond-haired girl—what was her name? Colleen? Yeah, that was it. With the blond gal, it had never taken. She was young, she was decent, but she didn't start his fire like Melina had. That woman could have suck-started a leaf-blower. She had to be pushing fifty, and he figured he'd keep on visiting her until she was seventy, at least. She knew what he liked.

Then the redhead showed up. All it took was a test drive, Melina whispering in his ear all manner of encouragement in that throaty voice she had, all the things she whispered to him when they were together. It was a kink and a half to him; John had only ever gone for one girl at a time. Having the woman he'd been banging forever telling him to fuck a new girl, and finding that he liked the new girl on her own damned merits …

Well, it was what he'd heard some city boy call an embarrassment of riches. He wanted to spend all his money at Melina Cherry's brothel. He wished for mail-order Viagra so he could get hard more often. He even considered going to the doctor and complaining he couldn't get it up. Sure, it'd be damned embarrassing but worth it if he got a regular supply of those little blue pills. He didn't normally truck with drugs, but fucking was an addiction he could get behind.

And behind it he was at the moment, buried up to his pubes in the redhead. It hadn't taken him long to remember Melina's name, because she practically insisted he scream it aloud in their every encounter. She had confidence when he had none, pushing a teenage boy around and pressing every one of the arousal buttons in his then-fledgling, gangling body—the one no one else but him seemed to want to touch. She could still pop his cock to boner in two seconds flat, even with her looks fading.

Names weren't his strong suit, though, and he was always and forever forgetting the redhead's name. Lucy? Something like that.

He was thrusting and she was moaning, just a little less sincere than Melina made it sound. God, but she got into it. Just thinking about Melina made him go faster, his hands on the redhead's hips and thrusting inside, smooth and wet satin ringing his cock all the way down. He could feel the build as he inched closer, his eyes firmly closed. He only cracked them every now and again when he was with her, still visualizing Melina Cherry, the back of her head—

He thrust with a gasp and felt the sensation on his prick disappear. It was the most damned odd thing; one minute he could feel his pubic mound against her taint, the pressure like the curve of her insides was pushing his cock up at a forty-five degree angle. Sloping up into her, like a hungry dog begging for more. More cat. Yeah. He was digging it.

The next minute, the pressure was gone, the smooth satin pussy was gone, and he went from feeling like he was fucking a sweet, tight snatch to feeling like he was fucking empty air. He blinked his eyes in confusion and sure as shit, he was fucking empty air. The redhead was gone, no sign of her pale, freckled back where it had been only a moment earlier. His hands had been lightly resting on her hips and now they hung motionless in space. He knelt there, knees creaking on the bed, dick hanging out into nothingness, already starting to lose altitude—

"What the fuck?" John asked, waiting for the joke, waiting for the girl to pop out from the closet or beneath the bed. He just waited, feeling slightly stupid now that he could see his sweaty, hairy, sunken chest, protruding belly and his deflating cock in the mirror that had been hidden by the redhead's sweet flame-red tresses only a moment before. He looked at his eyes in the reflection, bulging, trying to figure out if this was a dream.

"Hello?" he called, a little louder. There was no answer.

***

Arch felt the impact on the back of his head and knew he'd been suckered. If he'd had time to think about it, he might have held a little tighter to the flashlight, but the shock of the blow knocked it clean out of his grasp, sent it rattling and rolling away, spinning in a way that made the scene seem like something out of a disco.

He knew by the throbbing in the back of his head that this wasn't a disco, that the only dancing about to be done was him trying to dance the heck away from whatever was aiming to put a hurt on him. He tried to roll from the blow, mostly by instinct, but it was a struggle of its own to keep control of his body. The impact sent his head rattling; his shoulder hit the hard stone ground and a face full of dust was his reward for failing to land properly.

Something landed on his back with a lot of weight, and Arch felt that panic rise again from what he suspected was coming.

The dust was everywhere, the dirt filling his nose and the back of his mouth, prompting a cough, a tickle and a liquid gush from his nose where he'd hit. It was hot blood, pain in his lip and face and shoulder, and even as he fought back against the imperious weight on his back, he knew that this was a lousy position from which to begin a fight. Not a bad one for losing a fight, though.

Arch thrust blindly with the one thing he'd managed to keep a hold on. The blade of the knife found something above him, striking a skipping blow against something that was perched on his back, applying weight and pressure to grind him into the earth.

The weight vanished with a hiss and the sound of crackling flames, and Arch had almost a half second to breathe before something else landed on him, just as hard, driving the air out of him once more and filling his ears with the sound of something—something very not human—snarling hot, foul breath past the side of his head.

***

Hendricks didn't find much strength in his arms for swinging his sword, but he got it around anyway. He caught the first flame dog on the point of it, watched the orange fire turn dark and suck inward like some sci-fi movie version of a black hole. It provided him with just the briefest sense of satisfaction before the next one came, and he stumbled back in response to the speed of the damned thing.

He paid little attention to the crack of gunshots from his right. He could see out of the corner of his eye the effect Alison was having on the fiery dogs—not much, unfortunately. They were staggered a little here and there, and that was about it. He could use the hesitation, though, because they truly did move like dogs. Low the ground, running in a loping motion that carried them across the cracked and broken road that divided the square from the mouth of the alley where they stood. If Hobbs Green was a place the world had forgotten, Hendricks figured that these things were a very definitely good reason for that amnesia, and he found himself wishing he'd never even heard of this damned place. Very literally damned place.

The bonfire roared and rose higher, belching more of the flaming beasts out of its depths. They swept past Mandy, who had her arms raised like she was directing an orchestra or some such shit. "Shoot her!" Hendricks called out, hoping Alison would take the hint.

Shots rang out from his right, and he saw Mandy stagger, her bald head lowered from the impact. Her scalp was wrinkled, too, and had the scuff of black singeing all about it. Hendricks spared a thought to wonder how someone once presumably normal had gotten so fucked up, then he remembered the fucking fiery dog sucking her teat and figured shooting one of those out of your joyhole might just start the party on being fucking nuts. He brought his sword down across the neck of another dog, but it was utterly pointless; he'd killed two, and in the time it'd taken him to do so, a dozen more had emerged from the fire, charging in a flat run at them, a pack of burning wolves hungry for blood.

"Dear God, I hope that fucking kills her," he had time to whisper before another dog came at him. The worst of them were still coming, still charging. Right now they were held at bay by Alison's shooting, judicious pistol shots that made 'em squeal and bark, smoke and little gouts of flame coming out of their snouts as they flinched away for a second, more resentful of the pain than actually injured. Hendricks could sense the feral calculation behind those burning eyes, watched them hold off for reinforcements. He had a bad feeling about those growing numbers, watched a few start to peel off from the bonfire and snake sideways, and he knew for a fact that he'd have a hellfire hound nipping at his ass in just a few shakes.

Mandy's head came back up, and the dark eyes were replaced by flames of their own. Not content to be the bitch who bred flaming hell dogs, something had twisted her shit up and there was a literal fire oozing out of her eyes like her brain had fried off in a grease fire. She didn't look lost or dreamy anymore; she looked pissed and nuts, the black ash leotard scraped clean in all the wrong places, giving Hendricks a view of aging anatomy that seemed to fit just perfectly with his own personal vision of hell. Hell was a town like this, swarming with devil dogs and administered by some old naked lady.

"If I ever get old and go evil, I hope I have the fucking sense not to let my dick and balls hang down to my knees while I'm being a fucked-up crazy person," Hendricks said.

"I wouldn't worry about either of those happening right now," Alison said, in the middle of a reload. "If you make it out of here to get old, it probably won't be with your balls intact to get saggy." She dropped the mag out of the bottom of the Glock and didn't even bother to fetch it, slamming the new one home without racking the slide. Slick move, Hendricks thought, and her weapon belched a shot. He spared a glance to the magazine and saw it was completely dry; she'd had the presence of mind to count her shots. On a fifteen-round magazine. He would have squeezed out a low whistle of admiration if he hadn't been stabbing some asshole demon pup in the face.

"Less talk, more fight," Duncan said, whipping a fire-red dog so hard it flew through the air as its flames guttered to black and disappeared before it hit the ground. "Maybe spare your balls to sag another day."

"You really think we're gonna walk out of this alive?" Hendricks asked, whipping his blade around. "They're gonna be on our asses from the flank in less than a minute, I figure."

He felt Alison brush his side, felt his gun slide out of his holster and watched her hoist it up, drawing it as she forced her back to his like something out of a fucking John Woo movie; she had one eye on the side of him and one on the alley behind them. "Oh ye of little faith," she said.

"No faith, actually," Hendricks said, with a gallows grin.

***

Arch felt the hit, felt the heat from the thing that was on him. That skitter of pure, blind terror that snaked its way over his skin, that settled around his belly. He tried to arch his back, tried to throw it off, but it was so heavy. He bent his arm and thrust the blade at it, missing clean. He wondered where it was, figured it had to be close and down on his back. Felt it writhe on him like a snake, the sound of something like elastic straining—bicycle pants, he figured a little belatedly—and then caught a flare of hard pain right in the kidney.

He took a full lungful of dirt, coughing and sputtering, ready to cough up everything he'd ever breathed. The dry dust was like he'd inhaled a sandbox, grainy and wet from his saliva, hints of blood coloring the taste. He spat as he coughed, felt a glob fall between his lips and hang there, suspended just off the ground, last stringer dangling from his lip as the pain shot through his whole back again.

It felt like someone had taken a crowbar to him, like he'd been tackled without pads around the midsection. From behind. By a tiger. If an ache was a rumble of the body's discontent, but this was a full-throated scream from the lower back on up, the cry of a body and a mind in panic and terror about what was fixing to happen to it. Arch thrust himself hard against the ground and tried to roll to the side. It worked, and he found himself on top of the small-framed demon riding his back.

Arch threw an elbow back and felt it land on smooth fabric. He heard it make that noise, that rubbery squeak as his foe struggled back, still pressing into his back. Arch threw his head back and slammed it into something hard, driving the apex of his skull into something a little softer. He felt warm fluid splatter in his short hair and wondered if it was demon blood or snot, then drove his head back again, uncaring.

His elbow found its own purchase, and the creature behind him went slack. Arch scrambled and drove the knife blindly backwards into its side. There was a brief moment of fear as his senses caught up to his rational thought: what if this wasn't a demon at all?

Then the black fire burned hot in the darkness—just a flash of something darker than the cave in front of his eyes—and his world was righted again.

He was on his knees, the gravel biting into his skin under the leg of his pants, doing that slow chew into the kneecaps as he dove for the flashlight that was just out of reach. He wanted to see, needed to see, needed to spin it in a circle and vanquish the shadows around him, to have it confirm for him that all the things trying to get him in the dark were gone—

His fingertips just barely touched the black checkered grip when he got hit in the back again, and the beam that promised to be the light that would drive the darkness out of his world spun out of his grasp yet again as Arch tumbled back to the floor of the mine.

***

Hendricks was off by a few seconds, not that he was keeping count. The bonfire was belching those flame dogs still, the smell of sulfur from their fires clouding his senses and hanging thick in the air like low-hanging smog he couldn't even see. Alison's right-hand gun was firing him behind him now, the one she'd kept pointed down the alley. He had his doubts about how effective she'd be with it—it was his 1911, after all, that big-framed automatic—but he watched her catch two of the flaming dogs right in the middle of their big, Rottweiler-sized bodies and thought if he was gonna put his faith in an Almighty, he might direct it toward the Southern belle at his back who was pegging demons one-handed like they were a ten ring on a target at the range, not big fucking flaming demon dogs running at her with intent.

"You've only got eight shots," Hendricks cautioned her, though it was probably unnecessary. He brought the point of his sword forward and poked another hellhound. The only thing saving him at this point was the complete lack of pressure needed to deflate a demon. Fortunately, they kept running at him, and no matter how fast they came, he managed to give 'em the poke at some point in their attack.

From there it was just a second 'til they evaporated, leaving a more sulfurous stink hanging around them.

"We'll be dead long before she runs out," Duncan said from Hendricks's left. Their little triangle had gotten a fucklot smaller, with the OOC at his side. The dogs were still approaching slowly, though their numbers were growing sickeningly larger all the time.

"They don't seem to be running short of help," Hendricks observed. "Anyone think we have half a chance if we break and run?"

"Nope," Alison said. Dead certain.

"They'll run us down and tear us to shreds like Korean barbecue," Duncan said. "Minus the sauce." He paused for a second. "Well, I suppose in your case, the blood is like a sauce, maybe—"

"Listen to the demon gourmand," Hendricks muttered. "We're not cooked just yet."

"Your indomitable spirit is endearing," Duncan said. "But this fight is pretty damned near over."

"No," Alison said, "it's not. We just need to hold out."

Hendricks's ears perked up at that. "Why? Is the cavalry coming to save us?"

She did not answer, the sound of her guns firing in tandem covering any reply, the smell of the discharged bullets mingling with the sulfur of the hellhounds.

"At least it's not as hot anymore," Hendricks said as he raised the sword again. There was a demon dog coming right at him, flames trailing from its body—

A rifle shot cracked through the air around them and knocked the dog back, rolling it across the road with a yelp. Everything froze as it echoed through the town square, and Hendricks stared at the beast, which had come to rest at Mandy's blackened feet, fire-covered ears turned down in discouragement.

"What ... the hell was that?" Hendricks asked, turning his head just far enough around to see the smile perched on Alison's wearied lips.

"'Do not be terrified; do not be discouraged, for the LORD your God will be with you wherever you go,'" she said, drumming the words out with a steady rhythm.

"That's not an answer," Hendricks said, rolling his eyes, "and I kind of doubt your mythical savior is waiting on a hilltop nearby with a sniper rifle waiting to save us all from the fires of hell."

"No," Alison said, and he could hear the smile without looking at her, "but my other father is." He could feel her straighten with her back against his, her voice gain confidence and wash with relief as she spoke. "And while he might not have unerring and holy accuracy on his side, he does have the advantage of being a pretty damned good shot."

***

Arch could feel the end at hand, his struggles all down to naught. Much as he writhed, much as he jabbed that knife back looking for the substance of a demon body to pierce, he had no luck in the matter. These things were contortionists, in control of their bodies in a way that kept him from laying a stabbing on them. His elbow was locked, a demon hand blocking it. The whole fight, from the moment he'd been suckered from behind, had been an exercise in fighting in the dark against stronger things. Nastier things. Meaner things.

Arch's brain defaulted to scripture in moments such as these, the quotes sustaining him. The one that popped to mind now was from the book of Jeremiah, but the idea of hope and a future and prospering seemed like folly. After all, when a man was on his deathbed, his earthly travails were at end. Hope and a future and prosperity were out of the question, at least on the mortal coil. As Arch felt the thing—this last in a succession of 'things'—on his back, making itself ready to do him in, he was utterly certain that his time was spent. It produced just the faintest hint of trepidation; the doubts came and with all the requisite humility.

Did I do enough? Did I fight my hardest? Was it foolish to come here?

While he was sure the answer to that last was a resounding YES, in that split second before the final blow landed, he didn't get to the conclusion of his thought. He felt the force reverberate through his body, but it was lighter than the deathblow he'd expected. It was a shock, a stunning move, a body hammering against his in a haphazard, disorganized sort of way. Chest against his back, weight on his frame, a thump that tingled him from toes to fingers. It came again, then again, and Arch held himself still, considering it. It didn't hurt, not really.

The last impact produced a hiss after the hit, and he felt the flames of hell lick across his back as the thing on top of him disappeared in rush of the black fire from below. Arch rolled to his back, and found himself looking up at a white face in the dark, lit by the refracted beam of the flashlight.

Dr. Lauren Darlington stood there, a tire iron in her hand. He watched as it slipped from her grasp to hit the floor of the mine, initial thud muted by the sand, followed by a ringing echo when the long shaft of it came in contact with exposed rock. Its clatter could be heard all through the mine, he thought, still stuck on her horrified face.

"What ..." Her fingers came up to her cheeks, like she was trying to cover her eyes but not quite making it there, "... the hell ... was that?"

***

Another shot rang out, sweet thundering déjà vu for Hendricks, recalling all those recent incidents where the shot of a rifle preceded his ass getting pulled out of the frying pan it was dangling onto. Except this time the woman who'd been doing the trigger pulling up 'til now was standing just behind him, her back against his black drover coat.

"You been talking with your daddy?" Hendricks asked, "or did he just happen by—you know, decided it was a fine day for a drive down to Alabama to visit a town where the canine fire-breathers run free and wild and there's no bag limit?"

"I was texting with him," Alison said, "on the way down." A light went off for Hendricks, remembering looking back and seeing her peering at her lap. He'd thought maybe she was head down from fatigue or sorrow.

"You were faking that hobble on the way in here, too," Hendricks said, shaking his head. "You slowed us down so he could catch up."

"Carrying that Barrett miles over uneven terrain was a bad idea for me," she said. "But my daddy has lighter rifles, and he's a deer hunter. That means he can tread the rough ground pretty fair."

"Nice," Hendricks conceded as he poked another fire dog in the snout. It whimpered for a half second before it dissolved. "You could have let us know company was coming."

"Didn't think you'd take kindly to more people treading in on your demon hunting circle," she said. She eased off him, back toward the rear of the alley. "We're gonna need to start getting out of here now."

"They're still flanking us," Hendricks said, turning back in time to see Duncan dispense with one of five (five!) of the critters that swarmed up the alley from behind them. "Unless you think we should run through town." Hendricks chanced a look toward the square as another bellow of a rifle cracked out. "Your daddy is probably gonna get run down by those things pretty soon, you know."

"He can take care of himself," she said.

"Well, as much as I applaud his help, he's overlooking the square and we're fucked if we try and work our way to him," Hendricks said. "So I guess what I'm saying is … he's bought a couple minutes, that's all." He hacked the blade down and took one of the devil dogs' heads off. They were pacing themselves, he could tell. When they unleashed, it was not gonna be a pretty sight. Still more of them popping out of that bonfire all the time, too.

"Sometimes all you need to do is play for time, Mr. Hendricks," Alison said.

"I think we're about played out," he replied. He was all in favor of hoping for a change in the status quo, but this far from help there wasn't much hope for the quo to get a status update.

And then there was a brief flash of light and a red-haired, pale-skinned woman wearing jeans and a t-shirt appeared and kicked a hellhound so hard it flew across the road, and Hendricks felt a flicker of doubt that his lack of faith might maybe—just maybe—be a couple degrees off. It didn't last, though.

***

"Seriously, what the hell was that?"

Lauren Darlington didn't recognize the sound of her own voice. It sounded choked, strangled, like that—that *thing*—that had been about to throttle Arch Stan had jumped up and wrapped long, pale fingers around her own throat.

Arch Stan was on a knee now, eyeing her warily, nothing in his hand but a switchblade. She could see his eyes in the dark, the outline of his face, but that was it. He was a shadow, a slow-moving ghost that was crawling up to unfurl itself in her face. She'd had a tire iron in her hands but it was gone now, and she fixated on the knife in his fingers, looking at it with a mix of wonder and horror that congealed together, conspiring to make her want to recoil and run.

"Are you okay?" he asked, his voice sounding like he'd been a little choked himself.

"I am not fucking okay," Lauren forced out. "I am not at all fucking okay. I am miles from fucking okay. I am from here to Chicago from okay, *okay*?" She stared him down, took a step back because of the knife—finally, her brain unlocking her legs, though she didn't dare reach for the tire iron—and then stood there, feeling helpless, absolutely flummoxed by what she'd seen.

Arch seemed unaffected, his shadow moving to collect the flashlight that had fallen by the wayside. He stooped, scooped it up, and she could hear his breath and labor as he did so. It made a scratching noise, scuffing the rock as he retrieved it, a sound that reminded her of a record needle being removed.

She'd followed him to see what he was doing, this rogue, lying deputy who had been on her list, that ephemeral shit list that she'd kept for sixteen years. What she'd found was him getting his ass beat by—by—by—

By some guy in bicycle pants who'd disintegrated in a flash of black fire. She hadn't imagined that, had she?

She remembered them coming down the hill, those guys on the bikes, remembered wanting to jump the cliff's edge. What had that been? A delusion? The cry of a mind entering psychosis? This was shit straight out of a psych residency. People did not dissolve into flame when you beat them with a tire iron. That was not normal.

"They were demons," Archibald Stan said into the echoing darkness of the mine. He kept the flashlight out of her eyes, scanning down the shaft with it, back in the direction he'd been heading when she was following him. Which had been stupid, she had to concede.

"Oh, fuck you, holy roller," she said, in utter disgust.

That put the silence back in the tunnel. "Excuse me?" Arch Stan wore that shield of aw-shucks politeness like a home-stitched quilt, but she'd seen through it before.

"What kind of cock and bull are you trying to get me to swallow?" Lauren asked.

"You hit a guy with a tire iron, and he got dragged back to hell before your eyes," Arch said. "You decide if you want to believe me or not, but—" He made a clicking sound as the flashlight beam swept back around and finally hit her, effectively blinding her. "Either way, you might want to get out of here."

"Why?" She covered her eyes, blinking away from the beam. "Are there more of them?"

"I don't think so, but I didn't know there were any to begin with," Arch said. "No, I'm suggesting you leave because I'm leaving, and I'm taking my light with me." He started toward her but kept a healthy distance, steering wide of her as he approached.

"Fan-fucking-tastic," Lauren muttered, and she started to shuffle back, ready to make for the entry.

"Dr. Darlington?" he asked, and she stopped in her tracks, staring at the shadow hidden behind the flashlight. "Don't forget your tire iron."

"Fuck you very much," she said, and took a few steps forward before dropping to a knee and sweeping her hand around to find it. She ran a palm over the dust before jarring the handle, then wrapped her fingers around it and hefted it to her side. She stood, never taking an eye off Arch Stan as she gestured toward the mine entrance, somewhere out of sight down the tunnel. "Lead on." She followed him, fuming, through the dark, happy to let the silence between them fester.

***

"Hell descends and the crazy bitch appears," Duncan said. His baton was whipping around in a frenzy, fast enough Hendricks's eyes couldn't even keep up. Devil dogs were turning black and burning up faster than he could count.

Hendricks heard him and did not acknowledge him, not really wanting to chance offending her. She heard, he was sure. She heard everything. Hell, she'd just dropped into this blazing corner of Alabama without warning, and he would have bet she'd been in Midian just seconds earlier. It was damned curious what Starling could do. Curious and freaky, and not worth contemplating in detail at the moment. "Took you long enough," he found it in him to sputter out, but he did it with a little gratitude.

"I could not let you perish at the teeth of these things," Starling said in that flat, emotionless tone.

"Because you've got big plans for me to perish elsewhere, in a bigger and better way?" He tried to keep it light, but after the words left his lips he felt a quiver wondering if there was any truth to the question. She did not answer either way, instead sending another demon dog yelping its way back to momma.

Hendricks saw Mandy again now, encircled in a sea of the flaming pups. They were curled around her, a sea of flaming devils she could walk across to get to them, if she was of a mind to. Hendricks did not like that idea, either.

She turned away from them and Hendricks caught a glimpse of her back. The skin on her shoulders was wrinkled and burned on each of the blades, scarred and healed, like a burn crusted over and burned again. He had a vision of them raring up on hind paws, putting it to her from behind in the way that dogs did, and he felt sick to his stomach even as he brought his blade down with unusual violence, lopping the head off one of them.

He got the sense that whatever they had done to fuck her up, it went a lot deeper than just her lack of hair and the black dust that clung to her wrinkled skin like a leotard. Those scars bespoke something twisted and isolated that threatened to bring up his half-digested waffle.

"It would be best for your own survival if you began a retreat," Starling said, her back turned as she hurled another flame dog back to mommy dearest.

"It woulda been best for my survival if I'd never come here in the first place," Hendricks said.

"But then you would have missed the truth of things." Starling punched one of the leaping dogs in the jaw so hard it disintegrated into black flame, the disturbance carrying through ten feet of air before it finished sucking the thing back to its origin.

"You could have just *told me*," Hendricks said, exasperated. "'Hey, Hendricks, I know I'm a cold and frosty demon ass-kicker who moonlights as a whore, but I've now saved your life on multiple occasions, so listen up: there's a carnie in town who's going to have sex with some girl and she's going to give birth to flaming demon dogs that will destroy the town. Might wanna get on that.' Boom. And I would have, no day trip into the heart of darkness necessary."

She paused and looked back at him, her ice-white flesh and dark eyes causing his skin to tingle from the attention. "You needed to *see*." Without even looking, she punched another demon dog into oblivion. "You needed to *know*. You are being prepared."

"You make him sound like a meal," Alison said, pitching in with an even-toned reply of her own.

"Hell would spit such a rough morsel as he from its lips in the trace of a wing's flap," Starling said. "He needs to be coarsened."

"Before hell can properly eat me?" Hendricks asked. "Hell can fucking blow me, and I give less than a damn whether it spits or swallows after that."

"I'd be careful," Duncan said. "In case you haven't noticed, veteran demon hunter, the one thing creatures of the underworld have in common is lack of access to modern dentistry."

"Oh, fuck all of you," Hendricks said. He pushed gently against Alison's back. "She's right; let's bail." He felt her start to move back down the alley and he followed. "Duncan, you coming?"

"A few steps behind, but yeah," Duncan's voice reached him, full of strain. "Just gonna keep the redhead company while you two get a head start." The heavy smell of that sulfur reeked in Hendricks's nose. Another shot echoed in the distance. Hendricks wondered if he'd lost track or if the shooter had moved in the last few minutes. Probably the latter; it sounded closer now.

"Let's bug the fuck out," Hendricks said, rushing the way through the alley with his sword out front. They burst out the other side to find it clear of dogs and the woods looking awfully damned inviting. "Hope you're in the mood for a run," he said to Alison as he started humping it over the uneven ground.

She already had her gun holstered and was pacing him cautiously, her hair flashing as she kept her eyes out for danger. Smart girl. She edged over to him and jammed his gun back in his belt holster, the slide still cocked back and the chamber exposed. She never broke stride. "Bet I make it back to the car before you," she said and hustled up. He hurried behind her, and listened for Duncan's footfalls from the direction of town. It took a while to hear them, but they did finally reach his ears, along with another set that was lighter.

***

"I assume you weren't down that mining tunnel by pure coincidence," Arch said as they broke out into the daylight. The afternoon sun was hanging high overhead, taking its slow arc around the sky. Wafting white clouds rolled along, and the wind came rolling too, but off the top of the mountain.

"Yeah, I'm not doing a rotation in the local abandoned mine," Dr. Darlington quipped. The woman had a sour face, like she had just swallowed a dill pickle and maybe took a chaser of the brine as well. He'd seen her around town, and she didn't always look like that. Just when she was pointed at him.

"Why were you following me?" Arch asked, leaning warily against his vehicle. His khaki uniform bore dark stains down both legs and all across the chest; he looked like he'd been wrangling pigs or at least playing an afternoon football game, minus the grass stains.

"Why are you changing IV bags at a hospital?" She spat it back at him with a hostility that wouldn't have been out of place in a line of scrimmage with the bitterest rival team across from him.

"I ... don't know what you're talking about," he said with so little conviction that it didn't sound like he was within even a hundred miles of honest.

She gave a little smug smile in response. "I'm gonna enjoy watching you twist for this. And if not for this, it sounds like your sheriff has enough other stuff to bury you forever."

Arch straightened, felt his back tense all the way down. "What are you talking about?" Reeve had said he was going to come after Arch if Erin hit the skids. "Did something happen to Erin—Deputy Harris?"

"What did you put in that IV bag?" Lauren asked.

"I didn't put anything in an IV bag," Arch said, and this he delivered truthfully. "Is she all right?"

Darlington stared back at him, her hands clenched. She wore scrubs, he realized a little belatedly, and her car was parked just behind his cruiser. She had a cell phone in one of her pockets, and she pulled it up to look at the screen. "No news yet, which is probably good for you, since they would have called me if she died."

Arch took a breath of relief, letting his back muscles relax as he slumped back to the car. He closed his eyes. "Thank the Lord."

"No thanks to you, I think you mean."

"I didn't do anything to Erin," Arch said, cracking an eye open. That woman still looked fiercely sour.

"We sent the bag for analysis," she said, staring flatly at him, more than a little malice in her gaze. "We're gonna find whatever you put in there."

"You're not gonna find much of anything, then," Arch said, rolling himself a little along the side of the Explorer toward the door. Normally he wouldn't have been that cavalier with his duty uniform, getting it dirty on the side of his car, but it was already well and truly wrecked anyhow. The car and the uniform.

"Then why'd you change the IV bag?" Dr. Darlington asked.

"How do you know I did?" Arch said, pulling himself off the side and taking a breath of the fresh mountain air. It was a fair sight better than what he'd been breathing in the mine. "Is there some reason you always assume the worst of me, Doctor?"

That got a rise out of her. Those snakelike eyes went so narrow she couldn't have squeezed a fat tear out of either of them. "I know who you are, Archibald Stan, and I've known all along, even if nobody else wanted to believe the truth of you. You were a sorry, belittling, pious, hateful little shit when you were a child, and now you're a corrupt, bullying, power-mad murderer in a town going straight to hell." She had that low, loathing drag to her voice like every word of her soliloquy was sweet pain to spill out.

He just blinked at her. It wasn't exactly the first time someone had said something unkind about him, but it might have been the worst thing he'd heard that didn't have a racial epithet thrown in. "Well, answer me this, then, Dr. Darlington," he applied the full sarcasm to her title, something he did not normally do, "if I'm a 'power-mad murderer,' and we're up here in a deserted location all alone together …" He opened his car door, boosting himself up to get in but still throwing a venomous glare right back at her, "why haven't I just shot you dead and called it a happy day?"

He watched her face contort in reaction, that furious uncertainty dissolving as she realized either she'd put herself at stupid risk or that he might have been lying. He found that he did not care either way and tossed her an uncharacteristic salute as he started his car. His wheels tossed gravel as he floored it in reverse, narrowly missing her car with the Explorer as he wheeled around in the old, weed-filled parking lot of the mine. He left her in the dust, but the stings she left him with vexed him all the way back to town and beyond.

***

"On your left!" Duncan called just before he overtook Hendricks. Hendricks had been expecting this for a while, since he'd heard Duncan's footsteps coming from behind. He didn't glance back, but he knew Starling had to be close at hand as well.

She came alongside a moment later as Duncan passed him to match pace with Alison. The red-clouded sky burned overhead, casting a glare down on them like they were under a crimson light. "You are well?" the redhead asked, causing Alison's head to jerk around. Hendricks could read the expression on her face, but when she spoke in response he didn't quite expect what she said.

"What kind of rough, no-lube butt-fuckery is this?" Alison stopped hard and turned on Starling. "You sent us here—"

"She seems angered," Starling said, like it was a matter of no consequence. *Oh, the grass is green.*

"Can't imagine why," Hendricks said, coming to a stop himself. He put his palms on his knees this time and gave Alison a sour look for not doing the same. She looked completely unbothered by the run. Neither were Duncan or Starling, but that was different.

Hendricks heard the crashing of brush and turned his head in time to see the man he'd met earlier that morning—lo, those many hours ago when the sun was still well below the horizon—coming at them in the darkness. Hendricks could tell it was him by the bevy of flashlights that suddenly got pointed his way. That same slightly overweight, large-framed fellow—except now he had a hunting rifle snugged across his shoulder by strap and a pistol on his belt that looked like a real, old-fashioned wheelgun.

"Daddy!" Alison said with obvious relief and took off for him, feet crushing leaves with each step. She threw herself into his arms and sank into his chest.

"Baby girl." Mister—what was it he'd introduced himself as? Longcolt? Longholt, that was it. Mr. Longholt hugged his daughter tight, his greyish brown head of thinning hair bowing down to Alison's shoulder. Hendricks couldn't see his face, but that didn't stop him from looking.

"And now she is no longer angry," Starling observed. *The sky is red.*

"Even you mystical beings can't figure women out," Hendricks said.

"Don't be a pig," Duncan said.

"Oink oink," Hendricks said with an unintended snort at the end. He snapped his gaze to Mr. Longholt. "I take it we don't have to spend time doing the long explanation about what just happened back there?"

"Demons from hell," Mr. Longholt said, pulling his head off his daughter's shoulder. He didn't look old or frail, not one bit. He looked strong, maybe a little wary, like many a soldier in a war zone Hendricks had known. "That's what's going on in Midian right now?"

"In a nutshell," Hendricks said. He hadn't been able to formulate much of an opinion about the man when they'd met the night before, being in something approaching screaming pain, but this was more than a bit impressive. "If you don't want your town to turn out like this, we need to get back immediate-damn-ly."

"We need to keep moving," Starling said.

Hendricks turned his eyes to Duncan. "They following us?"

"Doubtful," Duncan said, shaking his head quickly. "But I still can't see in there. Someone mucked this place up, bad."

Hendricks blinked at the OOC. "Are you talking about the fact that this place is burned to the fucking ground?"

Duncan didn't even show a hint of emotion. "That too. But it's clouded over. Some kind of work like Spellman does, but maybe on a bigger scale. I thought it was cloudy before we went in, but it's kinda like fog; you can't see in front of you so it's hard to tell if there's anything going on inside." He glanced at Starling, and a hint of distaste appeared. "Red here doesn't seem to share my limitations, though, so if she says we should keep moving, we should keep moving."

"Roger that," Hendricks said, breaking into a jog again long after Mr. Longholt had started moving his daughter forward. Just another reason for the Army man to rise in his estimation. Between that and the impressive daughter he'd raised, Hendricks was beginning to think he'd been making a mistake running solo all these years.

***

Mick had some time off, so he went into town. The sun was starting to arc lower in the sky, heading toward its terminus on the western horizon. He was excited about the night's activities, about what the evening with Molly would entail. He had trouble with her name, because some time in the itty-bitty hours of the morning he'd remembered that the last girl he'd been with, in that Alabama slice of shit town, had been Mandy. It had popped right into his mind like only something long forgotten could, ringing triumph of random memory in his ears. She'd been a sweet little piece, hadn't she? Nice knees and everything. He wasn't all that curious about how she was doing, but if things fell into the usual pattern, she was probably still alive—if one could call what she was doing living.

As he looked around the town square, he felt nothing. Less than nothing, really. The urge was too strong, it was burning him up inside. Left unsated, in about another year he'd be a walking erection, a disaster area of demonic proportions. He wouldn't be able to be near anybody, his essence would be bleeding out in flaming bursts of uncontrolled emotion. He'd tried holding it back once, when he was young and denying what he was. That had been Italy, he thought, and a few hundred years back. It had sure as shit cost him, too, made him flee the country in a hell of a hurry. Bonfire of the vanities looked quaint by comparison.

No, this was the time, this was the place. Just another stop for the carnival, just another town. Except this one was already heading to hell anyway, so why not speed up the process a bit?

He could smell the scent of coffee coming out of the Surrey Diner and thought about stopping in for a bit. He had that plan with Molly, knew where to meet her and when, was ready to follow through with it. He looked at his watch, the face scratched with a half a hundred nicks in the glass, and bemoaned—not for the first time—the slow passage of the hours.

What the hell was there to do in this town?

He came with a half an inch of voicing that thought, and then the faint crowd around the square gave him an answer.

"Flame inside," came a dreamy voice, far off, from behind him. "Fire burns, runs through the trees." He turned to see a man standing there in clothes a hell of lot worse than his own, and his were not exactly new and fancy. The guy looked to be in his fifties, old navy shirt that was threadbare and worn, long-sleeved even in the heat. He wore long, stained trousers, too, some sort of heavy canvas-looking material. He was sweating, a stocking cap pulled down around his ears.

Homeless, Mick thought. Bum. Not the sort of thing you saw a lot of in a town like this, but here one was.

"I can see it burning like a lit match inside," the bum said, staring at Mick. The man's eyes were looking straight through him, and Mick felt just a little swell of panic inside as his essence rippled. "Oooh," the man said. "Pretty, it crackles like flame."

"Don't mind Jarrett," came a rough voice from behind him, causing Mick to pinwheel around. There was a guy in the alley next to him, wearing a white apron as he came out the side door of the diner, full trash bag in his hand. Looked older than the bum, and Mick realized he'd seen him before. Pat, wasn't it? He squinted and caught the nametag. His hair was grey brown, and he looked like he scowled more than he smiled. "Came home from Vietnam a little off, but he's harmless."

Mick tore his glance from Jarrett, the bum, to Pat. He hadn't met Pat before, but he knew who he was. He was the guy giving Mick the stinkeye from behind the counter of the diner when he'd been sitting there with Molly last night.

"The flames are rising," Jarrett said, like he was in some kind of fucking trance. Mick could still feel the nervousness, but at least now he had a plan. He eased away from Jarrett and toward Pat, taking odd note of the stains and marks down the apron on the old proprietor.

"I know you," Mick said, putting on a fake smile.

"I wouldn't say that," Pat replied, pausing after heaving the garbage bag into the open dumpster. He wasn't looking at Mick with suspicion, exactly, but it wasn't friendliness, either.

"You were the one giving me dirty looks when I was with Molly last night," Mick said, throwing some affable in there. It was all pretend, of course, but he kept his pace steady, trying to stage-manage the show and hoping that the bum stayed right where he was. A glance back showed that he was doing exactly that, though he'd taken to mumbling under his breath.

The alley was in shade with the side of the diner keeping the sun off of Mick's head. For this he was slightly grateful. He offered a hand to Pat. "I'm Mick. Nice to meetcha."

Pat glanced down at it like it was a foreign object, and Mick could see him weighing the options. Out of politeness he finally out thrust his own and took it, but Mick didn't miss that it was the hand that had been holding the garbage bag seconds earlier. Fucker. Mick didn't even feel remorse for what he was about to do after that. "Pleased to make your acquaintance," Pat said, putting the squeeze on Mick's hand, though by his tone he clearly wasn't.

Mick met his eyes, shook his hand once firmly, then glanced again back at the bum. He was at a good twenty paces away, and that was good enough for Mick.

"The fire," Jarrett whispered.

"What's he talking about?" Mick asked, nonchalant. He reached inside and started to play with something he'd only used once before, squinting at Jarrett like he held the secret of life.

"Like I told you, he ain't right," Pat said from Mick's peripheral vision. Mick knew he was far enough away to make this plausible. It was just a matter of effort, really. He pictured the bum in his head, pictured him in flames, rising—

"So hot," Jarrett said quietly. "Sooooo hot." The voice rose.

"It's a hot day all right," Pat said toward the bum.

Mick reached deeper, looked deeper, saw the middle of the bum. He didn't think of him as a person anymore, not that he cared all that much. There was a switch in there, a fiery middle, and all he had to do was—

"AIEEEEEEEEEE!" The shriek was instantaneous, and Mick found himself jumping back involuntarily just from the noise.

"Jesus!" Pat said from next to him, startled. "Simmer down, Jarrett!"

"Is this normal?" Mick asked, taking note of the first strains of smoke wafting from under the bum's dark shirt.

"He's usually fairly docile," Pat said. "But I have seen him get irate once or twice." The man said 'twice' like 'twiced,' like it had a d to end it. Southerners. It was barely audible over the bum's shrieks by this point.

The fire burst out of the belly of the bum's shirt like a door coming off a stove, and the next scream he let out was consumed by a belch of flame that rolled out of his mouth.

"Holy shit!" Pat said. He did not move to help and neither did Mick; the diner owner just stood there, stunned, and Mick stood right with him, though only feigning surprise. Inside, he was a big, bubbling pot of indifference.

The bum's screams died with the gout of fire that came out of his mouth and his skin was replaced with flame within a second, a blackened skull appearing within them like some object partially unearthed. The fire crackled as the bum fell to his knees, arms spread wide like he was ready for a hug or salvation or something. He was completely consumed by now, and Mick wondered just how alive he was under the orange blaze. His clothes, the threadbare, shitty things, had already blackened and peeled back. Bones were appearing now, obvious, as the body—what was left of it—toppled to the ground in the mouth of the alley and stopped moving.

Mick watched with detached interest, trying to plot his response for maximum effect. "Jesus," he said, putting a little acting into it, like when he had to fake excitement for someone who had won a prize at a booth, "did he just spontaneously combust?"

"I ain't never seen nothing like that," Pat said from beside him. "Jesus. I think he did."

"I know I wasn't anywhere near him," Mick said, trying to sound awestruck, "and neither were you." He cemented his alibi with this little lie. "He was just standing there and—I mean, holy, it was like the flames came *out* of him, it wasn't even like he was on fire on the skin or clothes or anything ..."

"Yeah," Pat said, nodding. The proprietor had not yet moved his gaze off the charred remains, the flames finally dying down. The whole alley smelled of them, smelled of burnt meat, and Mick covered his nose involuntarily. "There wasn't anybody anywhere near him, he just lit off like a firecracker." His nods came one after another, and Mick wondered for a moment if the diner owner's head wasn't going to bob right off his shoulders.

"We should call 911," Mick said, finally dropping that suggestion. Now that the damage was irreversibly done and his alibi was secure.

"Yeah," Pat said, but it came out with the air of a man who had heard and nodded but would not move without some external prodding.

"You should go do that," Mick said then thought the better of it. "*We* should go do that." Pat's gaze finally shifted off the body to look him in the eyes, a sort of blinking curiosity one might find in the eyes of a child looking for explanation on some simple fact. Mick provided it, happily, acting his way through. "I don't want to be alone with the …" He waved a hand at the smoking corpse, lying prostrate on the alley floor, the pavement scorched around it. "… With him."

***

Arch heard the "All units" call go out on the radio as he hit the outskirts of Midian. He assumed, the shudder of the car's deceleration running through the steering wheel to his arms, that it did not apply to him. He listened anyway, the particulars causing a very different sort of shudder, one prompted by the description of Jarrett Barnes, whom everyone in Midian knew, turned to flaming ash and dust in the middle of the square. Arch kept driving, kept shaking, and found when he reached his apartment that he had some trouble walking from the Explorer to the door of his apartment, and the fumbling for his keys was even worse.

Yes, this was Midian now, he decided. Bodies found every day, the town falling steadily into ruin. Was it the end of days? Maybe, he decided, as he finally sunk the key into the lock. The cool air of the apartment was not reassuring, though, as he closed the door and felt the lack of the apartment's other occupant especially acutely in the shaded dark of this place that did not feel like home.

***

They made it to the car faster than Hendricks had anticipated. The chatter was minimal, the breathing not as heavy as one might have expected given that there were five of them. Two of them might not have been human, but still—Mr. Longholt did not wheeze at all, and his daughter's panting sounds were minimal. Hendricks fought against the pounding of his own heart to hear, mostly, and found it somewhat surprising that there was no sound of dogs behind him, no patter of hellhound feet searing plant and leaf and grass and dirt as they pursued. When the town car came into sight he let out a breath of relief, one which sounded much like every other breath he'd drawn in the last hour or so—somewhat gasping.

"Why … aren't they chasing us?" Longholt asked. Leave it to Army to try and beat the Marines to the punch. "Last time they at least dogged us on the way out. This time, nothing."

"Because his girlfriend killed their queen," Duncan said, nodding at Starling, who stood next to Hendricks, but a lot more at peace than he was. So level was the OOC's tone that it took a moment for what he'd said to settle in Hendricks's brain.

"Wait, she did what?" Hendricks jerked his head around to look at Starling, who was staring straight ahead. "She killed Mandy?"

"You're not gonna cry about it, are you?" Duncan asked with something approaching a sneer. Like he was channeling Lerner's departed spirit. "But yeah, she chucked a wooden support from a collapsed building at her. Impaled her right in the middle of her little dog party. They all burst into black flames right off."

"Like a hive army in a movie," Alison said. "Kill the queen, kill them all."

"Let's not go digging too deep into that," Mr. Longholt said, his expression now curiously clouded.

"It's good to know, isn't it?" Duncan asked. "In case we fail tonight?"

Hendricks let that rest for a minute before cutting into it. "Yeah, it's great to know that if we fuck up and this carnie gets laid, all we have to do is murder a girl to save the town. I'm so very ecstatic about that. Somebody pinch me." He felt a harsh sting on his hand and looked over at Starling, who had done just as he commanded, as neutral as ever. "Didn't mean it in a literal fashion." Starling did not look sorry.

"We need to move," Mr. Longholt said. "So as to avoid having to consider that option."

"I guess I'll just play devil's advocate here—" Duncan said.

"Seems like that would be in your job description," Alison said.

"—and suggest that this is a very valid option," Duncan went on. "Maybe you lack the emotional distance to see what needs to happen here. One girl's life does not balance well on the scales against that of a whole town."

"Which is maybe gonna burn anyway, if cryptic prophecy chick over here is right," Hendricks said, nodding at Starling. He locked his eyes on her. "Well? Gotta any other helpful words of advice now that we've extracted ourselves from this mess I just had to *feel?*"

"You are unforged steel," she said, looking straight at him. "A sword without an edge."

"Oh, I think you're about to see my edge," Hendricks said.

"You are not ready," Starling said. "You must face the trials to prepare for what is to come."

"And you're just gonna lead me through 'em, like a pup at a dog show?" He didn't even like the way it sounded in his head, but it was even more bitter spilling out of his lips. "What am I to you? A pet? Like those ... things ... were to Mandy?" He waved his hand in the direction from whence they'd come and tried to glare at her, but she gave no hint to indicate that his anger affected her at all. "Is that what I am?"

She stared at him coolly, like always. "You are Lafayette Jackson Hendricks."

He felt his mouth dry. "And?"

She did not break off from his look, did not blink. "You have a task set before you."

He started to bark back at her about tasks he did not want nor need, but before the bile even had a chance to bubble out in hot, molten fury, it was as though he had blinked and she was no longer there. Empty space stood before him, the cloudy sky now more closely approximating a grey day than night, the smell of fire and sulfur nearly gone from the wind.

"That's a hell of a thing," Mr. Longholt said, staring into the space she had occupied.

"Neat trick, huh?" Duncan said, and he sounded a little pissed himself. He bumped lightly into Hendricks's shoulder as he stepped forward, like it could give him a better view to the empty space Starling had been standing in only a moment before. "Well ... you want to keep arguing about whether you ought to do as she said like a dog, or would you like to go see if we can save that town where you've been hanging your hat, laying your—lay?" Duncan grinned, and once again Hendricks had the sense that it was the sort of crack Lerner would have made, had he been here.

Hendricks felt like arguing, was all set for it, ready to let it fly, but the lack of Starling to rail against took all the starch out of his collar. He kept his mouth shut long enough for reason to prevail, never once looking away from the place that damned woman had stood as she spouted her matter-of-fact bullshit. "Let's just go," he said, and he turned away, tracing a path back to the town car one step at a time. He tossed the keys to Duncan, though, and headed for the passenger seat for himself as he watched Alison go toward her father's pickup. He spared only a fleeting thought about how it might be marginally more fun to be a fly on the window of that vehicle than the passenger in his own, seated next to the stoic demon for a hundred and fifty miles of highway and silence.

17.

Alison didn't exactly revel in silence, not when her daddy was right there. He gave her the space to start the conversation, and she appreciated that, watching the fence posts on the side of the highway whipping by as they blew past at eighty. The black town car carrying Hendricks and Duncan was just ahead of them, setting the pace her father was following. The air conditioner was turned up to full and blowing cold air at her, silent accusation for what had happened a hundred miles ago and more now.

"She wasn't the same girl," Alison said, breaking the silence herself, a plate crashing to the floor of the kitchen on a quiet night.

"No, she wasn't," her daddy agreed, nodding along without much else in the way of emotion. "I could see that plain as day, even through the scope."

"How do you reckon it's been for her?" Alison asked, genuinely curious. "All those years there with nothin' but those dogs for company?"

Her father just shook his head. "Girl wasn't right, that's for damned sure. Last time she was ... distant, for certain. But not like this. Her daddy ... I reckon he'd have been real disappointed to see how it all turned out for her. I find myself thinking that redheaded gal might have done Amanda a favor by putting her down."

"Like a dog," Alison said.

Her father held a silence for a second, guiding the old pickup truck between the lines. "Just like."

She held her thoughts for another minute, just letting them sift. "Did you ever think when we went there all those years ago ... that ... what happened there ... that it'd ever happen to our home?"

"Hell no." There was a silent shame there, she realized, unspoken. "It was one of those things that I couldn't explain at the time, not knowing about demons and whatnot. I still don't really know much, at least not like your new friend in the cowboy hat seems to. But I don't reckon anyone looks at the misfortunes of others like that—and I couldn't see what happened to her, her town, in any way except through the eyes of her daddy, because I knew him well—and wonders too hard about what would happen if a freak occurrence like that came to rest on his own home. It's a lot easier to think that something like that'd happen to someone else, anyone but you. So, no, I didn't ever think about it coming. Not to Midian." He swallowed hard enough that she saw his Adam's apple waver. "Not in a million years."

"More like thirty years." She sat there for a second and the reached out, resting a hand on his arm. "We'll stop it, Daddy."

He gave her a faint smile. "Damned right we will, sweetheart." But she could tell that in his heart of hearts, he was really not so certain.

***

Hendricks rapped the window, staring out. The sky was starting to show the first purple hues, and that didn't sit well with him for some reason. Veteran of Iraq, demon hunter who'd put the sword to more of the beasts than he could rightly count, and now he was getting squeamish—nervous, he corrected himself—wondering what was about to happen. He'd left home behind a long damned time ago, walked away at eighteen with not even a look back for very good reasons. With Renee, it had felt different for a while, like he could go home, just to a different one. When he'd been fished out of Lake Ponchartrain, that feeling had gone like yesterday's breakfast, flushed out of him. Nothing left but a hollow, hungry feeling that he'd filled by indulging in revenge. Sweet, sweet revenge against an endless, disorganized army of demons that he'd bested on every single occasion. Strong but solitary, he'd found stomping demons flat easier than knocking down doors or going on missions in Iraq.

He could hear a noise in the wheel well of the car as it rolled along the highway, and that noise was driving him half nuts. The steady thump of his knuckles against the glass didn't cover it, didn't nearly blot it out of his hearing. It almost seemed like it added to it, a drum beat for the music that was torturing his soul. If he'd believed in souls.

"Will you stop that?" Duncan asked him. The OOC didn't seem terribly put off by it, such was his calm.

"Sorry," Hendricks said, not really sorry. He did stop the drumbeat, though, letting his knuckles twitch idly in the same rhythm. He could hear the noise, that buzzing, screaming sound like he'd heard on the mountain as he hung out the window and felt the air streaking through his uncovered hair—

"Missing your girlfriend?" Duncan asked, and Hendricks could tell by the way he asked that he didn't really care.

"Missing your boyfriend?" Hendricks lobbed back.

Duncan didn't respond, and Hendricks sunk back into thought. That buzzing noise was a damned haunting thing. He imagined hearing it in dreams, wondered how much of it that it would take to drive him mad. He listened closer to the thrum of the tires on the highway and concluded that it probably wouldn't take all that much. Then he thought of Erin, lying in a hospital bed somewhere he couldn't even see her, hopefully surrounded by her family by now, and the sound became a buzzing in his head again, and before he knew it, he was drumming his fingers on the window without even being fully aware of it.

This time, Duncan said nothing.

***

"He just burned right up," Mick said to the skeptical-looking sheriff. The man had a really severe case of baldness going on, and a cynical look to match. It was just consuming his whole face, that don't-bullshit-me cop look. Mick tried to decide whether it was from the squinted eyes, those puckered lips, or some other feature. The sheriff had talked to Pat from the diner first, and Mick had listened to the man spin a short story about how the bum had been going on and on about fire and suddenly burst into flame. It had been filled with the requisite amount of "Holy shits!" and exclamations of "Jesus!" It hadn't given the sheriff much of anything to work with, though, and Mick was all about keeping that the case. "Never seen anything like that before, and I've worked the freak show tent for a few years, if you know what I mean."

"Yeah, the amazing elephant-pig fetus must pale in comparison to this," the sheriff said, unimpressed, as he made a notation on the itty bitty notepad he carried with him. "You see anything suspicious before the event?"

"The guy was rambling about fire," Mick said with a shrug. "Like the diner guy said, he was like a broken record on it. Couldn't get it out of his head for whatever reason."

"And then he burst into flames," the sheriff said, writing something else down. It took Mick only a second to realize he wasn't asking. "You weren't anywhere near him when it happened?"

"I never got closer than about ten feet from him," Mick said. "I was standing by, uh ..." He pretended to have to remember the name for a second, "... Pat, yeah, Pat, when he lit off."

"All right, then," the sheriff said, and flipped his notebook closed. "Do you have any contact information where I can reach you if we have any other questions?"

Mick stared at him, trying to screw up his face to look uncomfortable at giving a tough answer. "I mean, I go where the carnival goes, so you kinda have to get ahold of them to get me."

The sheriff lowered his head slightly. "You don't have a cell phone?"

Mick shrugged. "Never needed one."

"It's 2014, son, you might consider looking into gettin' one," the sheriff said, turning away from him with a sigh. "Thanks for your cooperation."

"Uh, you're welcome," Mick said, turning back to the mouth of the alley and the square beyond. They hadn't retrieved the bum's body yet, it just sat under a white sheet that was weighed down on two corners by stones. The wind whipped through every few minutes, disturbing the edges and moving the corners that were not weighed down. It was flapping lightly in the breeze now, like the dead man was trying to surrender by waving the flag.

Too late, you crazy fuck.

Mick looked past the body, burying that sense of self-satisfaction he felt running through him. He caught a glimpse of dark hair and saw Molly in the middle of the square with a woman who looked damned similar, though her hair was maybe a shade or two darker and she was wearing surgical scrubs. Was that normal in this town? Mick guessed it wasn't. He hesitated at the mouth of the alley and caught Molly looking his way. They were supposed to meet here, but he wondered at the presence of what damned sure looked like her older sister. Then Molly waved at him, and he shrugged it off, heading toward her at a walk. No reason to hurry; tonight was the night, and all he needed to do was play it cool.

***

Lauren felt a hint of sick as the guy—Mick—crossed the road toward them. Sick at the thought of Mick. Heh. Her scrubs felt dirty on her skin, and not just because of her shift. She felt like some dust or grime or something deeper had settled on them in that mine, had contaminated them, and the fact she hadn't had time for a long shower and a change of clothes was a source of aggravation. She'd wanted to be here for this, though, and since Molly had been ready to leave the minute she got home, she ditched any thoughts of being clean and not icky and heebie-jeebie free for the time being and walked her to the square. But seeing this Mick hadn't really helped matters. In fact, it had generated a nasty little sliver of doubt in her stomach.

Yes, he looked nice enough. Though she did have to frown since he was walking away from the mouth of an alley which contained—if she wasn't much mistaken—another body. Yet another body. Sheriff Reeve, naturally, was in close attendance.

Sweet fancy Christ, what the hell was going on in this town?

"Hey," Mick said, earning no points for wit. At least he hadn't said "Yo!"

"Hey," Molly replied, and Lauren felt like she should slap her daughter in the back of the head.

"Wasssssssssuup?" Lauren said, just for variety. It got them both to look at her, her daughter with flushed cheeks from embarrassment and the carnival worker with one of those perplexed expressions that Lauren so often found directed her way. "I'm Lauren," she added.

"Mick," came the reply. No, "I'm," to preface it, just the statement of a name. Nope, she didn't like him.

"Mick, this is my ... mom," Molly finally found voice to say.

"Oh, wow," Mick said, brows slightly inclined, "I woulda thought sister. Good for you."

Lauren tried not to dissect that statement for its obvious flaws, instead jumping to a more important question. "So, Mick ... is that a body over there?"

"Yeah," Mick said, apparently not concerned by this admission. "Dude just started screaming and burst into flames." He frowned, the expression revealing him to be kind of an idiot in Lauren's estimation. "You got a weird town here. Lot of people dying, it seems like."

Lauren cocked an eyebrow at him and knew if her father had been alive and standing here, he would have crafted a careful warning about how it could be one more by the end of the evening depending on how things went. "You caught us on a bad week."

"Bad month," Molly said, doing that inappropriate teenager laugh. She stopped after about two seconds. "Oh my God, that's not funny at all."

"At least you realized it, sweetie," Lauren said. She looked over at Mick. "So, Mick ... you're only in town for tonight?"

"Yep," he said.

Monosyllabic was never a great sign, but Lauren withheld her disappointment and moved gamely to the next question. "Have her home by eleven, please."

She searched his eyes for hints of intelligence, or, barring that, comprehension. "You got it," Mick said, fulfilling at least part of the requirement. He held out a crooked elbow to Molly, like some sort of gentleman. "Shall we?" His northern accent was plain as day to her, and she found for the first time in her life she didn't care for it. Usually it was such a breath of fresh air.

"See ya later, Mom," Molly said, flushed with delight as she hooked her arm in his. Lauren tried to smile, because that—it was innocent, right? Walking arm in arm with a man? Lauren watched them cross the street, and they even looked both ways. Mick said something to Molly that was lost in the wind between them, and Molly laughed, not even a look back over her shoulder at her mother. That knot in her stomach was growing bigger.

"Molly got a date tonight?" Sheriff Reeve's voice jarred Lauren out of her trance, watching them cross the square, talking, laughing.

Doing the normal things couples did. Lauren vaguely remembered that.

"Yeah," Lauren said, a little more tense now that she didn't have to hide it in front of her daughter. "He's not implicated in murder by any chance, is he? Because I wouldn't mind an excuse to put an end to *that*." She waved a finger gently in the direction of their laughing conversation as the two of them traced their way around the edge of the square.

"No, just a witness to another weird death," Reeve said, somehow not relieving her. "Jarrett burst into flames. Spontaneous combustion. Pat saw the whole thing, kid didn't come anywhere near him before it happened." Reeve sighed. "I swear, it's like this town is going to hell."

Something about that tickled Lauren, bringing her back to what Arch Stan had said. *They were demons.* Like that was a normal, natural thing. Well, maybe for holy, pious Archibald Stan, they were. "Hell, huh?" Lauren just kept watching Mick and Molly. Molly laughed again at something he said, and it sent a jolt through her as she compared the now with a memory of her as a baby, sitting on the floor, laughing. Such a delightful sound, so innocent and sweet and full of promise.

A promise this carnie knew nothing about and was now walking away with. Lauren felt her fist clench.

"You okay?" Reeve asked.

"Just contemplating murder," Lauren said.

"Sweet fancy Christ," Reeve said, "Please refrain. I need another body in this town right now like I need a hole in my head."

***

Arch's phone rang as he was pacing around the map again, a pen in hand and a mad gleam in his eye that he could feel. He scrambled to answer quickly and was only mildly surprised when Alison's name came up on the caller ID. "Hello?"

"Arch," she said with a sense of relief that was palpable to him even over the open line.

"Alison," he said, maybe with more than a little relief of his own. "Are you all right? Where are you?"

"Just passing Cleveland," she said. "We got a big problem, though."

Arch felt his teeth just about grind on that one. "Of course we do. How big?"

"Bigger than the bikers, that's for sure." Her voice was tight. "Arch, it could turn Midian into a wasteland."

He felt himself fall into the chair heavily. "Sounds about normal. What's the threat?"

"Someone with the carnival. Some kind of fire demon, sleeps with a girl there, and he somehow impregnates the whole dang town."

Arch felt his face twist as he tried to plumb the meaning of the nonsensical statement she'd just made. He didn't quite get it. "Say what?"

"I know, it doesn't sound right."

"Yeah, it sounds wrong," Arch agreed. "Which is about par for Midian's course of late. What's the move?"

"Get to the festival, find the demon, send him packing home with nothing but his black-flame soul."

"A plan I can endorse," Arch said. "What do you need from me?"

"It's spawns fire demons, so …" Her voice trailed off. "I dunno. You think a fire extinguisher would work?"

Arch didn't really know how to answer that, but it didn't matter because his mind jumped in a new direction. "Oh, wow. That can't be coincidence."

"What?" Her voice picked up. "What is it?"

"Jarrett just burned to death on the town square," Arch said. "I heard the all-call on the radio just before I got home."

"Sounds like our boy is already working," Alison said.

"Hmm," Arch said. "You sure it's a boy we're looking for?"

"Unless you know a lot of girls who can impregnate a whole town with fire demons?"

"Point." Arch scratched his face, scruff and all. "How do we do this?"

"We're gonna have to comb the festival looking for something unusual," Alison said. "The demon is going to try to knock up a girl there."

"So we're looking for teens who look like they're ready to have relations at the Summer Lights fest." Arch felt some of the thrill of hope, the certainty of direction fade. "Well, that should be …" He didn't even have the heart to say it.

"Like picking a horny teenage couple out of a pack of horny teenage couples," Alison said, finishing the thought for him. "Arch, if we don't, we're gonna have to kill the girl who gets pregnant. She becomes the queen of the demon horde that follows." She didn't sound any more hopeful than he did. Fairly desperate, actually.

"So if we can't find them, we have to kill a human being?" Arch asked, feeling the weight go out of his legs. Luckily he was already sitting.

"It's her or the town," Alison said. She said something else, but there was a burst of static and he couldn't hear it.

"Alison?" he asked. "Alison?" She was gone, signified by the double beep of his phone to let him know the line was dead.

Arch set the phone slowly down on the map, stared at the black screen, and all the dark X's marked over the colorful surface lines of the paper. Every one of them felt like a failure, and the black screen of the phone was the worst of all. It stared back at him with a dark reflection of his own face, his features blurred and consumed by the blank screen. It felt to him like he'd been subsumed by the darkness within it, like it had spread all over his features until all was in shadow, and he wondered if it was an omen for the immediate future.

18.

The sunset didn't stop the heat. Mick was picking his way across the field, Molly hanging on his arm like a lady at a fancy dance, and he could feel her sweating, though from anticipation or the heat, he wasn't sure. She was wearing a soft cotton dress that fell to mid-thigh, and he caught a look at those knees. What was it about that joint that moved him so? Bone and cartilage and connective tissue, but the way it moved, the way it could right-angle and twist, the pale skin stretched over it all—something it about it got to him.

They made their way through the short grass, heading toward the main gate. Cars were parked all around them, from the newest of the new to the old—Fords, Chevys and Dodges. Mick had seen BMWs before, but he didn't see many here. He figured this was the working man's entertainment, the blue-collar place of leisure. The carnival was already lit up, the Ferris wheel shining at him across the field. That'd be the place, he figured. It was a good place for it, even with the new, smaller boxes. He could do it sitting down, Molly astride him. He'd done it that way before, in tight places, though it'd been a few centuries.

That was the one downside to his condition. It sure felt good when it happened, but he would like to have done it more often. That rush of release, that feeling when it surged out of him and filled the girl, filled all the women nearby—that was a damned good feeling. Cathartic in its way. It wasn't just a little satiation; it was like drinking a river to drown your thirst on a hot day. Once you could handle it, there was nothing so sweet and relieving.

But Mick wasn't up for a leaving a trail of carnage that would have OOCs after him, looking over his shoulder every day of his life. This he figured he could manage, just this town, and he'd be done for a while.

He dropped Molly's arm from his and took her hand, meeting her shy eyes with his and smiling. She smiled back as they passed the entry gate without paying, just a wave from Joshua to let him know he was clear to proceed. He could tell she felt it by the look on her face; she was special. Tonight she was his lady, and he was gonna do everything to make her feel it, so that by the end of the night she'd feel obligated to let him feel *it*.

He felt her sweaty hand in his as they traipsed past the carnival games toward the midway by unspoken suggestion. He'd lead her where he wanted her to go. He felt the smile even as he took his eyes off of her, that anticipation breaking free and taking on a life of its own. This was where the fun began.

***

Hendricks was already ditching the car even as Duncan came to a halt in the wide field the festival was using for a parking lot. It took Hendricks a minute to realize they'd been at the edge of this field only a couple days earlier, and he hastily shot a look at the far end to confirm his suspicion. Yup. That was where they'd bagged that quantel'a after the downhill chase.

They'd fallen in behind Alison's daddy as they drove into town. Duncan had fielded a call from her on his cell phone. She'd been in touch with Arch. Hendricks had watched the conversation, the demon driving adeptly with one hand as he coasted down the off-ramp toward the Old Jackson Highway. He heard snatches of Alison's side of the conversation and of course all of Duncan's, ferreting out that there was some incident that had happened involving fire. Hendricks didn't care for the sound of it, but it did suggest that Starling was on to something. Not enough that he'd forgiven her for sending him down to that backwoods quarantine zone from hell, but he felt himself soften just a little.

Alison was out of the pickup truck door in a hot second, too. Hendricks caught sight of Arch waiting, leaning on his police cruiser, his uniform looking a little worse for the wear. Hendricks suspected he'd been up to something. It must have really been a hell of a thing if he hadn't even bothered to change afterward.

Hendricks watched Alison run into her husband's arms, watched them meet in a kiss that was equal parts relief and desire and fear. The interplay of emotions was all there, the warring of them, and he felt a few of his own as he watched it, unable to look away. He spared a thought for Erin, still lying in a hospital bed. He resolved to see her after this, and then hunt those fucking bikers down. Assuming they won this fight.

Assuming there'd be a fight.

"Bill?" Arch asked as he put his bride down, sweeping her to his side as he shifted his expression to regard his father-in-law. That was his name; Hendricks had forgotten and just taken to thinking of him as Alison's father. Simpler that way. Bill.

"Arch," Bill said, coming 'round the truck and offering his hand to his son-in-law. They shook with an easy familiarity, and the respect was apparent on both sides of the gesture. "I wish we were coming to this point of revelation under less strenuous circumstances."

"You've known about demons all along?" Arch asked. He kept a good mask on it, Hendricks thought, but it was clear there was something going on beneath it.

"Since you were a child, I reckon," Bill said. "I didn't know exactly what was going on here until Alison spelled it all out for me, though."

"Well, it's all in the fire now," Arch said. "And we're about to be too, 'less we get this thing stopped in time."

Duncan pushed up next to Hendricks. "Let's find this fiery fuck and put an end to him; get back to the business at hand."

"This is the business at hand," Arch said firmly. "Flaming destruction of the whole town seems like a priority to me."

"Whatever," Duncan said, waving a hand. "What's the plan?" There was a moment's silence, and he looked to Hendricks rather obviously.

Hendricks saw the shift of gazes his way, and felt more than a little discomfort. "Um … okay. So. We're hunting a, um …"

"A horny teenager," Alison said. "In a sea of them."

"Right," Hendricks said, and his eyes scanned the carnival in the distance. The Ferris wheel was the most obvious point sticking on the horizon, but he saw the tops of tents and the metal, lit metal frames of other rides as well. "I don't know how much good it'll do when it comes to the fight, but having a couple people spotting from a distance might be helpful. Scan the crowd, call out anything that looks unusual—"

"Through the scope of a rifle?" Alison asked and then looked to her father. "That could be done. There's a hillside overlook that runs around the side of the carnival. Good wooded cover."

"Good hunting up there, too," Bill said with a nod. "You know, in the fall. We should be able to drive up there from here; cross through the fence gate at the far end of the parking lot. It's Ed Claskey's land, he leaves the gate unlocked."

"Is that trespassing?" Hendricks asked, only marginally interested in the answer.

"He's a friend," Bill said. "So no."

"Sounds like hunting season's come a little early this year," Hendricks told them with a nod.

"Take these," Arch said, slipping off Alison and dipping into his car to pull out a couple of little plastic bags with something black and threaded inside. "Earphones for your cells. We'll conference call."

"No walkie-talkies?" Hendricks said with a smirk.

"Didn't have time to put much together," Arch said, tossing the baggies to Bill, who caught them both with a nod and handed one to his daughter. They both headed back for his truck, slammed the doors and didn't spare a lot of time getting moving, the pickup bouncing its way through the dirt parking lot.

"What about us?" Duncan asked. "Just start walking around the place?"

"Good a plan as any, I guess," Hendricks said. "I'll hang with you since I don't have a phone."

Arch just shook his head. "You may be regretting that before long."

Hendricks shrugged. He'd never needed one. "Let's get in there."

"Wait," Arch said, and Hendricks looked back at him. "You're gonna need a ticket to get in, hotshot."

Hendricks just blinked, the hot night bringing out the first beads of sweat under the brim of his hat. He hadn't even considered it.

***

Lauren had decided to go to the festival. It wasn't something she really wanted to do; it was something that she conceded was the crazy mother at work in her brain. She'd had a couple leaps getting to that point, but she'd finally bent her mind to do it, justifying it by saying she wasn't gonna be looking for Molly. It was a big event, the biggest in Midian, and indeed the whole of Calhoun County. She lived in Calhoun County, ergo her attendance at this major social event was no big deal. Natural, even. She couldn't avoid going just because her daughter was going, after all, she planned to laughingly tell Molly on the off-chance she ran into her daughter.

It didn't even sound true in her head, but she went anyway.

She was just about to park the car when she saw Arch Stan through a narrow aisle of parked cars. He was wearing the same dirty, fucked-up uniform he'd soiled in the mine, and he had that cowboy (!) walking a pace behind him, and one of those federal agents that had flashed a badge at her, if she wasn't mistaken. She stared a moment too long and nearly put her car into the trunk of a vintage Oldsmobile before she saw it and slammed the brakes.

She just sat there for a second, processing what she'd seen. A pious, corrupt asshole, a cowboy and a federal agent walked into a county fair ... It sounded like the setup to a bad joke to her.

She could feel her brow furrow in concentration as she mulled those three disparate elements while she searched for a parking space. To their credit, they did drive the thoughts of how Molly was doing out of her head almost until she reached the gate.

***

The song *California Girls* was playing on the tilt-a-whirl as Mick sat next to Molly and felt it jolt as it spun them. The hazy night closed in, laughter filling the air with the music, screams of delight as they went 'round and 'round. He felt her hand squeezed tight in his, an unexpected delight filling him. Benny was the announcer, and he was rhyming verses like he always did, amateur poet:

"Gonna go round and round!
Find yourself be spinnin' down!
We takin' 'round this tilt a whirl!
And when it stops—kiss yo girl!"

Mick could see the people in front of him laughing from the impromptu rhyme, giving in to the spontaneity of the unspontaneous moment. Benny had other rhymes, but Mick knew he'd pulled this one out just for Mick. Even so, he smiled at Molly. She smiled back, a nice tilt of her head that said she was thinking, *Why not?* So he gave it to her, a meeting of the lips for their first time, sweet and filled with promise. There was something in the heat of the night, in the touch of her slightly damp fingers to his, the interlacing as he squeezed her hand in his, of the taste of faint coffee on her tongue as his met hers. He wondered what she tasted on his.

They parted lips as the ride came to a stop, and Molly giggled with delight at Benny's next rhyme.

"Now we comin' to an end,
come on back and go 'round again,
but even if you're done and going on,
kiss your girl again before you take her home!"

Mick matched her grin and took Benny's advice as the soundtrack clicked in again. He was old enough to know that this wasn't how the Beach Boys sang about *California Girls*, but it wasn't bad, he reflected as he kissed her.

***

Arch stopped counting what he considered inappropriate public displays of affection from teenagers after the first dozen. He was fully aware that his bar was bound to be set lower than most, and he tried not to let it bother him as he moved through a crowd, the lights glaring like someone had let Las Vegas off the leash and spun it around him.

He'd conference-called Bill and Alison, and Alison had tied Duncan into their conversation. He could barely hear them even with the volume turned all the way up; the sound of people talking, shouting, jubilant laughs and the ringing of bells from booths and electronic noise from rides and games nearly blotting them out. The smell of something deep fried tickled his nose, reminding Arch he hadn't eaten in far, far too long.

"Looks like a big, happy carnival," Arch heard Bill's voice through his earpiece. He had to agree. Midian went all-out on this, the perfect time to celebrate the end of summer and herald the coming of fall with its cooler nights and shorter days.

"Nothing obvious so far," Alison concurred. He wondered if they'd split up to cover from different angles. He didn't ask, though, because he didn't want to be the one to tell his wife how to do her job, volunteer gig though it might have been.

"Just one big clusterfuck of lights," Duncan's sour voice came through. "Cowboy looks kind of out of place here." Arch heard something said in the background. "Simmer down, man in black."

Arch nearly bumped into two teenagers walking close together, casting them a gaze that he hoped looked like adult disapproval without venturing into creepy territory. They didn't even notice.

***

Lauren nearly ran into Sheriff Reeve. He was loitering, she realized, hanging about on the edge of the crowd, flying the sheriff's department colors so everyone would see law and order was present at the festival and they could relax. She wasn't an expert on security, but it seemed like a good strategy. Though it didn't look like attendance had suffered any from the shit that had landed all around Midian of late.

"Dr. Darlington," Sheriff Reeve said, ever the voice of politeness. She would have ducked him if she'd seen him coming, of course. "So lovely to see you. And not in your scrubs this time."

"But you're still in uniform," she said, nodding at him. "Making a showing to reassure people?"

"All business tonight," Reeve said with a nod. "Which is a shame, because I'm a pretty fair skee-ball player."

"The things you sacrifice for your work," she said, only slightly mocking.

"Tell me about it," Reeve said. "So-o … you're not here to commit murder, are you? Because … my official presence would frown on that. And I'm not ashamed to admit, I would probably cry at having to deal with another corpse."

"You may relax," she said. It was a county fair, for fuck's sake. She'd make nice with him for two minutes and be on about her business of darting between booths, pretending not to look for her daughter. "My intentions are more in the direction of the corn dogs, I think."

"Ill intentions for them, I suspect, but that's not a crime," Reeve said with a little humor. The man looked a little pallid, worn.

"Depends on what you do with them," Lauren said, scanning the crowd. "I was on an ER rotation, and this guy came in complaining of rectal pain—" She stopped herself, blinking as she realized she'd launched into the story without thinking about it. Reeve had an eyebrow slightly up, at least a little amused. "Sorry," she said, feeling mortified already. I did not stop to think before speaking." She lightly thumped her temple with a forefinger. "Long day."

"I can assure you," Reeve said, and his tone reflected the amusement, "I actually want to hear the end of this one. It sounds like a better story than any I've got from this week."

Lauren thought—just for a second—about protesting. She gave it up with only a thought of the bodies she'd seen in his company. "Right. Well." She pushed her embarrassment aside. "So, he comes in, and he's complaining of pain in his ass—"

"One sympathizes. I've felt a few of those of late," Reeve said.

"I doubt yours also carried a symptom of a wooden stick peeking from your anal sphincter like a telephone pole towering over a city street, though," Lauren said, trying to keep the smile from breaking out too early. It actually was a funny story, though not exactly safe for work. Except hers. This was life in the ER.

"Indeed it does not," Reeve said, with a smile of his own. "At least, not as yet. Go on."

***

Mick took her on the roller coaster next. It wasn't quite like the olden days, he reflected. There were bigger ones, better ones, ones that were fixed in place. Thrill riding was an industry, and companies like Walt Disney, Six Flags and Anheuser-Busch dominated the field, making his little piddly coaster that could be disassembled and put on trucks at the end of the day seem positively quaint compared to the excitement it had brought thirty years ago.

But then he got on the car and they started moving, and Mandy—no, wait, it was Molly—started screaming like it was the best damned thing ever, and he had to concede that maybe this old-fashioned ride still could get a girl lubed up. She gripped his hand tight, and he could feel the dampness of her palm against his as the ground dropped from underneath them, screams filled the air, and they shot down an incline at what felt like a ninety-degree angle. Mick just screamed along, but not out of fear.

***

"This is not gonna be good," Alison's daddy muttered as they both lay, prone, about fifty feet from each other. She could hear him because he was talking loud enough to be heard that far away.

She had her cheek against the rifle, eye a little back from the scope with the butt against her shoulder. The pad was already in place, but she had it safetied against possible discharge. "Can't imagine what you mean," she said back, conveying by tone that she knew very damned well what he meant. "Limited backstop, huge crowd … what could possibly go wrong?" She said it with sarcasm, but the idea of what would happen if she fired the big Barrett, even at her slightly downward angle, into the fair was the stuff of nightmares. She could easily kill half a dozen people with a poorly placed shot. More if she had to fire multiple times. People she knew, people who shopped in her store, people she'd grown up with, been to church with.

Plus, there was still absolutely no obvious sign indicating two teenagers were having carnal knowledge on the premises. The likelihood they'd do it out in the wide open seemed low, though, especially since she'd seen Nicholas Reeve wandering around in her scan of the crowd. She hovered her sights over the line of seafoam green porta potties, looking for any of them to be rocking subtly. That'd be a sign. True romance.

"What do you reckon?" she asked her father.

"Reckon if I were a betting man, I'd like to place some money on the long odds against us." He sighed. "But since I'm not, I reckon I'll just put my eye back to this scope and see if I can find a couple young adults rubbing up against each other like a flea-ridden dog against a fencepost."

***

They got off the roller coaster breathless, Molly flushed with that red-cheeked excitement that couldn't be faked. Mick didn't know if it was the night, the lights, the feeling of the place—music was playing, in the background, some old Springsteen song that was the kind of thing he could still get behind. The first fireworks started to go off overhead and the night was lit up like it was the Fourth of July. The air carried just the littlest hint of briskness, the first breath of fall, and it was a perfect, signature end to summer. Mick took a big breath in through the nose and smelled that whiff of cotton candy mingled with the suggestion of cool air coming. He looked over at Molly's cheeks, those happy, rose-red cheeks, and couldn't keep from smiling himself. He often thought humanity was a contagious condition, and in moments like this he felt like it was catching, just a little. "Wanna ride the Ferris wheel?" he asked with a grin. She nodded with a placid smile of her own, and their fingers met to interlace once more as he led her off to the night's capstone.

***

"You don't seem impressed," Duncan said as he and Hendricks charged through the crowd at a brisk walk. Brisk was the word for it, all right, Hendricks thought as they paced through the crowd. They passed a funnel cake booth and Hendricks nearly did a double take at the smell.

"My hometown did something similar," Hendricks said, catching his thousandth funny look of the night for the drover coat and hat. He had the coat all buttoned up and considered himself lucky the ticket taker hadn't asked him to undo it. He actually considered it lucky, too, that the night was just a little chilly for the locals. Not anything to write home about in Wisconsin, but for Tennessee it was something. He saw a few others wearing windbreakers.

"Oh, yeah?" Duncan didn't sound too impressed, either.

"Amery—the town I'm from—had this thing called the Fall Festival," Hendricks said. "Of course, in western Wisconsin, every town had its own little fair or carnival or whatever. I mostly went to the Fall Festival in Amery, but there was New Richmond Days, Good Neighbor Days down in Roberts, the St. Croix County Fair down in Glenwood City, the—"

"I stand in awe of your boring story," Duncan cut him off. He hadn't been quite this abrupt a few days ago, had he? Hendricks wondered if it was Lerner's loss or some sort of fatigue that was pinching the OOC's personality. "This is fucking pointless."

Hendricks didn't remember the demon swearing as much a few days earlier, either. "It's not looking too good for the home team, I'll be the first to admit." He glanced at a couple in their early twenties walking along. The guy had his hand around her shoulder, firmly cupping the girl's tit. It looked like a pretty decent handful, Hendricks had to concede, but they weren't really showing much sign of anything other than that, at least not yet. "Half this town's teenagers could be heading off to fuck right after this and we wouldn't know it." He paused. "Wait a minute."

"What?"

"We're not looking for a guy from this town," Hendricks said, shaking his head at the stupidity. He leaned in to Duncan and lifted the strand of black headphone wire off the OOC's shirt and spoke into the little lump of plastic. "We're looking for a total stranger, team. Keep your eyes peeled for a guy you've never seen before."

***

"That doesn't exactly narrow it down," Arch said, making his way slowly through the crowd next to a ball toss game. He was watching a guy in full bib overalls trying to knock over a series of bottles at ten paces. Arch hadn't watched for more than five seconds before he came to the conclusion the game was rigged. "The guy's a carnie, right? What do they dress like?" He stared at the booth worker, hard pressed to tell much difference between him and any of the other people he'd seen that night.

***

"Looking." Alison trained her eye through the scope again. She focused on a knot of school-aged kids and was a little shocked to find how young they looked. She tried to put it out of her mind that they were almost a decade younger than her, and when she'd figured out that she knew every single one of them, she moved the scope onward, taking only a moment to ponder that she'd violated a rule of gun safety by having her weapon continually pointed in a very, very unsafe direction.

***

Mick felt the thrill of upcoming victory as they passed Troy at the ticket-taker stand for the Ferris wheel. He got the nod and the arched eyebrows from Troy, which was like a compliment to his skills before the job was done. That was fine with Mick, though, because he could just about smell her cooch from here, and she hadn't even lifted her skirt or slid down her panties yet.

He took her hand as they made their way across the little platform to get on the wheel. He'd picked a carnival that had enclosed buckets—for privacy. This was always the place. He could have gone somewhere else, he supposed, but the truth was that the Ferris wheel was his favorite ride, too, and ever since he'd rode his first one in Chicago over a century earlier, he had never gotten over the idea of being lifted to breathtaking heights in the sky.

The bucket rocked as they stepped inside. He closed the door and watched Troy come by and lock it before pulling the lever and sending them up. He'd talked with Troy about this moment beforehand, and here in the heavily used, sweaty compartment, he stopped to stare at the weave of fiberglass that made up the inside of the bucket. It looked like little roots, connecting to each other, to him, like things of life that joined people and time and events together. His head always filled with these heavy thoughts just before time, like his mind was expanding in advance of the event itself. Soon he'd be tasting every woman in the entire carnival, smelling their sweat and perfume as he released himself into them. He could already feel himself stiffening with anticipation as he looked in Molly's eyes. He felt a gleam as he kept his hand on hers and willed the Ferris wheel into motion. It started on its slow path to the stop between the seven and eight o'clock positions, and he found he could barely wait a second more.

***

"I've got something," Alison heard her father say. "Young man I've never seen before, hand in hand with Molly Darlington. About to get on the Ferris wheel."

Alison pulled her eye off her scope for a second. She'd been trolling near the gates, scoping out the pretzel stand. She swiveled her weapon to the Ferris wheel and looked back through the scope, centering on the ticket taker. She saw a blur of motion, a couple moving to get in the bucket. "Got eyes on him," she said, watching as they stepped inside. "I don't know who he is, either."

***

"Heading that way," Duncan said in response to what Hendricks presumed was a voice in his headphone. He cuffed Hendricks on the shoulder and pointed toward the Ferris wheel that towered above everything. Hendricks shrugged and fell in beside the demon. They weren't far away, and it wasn't like Hendricks had anything else to do but follow the OOC.

***

"This has been a real special night," Mick said, looking over at Molly. He could smell that sweet aroma of sweat in the air, feel the hard bench beneath his ass, the wind creeping in through the slit of a window that overlooked the ten thousand lights of the fair below. The bucket bobbed from the motion, but gently, rocking them both with a Rolling Stones song faintly audible from the loudspeakers below as their lullaby. Or mood music, Mick thought. That was probably closer to right.

"It has," Molly said, and she was just a little sphinx-like, as if she were holding something back. Girls always did, though, in Mick's experience. Probably nerves.

The bucket started to move again, this time toward the nine o'clock, and Mick knew he only had about ten minutes left. He leaned in and kissed her, again, full and deep, parting her lips with his tongue, feeling hers press back gently. She broke from him unexpectedly, pulling away sooner than he would have thought. She looked out the slatted window on her side, out on the brightly lit parking lot below.

"What is it?" Mick asked.

She looked back at him and smiled. "Nothing. I just want to enjoy the ride."

So she was a little reticent. He'd run across this a couple times before, and it was easy enough to solve. He'd forgotten what it felt like to have a girl resist, he'd gotten so good at picking the ones that would put out. He hadn't even had to put his mouth on the wet snatches of the last two, something he didn't really enjoy save for what it got him. He sniffed audibly, could almost imagine his tongue dancing on her—

"What?" Innocent. She was looking at him, wondering what he was thinking. It was obvious, written on her face.

"I was just thinking how beautiful you look tonight," Mick said. He rested a hand gently on her thigh, and it wasn't there for more than a second before she jerked away from his touch like he'd burned her. Now it was his turn to frown. "What?"

"Umm ..." She swallowed heavily. "Let me just stop you there ... I'm okay with making out a little, but ... that's about it. That's the line." She had some strength in that voice, and it raised Mick's eyebrow.

He smiled. Things that were easy were never as worth it as the things that were hard. "It's okay." He turned on the charm. "I understand if you're, y'know, inexperienced. It's not a big deal."

She cocked an eyebrow at him, and something in the way she did it looked far, far different from anything he'd ever seen in this situation before. "What do you think is going to happen here?"

Mick felt a hot flush creep up his neck and settle in his cheeks. "I figured we'd, uh ... you know." He arched his eyebrows once.

Her expression got hard just as the lump in his pants showed the first sign of softening. "Listen ... I like you," she said gently, "but ... I'm sixteen."

"You're a woman," he said, a little flustered. "Baby, you're old enough to—"

"To make my own decisions?" She was sounding patronizing now, and that heat in Mick's cheeks belied just a little, tiny grain of anger. "I agree, which is why I'm saying that we're not going any farther than first base. Like I said, I like you. Which is why I'd like to enjoy our time together without feeling, like ... pressure and stuff."

"But ... but ... I took you all over this place," Mick said, lamely even to his ears.

"It was a good date," Molly said, still looking cool but with just a speck of pity mixed in, "but that doesn't entitle you to *carte blanche*." She smiled at him, but all he could see was this building rage in him that reflected back. "Can we just ... have fun?"

He could feel his hands shaking, and he grabbed one of the lap bars to stabilize himself as he watched her pale slightly from his reaction. "Oh, we're gonna have fun. You bet your sweet little snatch we're gonna have fun."

***

The scream cracked through the air as Hendricks and Duncan were loitering just outside the ticket taker's line. Hendricks didn't hesitate; he pulled up on the guardrail, mounted the platform and ran straight for the Ferris wheel. When he got to the box that was on the bottom, he paused just long enough to hear the next scream from the car that was climbing up to the space between the ten and eleven o'clock positions on the wheel. He gripped hard on the metal frame and started to climb.

***

"A frozen corn dog?" Reeve was chuckling at the end of her story. "Corn dog in the corn hole? Shiiit."

"That's what he eventually had to do to get the rest out," Lauren said with a smirk of her own, "though it wasn't at all frozen by that time."

"I bet you see some crazy damned stuff," Reeve said. "You know, other than corpses strewn randomly around your hometown."

Lauren blew air out through her lips and could feel the weariness settle over her. "Honestly, what I've seen these last few days trumps most of the stuff that comes through the ER."

There was a scream in the distance, echoing through the night as the crowd silenced abruptly. Lauren turned her head; it had come from the Ferris wheel and it was a thick, fearful one. A second one followed, and suddenly from below the lowest metal spoke of the wheel, she could see a man clad all in black, climbing the frame.

A man with a black cowboy hat on his head.

"What ... the ... fuck?" Reeve asked, staring up at the Ferris wheel from beside her. "I bet this shit doesn't happen at the Renaissance Festival." The way he said it reminded her of a plea for grace of the sort one heard in church. Minus the profanity. She started to respond, but the sheriff had already disappeared into the crowd, pushing his way toward the disturbance.

Another shriek sounded, and Lauren realized she could place it as female ... and young. It took only one leap of logic before she, too, was pushing her way through the crowd toward the wheel and whatever the hell was going on within it.

***

"Hendricks is climbing the Ferris wheel," Alison reported tensely, her rifle centered on the cowboy. She was trying to get some idea of what was going on, but the entire ride was closed off, each box providing only a thin viewing window a foot or so wide that stretched around the front of the cars. There wasn't even a window in the side doors, which totally cockblocked her efforts to figure out if something was going on. One of the boxes was rocking pretty heavy, though, the one heading toward the midnight position. She couldn't tell if Hendricks was heading that way yet, though, because he was just reaching the center of the wheel.

"I've got carnies everywhere!" Duncan's voice exploded in her ear. He sounded strained, and she lowered her scope to take in what was going on below. He did indeed have carnies everywhere: there were three surrounding him on the platform, anchored to each of his arms and one dragging him down by grabbing his legs. They appeared to be punching, kicking, and trying to tackle him.

Alison frowned; she had little doubt Duncan was fully capable of dispatching all three of them with minimal difficulty. She doubted he could do it without causing serious injury, though, and that sounded like something that would be better off being avoided.

"You're assaulting a federal agent!" Duncan's voice blasted through the microphone again, and she watched him shake one of them off with that. The other two clung stubbornly to him, however, leading Alison to believe they might not be the sorts that always complied with lawful commands. Or laws.

"On my way," Arch said tightly through the open channel, "but it's a bit of a fight to get through this crowd now that y'all have everyone's curiosity drawn."

A quick scan of the crowd, and Alison had to agree with her husband; there was a growing cluster around the base of the Ferris wheel, a swelling crowd of people watching the skirmish on the platform and Hendricks's climb. It was growing all the time as people gravitated toward the ruckus, filling the tight channels around the wheel with an ever-expanding mass of humanity.

***

"You led me on, you little slut!" Mick got out in a yell. He'd been struggling with her for a few minutes, lightly at first, but with ever-increasing force. She was resisting, and it was pissing him off more by the second.

"Because I said I'd come here with you?" She grunted it out as she put a hand against his cheek and forced his face away from her. "What, that means I automatically have to have sex with you? FUCK YOU!" She finished it and trailed into another scream that lit his ears. He hadn't hit her yet, just pushed and shoved a little. He was getting to the point he was about ready to backhand her into unconsciousness and just be on about his business.

She raked fingernails across his cheek, and he felt the sting as she ripped through the first layer of flesh on his shell. His essence boiled within him, and he slapped her down, hard. Her head hit the side of the car, and she slumped against the door.

"Finally," he said, and knelt down, dragging her to the floor of the car. She fell in the confined space, her head thumping against the floor as she dropped. He wondered how this would work, with her unconscious, if it would be the same? This had been easier before, hadn't it?

***

Hendricks was climbing to the side now, working his way up a forty-five degree angle, his feet extended and his back bent as he shimmied up the arm toward the box that dangled at the end of it. This was, he had to concede, an immense pain in the ass. It was a lot more fun to fast-rope out of a helo than try and climb this damned thing.

There was no screaming now, and the box dangled only ten feet above him. He could feel his sword hanging at his belt. His pistol was there, too, and he'd taken the time to reload it on the journey here. He was pretty clear about which of them he'd need more right now, though, and he doubted it'd be the 1911.

The screaming of his muscles seemed to diminish in the last few upward steps. And they were steps. He was leaning most of his weight on his legs, using them and the resistance of the soles of his boots against the metal to climb. It was an age-old thing, something he'd applied to climbing drainpipes in his youth. This time if he fell, though, it wouldn't just be a sore tailbone as a consequence.

He kept climbing the arm to the extension point where it met the joint above the car. Even at his sideways angle, it was going to require either a small leap or some fancy footwork to transition to the little running board on the bottom of the car. He swung and heard a collective gasp from below at his stunt work. He tried not to reflect on the fact that there were a few hundred pairs of eyes watching him, because the consequences of that particular bit of business were a whole 'nother matter, one that would probably rock his skull clear off its shoulders if he gave it time to think.

Instead, Hendricks positioned himself, anchored his hand inside the thin window of the box, and jerked the door open full force before freeing his hand to go for his sword.

He hadn't quite got it clear of the scabbard when the fucker inside—a demon with blazing eyes that shone through his facade—stood in surprise. The bastard probably hadn't even remembered that his pants were around his ankles and his tiny pecker was hanging out like a pinky finger dangling all by its sad, skinny self in the middle of a tangled black forest of pubic hair.

"Check out time," Hendricks announced to the startled demon as he moved his body and coat to hide from the crowd the sword that he pointed into the car.

***

Alison looked through the scope as Hendricks flung the door to the Ferris wheel's car open, and she saw the glint of his blade as he drew it, but everything else was cut off by the billow of his coat.

"I don't have a shot," she said into her microphone as she stared through the scope, willing Hendricks to move the hell out of the way. There was absolutely nothing behind the Ferris wheel except for an empty baseball field, red clay without so much as a soul on it visible even from here.

"Me either," her daddy said. She settled in to wait for the situation to change and was shocked at how fast it did.

***

Mick had thrown her panties out the little window, a "Hell yeah, fuck you," gesture to the girl who'd been such a pain in his dick. Not that it mattered to her now, but presumably she'd notice their absence later.

After.

He had gotten down on all fours and taken a deep whiff as he slid her dress up around her armpits. She smelled good, and he came up to his knees. The car wasn't yet at the twelve o'clock, and he didn't need that much time, he figured. He'd just dropped trow and slid his pants down around his ankles when he saw a set of fingers pop inside the window.

If Mick had been human, he would have shit himself right there. Fingers didn't just appear in the window of a moving Ferris wheel car at the top of its arc. The surprise made his stomach drop and he felt himself start to go limp, a feeling not aided a second later when that fucking demon hunter in the cowboy hat and black coat ripped the door open. Mick hadn't heard what he'd said over the shock and fury mingling in his essence at the humiliation. The fear was the worst, that uncertainty of getting so damned close to what he wanted and having this guy—this fucking guy—show up at the last moment to yank it away.

The cowboy had a sword in his hand, the point dangling just inches from Mick's face, and Mick found himself swallowing hard, letting the fury take over. Fuck this. He was a greater for a reason, and even if the sword was a holy object, he wasn't gonna let it matter. He reached out and grabbed it by the blade, felt it dig into his fingers, and ignored the pain. He shoved on it, hard, and watched the hilt hit the cowboy in the sternum. He fucked up his balance, tilting sideways, one of his boots losing footing and the other following suit.

The demon hunter tumbled out, fingers gripping the window but letting go of his sword. Mick had it by the blade, and stood there surprised for only a second while the cowboy caught himself on the window, four little fingers sparing him from a hell of a fall. Four little piggies.

Mick just smiled and stepped over the limp body of Molly—no, Mandy? Shit. Whatever. He stood at the door to the car and looked at the cowboy hanging there exposed, his fingers right there for the unfurling …

***

Hendricks was hanging there, fingers in fucking agony, the only thing keeping his ass from splattering on the grass below. He heard the requisite "oohs" and "aahs" and "HOLY LIVING FUCKS" out of the crowd below, but it was all background noise. His arm was twisted, holding all his weight, and he knew he didn't have an overabundance of time.

Plus, his sword was gone. He'd liked to have held on to it, but being as he'd been getting shoved out the door by the demon holding onto the other end of it at the time, it had seemed like a real good idea to part ways with it lest it continue to be used in just that manner.

Now he saw the demon reverse his grip on it, and suddenly Hendricks was staring down the blade. Not a sight he was used to seeing, but he had to reflect he might not have any more chances after this one to see it in this way.

"You ever heard that old saying?" The demon asked, the fire muted, barely visible in his eyes as he stared down the blade at Hendricks. "You live by the sword, you die by the sword?"

Hendricks just braced himself, and the blade rared back, ready to slide into him like a skewer to a pig.

***

"I have a shot," Alison said, "and I'm taking it." She saw the skinny little bastard with the blade pointed at Hendricks, and she stroked the trigger as she blotted out all else, aiming for center mass and compensating for that slight breeze.

***

Arch was in the crowd below when the roar of the big rifle belted out. A few ladies screamed—a few men, too, Arch reckoned. He'd heard Alison's warning and used the opportunity to push his way through the crowd. He caught a few glares that softened the minute they saw his uniform.

Duncan was still up on the platform, but all activity there had stopped; the demon and the two carnies that had been fighting him were all transfixed, staring up into the sky at the car above.

***

The roar of the rifle reached Hendricks's ears about a second after he watched the skinny little demon lose an arm at the shoulder. It took him a second to realize it had spun off, ricocheting on the frame of the door and twirling downward like a helicopter blade as it fell into the crowd below. Hendricks blinked and looked up to see the demon looking at him in muted astonishment. It hadn't been the arm that held the sword, but he was in sheer disbelief, the blade sagging from where it had been pointed at Hendricks's chest only a moment before.

"What the hell was that?" the demon choked out.

"Not a sword," Hendricks said, and swung his feet up to kick the demon in the legs full force.

***

Alison watched Hendricks swing back into the car after knocking the demon back. Once more, the black coat billowed as he stood framed in the entry, completely blocking her ability to see into the Ferris wheel's car.

"No shot, no shot!" she called into the microphone, trapping it between two fingers and bringing it closer to her mouth as she stared with one eye through the scope. "Duncan, get that wheel spinning! Hendricks needs to get his ass on the ground ASAP!"

***

Arch could hear Alison speaking over the chaos in the crowd, but he could only make out every other word or so. He heard the part about getting Hendricks on the ground and agreed wholeheartedly, so much so that he shoved his way through the last few people in the crowd and vaulted up on the platform that supported the Ferris wheel. "You!" he snapped at the carnie that had broken off from Duncan the minute he'd announced himself as a federal agent. Arch flicked his badge with a finger, causing it to catch the light and draw the youth's attention to it, snapping him out of his trance. "Get that car down here. Now." He didn't leave any room for argument, and the young man nodded, cowed, and headed toward the controls. The two that had been fighting with Duncan just stood back, still stunned, and stared up along with the OOC and the rest of the crowd.

***

Lauren was within a hundred feet of the Ferris wheel when the cowboy swung back in. She was making slow progress through the throng, and had resorted to crowd surfing tactics, jumping up and placing weight on peoples' shoulders to make them give way. She thought about just announcing herself as a doctor, but she somehow doubted that would impress in the middle of this spectacle of redneck theater. Gunshots, high-wire fighting and derring-do, oh my.

This close to the Ferris wheel, the crowd had congealed; there was simply no more room to maneuver. These were hardly a panicked herd, which was a surprise given that everyone had heard the gunfire. But it was equally obvious to anyone with a pair of eyes that whoever was shooting had done so at the mostly naked guy in the car that had tried to attack the cowboy. It was a surprisingly illogical progression for a crowd to make, in Lauren's estimation. They should have run like a herd of cattle, but apparently they were too busy watching the show.

Whatever the case, Lauren knew she'd gone about as far as she could go in this direction without a tractor-trailer with which to plow through the crowd. She looked left and saw the density of people lighten off to the far side of the Ferris wheel. It was stationed right against the fence to the ball field, and there was no one in the small no man's land behind it.

Lauren started working her way around the edge of the crowd toward that space, hoping for a better look but doubting she'd get one. Still, approaching from that side and climbing onto the platform from behind would be a better bet than trying to fight her way through a crowd too drunk on what they were watching to move the fuck out of the way.

***

Hendricks was balancing tentatively, his feet back on the solid ground of the running board but still painfully aware that this was not so solid as he might wish. The box rocked left to right, more than a sway, and Hendricks braced himself in the door frame, taking the shift in weight by tensing his thighs. That fucking demon still had his sword, but the bastard was a touch off balance, and that was about all the advantage Hendricks had.

He drew his pistol and fired from the hip, dimly aware that there was a body at his feet. The gunshot tore through the little car, the flash lighting everything up and the sound just about driving him backward from the force and recoil. It staggered the demon, though, so Hendricks pulled the trigger again. This time, when the flash lit the car, Hendricks realized there was a second door on the other side of the box, and he started wondering if there was a way to use this to his advantage.

***

Lauren had made it to the other side of the Ferris wheel when the shooting started. This time it was painfully obvious where it was coming from, the muzzle flash lighting up the car that was currently at the midnight position and starting its descent around. She hadn't heard a scream for a while, though, and part of that worried her in a distant sort of way as she crossed around the edge of the rail that sealed the Ferris wheel off from the grounds. A square of white cloth was lying on the dewy grass, discarded, and it took her eyes only a moment to realize they were cotton panties. She stooped to pick them up without thinking it through, and it was only a moment more before the size printed in the back gave her more reason than ever to be worried about what was happening above her.

***

"You fucking animal," Hendricks said, holding off on shooting the bastard again in favor of kicking him in the gut. The last two shots had made the fucker writhe, and Hendricks was highly in favor of more of that, but not at the expense of an ass-whooping. The sound of the box squeaking in its cradle at the end of the Ferris wheel arm was audible to him even over the ringing in his ears, and it sounded like that fucking buzz, that bee-like mechanical buzz, ringing in his ears like the crescendo of an orchestra. He rained another kick down on the one-armed demon's gut, watched him flop against the far door, minding his footing so he didn't trip over the girl. He braced himself and kicked the demon in the hand, heard the sword fall from his grasp. It was music, it was that buzzing, all in one, and it wasn't until the demon caught his next kick with a shoulder and punched him in the balls that his thinking caught up with his instincts, and the words "Oh, shit" formed in his head.

***

Alison peered through the scope, alarmed at what she was seeing. She was dead-on, a perfect view in the door of the Ferris wheel car. Hendricks had entered, had looked like he was getting the job done, and then suddenly he just crumpled. But the problem was his damned coat was still in the way. Any shot she took was going to go right through him, and it would be an utter miracle if it hit anything other than the cowboy.

"Arch, I got nothing," she said into microphone. "We're shut out here. Can you see anything?" She suspected she already knew the answer without even checking, but she had to do something.

***

"Arch!" Reeve's voice turned his head from where Arch stood on the platform, hovering over the carnie working the Ferris wheel. "What are you doing?"

"Getting that car down here," Arch replied. Reeve was staring out at him from within the crowd, shoulder to shoulder with a boatload of people, looked like he was in a bit of a squeeze.

"Did you hear that shooting?" Reeve called to him. Arch was a little surprised how quiet the scene was, all things considered. He supposed people were awed into silence.

"Saw it, too," Arch said, looking down at the sheriff.

"I sent Reines up there on that hill after the shooters," Reeve said. He pointed, and Arch followed where he'd gestured to see a Calhoun County sheriff's cruiser climbing up the side of the hill where Alison and Bill had stationed themselves.

"You sent Reines after the shooters?" Arch put a total lack of inflection into it, like he was stunned. "You sent Reines after the shooters, Sheriff? Up the hill?"

Reeve looked up at him like he was an idiot. "Yes, Arch, I sent Deputy Reines to arrest whoever is shooting rifles into my goddamned festival. Can you please, kindly, do your job and help me control the scene here so we can get up there and assist him?"

Arch just stared down at the sheriff and ignored the sudden, loud curse word that his wife practically shouted into his ear. "Yes, sir," he said. "I'll start by getting this car back down to the platform."

***

"Fuck!" Alison said, treading into territory she did not usually venture into with that particular word, at least not in Arch's earshot. It seemed appropriate, though. "We gotta move, Daddy."

"We're gonna leave that cowboy without any help," her daddy replied, loud enough she could hear him without the earphone. "You sure?"

"I still got no shot," Alison said, "and if we stay, all we're gonna do is get ourselves arrested and still not do him a lick of good." She pulled the rifle up, folding the tripod. She gave one last look through the unsteady scope and saw Hendricks's undefined shape still obscured by the black coat and the darkness in the car. "We gotta book it."

***

Mick could feel the car moving around the circle, time ticking down on the face of the clock. He'd hammed it a bit, got the cowboy to drop his guard and get riled, and then he kicked him in the balls to make up for what he'd cost Mick.

"You fucking shit," Mick said, reaching up and taking hold of the cowboy by the face with his remaining hand as the man clenched in spasming pain. "Why don't we find out if I can impregnate you?" He started to push the cowboy headfirst into the bench of the car. Knock him out, bend him over, flip that coat up and show him who was boss— "This is gonna burn."

"No, thanks," the cowboy said and brought the pistol around. Shit. Mick had forgotten about that little stinger. "I've already got a girlfriend," the cowboy said, and then he blind fired the gun right in Mick's face. Twice.

The pain was sudden and immediate, and it took Mick a minute to realize he'd fallen half out the back door of the car after the second shot, the dark sky lit above him and the outline of the spokes of the Ferris wheel all lit up around him. Mick held on, one-handed, to the edge of the doorway and watched as the cowboy tried to right himself then came staggering at Mick in an attempt to knock him out.

It was clumsy, it was stupid, and Mick was faster. The cowboy missed as Mick slid out of the way and let the little bit of momentum the man in black had carry him forward. He looped out of the car and—the lucky fuck—caught a grip on the spoke below as they passed the three o'clock position. Mick smiled down at the cowboy's one-handed hold, knowing that in about ten seconds his grip was going to be lost as the arm of the wheel slanted downward. It wasn't going to be much of a drop by then, maybe fifteen, twenty feet, but it'd be enough to put the fucker down so Mick could—

Mick felt a hard flare of pain in his own balls as someone hit him unmercifully in them while he was looking the other way. He turned in time to see Molly—or was it Mandy?—with that fucking demon hunter's sword in her hands, the blade plunged right into his crotch.

Mick screamed, lost the power of thought, and whatever grip he had left. He fell, sword still buried in his fucking cock and bollocks, and hit the dark, empty earth below. He could see that Molly whore above him, staring out of the door of the car—

***

Lauren had a clear view when Mick came plummeting out of the car. She had a very clear, rage-filled view of her daughter stabbing him with a sword, and she watched him fall. *I hope he's dead*, she thought, her mind filling in the blanks of what had happened above. It wasn't like it was real difficult; her daughter's screams coming from the car, her daughter's panties lying on the grass, her daughter's supposed love interest with a sword through his groin, put there by her daughter.

A + B = Rapist motherfucker.

It wasn't exactly a casual stroll she took over to him. It was urgent, it was hurried, it was full of fury and wrath and all manner of righteous, hateful indignation. She found him clutching himself at the site of the wound.

The cowboy fell right as she reached Mick, a shorter drop than the carnie had taken. She heard him land, heard him go, "OOF!" and gave him not a whit of attention.

Lauren Ella Darlington stared down at the bastard who had hurt her daughter, made her scream, made her feel all manner of unpleasant and unsavory things—

And she grabbed the hilt of that sword that was lodged in his nuts—visibly, obviously lodged in them, since his pants were nowhere to be found—and she plucked it out—

And rammed back in again, a little higher. Turned that fucker into a falsetto in one.

***

Hendricks watched the doctor—he was pretty sure it was her, the lady from the accident scene where Erin had gotten hurt—sever the demon's genitalia with his sword. He would have cringed, but he didn't really have any mercy left in his tank for the bastard, honestly.

"Mom!" The cry came from above, from the car that he'd just dropped out of. The girl was standing, framed in there, on her feet again. Hendricks traced the line back to the dark-haired, avenging angel standing over the demon and put it together.

"Get him in the heart," Hendricks said, just loud enough for her to hear him, as he struggled to his feet. She glanced at him blankly. "The heart," Hendricks repeated and mimed a stabbing motion.

The doctor stared at him uncomprehendingly for just a second, and then he watched the determination cross her face, twist it, all that rage pooling—

And she stabbed him in the heart, the motherfucker, and he glowed for a second before the black fire claimed him.

***

Mick couldn't believe it. It was the mother, the fucking mother. He couldn't have seen that coming, not in a million years. He was ready to burn her, too, like that fucking bum, but then she pulled the sword out of his balls and slid it a couple inches higher. That was a new level of desire to scream.

He was still too busy writhing from getting his junk severed to hear the conversation going on around him in anything other than muffled tones. He'd just about come out of it enough to hear the words "the heart!" when he felt a blade slip into his, and that was all she wrote.

Mick had about two seconds to open his eyes, pack his essence's metaphorical bags, and stare straight into the eyes of a pissed-off mother before the fires of hell dragged him down into a darkness the like of which he had never experienced.

***

Arch saw it all from where he stood on the platform. Saw the demon fall, saw Hendricks fall, saw Dr. Darlington mosey over and stab the bastard dead—with a little coaxing from Hendricks.

He took a quick look and found Reeve making his way up the platform on the far side. It was obvious to the crowd that something had happened on the far side, but the rush and the glut was making fast movement there well-nigh impossible. He made a quick gesture, something he hoped Duncan would see that Reeve wouldn't. The OOC gave him a nod of acknowledgment and plunged off the platform on the far side, ducking through the moving spokes of the wheel as he jumped and dodged to get to Hendricks.

"What the hell just happened?" Reeve called at him, stalking up the nearby ramp, only twenty feet or so away.

"Almost got that car down," Arch said, nodding at the one with the door open and flapping in the breeze. There was an outline of a girl in a dress, and he had his suspicions on exactly who it was, based on the good doctor's reaction to the demon ...

"Who gives a fuck about the car, Arch?" Reeve yelled. "What the hell is going on here? Did you see who came out of it?"

"Not really," Arch said. He doubted his lying face had gotten any better, but at least it was getting easier to spit them out now.

***

"Nicely done," Hendricks said, eyeing the woman with the dark hair, who was staring at the spot in the grass where the demon had burned his way back to hell. "Can I have my sword back?" He tried to be neutral about it, as much as he could under the circumstances.

The woman stared at the hilt of it like she could see through it and dropped her grip on it. The sword tilted toward the ground like some great tower falling to the earth, thudding gently in the wet grass.

"Thanks," Hendricks said, dodging past her to scoop it up. He brought the blade up in defense by pure instinct when he heard the thump of someone landing just in front of him—

"Time to go," Duncan said from where he'd just jumped off the platform. "We need to make an exit."

Hendricks looked left, then right, finding both ways starting to fill with people. Behind them, a ten-foot high fence cordoned them off from an empty baseball diamond, the red clay a pale shade of grey in the light of the Ferris wheel. "I'm not finding any exit signs."

"Aren't you with the FBI or something?" the doctor asked. "I could have sworn you were from the FBI."

Duncan's face twitched slightly as Hendricks stared at the OOC, wondering. "That's not gonna hold up under this scrutiny," Duncan said simply. "We need to motor."

"I'm open to suggestions," Hendricks said, "since I'm guessing this little clusterfuck isn't going to be easy to explain."

"Good," Duncan said and started toward him, "I'm glad you're open."

"To *suggestions*," Hendricks said as the OOC wrapped an arm around his chest and started dragging him forward like he weighed about as much as an empty suit, "not to—what the hell are you doing?"

Duncan jumped the softball field fence, just barely clearing it. Hendricks could hear the fence rattle, felt the heels of his boots click-clack the metal top of it as they passed. Duncan straightened him out after the landing, though, setting him back on his feet instead of just letting him drop. "Time to run, cowboy."

Hendricks blinked as the demon started off at a brisk run toward the nearest bleachers. Bereft of any other good suggestions, he tossed one last look back at the doctor, who just stood staring at him through the chain-link, and then he ran to follow the OOC.

***

Alison bounced as the truck hit a rut, the whole cab jouncing her a good foot in the air. She fumbled for her seatbelt when she came down, the uneven ground of the hillside they were running not doing her any favors. Her daddy was at the wheel and the rifles were stowed not very ceremoniously in the back, which was worrying. They were plunging down the thinly tread trail that Ed Claskey used to reach this part of his property, going at a speed that Alison knew her father hoped would keep them ahead of Ernesto Reines until they got to the main road. That was safety, that was escape, but until then, she had a feeling it was going to be a rough ride. They hit another rut and she bounced again, the pickup's shocks protesting the rough treatment.

"You'd think this wasn't your first time evading the law," she said to her father as he jerked the wheel, following the old rutted trail.

"That's definitely a first," her father said, his face screwed up in concentration, eyes darting to take in everything he saw ahead, "but it's not exactly the first time I've driven off road in a hell of a hurry." He spared her just a moment's look, a little glint in his eyes before the road ahead got his attention once more. Alison just braced herself and held on as they went, keeping one eye fixed in her rearview mirror, hoping against hope not to see red and blue flashing lights there.

***

Arch watched Duncan and Hendricks clear the fence in a jump just as Reeve got into view to see for himself. He didn't know how much of that the sheriff caught, but he was pretty sure he saw them hoofing it off into the night. It wasn't like a guy in a long black coat and cowboy hat was the sort of thing that just slipped the mind.

Reeve wheeled on Arch with a look that suggested betrayal, fury, and a mingling of a hot mess of emotions that Arch didn't even want to dip into. "What the fuck was that?"

"Guy in a cowboy hat running off into the night," Arch said coolly.

"You just stood here and watched it happen," Reeve said with a glacial reserve of his own.

"I may be a decent athlete, but I'd have a hard time leaping that fence to pursue," Arch offered.

Reeve's lips contorted long, like his jaw clenched. "You think I don't recall your friend the cowboy? Who I met the night your apartment was broken into?"

"I'm sure you recall my friend," Arch said, feeling a surprising level of calm. "I'm sure you also saw him climb the Ferris wheel just now, and not shoot a rifle from the hillside, not cause screams from inside the car—"

Reeve's face contorted again, but somehow he held back his spitting rage. "You're relieved of duty, Deputy Stan."

"For not pursuing someone who wasn't committing any crime except climbing an apparatus not designed for climbing?" Arch didn't even feel resentful; it wasn't like this was unexpected. He snapped out a response anyway.

"I'll let the district attorney craft the official charges," Reeve said with a rough satisfaction. "But I'm thinking aiding and abetting, obstruction of justice, some sort of corruption charge—"

"You don't know what you're talking about," Arch said with a surprising amount of calm.

"I know a dirty cop when I see one," Reeve replied.

"You wouldn't know your *ass* from a hole in the ground," Arch said and just dismounted the platform right off the side, over the railing and Jesus help anyone below. Thankfully for their own sakes, they moved.

"You better run, Arch," Reeve shouted from somewhere above him. "I'm coming for you!"

329

Arch just turned and looked up. "Why don't you try and catch a glimpse of what's really going on around here?" He met Reeve's gaze for a split second to let the man know he was serious and then started shouldering his way through the crowd with a purpose.

19.

Lauren stood in the dark after she watched the cowboy and the FBI agent—or whatever he was—retreat over the fence and flee into the night. She turned back to the Ferris wheel to watch it descend, her eyes on Molly, but she started catching snatches of conversation from the platform. It was about five feet off the ground, clear as day in front of her on the lit, raised metal structure, just through the crossbars of the Ferris wheel. Impossible to miss. And so dramatic, she couldn't help but look, even as she waited for Molly—thank God she looked all right, sweeping in a slow arc back toward the platform—to descend.

"I know a dirty cop when I see one," Reeve said to Archibald Stan, clear as if he'd just fired a gun.

"You wouldn't know your *ass* from a hole in the ground," Arch replied, testier than he'd even been that afternoon at the mine. The man looked strained, and he'd—had he actually just *cursed*? Holier-than-the-Pope Archibald Stan? He disappeared over the far edge of the platform, and she caught a glimpse of his legs under the metal girders that held the platform aloft. He'd jumped. Just walked away from the sheriff. From his boss.

"You better run, Arch! I'm coming for you!" Lauren listened to the words dully, blinking, and she looked down at her feet again.

Where that man—that rapist—she'd meant to kill—meant to stab right through the heart—had disintegrated into nothingness, eaten by what looked like ... black flames.

Demons.

She blinked and folded slightly again to see Arch Stan's legs as the man disappeared into the crowd.

He hadn't lied.

There were *demons*.

"MOM!" Molly dropped from a height of about five feet as the Ferris wheel car swung around, her Chucks clunking against the metal as she hit the platform and then squirmed around, charging through the slow-turning spokes—and damned near giving her mother a heart attack—as she followed the path that FBI guy had to get to Lauren. Lauren opened her arms and Molly slammed into her amidships, rocking her back. She did not care. Not a bit.

"Dr. Darlington," came Sheriff Reeve's voice from through the spokes of the wheel, his near-bald head looking almost as wrinkled as his forehead. "Are you all right?"

Lauren felt the weight of Molly in her arms, her daughter in her grasp, the full significance of what had just happened causing her emotional mind to tremble even as the logical, careful, assessing, doctor part of her tried to assemble it into something rational. "I'm …" She didn't take her eyes off of Molly, and she didn't answer. She just didn't have anything to say that made one damned lick of sense.

***

"Will you hold the fuck up?" Hendricks said, gasping for breath and feeling like he'd been gasping most of the day. He didn't feel much in the way of pain from the drop, which was fortunate; this was more from the flat-out, haul-ass run he'd done to try and keep up with Duncan. They'd skated the edge of the carnival, running the fence line, hiding behind cover as best they could, Hendricks wondering all the while exactly how this particular shitstorm was going to make landfall.

"Now is not a good time for stopping," Duncan said, slowing only a little. They were nearing the parking lot, and, Hendricks figured, some measure of safety.

"When would be a good time to stop and die?" Hendricks asked, barely getting out his smart-assed reply.

"When we're safely in Moscow, I think." Duncan ran on, leaving Hendricks cursing as they rounded the last curve in the fence and found themselves staring at the first row of parked cars.

"Fuck that, I ain't running that far," Hendricks said, trying to avoid doubling over. "We still got business here, you know."

"Yeah, well, enjoy your stay in the local jail while this town and county get destroyed by the rising tide of demonic chaos," Duncan said. "Should be a front row seat for the end of Midian."

Hendricks adjusted his hat on his head. It wasn't that bad ... was it?

Of course it was. The signs were all there. They'd been watching the water level rising all along; now it was just a matter of when it would pour over.

A car screeched to a stop in front of them, lights flaring. It took a second for him to work out that it was Arch's Explorer, and the man himself was sitting in the front seat. Hendricks staggered forward a few steps behind Duncan, slipping through the passenger door that the demon graciously opened for him as the OOC slid into the back. Arch did not spare the horses once they were both in, putting pedal to metal in such a manner that Hendricks's doubts about having to run were erased in an instant. "How bad is it?" he asked once they were out of the parking lot and streaking down a paved road toward town.

"We're gonna need to get as much of our stuff together as we can pack in ten minutes or less and vacate Midian proper," Arch said. The tension was apparent in every facet of the man's reply, from his form as he held the wheel with one hand to the slow delivery of each word with emphasis. "You get that, Alison?"

***

"I heard you," Alison said, the line still open. "Everybody made it out?"

"We're all clear," Arch replied. "Meet us at the apartment; we'll need to ditch the Explorer."

He hung up without another word, and Alison was left speechless anyhow. She did not look at her father as they slid down a back road. She didn't need to; she watched him unspool the earphone out of his own ear after Arch hung up. Watched him and saw the expression on his face turn to fear, something she had never really seen there before.

***

"So much for the town car," Duncan said from the back seat.

"That sucker would draw nothing but heat," Hendricks said. Arch glanced at the cowboy in the passenger seat. He didn't bother adding his chorus of assent. "Kind of like the Explorer now, I guess?"

Arch didn't take his eyes off the road. "You guess right." He swerved slightly to avoid a pothole. The emotions were roiling inside of him, a thousand—no, a million of them, all warring for space to stretch out and express themselves.

"I only need like five minutes at my place," Hendricks said.

"Same," Duncan said. "Assuming you mean for me to come with you."

Arch glanced into the rearview mirror, saw on the demon's face a cold, blunt look that wasn't without a little rage etched in between the lines. "You got anywhere else to go?"

"Depends on what you mean to do," Duncan said. "If you're just gonna hunker down and hide until this place slides off the map, I can think of other uses for my time."

"Oh, no," Arch said, the answer coming out more playful than he intended. "No, no, no. See, we're in it now. I just watched my career go up in smoke to save my hometown; if you think I'm gonna do that and just run so the next nasty thing that washes up on these shores can have free rein to finish the job? You got something else coming."

Hendricks was the first to speak up. "What do you got in mind, Arch?"

"We move out into the country," Arch said, "find a place where they won't look for us. Embrace the wide open spaces of rural American life." He felt his grip on the wheel tighten. "Then we start taking this war to the demons and doing it a lot harder than we have up to this point."

Hendricks just listened, composing his reply when his train of thought got derailed from the back seat.

"Fuck, yeah," Duncan said. "When do we start?"

***

"Are you all right?" Lauren asked. They were riding in the car, shaken, stirred, fucked up, really. Molly was taking it better than Lauren had thought she would. Maybe.

"No," Molly said, shaking her head. "And yes. Kinda? Sorta? I don't know?"

Lauren listened to her, and when she stopped speaking, gave her a nod. "All right answers."

"I know, in the abstract, that a lot of guys are assholes with a one-track mind," Molly said, and there was no hiding the raw edge of pain in her voice, "but Jesus. I thought I knew him better than that. I guess it was all lies."

"Some men are demons," Lauren said, realizing that there was more truth to that than she'd ever thought of before.

"You stabbed him with a sword," Molly said carefully.

"I did," Lauren said.

"And he went poof," Molly said. "Like a product of my imagination."

"You didn't imagine that particular asshole," Lauren said, keeping the wheel even in her hands. Ten and two, and for some reason the wheel looked like a Ferris wheel to her for a second. "He really did go up in a puff of smoke."

"I'm no doctor," Molly said with a healthy dose of sarcasm, "but isn't that supposed to be impossible?"

"Yep," Lauren said.

"So what's the scientific explanation for that?"

Lauren made as expressive a shrug as she could without moving her hands off the wheel. "I don't know. What's the scientific explanation for Jarrett Barnes spontaneously combusting?"

Molly sat in silence for a minute. "Some men are demons."

"Yep."

They rode the rest of the way home in silence.

***

Her daddy dropped her off a block away and Alison ran, ran all the way to the apartment. They'd talked it over and decided this was for the best; it would keep him out of the obvious scrutiny that was coming. He'd probably still get some of it, but if he stayed mostly out of sight during the exodus, he'd at least be able to help some rather than be forced to flee with them.

And fleeing with them—that was something Alison hadn't exactly been planning for at the outset of the day.

The Explorer was not in the apartment building's lot, and she figured for sure that he had not made it back yet. It sent a flutter of worry through her belly, primal concern that rooted there and crept up toward her heart.

She made her way down the side of the building to the apartment. The outside lights cast long shadows on the pavement, and she watched her own slip past smoothly, like a snake, or a slick of oil rolling down a river.

She tried the handle and found it turned without unlocking. Hesitant, she pushed the door open, heard the squeak of the hinges, and felt for the pistol she'd kept under her t-shirt.

Then she saw a shadow cross in the living room and froze, just long enough to realize it was Arch, and she went to him in a rush.

She fell into his arms with a sudden bleeding of tension that was astonishing in its quickness. She felt like jelly against him, all form lost in the moment of contact. He returned the pressure of her embrace, firmer than he had been lately, and kissed her in return.

"Oh, Arch," she said, looking up at him. Her eyes were dry; his were not, surprisingly. "I didn't think you were here."

"I let Duncan and Hendricks take the Explorer," he said. "We're meeting 'em out at the MacGruder place. We'll ditch the sheriff's car there and make for our destination."

"Why there?" Alison asked.

"Because we're going across the county," Arch said, "over by Culver. By the time Reeve gets all his ducks in a row, his crime scene at the festival contained, we'll be hunkered down—for now."

"Okay," she said, still staring in his dark eyes. She could almost touch the pain there, right at the top, it was so obvious to her. "What do you need me to do?"

"Pack a bag," Arch said, nodding once. "Clothes. Toiletries. All the stuff you'll need."

"For what?" Alison asked.

"For living," Arch said.

She shook her head. "Not what I meant. What kind of living? City living? Camping?"

Arch didn't think about it for more than a second. "War. Pack like you're going to war."

Alison felt a mask of steely calm descend over her. "Okay." And she got to work.

***

Duncan had taken seconds—like maybe thirty, total—to cram about fifteen fugly suits into his suitcase and carry it out the door, tossing it in the back of the Explorer while Hendricks watched, waiting to slam it shut as soon as the OOC was in. It was an amazing bit of efficiency in his view. And while he had been standing there, waiting for the demon, he'd found the case in the back of the Explorer and opened it up, making a mental note to make sure to bring *that* with them. It was like he'd run into an old friend, really.

Hendricks had taken slightly more time at his hotel room, but he was out of there in less than three minutes. That was the blessing of being the kind of guy who traveled light; he was only ever a few seconds from being ready to go.

Now he was driving down the back roads toward the rendezvous point, watching the curves and enjoying the silence with Duncan at his side.

Well, maybe "enjoying" was too strong a word.

"You hear that?" Duncan stiffened in the passenger seat.

Hendricks cocked his ears like a dog. Or imagined he did. Probably just tilted his head a little. Still like a dog. All he heard was the sound of the road, the sound of the wheel well, the sound of—

Buzzing.

Mechanical fucking buzzing.

He stomped the brakes and listened to the screech of tires as the Explorer fishtailed just a little on the back road. He peered through the windshield at the long, straight stretch of road ahead of him. "I'm not imagining it, am I?"

"Nope," Duncan said with a tightly wound coil of rage all his own. Hendricks could sympathize.

Hendricks opened the door and hit the pavement with boots a clackin'. He heard Duncan get out on the other side, the Explorer slightly fishtailed to expose the passenger side of the car—still dented and fucked up from the battle on the mountain—to the side of the road the noise was coming from. "Got a plan?" Duncan called as he came around to meet Hendricks at the lift gate.

"Yep," Hendricks said. He just opened the gate and pushed Duncan's suitcase aside to reveal his new best friend.

"You're gonna beat 'em to death with a plastic case," Duncan said. "Should be fun, if not terribly productive."

Hendricks didn't reply to the sarcastic dig. He just flipped the case open.

Duncan let out a low whistle. "You know how to use that thing?"

Hendricks just smiled. "You're goddamned right I do." He hefted the AR-15 by the handle and checked the mag—again. It was full up, with a spare already prepared. Sixty rounds of mayhem at his fingertips.

It was like coming home, the feel of it in his hands. The actions were reflex—pulling the charging rod, battering the switch with his palm to jerk the bolt forward—he'd done this a thousand times since he'd pinned his EGA, and as he came around the car to give himself a rest on the hood, he reflected that he couldn't have planned a better spot to do this if he'd had to.

"You unleash hell, and we'll wade in together to wipe out the stragglers with sword and baton," Duncan said. "Fair enough?"

"Works for me," Hendricks said and fiddled with the red dot sight. The last time he'd used one of these, the range was so close he'd just aimed down the side of the barrel.

He could see them now, emerging from the dark—the peloton, the bicyclists, the Night Riders, if they wanted to call themselves that fucking pitiful-ass name. He fired his first shot and watched the soft-shelled bitch riding at the front of the pack disappear in a cloud of black as his bike fell underneath him. The tightly packed group struggled to swerve. Some failed. Some didn't. Hendricks didn't give a fuck. He had a full mag and a sword at his side to cap it all off if need be. He fired another shot, and another. Watched the chaos break, watched the demons panic. He filled the air with lead, a small, satisfied smile working its way out onto his face.

Bikes fell.

Demons screamed.

Black flames writhed.

Lafayette Jackson Hendricks clutched the AR-15 tight against his shoulder through both magazines, and by the time he was done, the handful of the demons that remained were all heaped in piles, trapped under bikes, disoriented.

He didn't even get the chance to finish them off. Duncan—that sadistic, magnificent bastard—had run forward like a lion heading for a carcass. Hendricks lost count of how many times the baton rose and fell. Kinda like the number of shots he'd fired.

All he knew was that once it was done, there wasn't a single demon left alive.

They packed up without another word, tossed their stuff in the back and headed on down the road a little late. Hendricks couldn't pull far enough off the road to keep from scratching the Explorer's undercarriage with broken bicycles.

They went in silence for a little longer, and Hendricks figured he'd just confirm—just for himself—that he was one hundred percent right in what he was picking up off of Duncan. "Wanna talk?" he asked, throwing it out there.

"Nope," Duncan said. Simple as that.

Hendricks just shrugged. "Works for me."

***

Lauren couldn't get rid of that nagging feeling. It was on her ass like an overbearing attending physician on an intern, like naivety on a med student. Molly was fine, Molly was coping—as fine as could be under the circumstances, surprisingly okay for what had happened. She'd gotten her home, gotten her inside, handed her off to her mom with a flimsy explanation, one that left out some crucial details. She hadn't know what to say; her mom had given her the concerned look, the soft one that glossed over the problematic details in favor of motherly empathy—for now.

But answers were gonna be needed.

And that got Lauren in the car a little after midnight, after making just one call. Because she needed to know.

***

Arch turned Alison's car onto the dirt lane and took 'em down a half mile before making another turn onto a driveway. There was no mailbox on the stand, just a weatherworn place where it looked like one might have been a long time ago.

Duncan and Hendricks were in the back, apparently in a war to see who could say the least. Arch didn't mind that; they'd been silent as stones since MacGruder's farm, since they'd tossed their things in the back. Duncan's suitcase and Hendricks's duffel had joined Arch's and Alison's bags in her old car. Plus the AR case Hendricks had brought. Arch had pretty well forgotten it in the hubbub.

The car was made for city driving, not dirt roads, but it managed. It kicked up the gravel, rocks dinging on the undercarriage and in the wheel wells. It hugged the ground but chugged along, up the winding driveway.

Night had descended; the light holding it at bay around the festival was far distant. Arch's mind felt the pull of the gloom, felt the desperation of the moment.

This was the valley of the shadow of death, but he would fear no evil. He had no rod or staff, just a demon with a baton, a cowboy with a sword, a wife with a massive rifle, and a switchblade of his own to guard the flock.

That'd do.

It'd have to.

He stopped the car in front of the old house. It didn't look too bad, the exterior a little unkempt, the lawn overgrown by a few months. Shabby, but not post-apocalyptic.

Yet.

"Where the fuck are we?" Hendricks broke his silence with a doozy, finding a way to sprinkle his favorite word into the sentence. The man could squeeze it into a prayer, Arch figured. If he'd prayed.

"This is an old farmhouse," Arch replied. He glanced over the top of the house and saw Alison get out the passenger side. She gave him a reassuring smile. "Been here since 1892. It was owned last by the McCullough family, but now it's the property of Bank of America." He looked back at Hendricks. "Served the foreclosure papers myself."

"So we're uh ... squatting?" Hendricks asked.

"Why not?" Arch looked up at the two-story house. "They're gonna come after us for a lot more than that if they can."

"You really think they're gonna be able to prove anything?" Hendricks asked. "No bodies, no witnesses that can put together a cogent explanation of what they saw, nothing but a lot of bullets fired, mayhem caused, and demons slain. They ain't got shit."

"Oh, they've got bodies," Arch said, taking in the lines of the house. The siding didn't look bad at all. He let his gaze drift to the main reason he'd chosen this place; there was a manual pump in the yard, no electricity needed. "No bodies we caused, but they've got bodies. And a whole town of people looking for someone to blame."

"And your sheriff's gonna make us the scapegoats," Hendricks said. "Lovely."

"We're the most convenient targets," Alison said. "It's not like we have a reasonable explanation for what we've done."

Hendricks gave her a sidelong glance that Arch caught. "'We,' huh?"

Alison did not look back at him, her gaze instead transfixed on the house. Her finger came up to point at the porch. "We."

Arch followed the line of her finger and found the shape waiting for them under the eaves, in the shadows. The pale skin slipped out into the moonlight just as the car's lights hit their automatic shut off. He saw the dusky eyes, somehow, in the dark, and the red hair still seemed to glow, like a fire burned within each strand.

"Somehow," Hendricks said, "I'm not surprised to find her waiting here."

"Feels like you should be," Duncan said, "since none of the rest of us knew we were coming here until just now."

"Arch knew," Hendricks said, but low, like he was trying to keep her from hearing it. "How'd you know where to find us, Starling?"

"You were always destined to be here," Starling said, bare feet slipping down the squeaking, warped wooden stairs as she stepped out to greet them, with as close to an approachable look as Arch had ever seen on her forbidding face. "Welcome home." He had a sense there was more to it than that, and she beckoned them forward toward the door.

Hendricks went first, coaxed by her, then Alison. Arch followed next, with only a single backward glance for Duncan, whose face—usually so carefully neutral—now burned with some rage barely concealed beneath the surface. He followed, too, last in line, and they went, one by one, into the farmhouse, following the redhead's lead.

***

"Erin."

The words pushed into her mind, into her ear, like something sharp against spandex. It was rude, it was not pleasant, and she wanted to resist.

"Erin, wake up."

Erin Harris most assuredly did not care for that suggestion, not even as gently as it was worded, not with sugar on top, pretty please, not at all.

"Erin, I need you to wake up."

Erin had been awake and had not cared for it; she'd awakened earlier in the evening, seen her family—mom, pop, three brothers—the whole family, wagons circled for this special crisis occasion. She was dimly aware of that. But visiting hours had ended, and that lovely narcotic drowse that had been calling her name? She'd willingly, happily succumbed to it, running back into the darkness with arms (and more) spread, ready to hump that motherfucker all night.

"Erin."

One eye cracked open. The world was a blur, Vaseline smeared on the lens of the camera.

"Erin ... can you hear me?"

"Mmmm ... awaaaaaake." Her own words were slurred, dragged, drawled, dropped on their heads as babies.

"Good. Can you open both eyes for me?"

Erin did and didn't like that, either. Because then the goddamned bitch shined a spotlight in her eyes. The world was a cold, lonely, and evil place. Fuck it. She closed her eyes again.

"Your pupils are reactive and undilated. That's a good sign."

You know what else was a good sign? Slippery when wet. That one always made Erin chuckle.

"Erin."

She opened her eyes again. No bright light this time. No signs, though. Just a face. Framed by dark hair. Long, dark hair. Feminine.

Pretty, really. Enough that Erin felt a trace of envy. Doctor ... What was her name? Dr. Dolittle. No.

Dr. Darlington.

Yes.

That was it.

"Dr. Darlington." Erin's mouth felt heavy, swabbed with cotton and someone left it in there when they were done. Now it was all dried out and icky, and no matter how much she smacked her lips together, it didn't help.

"Very good, Erin. You've had some painkillers, so I know you're probably feeling a little—"

"Fuck yeaaaaah, awesome." Slurred. Just a little.

"That's good." The doctor's face came into view. She looked good. Rosy cheeks. Really rosy. Like she probably ran or something. Good circulation. That was what made rosy cheeks, right? Or angel kisses? Was that bullshit or the real deal? "Erin, I need you to tell me something."

"What's up, Doc?" She blinked her eyes, and the doctor's face swam into view. Serious. Earnest. Erin blinked again, and she was still there. The world felt sharp but draggy, and Erin didn't mind. Like she was drunk, but better, because she hadn't had to consume approximately OH MY GOD, MY WALLET IS EMPTY, WHAT IS THIS BULLSHIT? beers to get there.

"I need you to tell me something, Erin." The voice was so smooth. So nice. Not like the light shining. That was not nice. Not smooth. That was bullshit, that was. "I need you to answer a question for me."

"Shoot." Me up with morphine. Hehe. Yes. Fuck yes. MOREphine. She had it. Lots of it.

"I need you to tell me everything you know ... about demons."

Return to Midian, Tennessee in

UNEARTHED

Southern Watch
Book 4

Coming Early 2015!

A Note From the Author

First off, if you want to know when future books become available, take sixty seconds and sign up for my NEW RELEASE EMAIL ALERTS on my website, www.robertjcrane.com. Don't let the caps lock scare you; I don't sell your information and I only send out emails when I have a new book out. The reason you should sign up for this is because I don't like to set release dates (it's this whole thing, you can find an answer on my website in the FAQ section), and even if you're following me on Facebook (robertJcrane (Author)) or Twitter (@robertJcrane), it's easy to miss my book announcements because…well, because social media is an imprecise thing.

Come join the Southern Watch discussion on my website: http://www.robertjcrane.com !

Cheers,
Robert J. Crane

Acknowledgments

(In Order of Appearance)

Karri Klawiter – Cover Artist

Nicolette Solomita – First reader/Verifier that the book was not crap

Jerod Heck – Marine Realism Consultant

Sarah Barbour – Editor

Jeff Bryan – Proofreader

Jo Evans – Error Catcher

My parents – Edifiers

My kids – Exercisers

My wife – Aid and comfort.

No authors were harmed during the writing of this novel. Well…okay, maybe just one.

About the Author

Robert J. Crane is kind of an a-hole. Still, if you want to contact him:

Website: http://www.robertjcrane.com

Facebook Page: robertJcrane (Author)

Twitter: @robertJcrane

Email: cyrusdavidon@gmail.com

Other Works by Robert J. Crane

The Sanctuary Series
Epic Fantasy

Defender: The Sanctuary Series, Volume One
Avenger: The Sanctuary Series, Volume Two
Champion: The Sanctuary Series, Volume Three
Crusader: The Sanctuary Series, Volume Four
Sanctuary Tales, Volume One - A Short Story Collection
Thy Father's Shadow: The Sanctuary Series, Volume 4.5
Master: The Sanctuary Series, Volume Five* (Coming Late November/December 2014!)
Fated in Darkness: The Sanctuary Series, Volume 5.5 (Coming in 2015!)

The Girl in the Box
and
Out of the Box
Contemporary Urban Fantasy

Alone: The Girl in the Box, Book 1
Untouched: The Girl in the Box, Book 2
Soulless: The Girl in the Box, Book 3
Family: The Girl in the Box, Book 4
Omega: The Girl in the Box, Book 5
Broken: The Girl in the Box, Book 6
Enemies: The Girl in the Box, Book 7
Legacy: The Girl in the Box, Book 8
Destiny: The Girl in the Box, Book 9
Power: The Girl in the Box, Book 10

Limitless: Out of the Box, Book 1
In the Wind: Out of the Box, Book 2* (Coming December 30, 2014!)
Ruthless: Out of the Box, Book 3* (Coming Early 2015!)
Tormented: Out of the Box, Book 4* (Coming in 2015!)

Southern Watch
Contemporary Urban Fantasy

Called: Southern Watch, Book 1
Depths: Southern Watch, Book 2
Corrupted: Southern Watch, Book 3
Unearthed: Southern Watch, Book 4* (Coming Early 2015!)
Legion: Southern Watch, Book 5* (Coming 2015!)

*Forthcoming

Printed in Great Britain
by Amazon